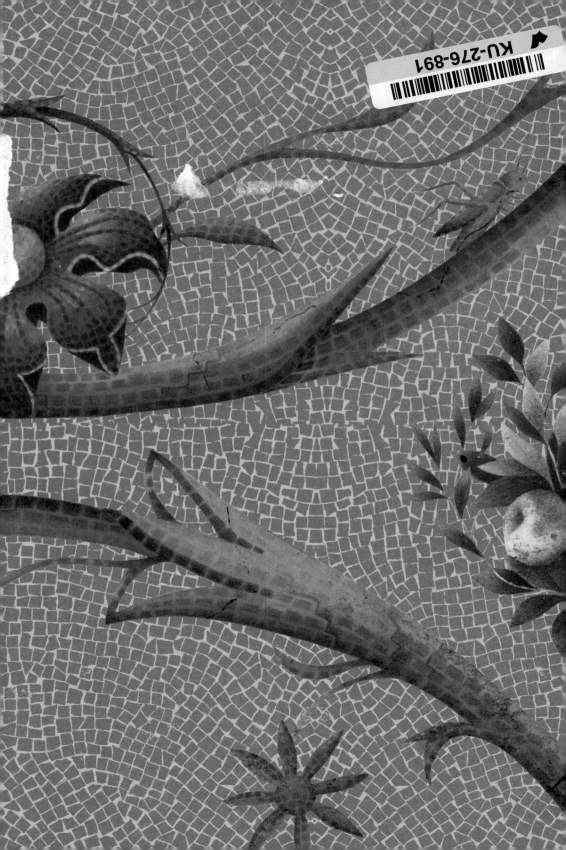

JAMES HYNES

Sparrow

PICADOR

First published 2023 by Picador
an imprint of Pan Macmillan
The Smithson, 6 Briset Street, London EC1M 5NR
EU representative: Macmillan Publishers Ireland Ltd, 1st Floor,
The Liffey Trust Centre, 117–126 Sheriff Street Upper,
Dublin 1, D01 YC43
Associated companies throughout the world
www.panmacmillan.com

ISBN 978-1-5290-9239-4 HB
ISBN 978-1-5290-9240-0 TPB

The poem on p. 184 is reproduced from *The Erotic Poems* by Ovid
translated by Peter Green (Penguin, 1982).
The extract on p. 228 is from *The Aeneid* by Virgil
translated by Robert Fagles (Penguin, 2006).

1 3 5 7 9 8 6 4 2

A CIP catalogue record for this book is available from the British Library.

Typeset by Palimpsest Book Production Ltd, Falkirk, Stirlingshire
Printed and bound by CPI Group (UK) Ltd, Croydon, CR0 4YY

MIX
Paper | Supporting
responsible forestry
FSC
www.fsc.org
FSC® C116313

Visit **www.picador.com** to read more about all our books
and to buy them. You will also find features, author interviews and
news of any author events, and you can sign up for e-newsletters
so that you're always first to hear about our new releases.

For Mimi

Qui invitus servit, fit miser, servit tamen.

The unwilling slave grows wretched, but is still a slave.

– Publilius Syrus, *Sententiae*

I Jacob, son of no one, father of no one, beloved of no one, a slave, a whore, a cinaedus, a eunuch, a murderer, a pimp, , possibly a Jew, possibly a Syrian, possibly the silt of the Nile, a labourer, an overseer, a cripple, a consumptive, an abandoned piece of property, a weathered piece of driftwood discarded by a receding tide, the sole remaining resident of a deserted town in an abandoned province at the bleeding edge of a dying empire, set down this history of my life. It will never be finished, for who will write my ending? But then no one will ever read it, because it will undoubtedly die with me, and I am dying fast. It will not long outlast the swift corruption of my body, it will survive me only as long as this papyrus lasts, mouldering untended in a crumbling house, nibbled around the edges by rats, feasted upon by beetles and cockroaches, soaked by the rain coming through the rotting roof, then bleached into silence by the infrequent British sun when the roof is gone. Or perhaps it will simply disintegrate, the way that all the other books in this library in which I write have already begun to flake away into dust. If it can happen to Tacitus and Cicero and Juvenal and Seneca and even the emperors Julian and Marcus Aurelius, then why should it not happen to me? I am just another author no one will ever remember, and this is just another book that changes nothing.

But I make this promise to you, the unknown reader who will never read these words: I will never lie to you. My life may have been wanton, but my page is virtuous.

I

An angry woman is boning a fish. She carves with a controlled rage, her fingers expert, her gestures unwasted. With a long, sharp blade, she slices the fish behind the gills, unseams the spine, and lifts off the pink fillet. She scoops out the blue intestines and tosses them aside. Then she lifts the head with two fingers under the gills and swings the naked spine at me.

I am a nameless child in the shadows, legs akimbo on a cracked flagstone in a corner of a kitchen. The fish head and its ladder of spine slither to a stop between my splayed legs. The fish's mouth is ajar, as if surprised to find itself naked on the floor. I don't know whether to laugh or cry. Is this a game? Maybe, maybe not. The fish's clouded eye fixes itself on my startled face, as if to warn me.

'It's you she's angry at,' it says.

The kitchen is full of shadow and stifling heat. It smells of smoke, onions and garlic, stale oil, and, yes, fish. Years of hot southern spices are baked into the blackened walls, a tang I can still feel in my sinuses. Along the back of a cement countertop are bottles of seasoning and spice, battered pots and pans, canisters of chickpeas and dried figs, and stained jars of olive oil, vinegar, honey, and garum. Above the countertop, hanging from hooks, are knives, tongs, a spatula, more knives, two ladles, assorted spoons. On a masonry cooktop along the adjacent wall, an iron pot is already on the boil. The morning's fire smoulders in the firebox below, red seams glowing in the ash. The only light comes through a low, square doorway, and beyond the doorway sunlight pours straight down into a kitchen garden, a knee-high jungle where chickens jerk their heads this way and that among the drooping leaves of heat-wearied plants. Beyond the garden is a whitewashed wall almost too bright to look at, and above the wall, a sky of flawless cerulean. Even now, after having lived most of my life under milky, shifting, inconstant British skies, the adamantine blue of that Spanish sky is still my Platonic ideal of the firmament – cloudless, boundless, depthless, perfect. It is the sky I would expect to see in heaven, if there actually were a heaven, and if I had any hope of going there.

Down the centre of the narrow kitchen is a stout wooden table, unsteady, unpainted, and crosshatched with knife cuts. Hunched over the table is the woman who is angrily boning fish. Under the table I see the ragged hem of her skirt. Her dirty toes clench and unclench against the flagstones as she eviscerates another. I have earlier memories than this, but they are just fragments – sunlight glittering on the sea, pellets of cat shit on a wooden floor, the smell of almond blossoms. This is my first coherent memory. It is the start of my story, and like all the best stories, says Horace, it begins in medias res. So when the serpentine head and spine of another fish skid to a stop near me, I am startled, but I do not cry. I already seem to have known not to protest. I already seem to know what will happen if I do.

'Still angry,' says the second fish head. 'And it's still you.'

In the stifling twilight of the kitchen, the woman's pale face shines with sweat. Her abundant hair is tied back in a bun, and the light through the doorway picks out unruly red strands round her face. She wears a blackened iron collar round her neck. She never looks in my direction, which is another way I know she's angry at me. Yet somehow the fish heads continue to land with unerring aim between my legs, a little boneyard of staring eyes and twisted spines. She knows where I am. She just doesn't want to look at me.

A shadow flickers past the doorway. I turn. There is nothing but sunlight glaring off the garden wall, a chicken bobbing her head, and leaves curling in the heat. I shift my gaze back to the woman, as she drives her blade into the next hapless fish. Then the light dims again. A sharply defined silhouette sways in the doorway, a man with bare legs and a short tunic. As I blink at him out of my dark corner, he steadies himself with a hand to either side of the door.

'Is this the pisser?' He breathes heavily through his mouth, as if he has just struggled up a hill.

The woman straightens, one hand on the tabletop. 'This is the kitchen.' She points with the knife. 'The latrine's next door.'

The man looks away, but he does not leave. He isn't tall, but the door is so low, the top of his head nearly brushes the lintel. Against the glare I can't make out his face or tell what colour his tunic is, but I can hear his laboured breathing. I see his legs trembling under him as if he has just put down a heavy weight. I hear the *snick snick snick* of the blade against the tabletop as the woman expertly savages another fish and stubbornly ignores the man. Then he draws a deep breath and pulls himself through into the kitchen. Light pours in after him. Now I can see he has tangled black hair and a patchy beard. Under the table I see his shoes. One of the straps has broken, and he has repaired it himself, tugging the two ends into a tight knot. His legs wobble as he stumbles across the flagstones toward the woman. She draws a breath, turns to face him, and stands as tall as she can. She sets her feet flat, she splays her dirty toes. Beneath the table I see the hand holding the knife slip into a fold of her skirt.

'What's *your* name?' The man stands close enough to breathe on her, and she turns her face away. He is only a little taller than she is. He lifts an unsteady hand and curls one of her flyaway hairs round his finger. She jerks her head away and steps back. But drunk as he is, he's quick, and before she can lift the knife, he's caught

7

her round the waist and swung behind her, clutching both her wrists. He doubles her over the edge of the table and squeezes one wrist against the tabletop until she grunts in pain and lets go of the knife. She pushes back against him, and he slams her against the table again and knocks the breath out of her.

'You want one of the wolves upstairs,' she gasps. 'I'm Focaria.'

'I have money,' he mumbles, 'I can pay,' and he grasps her round the waist with one hand while he claws her skirt up with the other, handful by handful. Under the table Focaria's toes clench as her heels are lifted off the floor. The man tenses his calves. He grinds the soles of his shoes into the flagstone. Focaria says nothing, her nostrils flared, her lips pressed bloodlessly together. With one hand she tries to find purchase on the tabletop among the slippery fish guts, with the other she reaches for the knife, but the man drops her skirt long enough to flick it off the table. The knife clatters against the floor, and Focaria cries out wordlessly as he shoves his hand again up her skirt.

If this is another game, it frightens me. Their scuffling and grunting bring me to the cusp of tears, but I'm too breathless to cry. Then, with a great hollow thump, the table lurches toward me. To keep from falling, the man lets go of Focaria and throws himself back on his heels. She falls to her knees, and while the man wobbles on his feet like a round-bottomed pot, she scuttles away under the table.

Now I do start to cry, and for the first time, the man notices me. 'What's this?' He sways toward me, one hand on the table, one touching the wall. He fills my vision, a faceless silhouette against the glare from the doorway. I cry even louder. He stoops and catches me between two blunt and callused hands, and he lifts me, howling, high off the floor. He reeks of wine and sweat.

'Who are you?' he says.

Now there's a question! Writing this memory now, at the opposite end of my life, I can only be impressed in retrospect at the man's drunken perspicacity. In vino veritas, you long-dead bastard.

'*What* are you?' He lifts me over his head and peers under my tunic, then he glances back where Focaria was a moment ago. 'He's too dark to belong to you.'

I squirm and scream, and he hoists me at arm's length so that my hands and feet don't strike him in the face. Swaying up near the blackened rafters, from a vantage I've never known before, I see the furthest horizons of my world and everything in it: the blazing doorway, the grimy walls, the scarred and slimy table. The cement counter, the masonry cooktop, the flagstones littered with fish heads. The poker and the little iron shovel and the leather bellows propped against the oven. The figure of a woman crouching in the far corner.

'Maybe he wants to watch,' the man laughs. 'Maybe he'll learn something.'

He turns, looking for Focaria, just in time to see a blur of pale face and flyaway hair as she charges out of the corner with the boning knife in her fist, thrusting up from her waist. The man shouts and twists away from her. His heel catches on a fish head, his feet fly out from under him, and he drops me as he lands on his backside. I scream as Focaria drags me out of the way by my arm. Propped on his hands, the man scrabbles for footing, but all he catches are fish heads. As skilfully as a street fighter, Focaria flips the knife in her hand so that the blade is down, and she raises her arm high over her shoulder. Her eyes are glittering and terrifying. My only consolation is that her rage is directed at the man and not at me.

Then another hand, huge and hairy, jerks Focaria off her feet by the collar round her neck. She sprawls, gasping, as the knife spins away over the flagstones. A new shadow looms over me, bigger than the first man, and kicks me aside. He stoops, grabs the front of the first man's tunic with both hands, and yanks him to his feet.

'The slut tried to—' the first man starts to say, but the new shadow, who is a head taller, slams him against the wall and pins the first man's wrists over his head with one hand. With his other hand, the new man slices the first man's face just under the eye with a short, sharp knife.

The cut man squeals. The hulking shadow drags him stumbling across the kitchen and flings him out the door. The first man flies into the sunlight and crashes through the plants in the garden, waving his arms, trying to keep his footing. The chicken erupts from the undergrowth, squawking and flapping, and the man recoils and crashes to the dirt.

The new shadow fills the door, dimming the kitchen again. Only a little light leaks around his broad back, his spreading gut, his thick calves.

'Don't come back,' he says. 'Next time I'll face-fuck you and cut your throat.' He wipes the blade of his knife with his fingers and slips it out of sight again.

'My money . . .' Among the trembling leaves the first man rises to his knees, one hand pressed to his cheek. 'My money's just as good as anybody else's.' Bright blood oozes through his fingers.

'Fuck your money, you cunt-licker.' The voice of the man in the doorway is rumbling and wet all at once. 'I don't need your fucking money.'

Between his legs, I see the first man stumble to his feet, trampling the plants around him. Somewhere out of sight, the chicken protests violently. The shadow in the doorway jerks his fist back, and the man in the garden staggers away, dripping blood on the wilting leaves. The new shadow turns back into the kitchen.

'Audo . . .' Focaria has pulled herself up by the edge of the table. In my corner, I am still howling like a dog.

The man Focaria calls Audo steps into the kitchen, and the light from the doorway falls across him. He has a fleshy, pushed-in face, a gut that strains over the belt of his tunic like a bloated wineskin, and meaty ankles mottled pink and white like hams. My gasping, desperate crying makes him scowl.

'Make that be quiet,' he says in his liquid rasp, pointing a blunt finger in my direction, 'or I'll send it back where it came from.'

'I wish you would.' Focaria rubs her throat where the collar bruised her. 'What am I supposed to do with him?'

Now Audo looks at me. I can hear him breathing all the way across the kitchen. His eyes are like currants pushed into a bun, and under his black gaze I instinctively swallow my sobs and snot. I am learning one of my earliest lessons: a slave does not cry.

'Put him to work,' he says. 'What's the problem?'

Focaria sighs. She is a slave, too, but a more useful one than I am at this point in my life, so she has some slight licence for backchat.

'Doing what?' Her voice is steadier now. 'He's too young.'

Audo's gaze narrows, and I fall completely silent. I am learning.

'Hit him.' This, I will learn, is Audo's answer to everything. Audo is a hammer, and every problem is a nail. 'A slave's ears are on his back . . .' he starts to say, but Focaria, testing the limits of her licence, finishes it for him.

'. . . he only listens when you beat him,' she says. 'I know, Audo.' She points at me. 'But I could hit him all day long, and it won't make any difference. He's a child. He needs somebody to teach him, and when am I supposed to do that? I have to cook and clean and shop. I have to run food into the tavern every night. I have to fetch water and wine up to the wolves and carry away their fucking chamber pots. How am I supposed to do all that *and* –' she jerks her head in my direction, but still does not look at me – 'look after him?'

She starts to say more, but she catches herself. Audo has put his head down. As a necessary piece of equipment, Focaria is less likely to be hit than I am, but she is not exempt.

'What do you want me to do?' Audo lifts his head. 'I'm not made of money.' This is another of his favourite sayings. It's what he says when he thinks he's being reasonable. Focaria sometimes repeats it mockingly behind his back, mimicking his coarse accent and calling him 'Pecunia'. Also behind his back, and never when he can hear her: 'It's not *his* fucking money, is it?'

Just now, though, she says, 'Send one of the wolves down to look after him.'

'One of the wolves?'

'Why not?' says Focaria. 'When she's not working.' Her voice is tight. She knows she's approaching the limits of his patience. 'All they do is sleep in the morning.'

Audo drums the tabletop with his meaty fingers.

'It doesn't have to be the same one every day.'

Audo sighs massively, like a bull pawing the earth.

'They can take turns. They can—'

Audo slams the table with both hands and makes it jump. Focaria breaks off and drops her gaze. He has not hit her, but such is the wonderful efficacy of violence that after a certain point, all you have to do is raise your hand to a dog, and it will cringe.

Yet Focaria seems to think she has one more inch of leeway. Under her breath, quickly, she says, 'I can't watch him every moment. If he hurts himself, you'll beat me. If he dies, you'll beat me. If I ask for help, you'll beat me. What am I supposed to do?'

Audo glares at her across the table, or rather at the top of her lowered head. He swings his gaze to where I sit on the floor, blinking, silent, breathless. Then he looks away toward the garden, and his face catches some sunlight. I can see the grey in his coarse black hair. I can see the red blossoms on his flattened nose.

'I'll send Euterpe down,' he says. 'In the mornings.'

Still not looking at him, Focaria mutters something.

'What?' says Audo.

Focaria hunches her shoulders, as if expecting to be hit from behind.

'Send Urania,' she says, still staring at the tabletop. 'Euterpe's too scatter-brained.'

'That was the old Euterpe,' Audo says. 'The new one's not so stupid.'

'Urania,' Focaria insists. 'How do I know the new Euterpe won't kill him?'

'It'll be up to you to make sure she doesn't.'

'Then what's the point,' Focaria says, much too sharply, 'if I have to watch them both?'

'*Enough!*' Audo roars.

Focaria cringes and clutches her elbows.

'Do you want to go back to sucking cock under the aqueduct?' he says.

'No, Audo,' whispers Focaria.

'Then what do you say?' says Audo.

It is settled. Euterpe is the best she's going to get. Focaria works her lips until the words come. 'Thank you, Audo.'

'Right.' He dips his head under the low lintel and squeezes into the garden. He stabs through the door once more with his finger. '*And* put him to work.'

Then he's gone. Focaria sighs and lets her shoulders loosen. She stares sourly through the doorway, tallying the plants the first man trampled in the garden. The chicken clucks past, jerking its head, swivelling its wide yellow eye. I start to whimper again in the corner, still shocked and bruised from being grabbed, dropped, and kicked. Sighing again, Focaria pushes the table back to its original position. She bends over, picks up the boning knife, and jams it, quivering, into the tabletop. Then she stoops, picks me up, and perches me on the edge of the table. She stares intently into my face until my whimpers subside and my tears stop. She swipes the snot off my nose and chin and flicks it away. Then she takes my jaw in her fishy fingers, not brutally, but not tenderly either, and she searches my face as if she has never seen anything like me before. In the light from the doorway I see her red hair. I see the freckles across her nose and cheeks. I see the bruise darkening her throat where Audo jerked her by the collar. I see her blue eyes, as hard and depthless as the sky above the garden wall.

'Your happy days are over,' she says.

Overnight the horizon of my world doubled in size, spreading out from the dark, hot, smoky kitchen and into the steep sunlight and tangy fragrances of the tavern garden. This was a narrow strip of dirt where Focaria grew onions, garlic, carrots, and beets, as well as basil, thyme, rosemary, mint, and other spices. It was bounded on one side by the kitchen with its sloping roof and smoking chimney and by the latrine with its rattling door of uneven planks, and on the other by the bright wall with its peeling plaster and a stout wooden door that led to the unseen street. At one end of the garden loomed the wall of the tavern itself, with a low arch into the main room on the ground floor and three barred windows peering down from under the eaves of the second floor. At the other end of the garden was the blank wall of the shop next door, and against it the sweating, masonry water tank and the weedy woodpile. The chicken and a petulant rooster also lived here, printing the dirt with their claws and fertilizing it with their droppings.

More importantly, the population of my world expanded to include Euterpe, the wolf Audo assigned to be my tutor. Each morning after cockcrow, as the early sunlight crept along the garden wall, I squatted outside the kitchen door while Focaria banged about inside. I drank a cup of water and tore at a piece of day-old bread, waiting for Euterpe to appear in the tavern archway, yawning and stretching in her red gown, still wearing her smudged make-up from the night before. Her mask, she called it. Sometimes there were bruises on her face or upper arms or around her throat. She winced if I touched them, but she never lost her temper or pushed me away. I was her Pusus, her Little One, and she was the second woman I ever knew, after Focaria. You might even say that I was

14

raised by a wolf, just like Romulus and Remus. And yet Euterpe was both a wolf and not a wolf. She was a Christian and not a Christian. She had the name of a Muse, but she was not a Muse. Euterpe was her name and not her name. She was my mother and not my mother.

In my earliest memory of her, we have already met, and we are nestled together against the cool bricks of the water tank. I already know her name, I already know the deep timbre of her voice, I already know the yielding warmth of her breasts. I know her smell of musk and sweat, of last night's perfume, and of something else, which I will later come to know as sex. She sits with her back against the tank and I sit on her lap or rest between her knees, and she teaches me the names of things in the world beyond the garden. That is the *sky*, that is a *cloud*, that is the *sun*. She lifts my hand and we point at each thing in turn. That is the *wall*, and beyond the wall is a *house*, and on top of the house is a *roof*, and the roof is *red*. She identifies for me the sounds from beyond the wall, but this is harder for me to understand, because there's nothing to point to. That's the sound of someone *walking*, and she walks two fingers up my arm. Tapping her fingers faster, that's someone *running*. That's the sound of women *talking*, like we're talking now. That's a dog *barking*, making her fingers yap. That's a mule *braying*, opening her mouth wide. That's a man *laughing*, and she tickles me until I squirm with my own laughter.

Occasionally Focaria steps into the kitchen doorway and tosses slops into the dirt for the chickens or plucks some leaves from the herbs in the garden. Sometimes, though, she just stands in the door and watches us. When Euterpe or I look back, she withdraws instantly into the kitchen like a rat into her hole.

Euterpe mostly teaches me by telling me stories, and here is the first one I remember. It's a story about the birds.

'In the beginning,' she says, her breath warm in my ear, 'God gave each bird a choice. She could do one thing well, or she could have the ability to do many things, but not very well. Do you see that bird there?'

She lifts my hand to point at the scrawny, dirty-white fowl strutting on yellow feet between the rows of the garden, turning its angry yellow eye this way and that.

'Chicken,' I say.

'Very good.' She gives me a warm squeeze. 'Now when God asked Chicken what she wanted to be able to do, Chicken said, "I want to be able to walk upon the ground, because that's where the food is." God granted her wish. And so Chicken walks upon the ground and eats all the worms and beetles she wants. Her choice was good, because she got what she asked for. But her choice is also bad, because she cannot fly. And so Chicken is enslaved by men, who steal her eggs every day and eat them. And she can't escape the fox if he gets into the garden.'

I shift in her lap. I don't know what a fox is, but I'm pretty sure I don't want to be caught by one.

'Don't worry,' Euterpe says. 'You're too big for a fox to eat. Now, do you see that bird way up high?'

We point together at another bird, with crescent wings and a split tail, darting to and fro against the hard blue of the sky, high above the red roof. 'That's a swift,' she says. 'Can you say "swift"?'

'Swift.' I follow it with my eyes as it streaks back and forth, up and down.

'Very good.' Another squeeze. 'Now, when God asked Swift what she wanted to do better than anyone else, she said, "I want to be able to fly, so neither man nor the fox can ever catch me." So God made Swift better at flying than any of the other birds.' She lifts my hand again, and we sway together as we trace the darting flight of the swift. 'Swift can never be enslaved, and she can never be caught by the fox.'

'That's good!' I say.

'But it's also bad!' Euterpe says. 'Because Swift flies so well, she has no need of feet, and so she can't walk upon the ground. And because she can't walk upon the ground like Chicken, Swift can only eat what she can catch in the air. She must always be hunting. So Swift can fly, but she can never, ever rest.'

I look from the strutting chicken in the garden, a slave to men and prey to the fox, to the swift in the air, never able to catch her breath or sleep. It's not much of a choice, and my lower lip trembles. Euterpe gives me another squeeze.

'The story isn't over, Pusus, there's one more bird.' She lifts my hand again. 'Look.' We point at a fat little bird atop the garden wall. It's not as striking as the chicken or as fleet as the swift. It's just a round, chestnut ball with another ball on top, with a short beak and a rusty red cap.

'That's Sparrow,' she says. 'Can you say his name?'

'Sparrow.'

'Good. Do you remember our story so far, Pusus?'

'Chicken can walk but can't fly. Swift can fly but can't walk.'

'Very good!' Squeeze. 'Now, what do you think Sparrow chose?'

I think it over. Unlike the strutting hen or the swooping swift, the sparrow just sits atop the wall and swivels his head. He rises slightly on his short legs, puffs out his chest, and lifts his blunt little beak. Then he settles, and he is once again a ball of feathers with a smaller ball on top. I look at Euterpe. She's watching the sparrow with her bright brown eyes.

'Remember,' she says, 'God told each bird she could choose to do *one* thing well, or she could choose to do *many* things, but none of them very well. Now luckily for Sparrow, he got to choose after Chicken and after Swift, and he learned from their mistakes. He learned that the best thing is to be able to fly *and* to walk.'

As if to prove her point, the sparrow rises up on his legs again and sidles one way along the wall and then the other. Then in a flash, he is aloft. He's not as graceful as the looping swift, but in a flurry of wings, he has flown across the street and onto the peak of the red roof.

'What's the lesson?' says Euterpe. 'Can you guess?'

'Sparrow can walk,' I say, '*and* fly.'

'Very good!' Another squeeze. In my life so far, this is the best feeling I know.

'Maybe Sparrow can't walk as far as Chicken,' Euterpe says, 'but he can walk well enough to fill his belly. And maybe he can't fly as quickly as Swift, but he can fly fast enough to escape the fox and keep from being enslaved by man.'

The chicken struts past us again. The swift streaks overhead. From the red roof beyond the wall, Sparrow looks down on them both, and on us.

'Remember Sparrow, Little One,' Euterpe murmurs in my ear. 'He's not excellent at anything, but just *good enough* at everything. It's what the philosophers call the Golden Mean.'

'What's a phil . . . phil . . . ?'

'Phil-oss-oh-fer.'

'Is that another bird?'

Euterpe laughs. 'A philosopher is not a bird, Little One. A philosopher is a person who helps other people learn by asking them questions.'

'Are you a philosopher?'

Euterpe smiles. 'Yes and no.' She kisses the top of my head. 'Remember the story of the birds.' She touches her lips to my ear. 'If you get to choose,' she whispers, 'be like Sparrow.'

Just like that, Sparrow became my secret namesake. Compact and self-contained, he perched atop the wall, he fluffed his feathers, he swivelled his head, he broke his short beak and chirped. In the days after Euterpe told me the story, I stopped sometimes to watch him from the garden, convinced that he was watching me back. I turned my own face from side to side the way he did, I looked at him with one eye and then the other, and I chirped at him in his own language, one Sparrow to another. Sometimes he just looked back, sometimes he chirped, but sometimes he replied by erupting into flight, his blurred wings beating the air as he rose, flying and flying and flying away from me, becoming a tiny outline of himself until he dissolved into the blue.

I'm a sparrow, too, I thought. Someday I'll fly away.

Focaria and Euterpe and the birds weren't the only residents of the garden. There was Audo, of course, and there were my aunties, the other four wolves who lived and worked upstairs in the tavern. Their names were a conceit of Granatus, our Dominus and the owner of the tavern. The grandson of a freedman and the son of a tanner, Granatus had properties and businesses all over town, the better to dispel the stink of the tannery. He had bought his way onto the city's curia, and though he would never rise any higher, he had hopes that one or both of his sons might be elected aedile or duovir, or join the staff of the provincial governor, or, who knows, even become a senator. His older brother was the bishop of Carthago Nova, and thereby, at least unofficially, the most powerful man in the city.

Granatus had a bit of Greek, so he named his wolves after the Muses and called the tavern itself Helicon, after the traditional home of the Muses. He hired a sign painter to ink the name in big red letters on the wall outside, but if he thought these touches of Greek sophistication would attract a more elite clientele, he was mistaken. The punters were still mostly sailors and fishermen from the harbourside, freedmen and slaves who worked up and down the street, and a few of the local shopkeepers and merchants, looking for what they couldn't get at home. The tavern also attracted seasonal grain harvesters and olive pickers, who spent all their wages in one night, as well as the farmers who came into market once or twice a year and spent a portion of their profits before taking the rest home to their wives. Long before I came to live there, it was so common along the street to call the tavern 'Helicunt' that it wasn't even considered witty anymore. I didn't know any of this yet, of course. It was a long time before I learned that Helicon was also a mountain in Greece, that a wolf was also a kind of animal, and that Clio, Thalia, Urania, Melpomene, and Euterpe had been goddesses long before they were whores in Carthago Nova.

Yawning, blinking, and hungover, the wolves came into the garden every morning to eat their breakfast of tavern leftovers from the night before. The morning was also their time to escape their cramped cells for a bit of fresh air and sunshine and to trade stories about the punters from the night before. Sometimes they sang together – the first music I ever heard – but sometimes they separated and went off on their own, just to be blessedly alone for a little while. At first, each one had a different name for me. Clio, a Gaul, called me Mouse, because I was small and brown and quick, I suppose. She was plump and ghostly pale, with limp, colourless hair, a mournful smile, and watchful eyes. Her shyness masked a streak of resentment that surfaced if one of the other wolves got something she didn't. Of all the wolves, she smelled strongest of wine in the morning. She never knew what to say to me, but only patted my head at arm's length and said, 'What do you know, Mouse?' Then she wrapped herself in her stained blue gown and settled into the thicket of ferns behind the stack of firewood. Here she hummed or sang wordlessly to herself, or caught up on her sleep, snoring gently with her mouth open.

The two youngest wolves, Thalia and Urania, were as inseparable as sisters, and they always sat together and groomed each other like cats – tweezing each other's eyebrows, shaving each other's legs, parting each other's hair and pinching out the fleas. Thalia was compact and shapely in her yellow gown, and she was quick to laugh, quick to take offence, quick to forgive a moment later. She was an Egyptian and a Christian, and she spoke more tongues than the other wolves put together – Egyptian and Greek and Aramaic and Syrian, as well as Latin – which made her especially popular among the homesick sailors and other travellers who passed through

Carthago Nova. She knew songs in each language, too, and when the wolves sang together in the garden in the morning, she led them in a clear, high voice until the others dropped away, closed their eyes, and just listened. She was dusky like me, and her hair was thick and glossy like mine, and so she called me Little Brother. Sometimes she chased me up and down the rows of the garden, calling out, 'I'll catch you, Little Brother! I'll catch you and eat you up!'

Her friend Urania was the only wolf who came from Hispania, from a village nearby, sold into prostitution by her father, a pig farmer, to pay his imperial taxes. She was popular with the rustic punters, because her first language was the old tribal tongue, and she spoke Latin with the same rough accent they did. She was tall and bony, with a bent nose and sharp cheekbones and black, undulating hair, and her green gown hung from her as if from a scarecrow, accentuating her shoulder blades and her clavicles and the points of her hips. She seemed to watch the world as if from a great height, smiling slightly at things no one else thought were funny. She didn't have a special name for me, but simply called me Pusus, like Audo and Focaria did. Usually she only watched as Thalia chased me up and down the garden, but sometimes she caught me, too, and turned me about between her long-fingered hands like a farmer evaluating a newborn piglet, as if trying to decide if I was going to survive or not.

'Why don't you sing with Thalia?' I asked her once, and Urania looked at me gravely and said, 'Because I croak like a frog.'

'What's a frog?' I said, and she only smiled and turned me loose.

Even more than the rest of us, Urania was always hungry. While Thalia and I played in the garden, she often lingered outside the kitchen door and stared into the gloom with her sunken eyes. 'You'll eat when you're fed,' Focaria muttered, slicing an onion as if she were cutting someone's throat. But then Urania, glancing over her shoulder for Audo and not seeing him, stretched her long

21

arm through the door and rapped the kitchen table with the edge of a coin. Without turning round, Focaria reached back and palmed the coin, then reached back again with a piece of dry bread or a handful of olives. Stooping through the door, Urania stuffed the bread or olives into her mouth, swallowed it whole, then folded herself out the door again.

Melpomene, the fifth wolf, called me Antiochus, because I may or may not have been a Syrian, and up to seven of the old kings of Syria had been called Antiochus. Behind her back, the others called her 'Queen of the Wolves', partly because she was shockingly old, partly because she was a freedwoman, and partly because of her superior manner. A couple of years before, when she had turned thirty, the minimum legal age for manumission, she had persuaded Dominus to let her purchase her freedom. He'd wanted to sell her to defray the cost of a younger Melpomene, but she had offered him instead more money than she was likely to have fetched on the slaver's block. Over the years, by giving each punter a little something extra and then persuading him to tip her a coin or two more than what he'd already paid Audo, she had saved enough – coin by coin, fellation by fellation, fuck by fuck – to buy herself. She had even raised enough to pay the emperor's tax on manumission. Most surprisingly, she made a deal with Dominus to stay on at Helicon and continue to work as a wolf. She had calculated that it was cheaper to rent her old cell and pay for her meals than it would have been to set herself up in her own crib on the street. Her regulars knew where to find her at Helicon. On her own, she'd have had to start again from scratch.

Punters paid Audo up front to have one of the other wolves, but Melpomene accepted her own money in her cell upstairs. Unlike the other wolves, who were slaves, she could leave the tavern anytime she wanted to – properly covered up in her mantle – and buy things for herself. She kitted out her cell with cheap drapery and scented candles and doused herself with more expensive oils and perfumes than the other wolves were able to. Where the others shared a single, cloudy hand mirror and an old, mismatched set of grooming implements of tin and lead, Melpomene had her own mirror, combs, and razor, as well as a kit of tweezers, brushes, and an earwax spoon, all made of silver and wrapped in a wallet of soft leather. She was the only wolf to wear a gown of white cotton, and the only one to wear jewellery – rings and bracelets of bronze, necklaces of glass beads and amber, and earrings that looked like gold but almost certainly weren't. She sometimes told punters she was a senator's daughter from Rome, and once a week she came back from the hairdresser's with her unnaturally yellow hair piled high above her head like a lady's. She was fine-boned and sharp-nosed and highly strung, with wide eyes and a pointed chin, and she often reacted to whatever happened or whatever was said to her after half a beat, like an actor milking a moment on stage. Now that she was a renter and not a slave, Audo no longer beat her, and though Dominus had made a rule that Audo was supposed to pay for his sex like any other punter, Melpomene was the only wolf he actually, grudgingly paid.

Behind her back, the other wolves said she made up in showmanship and enthusiasm what she lacked in beauty or youth.

'She dyes it,' Clio said about her hair. 'Every time she goes to the hairdresser, it comes back a different colour.'

'The gown's second-hand,' said Urania. 'She bought it off a grave robber.'

'Oh, please,' said Thalia. 'I'm more Roman than she is.'

'Don't laugh,' said Euterpe, who tried never to be unkind to anyone, even behind her back. 'We'd do it, too, if we could afford it. When a punter has Mel, he can pretend he's fucking his Domina.'

Once a week, all five wolves came into the garden for their weekly cup of atocium, a herbal concoction to prevent pregnancy and induce menses. Focaria brewed it with rue and dill from the

23

garden, sometimes with raw egg added at the last moment to make it less bitter. Audo supervised, if only to keep the occasion from turning into a party. Today, the wolves gather just outside the kitchen, stretching in the last cool moment before the day's heat. They talk in low voices, sneaking glances all the while at Audo. But he only leans against the tavern wall and absently bites his nails. As always, he smells of wine and unwashed armpit.

I'm excited, because all the people I know in the world are in one place, and I scamper from one to the other, trying to attract attention. Only Thalia pays me any mind. She extends her hand and lets me swing at the end of her arm.

'Who had the groaner last night?' she murmurs over my head.

'A groaner?' Clio widens her eyes. 'What do you mean, a groaner?'

Thalia glances at Audo, who is gnawing on the nail of his little finger. In a low voice, she moans. 'Ohhhhh.' She lowers her chin. '*Ohhhhhhhhhhh*,' she says a bit more dramatically. All the wolves laugh quietly.

'Was that what it sounded like?' whispers Clio.

'Like he was dying?' says Euterpe.

'Like he was already dead,' says Thalia, letting me swing.

'That one was mine.' Urania smiles to herself. 'He wasn't quite dead.' More discreet laughter.

'He sounded like he was dead?' says Clio. 'What does that sound like?'

Urania and Thalia exchange a glance, and together they groan, '*Ohhhhhhhhhh!*' They dip their heads and laugh.

Melpomene is watching Audo. 'Not so loud,' she says under her breath.

'What were you doing to him?' whispers Euterpe.

'Nothing special.' Urania shrugs. 'I thought he was going to burst into tears.'

'I didn't hear him.' Clio, always afraid of missing out. 'Did you hear him?' she asks Euterpe, who shakes her head.

Melpomene, a little apart, suggests, 'He sounded like a professional mourner.'

'And about as convincing,' murmurs Thalia, and they all laugh again, even Melpomene.

'Quiet,' grumbles Audo, but he makes no move away from the wall. It's bad for business for the wolves to laugh openly at the punters, but in the privacy of the garden, even he doesn't think it's worth exerting himself over. As violent as he is with each wolf individually, he usually scruples not to strike them when they are all together. Meanwhile, I keep tugging on Thalia's arm, and she keeps ignoring me.

'Was he young?' Euterpe asks.

'No,' says Urania, 'he was old.'

'Older than us,' says Thalia, 'or *old* old?'

'Old enough to be my shit of a father,' says Urania. 'I had to help him get started.' She thrusts her little finger in and out of her mouth.

'Maybe he thought you were going to bite it off,' says Thalia.

I tug harder on her arm and call her name. 'Thalia! Thalia!'

'I wish I had,' Urania says. 'I thought he was never going to come.'

I yank on Thalia's arm – '*Thalia!*' – and she snaps, 'Stop it!' and jerks her hand away. I land on my backside in the dirt, but before I can start to cry, Euterpe catches me up and balances me on her hip, my legs around her waist. She rocks me from side to side. 'I didn't hear him,' she says.

'I didn't hear him, either,' says Clio.

'I'm not surprised,' says Melpomene. 'You make so much noise yourself, gasping and grunting.'

Thalia and Urania glance at each other. Euterpe says, 'Really, Mel . . .'

Clio gets red in the face. 'You can't talk to me like that.'

Audo looks up from his fingernails but says nothing.

'You wheeze like an old mule carrying a sack of wheat up a hill,' Melpomene announces. 'That's not what a man wants to hear when he's in the saddle.'

Clio sputters, and Euterpe says, 'That's unfair, Mel.' I tug at Euterpe's springy hair and she gently flicks my hand away. 'You get to pick and choose.'

Audo grunts and shifts against the wall. He is flexing his right hand. On the back of it, under the black hair, is the faded blue tattoo of an eagle with its wings spread. One day Focaria will explain to me that this is a sign that Audo used to be a soldier. 'Watch out for the eagle,' the wolves sometimes warn each other, or, 'The eagle's on the hunt,' on those days when Audo is in a worse mood than usual. Now he squeezes his fist and flexes the eagle's wings, and the wolves fall silent and stare at the ground. Riding on Euterpe's hip, not understanding what the silence means, I seize my opportunity.

'Ohhhhhh,' I say in my piping little voice.

Thalia and Urania start to laugh behind their hands. Clio gasps. Melpomene widens her eyes. Euterpe looks sidelong at me.

'*Ohhhhhhhhhh.*' I have no idea what it means. I only know it makes them laugh when Thalia does it.

I draw a breath to groan again, but now they are all staring at me, even Audo, and I shrink against Euterpe. All the wolves burst into laughter, even Melpomene.

'Mouse!'

'Little One!'

'Listen to *you*, Antiochus!'

'Little pitchers have big ears!'

'*He's* more convincing!' says Thalia, and they all laugh again. Even Audo represses a smile, and I bury my face in Euterpe's spicy neck.

'What's so funny?' Focaria, in the kitchen door, dangles a small black kettle from one hand and a tin cup in the other. She is not laughing. The wolves glance round at each other. How long has she been standing there? 'It's ready.' She hoists the kettle and waggles the cup.

Still smiling, the wolves cluster round the door. 'One at a time,' Focaria says.

Melpomene pushes ahead of the others. Clio bristles, but no one complains. Melpomene is paying for her dose, after all, and she holds her hand out for the cup as Focaria dips it into the pot. She downs it in one gulp, tightening her lips at the taste, then hands the cup back to Focaria and shoulders through the other wolves, through the arch, and out of sight. The others let Clio go next, and she smacks her lips and sticks out her tongue afterwards. Urania takes a deep breath as if about to plunge into deep water and throws it straight down her throat. Thalia takes each tentative little sip as if hoping the next one will taste better. Finally Euterpe, still holding me, swishes it round in her mouth before she swallows.

As she returns the cup to Focaria, I hold out my hand and say, 'Me.'

'No.' Euterpe swings me away from the doorway.

'*Me*.' I twist in her arms, still reaching for the cup.

'Let him have some,' says Thalia. 'What could it hurt?'

'Let him see what it's like,' mutters Clio.

'There's a bit left,' Focaria says.

'He's just a boy,' Euterpe says. 'He doesn't understand.'

Focaria waggles the empty cup. 'Would you like some?' Her eyes are maliciously bright. 'I guarantee you won't get pregnant.'

'I want!' I am starting to cry. 'I *want*!'

Under all that fat, Audo still has the reflexes of a soldier, and he launches himself from the wall so suddenly that the wolves all scatter like birds. He grabs Clio bruisingly by her arm and spins her so that she stumbles through the archway. He swings his eagle at Thalia, who ducks and scurries after Clio through the arch.

Urania dances behind him and follows the others. Now Audo storms toward Euterpe, who turns to put herself between his fist and me. He kicks her backside so that she staggers toward Focaria, who retreats into the kitchen, sloshing atocium out of the kettle and into the dirt.

'For fuck's sake!' Audo bellows, only inches from Euterpe's ear, and his sour breath washes over us. Hunching her shoulders as he slaps the back of her head, Euterpe crushes me against her breast and ducks through the door into the kitchen. In the gloom, the two women each hustle round the table in opposite directions, putting it between them and Audo. They huddle together on the far side, while Audo blocks the light in the doorway. Focaria has lost the tin cup, but she holds the kettle before her with both hands. Euterpe has wrapped me tightly in her arms, and I am sobbing into her neck.

'Keep him *quiet*!' Audo breathes heavily in the doorway. 'That's your *job*.'

Then just as suddenly, he is gone, leaving Focaria and Euterpe blinking in the glare.

Focaria exhales. She sets the kettle on the table. Euterpe rocks me from side to side. Her heart pounds against mine.

'That was my fault,' Focaria says.

Euterpe jiggles me up and down. 'He's just a child.'

'I know,' Focaria says. 'I'm sorry.'

'He's just a *child*.'

Focaria reaches for the kettle. 'He can have some if he wants.'

Limb by limb, Euterpe peels me off her and sets me on the tabletop.

'You're getting too big for me,' she says.

I am beyond crying now into hiccupping. She strokes my hair and kisses my cheek, my forehead, my nose. Focaria steps away and comes back with the tin cup.

'No,' Euterpe says. 'He won't like the taste.'

'It's only water.' Focaria offers the cup, and Euterpe holds it to my lips and steadies my head with her other hand. 'Just a sip, Little One.'

There is still a bitter taste of atocium in the cup, but I gulp the water anyway.

'He won't be a child forever,' Focaria says. 'He'll be groaning upstairs himself, soon enough.'

Euterpe winces as if at a sudden, private pain. In spite of my size, she picks me up again and rocks me.

'I know.' Her breath is warm against my ear.

'You're good to him,' Focaria says.

'Thank you,' says Euterpe.

'That's not a compliment,' says Focaria. 'It's just an observation.'

Euterpe looks at her.

'You may not be doing him any favours,' Focaria says, 'in the long run.'

'I know that too,' Euterpe says.

'I could help you with him.'

A sharp look from Euterpe. 'I thought *I* was helping *you*.'

I am mostly calm again, and I gaze past Euterpe's shoulder at Focaria. She reaches up to flick at a spike of my tangled hair.

'I could teach him to work.' Focaria pulls her hand back and shifts her gaze to Euterpe.

'Yes,' says Euterpe. 'You could be his father.'

Focaria rolls her eyes, but Euterpe smiles. 'It's a joke,' she says.

The two women gaze at each other for a long moment.

'We could both be his mothers.' Focaria lifts her hand again, but this time she lets the tips of her fingers brush Euterpe's hair and cheek. Euterpe does not lean into it, but she does not pull away, either. The two women breathe each other in, and with each breath, the iron collar around Focaria's neck rises and falls. At last Focaria draws her hand back.

Euterpe kisses me. 'Would you like that, Little One? Would you like to have two mothers?'

My eyes meet Focaria's. She mouths the words, 'Say yes.'
I bury my face in Euterpe's hair.
'Yes,' I say.

And so Euterpe was my mother in the morning and Focaria was
my mother for the rest of the day. Euterpe sat with me while Focaria
left the garden to fetch water from the fountain and do her shopping, returning with her wicker basket full of vegetables or bread
or fish. When she thought Audo wouldn't catch her at it, Focaria
sometimes joined us for a little while, until Euterpe had to go
inside or leave for the baths. She would bring Euterpe and me a
piece of fruit to share as we sat against the water tank and watched
the shadow of the wall behind us retreat across the garden toward
our toes. The two women sat touching shoulders with their backs
to the tank, murmuring together and even laughing. Sometimes
their fingers intertwined. I played in the dirt a little distance away
and pretended not to watch.

Late in the morning nearly every day, the other wolves came
down into the garden for their trip to the baths, and Euterpe stood
and brushed herself off. She kissed the top of my head and
murmured, 'Time for the Parade of the Wolves,' and joined the
women whispering at the unpainted wooden door that led to the
street. When Audo came out, they fell silent and arranged themselves into a line: Melpomene in front, and then, in no particular
order, Clio, Thalia, and Urania, with Euterpe usually last. Over
their colourful gowns they wore pale linen mantles that covered
them from throat to toe. The mantles were fitted with hoods, too,
which Euterpe, Thalia, Urania, and Clio put over their heads when
they left the garden, while Melpomene walked with her head bared.
Without a word, Audo opened the door and shepherded them into
the street, bringing up the rear. As he pulled the door shut behind
him, I rushed to the wall, where I could hear the slap of their
sandals as they moved away up the street. I listened until I couldn't

hear them anymore, like a dog who doesn't believe his mistress will ever come back, until she does.

'Why can't I go?' I always asked, and Focaria said, 'You're too young,' or 'When you're older,' or 'You're not that dirty.' Instead she washed me herself in the kitchen, stripping my tunic over my head and scrubbing me top to bottom with a scratchy sponge and a bucket of water.

'Why don't you go?' I said.

'I go when Audo can spare me. And Audo usually can't spare me.'

'Why not?'

'Because I do everything around here that Audo doesn't do, and he doesn't do much.'

'What are the baths like?'

'Wet.' She made the sponge burn a little. 'Quit wriggling.'

Still, Focaria was not as rough as she used to be, before Euterpe. She taught me how to scour a pot, how to scrub the kitchen floor with a brush. She taught me how to scrape last night's ashes out of the firebox while keeping aside an ember to light this morning's fire, and how to keep the new fire lit by pumping the wheezing old bellows. She sent me into the garden to fetch firewood, to carry water in from the tank, to pitch ashes into the latrine to absorb the smell. She showed me how to water the herbs and vegetables in the garden without drowning them, how to start in the far corner of the kitchen with a broom and sweep toward the door, how to carry a bucket of water with an underhand grip rather than over-hand. She might grasp the top of my head and turn me to look at what she wanted me to see, she might forcefully place my hands on the broom handle, but she usually hit me only when Audo was watching, more for his benefit than for mine.

Meanwhile, during our time together every morning, Euterpe told me stories meant to astonish me about the world beyond the garden wall – where the sun goes at night, where the moon is during the day, why the stars move so slowly, why the wind blows, why rain falls from the sky. She also instructed me in the difference between men and women, opening her gown and lifting the hem of my tunic to show me the difference between our legs. She told me that I was circumcised and explained what that meant, though I didn't really understand. She told me that men, like Audo, and women, like her, came together somehow to make children, though I didn't really understand that, either. She told me that every child grows inside a woman's belly, and that every child has a mother and a father, even if the child doesn't know who they were.

'Is Audo my father?' I asked her, and she said no. 'Are you my mother?' I asked her, and she said no. 'Is Focaria my mother?' I asked her, and she said no.

'Where do I come from?' I asked. She said she didn't know, but it had to be further south than Hispania, someplace where the sun burned hotter than here and turned the skin of the people dusky, like mine. She was even darker than I was, and she told me she came from a land called Mauretania. Because I was circumcised, I had to have come from somewhere in the east – the same place where the sun comes from every morning – some land where mothers and fathers trim the tips of their male children. So I might be a Jew, she told me, whatever that was, or I might be a Syrian. I might even come from Egypt, where, she told me, a long snake of water called a river flowed through seven mouths into the Mare Nostrum, turning the sea brown, like the people, with the silt of the Nile.

All of this inspired many questions. How can water be like a snake? What is the Mare Nostrum? Where are my mother and father? Why is the sun hot? Why is the moon cold? Does Audo know where I came from? Does anybody? How does a child get out of a woman's belly? Is it violent and bloody like Focaria cutting the guts and spine out of a fish? Does it leave the woman empty and glassy-eyed afterwards?

Rather than answer these unanswerable questions, Euterpe often tried to distract me. I was lucky, she said, that I didn't come from someplace where the people were monsters, half human, half something else. Near the cave where the North Wind rises, she told me, lived a race of men who each had a single eye in the middle of his forehead, and in a hidden valley in the mountains lived a people whose feet were turned the other way. Having shown me the difference between our legs, she told me there was a race of people who each had a penis *and* a vagina. There were people who had two pupils in each eye, people with the heads of dogs who barked at each other instead of talking, people with one leg each who hopped everywhere they went, people born with hairy tails like a cat, people who had enormous ears that covered their bodies, people who had no necks and whose eyes were in their shoulders. She told me about naked wise men who lived in the desert and who spent all day, every day, just staring at the sun as it moved across the sky, shifting from one bare foot to the other in the hot sand.

I don't think she intended to frighten me with these stories, but I don't think she understood the effect they had on me. The street just beyond the door, she told me, was full of ordinary things and ordinary people that I would very soon see for myself. The strange creatures she told me about may not actually be real, or if they were, lived very far away from us. But as much as I loved Euterpe, I didn't believe she was telling me the whole truth. For a little boy whose only world was a cramped, smoky kitchen and a narrow garden ten paces across, anything beyond the garden door was very far away. And to hear Euterpe tell it, most of that world was full of monsters.

And in my imagination, I associated most of these monsters with men.

*   *   *

Apart from the drunken punter who had wandered into the kitchen and attacked Focaria, Audo was the only man I'd ever seen up close. He, too, was at least a little drunk all the time, and just on principle, he hit Focaria and me every time he came into the kitchen. Once in a while he came and went without striking us, but that was even more unnerving, his way of making us grateful to him for not inflicting a bruise. Sometimes Focaria said, as soon as he came into the kitchen, 'Just hit me, Audo, and get it over with.' Most of the time he showed us the eagle, even if it was just a tap to remind us he could do much worse. 'Stew's too thick,' he'd say, and slap the back of Focaria's head. 'Don't let the fire go out,' he'd say, and slap the back of mine.

Now and then a punter passed through the garden on the way to the latrine, darkening the doorway during the day or staggering at night through the fan of yellow light cast by our lamp. From my corner, where I sometimes tried to sleep even while Focaria was still working, I could hear his tuneless crooning in the latrine as he aimed more or less into the hole, or his clenched curses as he strained on the seat. Sometimes he didn't make it to the latrine and pissed against the garden wall or fertilized the turnips with a pungent coil. Sometimes I heard the spatter of vomit amid the plants in the garden, and one of my jobs in the morning was to sluice the mess off the leaves or turn it into the soil with a trowel.

I heard men more often than I saw them. Every night Focaria carried pots of stew, skewers of grilled meat, and platters of bread through the arch into the tavern, and every night she came back muttering 'drunken pigs' or worse. Some nights she forgot about me, and I sat against the water tank as the dark amplified the uproar from the tavern, a rumbling murmur that swelled to shouts and harsh laughter, then subsided to a murmur again. Sometimes I heard a man singing, or two men singing in harmony, or all of them singing raggedly together. Now and then I made out the words, though I didn't know what they meant:

My dirty girl, I pinch her breast
I pound her in her cuckoo's nest
My dirty girl, she fucks the best
I love my dirty girl!

Late at night, as the men's voices died away up the street, I heard different sounds from the three barred windows under the eaves of the second storey. I wasn't even sure these sounds were made by people because they weren't words or songs, only grunts and gasps and groans, or high-pitched chirping like a bird's, or whimpering like a child's, or keening like an animal in pain.

One night I'm startled awake by the slapping steps of a runner reverberating up the empty street beyond the garden wall. Lying in my corner among the cockroaches and mouse pellets, I open my eyes wide to the twin curves of Focaria, shoulder and hip, lying on the other side of the dying fire in the oven. The thudding footfalls come closer, and I hear two men in the distance shouting. The runner slaps to a stop just beyond our wall. Focaria lifts her head and looks to see if I'm awake.

Across the garden, the man beyond the wall pants like a beast. The two shouters converge on him, their footfalls slapping from opposite ends of the street. Now the gasping man is hammering on the garden door. I flinch as if he were hitting me. Focaria puts her finger to her lips.

'Help!' His voice is pitched high. 'Help me!'

I begin to whimper, and Focaria crawls to me through the red glow of the fire, her hair swinging, her eyes two black pools. She creeps round behind me and pulls me against her. Her iron collar presses against the back of my neck. Her hot breath rasps in my ear. She puts her hand over my mouth. It smells of fish and onions.

The pounding stops. The man beyond the door whimpers like a child. I can't make out what he's saying, but he's begging for his life. From our corner by the fire, through the legs of the table, I see only the black rectangle of the kitchen doorway.

There is a meaty thump against the door and a piercing cry. Focaria and I both flinch.

'Don't listen!' she hisses, but I hear grunts and curses and the scuffle of feet, then a sharp, wet sound, *snick snick snick*, like Focaria gutting a fish.

She tightens her arms around me. Her rough palm squeezes my mouth.

'Ohhhhhh,' the man outside groans. '*Ohhhhhhhhhhh . . .*'

Something slides down the garden door. The groaning becomes a wet, choking gurgle. Someone murmurs something, someone else laughs. Then silence.

Wide-eyed and breathless, Focaria and I stare into the black kitchen doorway, an opening we cannot close, a wound that will never heal. In the darkness I see the man Audo gouged with his knife one morning, I see the blood oozing through his fingers. With her other hand, Focaria covers my eyes and whispers.

'Nothing happened.' Her lips against my ear. 'You're having a bad dream.'

In the hot darkness behind her palm, I strain toward the silence, but there is no more running or gasping or groaning. We don't even hear the other men walk away, just the dry sifting of ashes in the fire. Neither of us speaks. Eventually, Focaria's arms around me loosen. Her hands slip from my mouth and my eyes. Her breathing becomes steadier. Still folded in her loose embrace, my own heart slows, my breath comes slower. At last, just as I'm falling asleep, I hear water trickling somewhere nearby, falling endlessly in a steady stream, all night long.

Perhaps you are already wondering, are these his actual memories, or are they only scenes he has invented or imagined, like a poet or a dramatist? Reader, I swear I have kept my promise not to lie to

36

you, but I have lived long enough to understand that memory is a shell game. The indelible image in my mind might have originally been placed under the cup of truth, but it might also have been placed under the cup of mistake, or the cup of fantasy, and over the years the cups have shifted places so swiftly under the conjuror's hands that finally even the conjuror himself no longer knows which is which.

Unlike Euterpe, who was a philosopher and not a philosopher, I am decidedly not a philosopher. She told me only half the story – a philosopher, it turns out, is someone who asks people questions, but then tells them their answers are wrong. I have met one or two philosophers in my time, so I know what I'm talking about. I don't have the philosophical temperament myself. I have no answers. I don't even know what the questions are. I'm just a tired old delicatus, a slave who, against the odds, has lived much longer than he or anyone else ever expected him to, and who has educated himself much too far above his station. I promised not to lie to you, reader, but I cannot promise that everything I remember is true.

The weathered old door to the street was stouter than it needed to be to protect the kitchen garden of a tavern. It was probably Audo's handiwork, a door more suitable for one of the massive forts where he'd served along the German frontier. It was fashioned from thick, upright beams banded with iron and reinforced with a pair of planks across the door in a giant X. It turned on iron hinges that Focaria regularly lubricated with oil or fat, and it could be locked from inside by a massive barrel bolt that only Audo could open with one hand. The ends of the planks, top and bottom, were worn splintery and soft from years of scraping against the lintel and the doorstep. Flakes of paint deep in the crevices of the wood showed that, on the inside at least, the door had once been red.

The morning after the stabbing, Focaria hauled back the bolt with both hands and scraped the door open just wide enough to peer out, while I peeked out of the kitchen with my heart pounding. No one was there, but Focaria sluiced the doorstep with three buckets of water before pushing the door shut and bolting it again. She caught me watching and shooed me back inside.

'Nothing to see,' she said. 'You had a bad dream.'

'You had it, too,' I said.

She swatted the back of my head. 'No, I didn't. Now fetch the broom.'

That morning, I started to make a mental map of my little fallen paradise. From every point in the garden, I learned the quickest route back to my own dark corner of the kitchen, and I learned the other hidden places where I could dash if the door suddenly opened with no warning. There was the dank space behind the water tank where Clio sometimes took her naps. There was the reeking space behind the door of the latrine, full of fat, buzzing flies. There were the weeds behind the woodpile, crawling with spiders and mice. None of these places were pleasant, but all of them were the right size for a boy to hide from anyone or anything that might come through the door. There was also the tavern archway, where Audo came and went, but I was forbidden to enter Helicon, and anyway, the obscene songs and raucous laughter of the punters were nearly as frightening as the violence in the street.

Out of sheer exhaustion I fell asleep every night, but now all it took were footsteps or a loud voice in the street to jolt me awake. I lay with my heart pounding and my eyes wide open, straining at the darkness until I fell asleep again to the steady trickle from the neighbourhood fountain. Then just before dawn, I woke to the ear-splitting crowing of our rooster. I became an anxious student of the sounds that floated over the wall – the women greeting each other at the fountain, the clatter of shop shutters, the barking of dogs – but especially the voices of men. A shopkeeper driving a peddler away from his shopfront with curses and kicks, the idle boys at the corner, singing at a higher pitch the same obscene songs as the punters in the tavern, the city crier announcing a reward for a runaway slave in a staccato singsong: 'FIFty denarii for the return of FORtunatus, a GREEK boy, FIFteen years of age . . .' Before I had ever seen one, I heard the creak of a cart, the rumble and crunch of its wheels, the *clop clop clop* of the mule drawing it on, the tinkling bell in her harness, the carter murmuring 'old girl' into her ear. Then I'd hear the carter trading insults with another mule-teer who was bringing his cart the other way, until one of them relented and backed up, and whatever I was doing – pulling weeds, scrubbing out an iron pot, hauling water one bucket at a time to the kitchen – I froze and watched the door intently, wondering if those old planks were thick enough and the barrel bolt strong enough to protect me at the inevitable moment when a blade went *snick snick snick*, and one of the men laughed while the other's last breath bubbled from his lips.

I also learned about men from the wolves. One day when Audo was out, they sat together in the early morning shade and talked about their fathers. Clio said she didn't know who her father was. Thalia talked tearfully of being torn from her father's arms by a soldier. Euterpe shook her head and refused to speak about her father. Urania, for once, was the most talkative. She told a long story about her father taking her from their farm one day and into the nearest village, where he hired a cart to carry them, for the first and last time in her life, past the big stone boar that marked the boundary of her tribe and all the way into the city. Here he sold her to a slave dealer to pay for the emperor's tax. The last thing she ever heard her father say was, 'Sell her far away from here. I don't want her wandering back.' But the dealer sold her to Audo, and here she was.

Then their talk turned to Audo himself. 'Wasn't he a soldier?' Clio wanted to know, but the others didn't know much more than she did. By now, Focaria had come into the garden to pinch off some leaves of basil, and she hovered near us, listening but not saying anything.

'He never talks about it,' said Urania.

'Is that strange?' said Thalia.

'I've never met a soldier yet,' said Urania, 'who didn't want to show me his scars and tell me how many men he killed.'

Focaria barked a laugh, and we all looked up.

'Of course he doesn't talk about it,' she said, clutching her fistful of basil. 'The army threw him out. He didn't *retire*.'

'How do you know?' said Euterpe.

'Think about it.' Focaria loomed over us. 'When you retire from the army, they give you money and a plot of land. If Audo *retired* instead of being kicked out, he'd be sitting on his ass in Germania somewhere, watching his brats plough his fields and milk his cows, not sleeping under the stairs in a tavern a thousand miles away, herding whores.'

She walked back toward the kitchen. 'I know a thing or two about soldiers,' she said.

And yet, strange as it may seem to you, reader, it simply didn't occur to me at this stage in my life that I had anything in common with men, with these large, loud, hairy, violent, untrustworthy creatures. Although Euterpe had shown me how she and I were different between our legs, I didn't know then how much difference that difference made. I was only a boy, and the only people I loved, and who loved me, were women. Nothing human is alien to me, says the playwright, but men were alien to me, because I didn't think they were people. It never entered my imagination that I might grow up to become one of them. And, in the end, as it happened, I didn't.

I lived in this state of alert for weeks after the night of the stabbing. As I weeded the garden, I watched the door. As I fetched wood to the kitchen, I watched the door. As I lit the fire in the oven, even though I could not see the door, the thought of it prickled the back of my neck, as if the door were watching me. When Audo

40

led the wolves out for their daily parade to the baths, I hid in my corner of the kitchen or in the latrine or behind the woodpile until Focaria bolted the door behind them. Only when I was sitting with Euterpe did I let my guard down, distracted by her stories, by the warmth of her touch, by the mellow sound of her voice.

When the moment I've been dreading comes at last, I am sitting cross-legged in front of Euterpe with my back to the door. I'm rapt as she traces a map in the dirt with her finger and tells me about our two boy emperors. She is explaining to me that our garden is only part of a tavern, which sits on a street, which runs through a town, which sits by the sea, which sits in the middle of the earth. She draws the shape of an egg in the dust and says, 'This is the sea.' Then she draws another, larger egg around the first one and says, 'This is the empire.'

The empire, she says – the garden, Helicon, the street, the town, the sea, and all the land around the sea – is inhabited by millions of people, and all of these people live under the authority of a single man called the emperor. I stare very hard at the two eggs, one within the other.

'How many people is a million?' I say.

Euterpe swipes up a handful of soft dirt. 'How many grains do you think are in my hand right now? How long would it take you to count them all?'

I can only count to twenty, on my fingers and toes. She slowly pours the dust back onto the ground. 'It's more people than that,' she says.

I'm speechless for a moment, then I say, 'And the emperor tells them all what to do?'

'Well, he's in charge.'

'Is he like Audo?'

'Sort of,' says Euterpe, 'only nicer.'

This is equally hard to understand. Audo may be a disgraced soldier, but he is the most powerful person I know, and he makes everyone do what he wants by hitting or threatening to hit them. How can one man threaten to hit a million people? And how can he do it by being nicer than Audo?

The emperor, explains Euterpe, has helpers who act as his eyes and his hands. 'Right now, in fact,' she says, 'there are two emperors, so each one only has half as much to do.'

Two Audos! How would that work?

'Not only that,' Euterpe says, 'but the two emperors are both little boys, not much older than you.'

Again, I am speechless.

'Each one rules a different half of the empire,' she says. 'Arcadius rules the east, where you came from, and Honorius rules the west, which is where you live now.'

This is too much to believe. How can two little boys rule the empire? I'm a little boy, and I can't imagine telling Focaria what to do, let alone Audo. I can't even imagine telling Thalia or Urania what to do, even in jest, even if there were two of me. It doesn't make any sense. How can two little boys at the top be in charge of everybody, when there is one little boy at the bottom who is in charge of nothing, not even himself?

'How could . . .' I stare at the dirt, trying and failing to imagine each invisible grain as a person.

'How could what?' Euterpe bends closer.

'How could anyone tell Audo what to do?'

At that moment, there is a pounding at the door. I leap straight to my feet, instantly terrified, and instantly furious at myself for letting down my guard.

'Little One!' laughs Euterpe, and grabs my wrist.

'Let me go!' I hiss, afraid to speak any louder. I lean away from her, trying to break free.

The hammering pauses.

'Audo, you lazy savage!' drawls a voice from the other side. The hammering starts again, filling the garden. 'Open the fucking door!'

I twist and turn and whimper in Euterpe's grasp, but she pulls me onto her lap and pins my arms in her embrace. 'It's all right,' she says, 'it's only Dominus.'

The hammering goes on and on until Audo staggers out of the tavern, rubbing his eye with one hand and adjusting his crotch with the other.

'Coming,' he rasps, and he yanks back the bolt and hauls the door open.

I go stiff as a hare in Euterpe's arms. If I had not already emptied my bladder this morning, I would be peeing myself. I expect to see someone even larger than Audo come through the doorway, one of Euterpe's monsters with one eye, one leg, and a tail. I expect to see him stab Audo and fling him one-handed across the garden. I expect to see him turn the burning eye in the middle of his forehead on Euterpe and me, in the last moment before we die.

But it isn't a monster. It's just a trim young man with two legs and no tail, and two ordinary eyes right where they're supposed to be. He's smaller than Audo, but he strides in as if he owns the place. Which, as it happens, he does.

'Peace of Dominus be with you,' he says in a singsong, flicking his hand at Audo.

'Peace of Dominus,' mutters Audo, who closes and bolts the door again. Then, to my astonishment, he backs up. He's a head taller than this new man, and yet he lowers his eyes, hunches his shoulders, and rubs his palms together.

'Were you still sleeping?' The man is not only shorter than Audo, he's slimmer and much younger, almost as young as one of the wolves.

'It's early, Your Honour.' Audo is nearly whispering. I have never heard him speak so quietly.

'Really.' The young man saunters up a row of the garden, knee-deep in the drooping leaves. He has a smooth face and thick dark hair, swept back and glistening with oil. He wears a white tunic

43

of much finer stuff than Audo's or mine, almost as fine as the stuff of Melpomene's gown, with a repeating blue pattern along the hem and the cuffs of his short sleeves. He looks back at Audo.

'I've been up for several hours already,' he says. 'And I don't have nearly as much to do as you do.'

'No, Your Honour.'

'We don't pay you to sleep.'

'No, Your Honour.'

The young man pauses, hands on hips, in the middle of the garden. His eyes flicker over Euterpe and me. Then he turns, laughing.

'I'm only kidding, Audo.' He walks back to the bigger man and claps him on the shoulder. 'You have to sleep sometime.'

'Yes, Your Honour.'

The young man fans the air between them with his hand. 'Oof,' he says. 'Happy is the nose that can't smell German.'

Audo makes a choking little chuckle, but the young man takes his elbow. 'Come, you smelly beast,' he says, guiding him into the tavern, 'show me how well you've done this week.'

To my continuing astonishment, Audo not only does not hit the smaller man, he allows himself to be led. Euterpe loosens her arms around me, but I still cling to her.

'That's Dominus?' I already know that Audo is not the owner of Helicon, that he merely runs it for a man named Granatus we all call Dominus. But I have always assumed Dominus is even larger and more frightening than Audo, not a trim young man in a fancy tunic. As I understand the world, the big ones rule the little ones, never the other way around.

'That's his son,' says Euterpe. 'But he's Dominus too.'

'Are there two of them?' I ask. 'Like the boy emperors?'

'Yes, but they're not brothers. They're father and son.'

'Why do they have the same name?' I say.

'I don't think they do. Granatus is the father,' she says, then, nodding toward the archway, 'and that one is his son. I don't know his name.'

44

'And he's Dominus, too?'

'Yes.'

'So why did he call Audo "Dominus"?'

'What?'

'He said, "Peace of Dominus be with you."'

'That's a different Dominus. He was referring to God.'

My eyes widen. 'There are *three* of them?'

'Dominus is not a name. It's *what* they are, not *who* they are.'

'I don't understand,' I say.

Euterpe sighs. Just then there's another knock on the door, but not as loud. I start, and Euterpe wraps me tightly in her arms again.

'Audo!' It's Focaria, her voice as sharp as her knock.

'Focaria's back.' Euterpe is relieved. 'She'll explain it to you.'

At that moment, the young Dominus's voice, loud and confident, precedes him through the tavern arch, and he reappears carrying a leather pouch bulging with coins, idly dangling it by its draw-string. Focaria knocks impatiently on the door again, and Audo reappears as well, edging his bulk deferentially round the younger man to the door. Audo pulls back the bolt, and Focaria storms in under his arm, a wicker basket full of bread on her back.

'That *fucking* baker.' Her fists are clenched around the basket's linen straps. 'Renatus tried to short-change me again. You need to have a fucking word with him.'

Audo grabs her shoulder and jerks her so that she notices the younger man in his expensive tunic. She stops short and lowers her head.

'Dominus,' she mutters.

But Dominus has not noticed her. He is sauntering through the garden toward Euterpe and me, swinging the pouch. The wolf and I shift against each other, and her arms around me loosen. We tilt our faces up as he stands above us.

'Peace of Dominus be with you,' he says.

'Peace of Dominus,' says Euterpe.

45

'Which one are you?' he says.

'Euterpe, Dominus.'

She lowers her gaze to the dirt, but I stare openly up at the young man. He is less hairy than Audo or the punters I glimpse staggering to the latrine. His eyebrows have been plucked, like a wolf's. Like Melpomene, he wears a bracelet and rings – of real gold – on his fingers. He even smells good, like Melpomene does early in the evening.

'You're the new one,' he says to Euterpe. 'How long have you been here?'

'Almost a year, Dominus.'

'Really.' He bounces the leather pouch on its string. It clinks, full of coins. He glances back at Audo, then lowers his voice. 'Have I had you yet?'

'No, Dominus.' Euterpe starts to shift me off her lap.

'Not *now*,' he laughs. 'It's too early in the day for that.' He lifts his chin at me. 'Is this your son?'

'No, Dominus.'

'Don't lie to me,' he says.

Euterpe lifts her face, just enough to peer up at him. 'No, Dominus, he is not my son.'

He shifts his gaze to me. 'Is this your mother?'

I open my mouth, but nothing comes out.

'I'm truly not his mother, Dominus,' Euterpe says.

'Let him answer.'

I peek at Euterpe, but she is staring at the young man's feet. His shoes are new and very clean, and his toenails are as smooth and manicured as Melpomene's, though they aren't painted.

'I look after him.' She keeps her voice low. 'When Focaria is out.'

'Well, he can't be Focaria's,' he says. 'He's a dusky little monkey.'

'No, Dominus.'

'Audo!' He turns to call across the garden. 'What's this boy doing here? Why haven't I seen him before? Where did he come from?'

46

Across the garden, Audo lets go of Focaria's shoulder. She stays put, watching from under her eyebrows as Audo minces up one of the rows of the garden.

'Focaria keeps him out of sight, Your Honour,' he says. 'As your father directed.'

'Well, there's Focaria.' The young man gestures lazily at the cook, who stands with her head down and her thumbs still hooked through the straps of her basket. 'And yet here's the boy, with . . . with . . . which one are you again?'

'Euterpe, Dominus.'

'She looks after him in the morning,' Audo says, 'while Focaria—'

'Whatever.' The young man waves his hand. 'I don't need to know all the details.'

'Your Honour.' Audo ventures a bit closer, and he stoops to whisper something that only the young man can hear. Dominus lifts his eyes to the sky as he listens, and he swings the clinking pouch at the end of its string.

'Ah,' he sighs when Audo finishes and steps back. 'I see.' He turns and smiles down at me. 'You're a lucky boy. Everyone else has to pay to spend that much time with, um, Euterpe.'

Audo makes his choking laugh again. Behind him, Focaria shuffles her feet and taps her fingers on the straps of the basket. Euterpe breathes through her nose.

'Not me, of course.' The young man laughs at his own joke. 'I don't have to pay for anyone, do I, Audo?'

'No, Your Honour.' Audo ventures a weak smile.

'But you do, don't you?'

'Your Honour?' Audo's smile freezes.

'Pay for a wolf's services.'

'Of course, Your Honour,' Audo says much too quickly.

'Still, I'm sure they give you a little something extra.'

He pauses. Audo clears his throat. Euterpe stares at the dirt. Focaria sneaks a glance at the kitchen door.

'Never mind, I'm only joking.' Dominus sighs. 'I don't know why I bother.' He starts toward the door and Audo dances clumsily out of his way. 'Have Focaria start taking him with her when she goes shopping. He can . . . carry things or something.'

'But your father, Your Honour . . .' Audo says, licking his lips.

'My father's not here.' The young man pauses at the door and lifts his chin in my direction. 'That's just a bit of trash from the stews of Antioch. Or Alexandria. Maybe Jerusalem.' He sighs. 'Whatever. Put the boy to work.'

'Yes, Your Honour.'

'That goes for everybody.' The young man waggles his fingers. 'Why are you all standing around?'

The rest of us wince where we stand or sit, as if each of us has just been pinched.

Dominus sails toward the door. 'A good week, Audo.' The last we see of him is his hand in the air over the top of the door, hefting the pouch like a ball. 'Peace.'

For a moment after he is gone, silence. Breathing heavily, Audo stares dully at the open door. Then he slams it and turns toward the arch. Focaria cringes away from him, putting up her hands. But Audo only sails past her into the tavern, and Focaria scuttles into the kitchen. Euterpe hoists me to my feet, kisses me quickly, and hurries through the arch after Audo.

In the kitchen, Focaria is unloading the basket.

'Why do they all have the same name?' I watch her from the other side of the table.

'Why does who have the same name?' She is separating the loaves of bread into two wooden bins, one for the day-old, wholemeal bread we eat, the other for the fresh white bread we serve to the punters. A symbol is pressed into each loaf, the baker's mark, combining (I later learned) the Greek letters *chi* and *rho*.

'Dominus,' I say, 'and the other Dominus. And God. Euterpe said you'd explain it to me.'

'Oh, she did?' Focaria slaps the flour dust off her hands. She stuffs the basket into the corner and jerks the broom away from the wall.

'She said Dominus is *what* he is, not *who* he is,' I insist. 'I don't know what that means.'

'She leaves the hard ones for me, doesn't she,' mutters Focaria. She thrusts the broom at me. 'Start sweeping, and I'll tell you.'

I start to scrape the floor where I stand, and she pinches my earlobe and drags me round the table. 'Start in the *corner*,' she says. 'Sweep toward the door. How many times do I have to say it?'

I put my head down and sweep.

'Our Dominus, the one who owns the tavern,' she says, shifting pots and pans with no apparent purpose, 'is Varius Granatus. The one who was just here, the young Dominus, is his son.'

'They're both Dominus?'

'Yes. But it's not their name.'

'What's the young Dominus called?'

'His name is Calidus.'

'Like Pusus is my name.'

'No,' Focaria says. 'You don't have a name.' She picks up a pot from the stove. 'Look.'

I stop sweeping.

'This pot,' she says, 'doesn't have a name. It's just a pot.'

I can't always tell the difference between when she's angry at me and when she's angry at something else. In fact, I'm not always sure when she's angry and when she isn't, mostly because she always is.

'Pusus isn't your name,' she says. 'Pusus is just another word for boy. Just like Focaria is not my name. It's just another word for cook. I used to have a name, but I don't anymore. Now I have this . . .' She runs her finger round the inside of the iron collar that sits across her collarbone. 'I don't know if you *ever* had a name.'

49

I clutch the broom before me in both hands.

'Look,' she sighs. 'Pusus and focaria are just words for a type of thing. Just like *table* is the word for this,' rapping it with her knuckles, 'and that's the *wall*, and that's the *door*, and that's the *sky*.' She points at each in turn. 'They don't have names. A wall is a wall. A door is a door. The sky is the sky. It's just what they are. Do you understand?'

I don't, but I nod anyway.

'The world,' Focaria goes on, 'is divided into free people who have names and slaves who don't, because they are things and not people. The Dominus named Granatus is a person. So is Calidus. Audo is a person, too, though not nearly as important a person as Granatus or Calidus. Even Melpomene is a person, though just barely. You and I and Euterpe and the wolves, we're not people. We are things, like this pot. When this pot is broken, Dominus can get another one. When I am broken, he can get another cook. When he doesn't need you anymore, he can get another boy. And that new pot will be called a pot, that new cook will be called Focaria, and that new boy will be called Pusus. The words don't belong to us. Nothing belongs to us. We belong to the word.'

'And what about God? Why is he called Dominus, too?'

'God is Dominus of them all. Even masters have masters. Do you understand?'

I shift my grip on the broom.

'Anything else?' She starts to turn away.

'Are you my mother?' I say.

Focaria sighs. I have asked her this question before, just as I have asked Euterpe. Both of them have told me no, with varying degrees of patience and exasperation. But this time is different. This time, because she asked, I'm hoping Focaria will tell me something I don't already know.

'Come here.' She beckons me.

I walk warily around the table. Focaria takes the broom from me and leans it against the wall. I hunch my shoulders, expecting her to pinch or slap me, but instead she kneels down so that we are eye to eye. Very carefully, as if for once she is afraid of hurting me, she takes my wrist and holds it next to hers.

'Look,' she says. 'How are we different?'

I say nothing. I don't want to be pinched again.

'It's all right,' she says. 'Tell me how our arms are different.'

'Mine is thinner?'

'That's true,' she says, 'but that's not what I mean.' With her other hand, she squeezes our wrists together. 'What else?'

'Yours is longer?'

'Look again.' We are near the door, and she shifts me so that the sunlight falls across our arms.

'Mine is pale,' she says at last, 'like the belly of a fish. Yours is almost brown, like faded leather. Do you know what that means?'

I shake my head.

'That means I can't be your mother. Mothers who have skin like mine . . .' The white flesh reddens where she pinches herself. 'They don't have children with skin like yours.' She touches my wrist with the tip of her finger. 'Look at me,' she says.

The light picks out a few stray hairs that have escaped from her bun, as well as the creases at the corners of her eyes.

'My eyes are blue and my hair is red. Your hair is black and your eyes are brown. I'm from a place far away in the north where the sun hardly ever shines . . .'

'Britannia,' I say.

'That's right, Britannia.' She purses her lips together, almost a smile. 'Where it rains all the time and all the people are as pale as I am.' She touches my arm again. 'You come from a place much further south, where the sun shines all the time, and all the people are baked brown.'

'How did I get here?'

'You're a mistake,' she said.

51

'A mistake?'

'Actually, two mistakes.' She holds my gaze. 'Dominus bought you from a ship captain, instead of from a proper slave dealer. You were a bargain, apparently. That was his first mistake.'

Dominus can make mistakes? This is news to me.

'The second mistake,' Focaria goes on, 'was that the captain said you were a girl, and no one thought to look until Audo dropped you off in the kitchen and I took a peek. By the time I told him, the ship was gone, and it was too late to get the money back.' She almost smiles again. 'Audo hit me and broke one of my teeth. The thanks I get.'

'So I was supposed to be a girl?'

'It doesn't matter now. You're here.'

'Why did the captain sell me? Was he my father?'

'That doesn't matter, either.'

I think about this, and then I say, 'Because I'm a thing.'

'That's right.'

'Was my mother a thing, too?'

'I don't know,' Focaria says. 'Probably.'

'What happened to her?'

'I don't know.'

'Does she know where I am?'

'No.'

'Will I ever see her again?'

'No.'

'Maybe . . .' I start to say, but Focaria takes my face firmly between her two rough palms. She forces me to look into her cool blue eyes.

'None of this matters.' She is almost whispering. 'You will never know where you came from. You will never know your mother. She might as well be dead. She probably is. Your life is going to be short, and it is going to be hard. And the sooner you accept that, the better off you will be.'

We gaze into each other's eyes. I have never seen her like this before. Her anger has been transformed into something like sadness. She looks as though she is about to cry. As I write this, at the other end of my life, I can still see her face before me in this moment, and yet, as I have already warned you, I can't say anymore if this is a real memory or just my imagination. I have stroked this image of Focaria's face like a coin for many years, and whatever meaning may have been stamped on it has long since been rubbed away.

At last, she says, 'Do you understand?'

I nod.

'All right.' She lifts her hands from my face and pushes herself to her feet with a grunt. She hands me the broom again.

'Get to work,' she says. 'Tomorrow I'm taking you outside.'

Now that I know that Focaria means to take me through the door in the morning, I lie awake after she goes to sleep, listening to the sounds of the street. Most of them are ordinary – the trickle of the fountain, the yowling of a cat – but then I hear men shouting in the distance, and I'm wide awake for the rest of the night. In the morning I say nothing, but I watch Focaria carefully. She gives me half a pear with my bread and cup of water. When I'm finished, and her back is turned, I run from the kitchen and hide in the latrine. Crouching in the reek, batting at the flies, I hope she won't find me, I hope she will go out and fetch the morning's water all on her own, the way she always has before. Through a crack in the door, I watch her cross to the water tank, pick up our two battered buckets, and carry them to the street door – so far, so good – but instead of going back for the yoke so she can carry both buckets at once, she crosses straight to the latrine, jerks the door open, and hauls me into the sunlight.

'No!' I drag my feet in the dirt, I twist in her grasp. Focaria tightens her grip and pulls harder, and my heels leave two furrows like a double-bladed plough. Only when we reach the door does she look down at me. Her eyes are like hard blue stones.

'Do you remember what I told you yesterday?' she says.

'No!' I lie. 'I forget!'

Still clutching my wrist, she unbolts the door with one hand like Audo and hauls it open.

I shout wordlessly and pull away from her as hard as I can. She yanks me nearly off my feet, and a moment later, I am in the street.

My shout dies in my throat. I can hardly breathe. None of the wonders Euterpe has shared with me are as astonishing as that first moment beyond the garden wall. There are no dog-headed men, no women with cat's tails, no naked wise men following the sun like sunflowers. Nor is there a groaning man bleeding to death. There is only morning light slanting across worn paving stones, yet the horizon of my world recedes from me like a wave, as if I were a pebble dropped into a fathomless pool. In fact, I'm as breathless as if I were drowning.

Can a pebble drown? I told you I wasn't a philosopher.

I have been pulled into a river of sunlight. The sun hangs low over the far end of the street, and light pours between the houses on either side. To the right, away from the sun, the light washes against the walls and the red roofs of long, low warehouses before spilling through a tall archway into an immensity of azure sky and glittering water, my first sight ever of the harbour of Carthago Nova. Against the water sway black sticks, which I will later learn are the masts of ships, and below the masts, along the quay, wriggle the silhouettes of men, lifting, shifting, carrying, loading. Above the masts wheel flocks of white gulls, picked out in every detail by the exacting light, which somehow magnifies even their piercing cries. On the far side of the harbour, the light falls full upon an enormous, humpbacked mountain that rises halfway up the sky above the city wall. The mountain is as red as a rusty iron pot, its dry rocks furred over with dull green scrub the colour of olives.

I reach for Focaria, but she has left me all alone on the narrow pavement at the edge of the street. I back up until my shoulders are pressed against the rough plaster of the wall. Outside the garden, away from the odours of herbs and latrine and Focaria's cooking, I smell grit and rubbish, I smell woodsmoke, I smell horse shit and dog turds. At the back of my sinuses, though I don't know it yet, I smell the briny tang of the sea and dust from far-off Africa. Directly across from me is the blank wall of the house opposite, painted red as high as a man's shoulder and then whitewashed above, where a line of letters I can't read is fading in the sunlight. In the middle of the wall is an old door faced with battered metal panels that have turned green with verdigris. It stands ajar, and in the shadowy hall I see a figure napping upright on a stool, his head tipped back against the wall, his mouth open. Now the horizon of my world recedes even further, beyond my comprehension – am I to understand that every wall has a door, and that every door leads into other rooms, and that every room has other people in it, and that they all just go on for ever?

Focaria comes out of the garden with the two buckets and sets them down long enough to pull the door shut behind her. Then she lifts a bucket with each hand and starts up the street, to the left, away from the harbour.

'Come,' she says, but I dig my fingers into the crumbling plaster behind me.

'Euterpe won't know where I am.'

Focaria keeps walking. 'You'll be back before she wakes up.'

The safety of the garden, the only world I know, is only steps away, but Focaria herself is striding away from me with an empty bucket dangling from each hand, into the dazzling haze of sunlight. The street dives into the distance, narrowing as it goes, tall houses on either side crowding closer together the further away they are. The sun glitters off the paving stones ahead, it glares off brightly whitewashed walls. The slanting light casts long patches of shadow under awnings and balconies, it limns the shoulders of tall figures in the street, it makes haloes round their heads, it shines between their legs. They don't look like Euterpe's monsters, but I can't see their faces with the sun behind them. Even the air seems to glitter. Starting at the tips of my toes, the fitted stones of the street seem to run forever, diminishing as they go, while two wagon ruts up the middle draw closer to each other the further away they get but never quite meet. It never occurred to me that the street could run so far I couldn't see the end of it. The patchwork paving stones are like all the kitchen floors I could ever possibly imagine, laid end to end and stretching forever. The work it must take to keep it clean! You'd be sweeping for the rest of your life!

And the noise! All the sounds that nearly exhaust themselves climbing the garden wall to reach me are now louder than I've ever heard them before. The ring of the blacksmith, the rasp of the carpenter, the tap of the tinsmith, the brass voice of the crier announcing another runaway, 'MONica, an AFrican, aged SIXteen . . .' The creaking gulls in the harbour behind me, the ceaseless splashing of water nearby, a couple of men shouting jovially back and forth across the street. Two girls laughing, a baby crying, a dog barking. I hear a rhythmic thumping, *whump whump whump*, and the sound of deep voices singing along with it. Up ahead, a large, complicated black shape resolves itself out of the haze of sunlight, wheels rumbling, bell tinkling, hooves *clop clop clopping*. Is that the box on wheels Euterpe tried to explain to me? Is that a cart? Or is it one of those strange creatures from where the North Wind lives, come to devour me?

I burst away from the wall and race to catch up to Focaria. I clutch the back of her skirt, to put her between me and the approaching monster. She looks down at me.

'Here.' She holds out one of the buckets.

I look past her at the approaching cart.

'Take it,' she insists, and I take the bucket's handle with one hand. 'Come,' she says, and I follow, clinging to her skirt with one hand and banging the bucket against the pavement with the other. Without stopping, she plucks my hand out of her skirt.

'Pick it up, Pusus,' she says. 'Use both hands.'

Now I'm trotting after her, both my palms under the greasy handle of the bucket. The cart is becoming sharper up ahead, filling the street. Euterpe was right, it is a box on wheels! The mule is swaybacked and bony and wearing leather blinders. It nods its long head, jangling the bell in its harness, and it sputters in a great sparkling cloud of droplets. A long-legged man in a ragged, wide-brimmed straw hat draws it along with his fingers hooked through the bridle. He is murmuring in the mule's drooping ear. The tired clopping of its hooves becomes the loudest thing I have ever heard, reverberating off the walls on either side. Focaria draws me onto the pavement as the cart's wheels crunch past us in the wagon ruts, close enough to touch. Euterpe was right about the wheels, too – they are taller than I am, they could crush a little boy without hesitation. If the wheels miss me, the cart above them is stacked with bundles of firewood that look ready to topple and crush me anyway. Then man and mule and cart have passed, the clopping and the crunching diminish, and the cart recedes down the street toward the harbour, shuddering from side to side.

'When you're out here on your own,' Focaria says, 'remember to look both ways before you cross the street. Last thing I need is for you to get trampled.'

'On my *own*?'

'Here we are,' she says, and she draws me by the shoulder into the street again.

Across from us is the source of the splashing water I hear late at night, when all the other sounds die away. A stone trough rests half in and out of the street, and at one end a ceaseless stream pours out of the worn mouth of a stone fish. The overflow dribbles through a notch in the trough and into the street, and the pavement all around the fountain is slimed with grit and mud. But this morning the purling of the water is overwhelmed by the buzz of conversation and the clatter of laughter from a group of women clustered round the fountain, each holding a bucket or two, each waiting her turn. At the centre of them, closest to the water, a tall, ebony-skinned woman with a prominent jaw seems to be conducting the conversation, bestowing a glance here and there, leading the laughter when someone (usually her) makes a joke. She seems to be directing the distribution of water as well, dipping her head to allow one woman and then another step to the trough ahead of her. Apart from the wolves, these are the first women I have ever seen, and I had no idea there could be such variety. One is old and fat and dark, another is younger and fatter and as pale as Focaria. One small, grey woman has drooping eyelids but a watchful gaze, and when the others laugh, she only smiles. Another is thin and hollow-eyed, and she waits until everybody else laughs and then laughs louder than all of them put together. Two are girls no older than the wolves, one short and one tall, like Thalia and Urania, but actual sisters (I will later learn) with similar round faces. Unlike Thalia and Urania, they go without make-up, coil their hair tight round their heads, and wear long dresses that cover them from throat to toes. But their eyes light up at the sight of me the way Thalia's do, and one of them calls out, 'Who's your little friend, Focaria?'

'Nobody,' says Focaria, drawing me to the edge of the crowd. 'Just Pusus.' Just a boy.

Standing slightly apart from the others, a pale, bony girl waits with two buckets at her feet and a narrow wooden yoke propped on end against the wall. She's younger than the two girls but older than me, and her coarse yellow hair is pulled back tight into a bun. She says nothing to us as Focaria and I stand next to her. She doesn't even look at us, but only stares down at the pavement just beyond her bare toes. Twice I see her glance up, once at the lantern-jawed woman at the centre of the crowd, then across the street at

58

a tall man with deep-set eyes and bushy eyebrows who is putting back the shutters of his shop, the one that shares a wall with the tavern garden. The morning light falls along the counter that runs across the front of the shop. Within, rows of rusty red amphorae laid on their sides in wooden racks recede into the shadows.

One by one each woman dips her bucket and waddles away, dripping coins of water on the pavement. As the crowd diminishes, the pale girl nudges her buckets closer to the trough with her foot, shifts the yoke with one hand, and shuffles sideways. Then she leans back against the wall and stares at her toes again. From the shadows among his racks of amphorae, the shopkeeper glances in her direction.

The remaining women all shout as the hollow-eyed woman dips her bucket a bit too enthusiastically, sloshing water over the side of the trough.

'Easy, Lucilia,' says the tall woman, dancing back from the sloshing water. 'Leave some for the rest of us.'

'I beg your pardon, Afra,' says Lucilia, and she hunches her shoulders and glances nervously from side to side as she hefts her brimming bucket away with both hands. Only the watchful, grey-haired woman and the two girls remain, and they turn deferentially to Afra.

'Balbina, you go ahead,' she says to the grey woman. She snaps her fingers at the slave girl with the buckets and the yoke.

'Tacita,' she says sharply, and the girl looks up. Afra circles her hand to indicate Balbina and the two girls. 'You go after these three,' announces Afra. 'I need to speak with my husband.' Then she lifts her long jaw and sails across the street toward the shop. The tall man, Priscianus the oil merchant, watches her from under his bushy eyebrows as he arranges jars of various sizes and colours along the countertop. Afra plants herself at the front of the small group that is already gathering to buy oil, and she conducts her business loudly, while her husband says little.

'Pay attention.' Focaria grips the top of my head and directs my wandering gaze to the fountain. Only Tacita is ahead of us now. She's already standing on the worn stone step next to the trough, holding her first bucket directly under the stream of water flowing from the fish's mouth.

'See that?' murmurs Focaria. 'She never dips the bucket in the water.'

Her arms taut, the slave girl lifts the full bucket away from the trough. She fills the second bucket and sets it at a distance from the first. Then she plucks the yoke from the wall. From each end of the yoke hangs a short length of cord with an iron hook at the end, and stepping between the buckets, she deftly hooks the handle of each bucket. Then she stands, holding the yoke with both hands, high enough to pull the cord tight, but not high enough yet to lift the buckets. Her face blank, Tacita watches the shop across the street until Afra sings, 'Ta-ra, then, dear,' and waggles her fingers at her husband as she walks away.

'Are you still here?' she says to Tacita. 'What are you waiting for?'

Tacita lowers her eyes, gets her shoulders under the yoke, and slowly stands. The yoke bends and the buckets sway, and as Afra strides down the street toward the harbour, Tacita trudges after her step by careful step, her calves straining. She's so slight it looks as if the water weighs more than she does, but she spills much less than the other women did. Across the street, even as he murmurs to his first customer of the day, Priscianus watches her walk away. When Afra reaches the house across from our garden, she sails through the door, and we hear her shouting at the sleeping porter to 'Wake up, you lazy boy!' Tacita carefully points the yoke through the door and follows her inside. As soon as the back end of the yoke and its gently swinging bucket slide through, the door shuts behind her.

'Pusus! Pay attention!'

Focaria has already filled her bucket, and she hauls me up onto the stone step next to the trough, where I stare at the water streaming from the open mouth of the stone fish.

60

'Does it ever stop?' I say.

'Nothing lasts for ever,' says Focaria, and she presses my hands around the handle of my bucket and helps me hoist it as high as I can.

'Right under the fish,' she repeats. 'Never get water out of the tank. You never know what's in it, especially in the morning.'

As I stagger down off the step with the brimming bucket, Focaria is already carrying her bucket back toward our doorway, leaning to one side with her other arm out for balance. I walk slowly after her carrying my bucket before me with both hands, the way I usually do. Before I'm even halfway there, Focaria shoulders through the door and disappears into the garden. I try to call out, but all I can do is squeak. The rope handle cuts into my palms. My legs tremble, my arms shake, I splash water with every stuttering step. If anything, the door seems to be getting further away the faster I try to go. She has left me on my own in the street.

'Wolf!' someone shouts, and now a pack of running boys streams past me at full tilt toward the harbour, their limbs flashing, their hair flying behind them. As the slap of their bare feet reaches its pitch, I set the bucket down hard, spilling some of it. I hunch over it on my knees, partly to protect it, partly just for something to hang on to. The boys, not much older than me, flow and weave through each other like swifts, laughing and hooting and shouting. The one who called me 'wolf' dances backwards, barefoot and bare-chested, wearing only a loincloth. He slows and stops and starts toward me. Two other boys turn and follow him, the three drawing together as if closing a net. Their hair is lank, their eyes are avid, the sun gleams in the sweat on their skin. The first boy watches me the way Thalia does when she says she wants to eat me up, but without affection, as if maybe he actually does.

'Pusus!' shouts Focaria. She's marching across the street from the garden door. I half expect to see a boning knife in her fist.

The two other boys bolt, but Focaria has blocked the first boy's escape. He prances from side to side on the balls of his feet.

'Pusus!' she shouts again, but she's not looking at me, she's looking at him. Of course: Pusus isn't his name, just as it's not mine. He's only a boy, like I am. She claps her hands as if shooing a cat, and he dances out of her reach, thrusting his face in my direction one last time.

'Wolf!' he shouts, and then he's gone, howling like a dog all the way down the street until he passes under the shadow of the harbour arch. Focaria drags me up from the bucket and hauls it and me into the garden. She shuts and bolts the door, then carries the bucket to the water tank. I trot after her.

'Am I a wolf?'

With one hand Focaria lifts the wooden lid of the tank.

'No.' She hoists the bucket. 'Not yet, anyway.' Pours it in. 'You might not be, if you're lucky.' Sets the bucket down, lifts its mate. 'But you're probably not that lucky.' Empties the second bucket.

As I puzzle over this, Focaria puts the bucket down, replaces the lid with a hollow thump, and turns to me.

'Fetching water's going to be one of your jobs from now on,' she says. 'Do what Tacita does, and you'll be fine.'

'Who's Tacita?'

'The slave girl across the street.' She lifts her chin toward Priscianus's house. 'She knows what she's doing.' Focaria ticks off Tacita's virtues on her fingers. 'Always goes to the back of the line. Doesn't talk to anybody. Fills the bucket straight from the spout.'

I'm not really listening. My head is still spinning from everything I've seen since she dragged me through the garden door.

'Do you understand?' Focaria says. 'She doesn't speak. She does her job and goes home.' She gestures at the yoke propped in the corner. 'When you're bigger, I'll show you how to use that, so you don't have to make so many trips.'

'But I'm not a wolf?'

Focaria purses her lips. I know that look. I'm about to be pinched or maybe even slapped. But then she sees something behind me, and her lips tighten in that smile she wears when something secretly amuses her.

'She'll explain it to you,' she says, and I turn to see Euterpe coming through the garden, rubbing her eyes and yawning. She's still wearing her smudged make-up from the night before.

'Explain what?' She gives us a broad smile that says she's equally happy to see both of us.

'Someone called him a wolf this morning.' Focaria is already heading for the kitchen.

'What? Who?' Euterpe catches the cook's hand as she passes, and the two women let their fingers slide past each other.

'Some boy,' says Focaria, 'in the street.'

'In the street?' Euterpe looks surprised. 'What was he doing in the street?'

'You heard Dominus yesterday,' Focaria says over her shoulder. 'I took him to the fountain.'

'You took him *out*?'

From the kitchen doorway Focaria favours us both with her secret smile.

'Our little boy is growing up.' She laughs. 'You're going to have to stop telling him lies.'

'What does that mean?' Euterpe says, but Focaria has already stepped into the shadow. Her voice floats out of the kitchen.

'You're the teacher!'

Euterpe and I settle into the shade beside the tank, our usual place. Before she can say a word, I act out for her my visit to the fountain, as well as everything I've learned from Focaria since the day before. I serve as my own breathless chorus.

'Focaria says her name isn't Focaria and my name isn't Pusus, and she says that some people are people and some people are things, and she says that I was supposed to be a girl, but I'm really a thing like a pot and a pot doesn't have a name and I don't have a name either, and the other Pusus says I'm a wolf, but Focaria says I'm not, though maybe I will be if I'm not lucky, but right now I'm just Pusus.'

Through the kitchen door, I can hear Focaria chopping, *snick snick snick*. But I scarcely notice, because I have questions. 'So what is my name? Is it Little One, or Mouse, or Antiochus? Is your name Euterpe, or is Euterpe what you are? Are you a thing or a person? Do you know where you come from? Why can't I know my mother?'

Euterpe sighs and folds me onto her lap.

'I know what I am,' she whispers into my ear, 'because I know where I came from.'

'So how come . . . ?'

'Shhh,' she says, and holds me tighter. 'Just because you *don't* know, doesn't mean that's a bad thing. Not knowing can be a gift.'

I say nothing, but I stir restlessly in her embrace. What does she mean? How can not knowing anything can be a gift?

'Listen,' she says, and then she does what she always does when I'm confused. She tells me a story.

Once, says Euterpe, there was a king named Numitor.

'What's a king?' I say.

'The man in charge. Like the emperor I told you about.'

'Like Audo?'

'Sort of,' she says. 'Don't interrupt.'

So, she continues, Numitor had two children, a daughter named Rhea and a son named Amulius. But Amulius wanted to be king instead, so he killed Numitor, his own father. And because Rhea saw him do it, he locked her up in a room so she could never tell anyone.

'Why didn't he just kill her, too?'

'Because she was his sister.'

'But he already killed his father.'

Euterpe squeezes me. 'Just listen . . .'

But even though Rhea was locked alone in a room, a god managed to visit her. Euterpe has already told me about God, who lives in the sky and is even bigger and stronger than Audo. God sees everything I do, all the time, even when Audo can't. Unlike Audo, though, God is kind, and Euterpe has told me that I, too, should aspire to be kind, like God. When I ask why I can't see him, she says that the only way to meet God is to live a blameless life, and that's not very likely. So it turns out that God is just one more father I'll never know. But back when this story took place, she continues, there was more than one god, and one of them was a god named Mars, who because he was a god could walk through walls and locked doors. So he came into the room where Rhea was, and together they made a child. In fact, they made *two* children.

'Two?'

'Yes, two little boys. Twins.'

'Like the two emperors?'

'Sort of. Just listen . . .'

I still can't imagine how one boy can come from a woman's belly, let alone two, but Euterpe continues: When Rhea's two sons were born, Amulius was very angry, so he ordered one of his slaves to steal the two boys and kill them.

'Why didn't he do it himself?'

'Because he didn't want to anger the god.'

'But then why kill them at all?'

'*Listen* . . .'

The slave didn't really want to kill the babies, either, says Euterpe, so he put them in a basket in the reeds next to a river, where he figured some animal would eat them or the water would rise and drown them. At least he wouldn't have to do it himself.

I gasp, but Euterpe hugs me. 'Don't worry,' she says. 'Something wonderful happens.'

'Their mother comes to save them?'

'No, Little One, I'm sorry.' She kisses me. 'They never see their mother again.'

Is every boy in the world like me? I start to cry, so Euterpe holds me tighter. She smells just as she always does, a mingling of her own scent and of all the men she was with the night before. As I write these words now, many years later and far away from Carthago Nova, I can smell it as if she were here in the room with me. It's what a mother smells like.

'No,' she says, 'the two little boys are rescued . . . by a wolf!'

I sit up straight in her arms.

'Yes!' Her eyes are bright. 'And the wolf takes them both home and raises them as if they were her own children.'

'Like you?'

Euterpe's eyes fill with tears. She holds me close again so I can't see her face. 'Yes,' she says, 'just like me.' She holds me tightly. 'Do you remember the empire I was telling you about yesterday?'

Someone sighs, and we both look up. Focaria is a few paces away, a trowel in one hand and an onion in the other.

'What nonsense are you telling him?' she says.

Euterpe ignores her. 'Those two little boys,' she says, 'are just like you. They never knew their parents, and they were raised by a wolf.'

'Oh, for fuck's sake,' mutters Focaria.

'But they grew up to be kings anyway,' Euterpe says.

'This isn't helping,' says Focaria.

'And they founded an empire,' says Euterpe.

'That's enough.' Focaria clutches the shoulder of my tunic and hauls me out of Euterpe's grasp. 'Go inside and get the fire going.' She swats me on the backside with the flat of the trowel. I trot a few steps, but then I look back. Euterpe is standing now, and she and Focaria are whispering furiously at each other.

'. . . life as it is,' says Focaria.

'. . . a little hope,' says Euterpe.

By now the sun is higher in the sky, and the shadow of the wall casts a meridian across the garden. Euterpe and Focaria are on the dark side of it, and I'm standing in the light.

'Did they have names?' I call out. 'The two boys.'

The two women stop arguing and look at me.

'Or were they just things, like me?'

Focaria starts to speak, but Euterpe touches her arm.

'Their names,' she calls out, 'were Romulus and Remus.'

'Why fill his head with lies?' Focaria mutters, but Euterpe steps out of the shadow.

'Focaria says I'm a thing, like the iron pot,' I say. 'You say I'm like the emperor.'

Focaria gives a short bark of a laugh, and Euterpe shushes her.

'You can be both,' she says.

'No he can't,' mutters Focaria.

'I don't understand,' I say.

Euterpe approaches and cups my face between her hands. 'For all you know,' she says, 'your mother could be the daughter of a king, like the mother of Romulus and Remus. Don't ever forget that.'

Behind her Focaria groans, but Euterpe holds up her hand.

'Promise me you won't forget,' she says to me. 'I want to hear you say it.'

'I promise,' I say.

'Good.' Euterpe pulls her red gown tightly about her. 'Now go inside and do what Focaria tells you to.'

Reader, I worry I may have aroused in you the false hope that the truth about my origins will be revealed at some point in this narrative. Focaria revealing my sale under false pretences, Audo whispering to Calidus, Euterpe telling me the story of Romulus and Remus – these memories seem to hint that that I intend to reveal my own parentage eventually. Perhaps you even suspect that I may rise triumphantly like the hero of a Greek novel, sold into slavery only to be restored to his estate as a dutiful son, a blissful bridegroom, and a wise prince.

If this is true, someone will show up in the final scene and reveal my true identity, as the son of a god or a senator, or, in a pinch, the illegitimate child of a bishop. The world will be set to rights, justice will be served, the guilty punished, the wronged man redeemed, the oppressed liberated. The lovers separated by pirates will be joyfully reunited, their virtue miraculously intact. After a lifetime away, the hero will come home to reclaim his household and his wife, or he will found a city in his name that will become the seedbed for empire. He might even be crucified and, three days later, rise from the dead. At the very least he will reveal who he really is, even if who he is, is nobody.

He won't. This is not that kind of story.

No one knows who I am, least of all me. No one knows how I became a slave, least of all me. Perhaps my parents were slaves, and I was born a slave. Perhaps, like Euterpe, my mother was a slave, and my father died or renounced me. Perhaps my father was a slave, and my mother, out of shame, abandoned me on a dung heap. Perhaps they both abandoned me, and I was rescued from exposure by someone else, who sold me to a slaver. Perhaps they sold me themselves, to settle a debt or because they couldn't afford to keep me. Perhaps my parents died and their families sold me because they didn't want me, or just needed the money. Perhaps my parents and I were captured by Galatian slave raiders or survived the sacking of a city, and we were sold to different buyers, never to see each other again, never to know where the other two went. Perhaps I was handed round the Mare Nostrum like a worn coin, in transaction after transaction, until the sea captain wrapped me in swaddling, mislabelled me as a girl, and sold me to Dominus.

The truth is, I will never know, and neither will you. No touching final reunion will ever be performed in this play. Nothing will be revealed or redeemed or healed. The story will simply stop. The players will run out of text. They will walk off the stage in mid-scene or even in the middle of a line. Suddenly the main character – don't call him the hero – will simply be gone, and you will never see him again. He will die alone at some undetermined time in the future, out of the sight of history. He will leave the world the way he came into it – alone, unknown, unrecorded. Nobody, not even he, knows where he came from, and nobody will know when and where he goes.

I take it back. Perhaps the story will round off, after all.

At first I was allowed out on my own only to fetch water, and I took over Focaria's job of topping up the tank every morning. I nearly wore a rut in the street between the garden door and the fountain, hauling one sloshing bucket at a time until my palms were blistered and my back and calves ached. With each trip, I had to go to the back of the line. Afra enforced a strict hierarchy at the fountain: free women first, then freedwomen, then free children, then slaves. A slave boy was not only required to stand at the end of every line, he was invisible. This worked to my advantage. As the women talked and laughed over my head, I learned their names and who they were. The two girls, Perpetua and Felicitas, were the daughters of Tullus the carpenter, and they listened more than they talked, befitting their youth. And when they did talk, it was usually only with each other, whispering in each other's ear or simply exchanging a look that made them laugh behind their hands. Grey-haired, watchful Balbina, the sister of Renatus the baker, kept her own counsel, merely smiling when the others laughed and speaking only to share a mild interjection such as 'Bless me' or 'My good-ness'. But she listened with keen interest, following the play of gossip from one person to another with her heavy-lidded gaze.

Hollow-eyed Lucilia, the wife of Nazarius the fuller, talked too much and too freely, and I learned more about her life in a week than I learned about all the others over the course of months. After only a few trips to the fountain, I already knew that she had been the only surviving child of the man who used to own the fuller's shop. The shop had been her dowry when her father's freedman Nazarius married her and took it over, because his new father-in-law didn't have a male heir. Nazarius turned out to be a more potent father than his former owner, and he and Lucilia were the proud parents of a son, on whom they were lavishing an expensive education. They also had a daughter, but all their hopes were on their boy. 'Our little Lutatius excels at grammar and rhetoric,' Lucilia loved to say. 'Someday he'll be an aedile or even a decurion. As a freedman, of course, my husband cannot hold office . . .' Lucilia never mentioned her husband by name, and once every couple of weeks or so she arrived at the fountain with a black eye or a purple bruise around her throat. Before anyone asked, she cheerfully explained that she'd tripped or walked into a doorpost. On those mornings, Afra, wife of Priscianus and unofficial Queen of the Fountain, stiffened her long jaw, put a sisterly arm around Lucilia, and ushered her to the front of the line, even ahead of herself.

Not that Afra ever carried her own water. She busied herself with conducting gossip and arranging the hierarchy at the fountain before invariably excusing herself to have a word with her husband as he opened his shop. Meanwhile Tacita, her slave girl, leaned silently against the wall with her two buckets and the yoke, staring at her toes. When her Domina wasn't looking, she looked across the street at her Dominus, and when his wife wasn't looking, Priscianus looked across the street at Tacita.

'Why are you taking so long with the water?' Focaria demands to know one morning when I'm dragging a bucket across the garden, spilling most of it into the dirt. 'Why aren't you using the yoke?'

'You haven't shown me how to use it' isn't an acceptable answer, so after she steps back into the kitchen and forgets about me, I grip the handles of both buckets in one hand and drag the yoke by the other into the street. The buckets bounce against each other and the back end of the yoke scrapes over the wagon ruts in the street until I drop them all with a clatter on the other side. By now there's no one left at the fountain, although Tacita's two buckets and her yoke are still propped against the wall. Neither Tacita nor Afra are in sight, and that's a bit of luck, because it means I can fumble with the yoke and my own buckets without being watched.

I fill one bucket and then the other. Trying to remember how Tacita did it, I lay the yoke out on the pavement between the buckets. But snagging both handles at once with the hooks dangling from the ends of the yoke is trickier than it looks. No matter how carefully I try, once I get the second handle, the first one always jerks loose. A couple of passing men laugh at me, and I stare at the pavement until they pass, then I square my shoulders to try again. When I look up, Priscianus is coming out of the gloom at the back of his shop, and here comes Tacita from the same direction, walking briskly toward the fountain and tying up the bun at the back of her head. I step out of her way.

'I'm sorry,' I say, 'but I can't . . . I don't know how . . .'

Tacita says nothing. She glances back at Priscianus, who looks away. Then she stoops over me and holds up her finger: *attend*. Without saying a word, pushing and pulling at me like a doll, she shows me how to steady the yoke by draping my arms over each side of it for balance, then how to flex my knees to hook each handle at the same time. From behind his counter, Priscianus shoots glances in our direction, but Tacita ignores him. Once I have my buckets off the ground, she shows me how to point the yoke ahead of me and how to walk in a slow but steady rhythm. Then she walks me back across the street toward the garden door. When I go too fast, she gestures for me to slow down. When the buckets swing too much, she shows me how to shift my shoulders. The weight makes my calves burn, but with Tacita walking silently beside me, I find a rhythm. Step by step, I swing the yoke slowly

71

to point it through the doorway. Inside, I carefully kneel and set the buckets down without spilling them. My legs are trembling, but I'm exhilarated. I have splashed more water than Tacita would have, but I have not spilled the buckets.

I turn, but Tacita is not there. Through the door I see her at the fountain with her back to me, lifting one of her own buckets under the spigot.

'See?' Focaria calls from the kitchen. 'You figured it out.'

I get under the yoke again, carry the buckets to the tank, and pour them in. When I hurry back into the street to thank Tacita, she is gone.

Focaria begins to take me with her when she does her shopping. I become her mule, carrying the wicker basket on my back. It's woven of spartaria grass and hangs from linen straps, and it's almost as tall as I am. It's surprisingly heavy even empty, and the more she puts in the basket, the more it tugs me back on my heels, until I learn how to find my balance. I also learn my left from my right by which direction we turn when we step out the garden door. If we're going toward the rising sun to buy bread, we turn left. If we're going toward the harbour to buy fish, we turn right. Left, bread. Right, fish.

On my first trip to the harbour, I trot just behind Focaria like an anxious little dog until she says, 'If you step on my heels, I'll slap you senseless.' So I hang back as we approach the city gate. Here the beggars live; abandoned slaves and labourers with missing limbs or sightless eyes who can no longer work, nearly naked men with scraps of loincloth and bristling, untrimmed beards who huddle all day in the shadow of the gate. Focaria marches straight through them with her gaze fixed, ignoring the fingerless hands thrust in her direction as men crawl or limp or hop toward her, their murmurs reverberating off the barrel vault above: 'Your blessing, Domina.' 'A coin, Domina.' 'Peace of God, Domina.' Only the blind ones reach their hands out to me, because the others can tell at first sight that I don't have any money.

A few steps onto the harbourfront, the pavement is slick underfoot with crushed vegetable matter and gritty with spilt grain. Almost immediately I lose sight of Focaria among the waists and backsides of all the men towering over me. Here are more men than I've ever seen before, maybe even all the men in the world. They come in all sizes, shapes, and shades, and though I don't know it at that first moment, I am looking at Jews and Arabs and Greeks and Gauls and Italians and Syrians and Persians and Libyans and Africans and Ethiopians, some in tunics, some in colourful robes, some in skullcaps or turbans or headdresses. All of them are talking at once, arguing, laughing, exchanging purses of coins, putting their heads together to consult a manifest, slapping hands to make a deal on the spot. The aedile in charge of the harbour, a short, fat man in the first toga I have ever seen, sails in a straight line through the uproar, accompanied fore and aft by two slaves – a big one in front to clear the way and a smaller one trotting behind with a wax tablet for taking notes. Behind them trail a gaggle of angry men, merchants and ship captains who each want a word with him about the unreasonable customs duties or the shameful state of the docks or the disgracefully unfair assignment of berths. And all around them are slaves and labourers, barefoot men with ropy muscles wearing only breechclouts, shuffling endlessly in long files like ants between the ships along the quay and the shadowy doors of warehouses, stooping under bales of cotton, rolling rumbling tuns of salt fish across the paving stones, dragging two-wheeled carts stacked with sacks of grain, or carrying between them, one man to each handle, amphorae of wine or oil that are taller than I am.

How big the world is turning out to be! Through the files of men I see ships and fishing boats rocking in the harbour all along the quay, their sails furled, their masts ticking from side to side.

The fishing boats are low and unadorned, but painted in vivid colours, solid red or yellow or blue. The cargo ships are patterned in jaunty colours, just as vivid but more weathered, and some of them have black-rimmed eyes on their prows to see in the dark, and sterns that rise higher than the rest of the ship and curve into the neck of a swan. Between the ships I see reaches of rippling green water, and closer to the quay, a sluggish swell with a greasy sheen and floating turds, where the city's sewer empties into the harbour. Overhead, slowly spinning bales and barrels swing from wooden cranes, palm trees droop over the water, masses of gulls wheel over the fishing boats. Above it all, the vast bowl of sky rests on the sharp ridges of mountains all round, and its hard blue surface echoes with all the talking and shouting, the scraping of feet, the rumbling of wheels, the rattle of pulleys, the screaming of gulls, the slapping of water against the quay, and the dry rattling of palm fronds in the sour, salty breeze off the sea and the faecal reek of the harbour.

'Hey!'

Somebody hits me. It's Focaria. She hooks her fingers through the strap of the basket and snaps, 'Keep up!' She drags me in a herky-jerky progress along the quay, stopping short for a mule cart heaped with jars, nearly yanking me off my feet to hustle in front of a coffle of shackled and shuffling slaves, then barking 'Make way!' to insinuate us through a chain of fisherman swinging bulging baskets of fish, one at a time, off their boat and onto the quay. Here the proportions of the tavern are reversed, and there are only a few women. Most of them are like Focaria, slaves or wives doing their morning shopping, but at least one is a street wolf, yawning through the crowd with gaunt eyes and smeared make-up, on her way back to the other homeless wolves who sleep under the arches of the aqueduct. Each woman, slave or wife or wolf, draws the gazes of men as she passes. Even Focaria, old and worn as she is, draws a skein of turned heads through the pattern of men as she drags me along.

We stop at a blood-red fishing boat, and Focaria hails the boat's captain, whose name, appropriately, is Rufus. His curly hair isn't particularly red, but his muscles slide under a skin that is as deeply tanned as the rind on a baked ham. Broad-chested and short-legged, he stands with one foot on the quay and one on his rocking boat, pointing at one basket of fish after another while Focaria tells him how much of each kind she wants. Beyond Rufus's boat, other boats are tied up to weathered pilings that rock queasily in the slow swell. Staring at the shifting, mossy heads of the pilings, I start to feel as if the quay itself is moving under my feet. The doomed fish spilling from the baskets flop and suffocate, crabs in wooden traps wave their useless pincers, a boneless octopus writhes and stains the paving stones with black ink. Above me, nearly naked boys swing one-handed from the rigging like monkeys, their tanned skin glistening. These are the same boys who rushed me in the street not long ago, and the one with bright eyes catches sight of me from aloft.

'Wolf cub!' he shouts, and the other boys pick it up, rivalling the greedy gulls with their hooting. I hide behind Focaria, who pauses in her haggling with Rufus to make a rude gesture at the boys and curse them in the incomprehensible tongue of the Britons. Then she drags me in front of her so she can load the fish she just bought into my basket.

'Ignore them,' she mutters.

Some of the fish are still wriggling, and the weight of them pulls me back on my heels. At that moment, all of it – the overpowering reek, the slippery fish sliding against my back, the uneasy sway of the pilings, the laughing boys silhouetted against the blazing sky – overwhelms me, and I vomit copiously into a basket of fish. The boys above shriek with laughter, and the leathery captain curses and lifts his hand to me. Focaria pushes me behind her.

'Sluice them off!' she snaps. 'What's in this boy's stomach is no worse than what's in the water.'

'You're lucky your mother's here,' says Rufus. 'I'd cut you up and use you for bait.'

Focaria drags me away by my wrist. 'I'm still not your mother,' she says under her breath.

At another boat she fills the basket with more fish, the slimy water soaking the back of my tunic and slipping down the crease in my backside. To keep from getting queasy again, I lift my eyes past the swaying masts to where a galley is slicing through the harbour, the blades of its oars flashing as they rise and twist in ragged unison. The captain is training his rowers, and sometimes the galley surges, water foaming to either side of the cutwater, and sometimes the blades dig into the water until the ship slows and stops and rocks in the swell. Beyond it, between the pair of mountains that frame the harbour mouth, the horizon is a tremulous line between the hard blue of the sky and the glittering sea.

Focaria follows my gaze as she puts one last fish in my basket, and for a moment we watch together as the galley coasts like a long, narrow water bug, its dripping oars lifted free of the water.

'I came here in one of those,' she says quietly. She hangs her coin purse in the folds of her skirt.

'Where's here?'

'What?'

'Where are we? What's this place called?'

'What place? The quay?'

'No, this place. Where we live. Does it have a name?'

'Carthago Nova.' She hooks her fingers through the basket's strap and marches me through the crowd toward the city gate. 'That's just the name of the city. The name of this country,' she says, waving her other hand to include everything from the slimy pavement at our feet to the dry red mountains hulking over the rooftops, 'is Hispania. Any other questions?'

I know I shouldn't, but I ask her another question anyway. 'Is what Euterpe says true?'

76

'What?' she laughs. 'That you're the son of a king?'

'Not that,' I say.

She stops suddenly at the centre of a little eddy in the crowd. '*What?*' she says.

'Is it true,' I say, 'that the emperors are two little boys like me, and that they're also like Romulus and Remus, and that they're nicer than Audo, and that they don't hit anybody?'

As merchants and sailors and slaves swirl around us, Focaria and I stand in a little pocket of stillness, and she briskly answers my questions.

'Yes,' she says, 'the emperors are little boys, but they aren't like you. I don't know about Romulus and Remus. And yes,' she continues, 'they may very well be nicer than Audo, but that's only because almost everybody is nicer than Audo. But no,' she concludes, 'that doesn't mean they don't hit anybody. Or if they don't hit anybody, it's because they have people to do it for them.'

As men tower all around us, she bends over me and says, 'This is how it works. God hits the people on top to make them do what he wants. Then the people on top hit the people just below them to make them do what they want. Then those people hit the people just below them, and they hit the people below them, and so on, until they get to Audo, who hits me to make me do what he wants, and I hit you to make you do what I want.'

'Who do I hit?' The men over my head are blotting out the sky. I'm afraid I'm going to be sick again.

'Nobody,' Focaria says. 'It's hitting all the way down, and you're at the end of the line.' She grips my chin. 'Remember what I told you? About what you are?'

I nod.

'Say it,' she says.

'I'm a tool,' I say. 'Like the pot.'

'That's right,' she says. 'Do you ever hear the pot asking questions?'

'No.'

'All right, then.'

She lets go of my chin, arches her shoulders, and presses her hands to the small of her back. Then she grabs my hand and plunges with me into the crowd, and I stumble after her with the weight of fish on my back, past the moaning cripples under the arch and all the way up the street to Helicon.

One morning when Focaria's back is turned, I take a pear from the kitchen. I don't have a coin to pay her, the way Urania does when she's begging for food. But the pear has begun to go soft and discoloured, and perhaps Focaria won't miss it. I sneak it out in my tunic, next to my racing heart, and hide it behind the water tank. Then I keep watch all morning across the street until I see Tacita on her own, without Afra, filling her buckets from the fountain. Once again it's late in the morning, and no one else is at the trough. In the kitchen Focaria is furiously chopping a carrot as if it owes her money, so I fetch the pear and dash into the street, darting through passers-by. The girl's back is to me, and she's already lifted her yoke and started to walk away in her slow but steady rhythm. I match her pace and slip the pear without splashing into one of the swinging buckets. Either she's glimpsed me out of the corner of her eye or she's so attuned to the yoke that she can sense the slightest shift in weight, but she stops and turns to look at the pear bobbing in the bucket. Then she looks at me.

'Thank you,' I say, 'for showing me how to . . .'

Tacita glances over my head at Priscianus. He's watching us from his shop, and when he sees us facing in his direction, he turns away. Then Tacita looks down at me.

'I'm Mouse.' I almost say 'Sparrow', but for some reason, I decide to keep that name to myself. 'That's one of my names, anyway. What's yours?'

I already know, of course, but I want to hear her say it. Maybe, like me, she has the name she was given and a secret name she calls herself, one that only she knows.

The girl turns away and starts down the street again, walking fast. I trot to keep up. But before I can speak to her again, I hear Focaria calling. I race back to the garden door and pause long enough to watch Tacita turning the yoke into the doorway of Priscianus's house, the buckets swinging just so, never spilling a drop. Then the lazy porter rises from his stool and closes the door.

The next morning Focaria and I turn left, toward the sunrise. Today the basket is stuffed with the wolves' stained gowns and bedclothes, because Focaria is taking me to the fuller. She tugs me along by the strap again, sometimes up the middle of the street, sometimes up the pavement, weaving this way and that. We pass the line of women at the fountain, who are too busy gossiping to notice us. I lift my hand to greet them, and Focaria nearly tugs me off my feet.

'Don't talk to anybody,' she says.

The adults in the street tower over me like the men on the quay as I fall behind Focaria under the narrow ribbon of blue sky overhead. Houses and shops loom over us on either side like closed and open faces – tall houses with massive doors and narrow, barred windows, in between wide-open shopfronts with counters that stretch all the way across the opening. Trailing Focaria's backside, I see for the first time the sources of the rhythmic chorus I listen to every day from the garden – the tapping tinsmith at his bench, the carpenter's rasping saw and the smell of sawdust, the clang and sparks and smoke of the sweating blacksmith. I hear the thump of the butcher's cleaver, and through his doorway, strung with loops of sausage, I see him in the shadows of his shop, his head haloed with flies. He's hacking the legs off the carcass of a pig, its body splayed on the block with its ribs exposed, its miserable snout pointing at the ground. The reek of blood and flesh pours into the street.

Without looking, Focaria grabs the strap of the basket and hauls me along faster. Up ahead I hear that rhythmic thumping again, *whump whump whump*, and the deep singing of men. I can almost make out words. We pass a cookshop where men slouch against the counter and eat with their fingers out of wooden bowls. We pass a barber carefully scraping the wattles of an old man, who lifts his chin and purses his lips like a fish. A greengrocer's bins push out across the pavement, heaped with apples, pears, turnips, and beets, and we make a wide berth around a woman arguing with the grocer over the price of figs, while a bored slave rolls his eyes behind her.

'Are you kidding me?' the woman is saying. 'Last week they were half that.'

'Last week,' shrugs the grocer, 'they were twice as easy to get.'

Whump whump whump. Now the thumping is even louder than the hammering of the blacksmith, and I can pick out words from the song, *walking, slow, nowhere.* Up ahead is a wide shopfront bordered by coloured tiles, and dead centre above its doorway is an image of a round-eyed bird, which I will later learn is an owl. To one side of the doorway a man has lifted the front of his tunic to piss into one of a row of knee-high, wide-mouthed crocks. He stares blankly at the wall and sighs, then he shakes off the last drops and walks away. Out of the shop comes the sharp tang of urine, a wave even stronger than the stench of the butcher's. A moment later, Focaria has marched me into the establishment of Nazarius the fuller.

A counter runs along one side of the shop, and behind it is a wall of wooden cubbyholes, each stacked with cleaned and folded laundry. Focaria tugs me up to the counter and starts yanking our laundry out of the basket and heaping it on the countertop. Nazarius, a wiry and energetic man with hairy arms and the densest beard I have ever seen, sweeps the soiled gowns and bed sheets out of sight. As the basket slowly lightens on my back, I stare into the high-ceilinged room beyond. To the left, a couple of slaves with wooden paddles beat dry clothes spread across wooden frames, *whump whump whump*. To the right, five male slaves in breechclouts each stand in a stone tub, each man resting his forearms on the little walls between each stall, each man treading in place, squishing underfoot linens soaked with a mixture of water and urine. In the stall nearest the door, a stout, red-faced slave with a mellow baritone leads them in song, call and response:

> Here I come, walking slow
> *I ain't going nowhere*
> It don't matter how far I go
> *I ain't going nowhere*
> When I get there, hear me say
> *I ain't going nowhere*
> I'll lie down and sleep all day
> *I ain't going nowhere*

In the middle of the room under the skylight, women slaves kneel on a step around a wide, raised basin, wringing garments tightly and slapping them on the lip of the pool. The women are singing along with the men, all the slaves treading and wringing and slapping to the rhythm of the song. All the way at the back, I see Lucilia and her young daughter moving through a vividly coloured labyrinth of drying laundry, slung on wooden beams suspended from the ceiling. Lucilia is testing each piece between her palms – a white sheet, a purple dress, a red napkin, a pearly handkerchief – then she pulls the dry ones down and hands them to the girl, who drapes each one over her arm.

'Who's this, then?'

Nazarius is pursing his lips at me over the counter. The basket is empty, and Helicon's pressed and folded gowns and sheets from a couple of days before are stacked on the counter.

'Just Pusus.' Focaria starts to push our clean laundry down into the basket, forcing me back on my heels.

'Does he have a name?'

The fuller looks as if he knows some secret about me and wants me to know he knows it. I already know one about him, from the chatter of his wife at the fountain – that he used to be a slave in the fullery he now owns, that once upon a time he was one of the singing men in the treading tubs, forever smelling of piss. Now he's working hard to ensure that his son will rise higher than he'll ever be able to, and to ensure that his daughter will marry better than his wife did. But on the mornings when Lucilia is not at the fountain, the women whisper, *You can still smell the piss on him.*

'Not really,' Focaria says, answering Nazarius's question.

Nazarius, hands on hips, calls down the length of his laundry.

'Lucilia!'

His sharp cry causes a stutter in the work of the laundry as everyone – the beaters, the walkers, the wringers – all pause and turn to him. Even Focaria stops pushing laundry into my basket. At the far end of the shop, Lucilia looks up sharply and pushes the girl behind her.

'Is this him?' Nazarius gestures at me with his thumb. 'The little chap from the fountain?'

The whole shop is momentarily still. Everyone watches in silence. Lucilia peers at me down the length of the shop.

'Yes,' she calls out.

'What's his name?' shouts Nazarius.

'I don't know,' Lucilia says. The girl peeks out from behind her, and Lucilia pushes her out of sight again.

'Mouse,' I pipe up.

'What's that?' Nazarius turns to me.

'But sometimes,' I say, 'Melpomene calls me Antiochus.'

The lead slave in the washing stalls coughs to catch the attention of his brothers, and he starts treading again, without singing. The others put their heads down and start treading as well. The beaters resume their paddling, and the wringers start splashing and slapping again.

'Melpomene!' says Nazarius. 'I know Melpomene.' He winks over my head at Focaria.

'You'll be seeing more of him.' Focaria gives one last hard push on the clean laundry on my back, and I grab the edge of the counter to keep from falling backwards. 'Soon he'll be coming instead of me.'

'That's a pity,' says Nazarius. 'I enjoy seeing your smiling face.'

She pushes coins across the counter at him. 'Don't think you can cheat him.'

'Have I ever?' says the fuller, palming the coins out of sight.

'There's always a first time.'

'So, Mouse.' Nazarius leans over the counter. 'See that boy across the street? The good-looking one in the front row?'

I look up at Focaria, and she nods curtly in the direction Nazarius is pointing. Through the passers-by beyond the shop door, I see, in the shadow of a portico across the street, a group of boys and a couple of girls slouching on narrow wooden benches as a tall man paces back and forth in front of them, idly swinging a stick. With his eyes lifted to the ceiling of the portico, the schoolmaster is declaiming something, pausing so that his students can repeat it back in ragged unison.

'Lutatius!' shouts Nazarius, and a nodding boy on the end of the front bench lifts his drooping head. The schoolmaster sees him and whacks the boy across his thighs with the cane. As the boy sits bolt upright, the schoolmaster salutes the fuller with the stick.

'That's my boy,' says Nazarius. 'Maybe someday you'll have a son like that, learning to read and write.'

Focaria tugs on the strap of the basket. 'Let's go.'

Nazarius leans over the counter. 'See you soon . . . what's your name again?'

I blush, but before I can answer, he laughs and turns away. The men in the stalls have started singing again, everyone working to the rhythm. At the far end of the laundry, Lucilia and the girl have disappeared.

Back home, as we come through the garden door, I ask Focaria, 'Am I going to learn to read?'

'No,' says Focaria, without breaking stride. But then, halfway through the garden, she stops and looks down at me. 'You're going to have to learn how to count, though, aren't you?'

'I can count to twenty on my fingers and toes,' I say with pride. 'Euterpe taught me.'

'Well,' says Focaria, 'you're going to have to do better than that.'

And so Euterpe begins to teach me arithmetic, using pebbles in the dirt to drill me in addition and subtraction. She also teaches me the hand gestures everyone uses for one, two, three, four, and so on. I learn them quickly. It turns out I'm pretty adept at doing sums and even division in my head.

'You have hidden gifts, Little One,' Euterpe says, so she also tries to teach me the numbers one through ten in her own language – *yan, sin, krad* – and laughs when I stumble over the pronunciations.

'Who taught you to count?' I ask, because I don't like her laughing at me.

'My father.'

'You knew your father?' I know she doesn't like to talk about it, but I ask her anyway.

She hesitates. 'Yes.'

'Did he sell you to Dominus?'

Euterpe closes her eyes. I know I'm touching a place that hurts. I say, 'Urania said her father sold her to pay his taxes.'

'That's not what happened to me.' She taps the dirt next to the pebbles. 'Tell me, Little One, how many are in this row?'

'Nine,' I say. 'Where is he now?'

'Who?' She fusses with the pebbles.

'Your father.'

'He's dead.' She arranges the pebbles into three rows of three each.

'What else did he teach you?'

She looks at me. There is always something sad about Euterpe, but now she looks like Focaria does when she is about to get angry.

'He taught me how to read.' She picks up one of the pebbles and rolls it between her thumb and forefinger.

Euterpe has taught me the alphabet, drawing the letters with her finger in the dirt and rubbing them out if Audo passes by, but I don't know how to put them together into words. I can pick individual letters out of the writing on walls in the street, and I can also pick letters out of the graffiti drunken punters have scratched on the garden wall, in between their crude drawings of yawning cunts and big cocks. I know the letters mean something, but I don't know what. There are also letters on the iron collar around Focaria's neck, and one day I asked her what they said. She weighed whether to ignore me, hit me, or tell me, then she said, 'They say "fugitive".'

'Is that your real name?'

'No. It's one of those names that isn't a name. It's what I am, not who I am.'

'Is it another word for cook?'

'It means I tried to run away.'

'Run away?' I said. 'Where did you go?'

'It doesn't matter,' Focaria said. 'They caught me and brought me back. Now I have to wear this,' tugging at the collar with her finger, 'for the rest of my life.'

Now, in the garden, I say to Euterpe, 'Was it in a garden, like this one?'

'Was what?' She rolls the pebble between her fingers.

'Where your father taught you to read.'

'Yes,' she sighs. 'In his house. In Cartenna.'

'Where's Cartenna?'

'Mauretania.'

'Where is . . . Maur-e-tania?'

'South of here. Across the sea.'

'Did he draw letters in the dirt?'

'No.' Euterpe lets go of the pebble. 'He taught me with a wax tablet and a stylus. He showed me how to write the alphabet, in both Latin and Greek. Then he taught me how to read from books.'

'What's a book?'

She tips her head back against the water tank. 'Perhaps Focaria's right,' she sighs. 'What good is it to teach you what you'll never need to know?'

'But I want to know everything,' I say.

'Of course you do.' She runs her hand over my hair. 'So did I. And my father, he tried to teach me everything. He taught me how to read, he taught me poetry, he taught me philosophy, he sat with me over books and opened the world to me. I hung on his every word.'

Perhaps without meaning to, she slowly tightens her fingers on the back of my neck.

'Everything he told me,' she says, 'was mysterious and beautiful, and all of it – all of it, Little One – all the philosophy I mastered, all the stories I memorized, all the poems I recited to his delight . . . all of it was completely useless.'

'Why?'

'Because he died.'

'Who killed him?'

Euterpe catches her breath. 'How did you know someone killed him?'

One of the few things I know about men is that they die violently. It has never occurred to me that they could die any other way. I say nothing. She looks at me as if she has no idea who I am.

'You're hurting me,' I say.

Euterpe relaxes her grip. 'I'm sorry.' She kisses me. 'It's just that it's very sad,' she says. 'What happened to him.'

'What did happen to him?'

She peers for a long moment into my eyes. 'If I tell you, you must never repeat it. Not even to Focaria.' She holds my gaze until I nod. 'And you must never ask me again.'

I nod one more time, and so she tells me, just this once, her story.

Her father, she says, was a Christian priest in Cartenna, in Mauretania, across the sea. Priests were not supposed to have wives or children – 'Why not?' I ask, and she says, 'Don't interrupt.' – but her mother was a slave in his household, and somehow he found himself not only with a child, but a daughter. Euterpe's early life was a bit like mine, because she was only rarely allowed to leave the house or the garden, and she was never allowed to say whose daughter she was. But unlike me she knew her father, and he came to love her in spite of himself and in spite of the sinful circumstances of her birth.

He began to teach her the way he might have taught a son. They sat in the garden of his house, which Euterpe says was much nicer than the garden of Helicon. There was a little fountain, and a pear tree, and singing birds. There were pebbled paths that wound between beds of flowering pink tamarisk. Here, father and daughter sat for hours. He started with numbers and letters, then Latin and a little Greek, then poems and stories, then the teachings of men like Seneca and Epictetus and Plotinus. Meanwhile, Euterpe's mother was a bit like Focaria, asking her Dominus time and again what was the point of his teaching his bastard daughter a lot of nonsense she would never have any use for? Especially since the hours he spent with her took away from the time her mother needed to teach her more useful things, like cooking and cleaning and sewing and spinning, the proper pursuits of a girl, and a slave.

'I think my father loved me more than he loved my mother,' Euterpe tells me. 'I'm not sure he ever really loved her at all.'

He told his daughter about his work as a priest, preaching to his flock, administering the sacraments. He told her about the Jew named Jesus of Nazareth, who was crucified by the empire and rose from the dead after three days. Here Euterpe pauses to ask me, 'Do you know what a Christian is?'

'Thalia is a Christian,' I say. 'So is the young Dominus.'

'We're all Christians now,' Euterpe says. 'Everyone is. By order of the emperor.'

'Am I a Christian?'

'I suppose, if the emperor says so.'

'Are you a Christian?'

'Yes and no.' She gives me a sad smile. 'It depends who you ask.'

'I don't understand,' I say, and she says, 'Neither do I. Now listen,' and she tells me that for many years, long before either of us was born, the empire had tried to destroy the Christians, until an emperor named Constantine decided that he was a Christian, too. Even after that, though, there were still different kinds of Christians, and they were forever fighting over which one of them was right. The fighting was especially bad where she grew up, in Mauretania. One kind of Christian, called Catholics, believed they should make peace with the empire. Another kind, called Donatists, believed that Christians should not let any earthly power tell them what to do. They believed Christians should live as the saints and martyrs did, pure and unsullied by the world. They believed that only Christians who were blameless could enter the kingdom of heaven.

'What's heaven?'

'I'll explain later,' she says.

Even among the Donatists, there were disagreements. 'Just like Focaria and I disagree with each other sometimes,' she says, 'even though we're both afraid of Audo.' Most of the Donatists believed

88

that they should force the Catholics to renounce their beliefs, by violence if necessary. And other Donatists, who followed a leader named Rogatus, believed Christians should never be violent, that they should try to win over the Catholics by persuasion alone. So instead of fighting the Catholics, the Donatists ended up fighting each other.

'My father was a gentle man,' Euterpe says. 'He followed Rogatus.'

'What did they do to him?' I remember the *snick snick snick* of the knife outside the garden door.

Euterpe takes a deep breath. 'This is the hard part.'

One night, she says, a group of rough men from the countryside came to her father's house and dragged him out of bed. Her mother told Euterpe to hide and then followed the men into the garden. But Euterpe watched from a window as the men forced her father to his knees and told him that, like Saul on the road to Damascus, he had to lose his vision so that he might see the light. Then they held him down and poured a mixture of lime and vinegar into his eyes. As he lay screaming, Euterpe's mother flew at them, calling them scum and criminals. One of the men knocked her flat and shouted, 'When you have Christ, whore, you cannot be a criminal!' As Euterpe watched, the man kicked her mother until she curled up into a ball, then the other men dragged her father away in his nightshirt, blinded and barefoot. The next day, someone came to the house and whispered quickly through the bolted door that the priest had been taken to the headland above the town and thrown off a cliff into the sea.

Euterpe has started to cry. I look down into the dirt between us.

'If Christians are always fighting each other,' I say, 'why do they always say, "Peace be with you"?'

Euterpe bursts out laughing. 'You're too smart, Little One.' She presses her tears away with the heels of her hands. 'My father once told me that savage beasts in the wilderness aren't as vicious to men as Christians are to each other.'

'Did your father ever hurt anybody?'

'No.' Euterpe swallows. 'He couldn't bring himself to hit me when I misbehaved. He never even hit his slaves.'

I'm confused. Focaria says this is what slaves are for. If a master doesn't hit his slaves, he may even be inviting the slaves to hit him, which upsets the order of things.

'He wouldn't even defend himself.' Euterpe's voice is trembling. 'He wouldn't take a life, even if it meant saving his own.' She shudders. 'Not even if it meant saving my life, or the life of my mother.'

'Did they kill her, too?'

'No. They sold her. They sold us both.'

'Why?'

'I wasn't his daughter, not legally.' She takes a deep breath. 'I told you, a priest isn't supposed to have children. My mother was a slave, and so was I. When our Dominus was killed, his family sold us to a dealer, and we were separated.' She stares at her hands. 'And thanks to my father, I didn't know how to sew or clean or cook. That's how I ended up in Hispania.' She smiles. 'The best educated whore in Carthago Nova.'

She closes her eyes and takes deep breaths. Somewhere a dog is barking. I want to make her feel better, but I don't know what to say. Instead I ask her, 'Did you have a name?'

She opens her eyes. 'A name?'

'What did your father call you?'

She stares at me for a long moment before she answers. 'Illi,' she says. 'It just means, "my daughter".'

'Can I call you Illi?'

She brushes my cheek with the backs of her fingers. 'No, Little One,' she says. 'I'm Euterpe now. I'm not anyone's daughter anymore.'

'Oh.' I poke at the pebbles arranged in a grid, three on a side. 'Are you still a Christian?'

Euterpe bursts out laughing again. She laughs so long that she infects me with it, though I don't understand what's so funny. When she catches her breath again, she scoots me around in the dirt, obliterating the grid of pebbles, so that she can look me directly in the eye. She says, 'Here's how it is, my darling Little One. I'm a daughter, but I'm not a daughter. I'm a wolf, but I'm not a wolf. I'm a woman, but not a woman. I have the name of a Muse, but I'm not a Muse. I'm a Christian, but not a Christian.'

'I don't understand.'

She touches my nose with her finger.

'That's philosophy,' she whispers.

'What are you telling him now?' Focaria is standing over us, holding two cups of water.

'Oh,' Euterpe sings out, 'lies and platitudes.'

'Ah. The usual, then.' Focaria hands us each a cup and squats beside us. She lifts her hand to Euterpe's face and brushes away the tears with her thumb. For a moment, Euterpe closes her eyes and leans into the cook's palm. Then they separate, and Euterpe drinks. She says, a little too brightly, 'He's good at counting.'

'Is he?'

'He can add and subtract in his head.' Euterpe strokes my shoulder. 'Multiply and divide, too.'

Focaria looks at me. If she is impressed, she will never say so.

'You'll have to teach him about money,' says Euterpe.

'I suppose so,' Focaria says.

The next morning, Focaria lays some coins out on the kitchen table and shows me how to tell them apart. The images of the emperors on one side are useless, she says, because they all look the same. The late emperor Theodosius – the man who made me and everyone else a Christian with a stroke of his pen – looks exactly like his son Honorius, who looks exactly like his brother Arcadius, each one a fat-cheeked profile wearing a diadem. You have to look at the other side of each coin, she says, to see which is which, and she flips them over, one at a time, with her burnt and knife-scarred fingers. In the glare from the garden, I peer closely as she explains the differences between them.

'This one,' she says, touching a silver coin showing a seated man holding a ball and a sceptre, 'is worth sixteen of these,' touching a bronze coin showing a man dragging someone by the hair with one hand and holding a banner with the other, 'which is worth two of these,' touching another bronze coin which shows three men in a row, each holding a spear and shield. 'Got that?'

Before I can answer, she saddles me with the basket and leads me into the street. We turn left, but after passing the fountain, we turn right into a narrow passage between the blacksmith and the butcher's shop, then through an irregular, rough-hewn doorway in a massive old wall. We come out into a huge, colonnaded garden, much larger than the tavern's, and much more unkempt. Apart from the harbour, it's the widest space I've ever been in, full of desiccated palm trees and squat, spiky shrubs and a few fruit trees gone to seed. The columns are stained and cracked, and a couple have toppled over into the undergrowth. Most of the paths through the garden are overgrown, but the main one up the middle is well-worn and littered with brown, curling palm fronds. Between the scaly palm trunks and through the spiky leaves I see the gleaming faces of boys, possibly the same ones who accost me in the street or jeer at me from the rigging of harbourside ships. They track us as we pass, rustling through the garden, whispering and snickering – *Wolf cub! Who's your father?* – but when one of them springs onto the path ahead of us, Focaria stiff arms him and knocks him to the ground.

'Fuck off,' she says, then grabs the strap of the basket and hustles me up the path, through another dank, echoing passage, up a ramp, and into the reverberating racket of the old theatre of Carthago Nova.

This is even bigger than the overgrown garden. To our right is a vast half-shell carved out of the hillside, with rows of weathered stone seats climbing in ranks to the upper rim, above which a crumbling temple rises from the hilltop against the vivid blue of the sky. To our left is the old stage with two storeys of cracked columns and tall doorways along the back. I don't yet know what a theatre is, of course, but it doesn't matter, because it's been years since anybody staged a performance in this one. These days the lower rows of seats are built over with four concentric platforms of merchants' booths, some with wooden roofs, some with roofs of woven spartaria grass or palm fronds, separated by partitions of brightly painted wood or stained white canvas. The theatre reverberates with voices, as shoppers edge past each other up and down the steps, or squeeze along the curving wooden platform before each row of booths, stopping to finger the merchandise and exchange abuse with the vendors.

Focaria hauls me along, elbowing her way without apology through a crowd gathered in the semi-circular space between the lowest row of booths and the stage. They hardly notice her, because they're all gazing up at something on the stage, which I'm not tall enough to see. Only when she drags me up the scalloped steps can I turn back to see eight or nine slaves – men, women, and children – all standing in a line across the stage, all of them naked, all of them shackled at their wrists and ankles, all of them staring gloomily at their feet or into the distance. They all have little wooden signs hung round their necks. The slave dealer is a stocky man with a pointed beard and a short tunic, and he paces back and forth before them, wielding a quirt and barking his pitch in a sharp voice that carries over the cacophony of the market. He thrusts the quirt under the chin of a dark-haired girl who's not much bigger than me. She's one of several slaves whose feet have been rubbed with white chalk, which I later learn means they're imported.

93

'First-rate girl from Syria,' declaims the dealer in a diffident singsong. 'Strong, not too stupid, knows Latin. Good temperament, no diseases, all of her teeth. Only a year or two away from bearing children.' He touches the tip of the quirt to the hairless slit between her legs. 'She's intact. I can guarantee it.'

The girl flinches, but she keeps her eyes straight ahead. I wonder if she can see me watching her from the steps, but she seems to be staring at nothing. She's wiggling the big and middle toes of each foot, distracting herself with the feel of the chalk dust between them.

Focaria and I insinuate ourselves through the crowd along the second row of booths, through a susurrus of haggling and gossip. There's no particular order to the merchandise — we pass heaps of bruised fruit, bright displays of cheap jewellery, battered pots and pans swinging from hooks — which means it's just like the street, only narrower and more crowded. Here in the old theatre are merchants who can't afford to rent or buy a permanent shop. Some are trying to work their way up to the street, while others are just offloading goods that fell off the back of a cart, as they say, and who will melt into the countryside when the goods are gone. There are bolts of fabric in dishevelled heaps, incomplete sets of second-hand tableware, day-old cakes and pastries. One stall brings me up short: it's a woman selling whistling songbirds, bright little creatures hopping about in wicker cages and chittering away. Sunlight lances through a hole in the stall's awning, and the shaft of light illuminates a sparrow in one of the cages, clutching its perch, its little feet tucked right under its belly, its head pulled down on its chest, its eyes dull. It's silent, and my breath comes short as I realize that Euterpe's story wasn't true: even a sparrow can be a slave. Then Focaria's hand falls on my shoulder.

'Keep up,' she says, dragging me away.

Now my instruction in the use of money begins in earnest. We stop at one booth to buy apples, then at another to buy garum, and Focaria negotiates with each vendor in a brisk patois, mingled with insults. She pauses each transaction to calculate the price out loud for my benefit, then shows me which coins to give the man and how many we should receive from him in change. She snaps at the vendor if he tries to short-change us, which he always does. Then she hauls me back along the aisle and up the steps to the next row of booths. After she's reached a price with a man selling spices, she hands me the coin purse and makes me choose the right coins. To my secret satisfaction, and her unspoken surprise, I pick them out without hesitation.

She drags me to the end of the aisle and jerks me up the steps to the fourth and topmost row of booths. On the stage below, the slave dealer has made a sale. He's bent over to unlock the ankle shackles of a deep-chested, red-haired man, while the buyer, a fat man with a pink scalp and a fringe of dirty grey hair, jiggles his coin purse and looks his new purchase up and down. The Syrian girl, meanwhile, has lifted her deadened gaze into the upper reaches of the theatre, surveying the crumbling rows of empty seats.

This last row of booths is too far to climb for most shoppers, so it's the cheapest and least desirable location. Some of the booths are empty and roofless, the sun glaring down into their dusty and splintered interiors. We stop before three adjoining stalls that are separated with low wooden partitions and rented out to three vendors, all of them in the translucent shade of the same stained, patched canvas roof. On the left, a weedy, slope-shouldered young man has set himself up as a scribe. He sits behind a little table, his eyebrows raised, his pen scratching, as a woman with a baby on her hip laboriously dictates a letter.

'Slower, please,' murmurs the young man without lifting his eyes, and the woman sighs, shifts her infant, and repeats her last sentence more slowly.

On the right, a plump moneylender with protuberant eyes also sits behind a little table, flicking at a clicking abacus while a man perches on the edge of a stool across from him and wrings his hands between his knees. The moneylender's slave and bodyguard, an intimidating man with a broken nose, sits in the shadows at the back of the stall. In the middle stall, behind yet another table, sits a gaunt, long-faced, grey-skinned woman with kohl-rimmed eyes and too much lip paint. She's made up like a wolf, but she's much too old. She sits chin in hand, absently gazing down at the slave auction below, where the dealer is unlocking another sale from its shackles.

I have no idea why we're stopping here. Surely Focaria has no one to write to, and less reason to borrow money, and the gaunt woman apparently has nothing to sell. But as soon as she sees Focaria, the woman lifts her chin off her hand and sits up straight.

'Focaria,' she says in a gravelly voice.

'Opitria.' Focaria makes me stand just outside the booth, at the edge of the low partition between Opitria and the scribe, then she perches on the stool across the table from the woman, with her shoulders hunched and her elbows drawn in.

'Dream or the future?' says Opitria, half turning in her seat. Behind her, in the shadows at the back of her booth, is a low cabinet stuffed with books, both scrolls and codexes, the first I've ever seen.

'Future,' says Focaria, keeping her voice low, as if hoping I won't hear.

'Are you a Christian or not a Christian?' asks the fortune teller.

'You always ask me that,' says Focaria. 'Are the questions different for Christians?'

'No, but the answers are.'

'Which is cheaper?'

'It's the same for everybody,' Opitria says. 'Christian or not Christian?'

'I tell you every week,' says Focaria. 'I'm not a Christian.'

'You might change your mind. One week you're not a Christian, next week you are. I see it all the time.'

96

'Or the other way round.'

'That never happens,' says Opitria.

The fortune teller holds out her creased palm. Focaria plucks a single coin out of her dress with two fingers. She's skimmed it off the allowance Audo gives her or earned it selling leftovers to Urania. I shift from foot to foot behind her.

'Read me the questions,' she says.

'We do this every time,' says Opitria. 'You should know them all by now.'

Focaria deposits the coin in her palm. 'Read.'

Opitria tucks the coin away and turns slowly on her stool to the cabinet behind her. She runs her finger along the shelves, pulls out a book, and presses it open with both hands on the table between her and Focaria, making the parchment crackle.

'Number one,' she sighs. 'Will I defeat my opponent in trial?'

'No,' says Focaria.

'Number two. Will I serve in the army?'

'No.'

'Number three . . .'

Bored, I turn away and look down the well of the theatre at the stage. Now a buyer is expressing an interest in the Syrian girl. He's squatting before her and running his hands up and down her legs and along her arms, feeling for sores or lumps or scars. Meanwhile the slave dealer chatters his pitch over the man's shoulder, trying to distract him and make the sale. I can't hear the dealer at this distance over the sea of voices, but I don't care, because I'm transfixed by the girl, whose eyes are wandering over the empty seats above me. For a moment I think her gaze meets mine, and I catch my breath. She's Syrian, said the dealer, and it's possible I'm a Syrian, too! She looks close to my age! What if we come from the same place? What if we're related somehow? What if she's my sister?

'Helicon?'

I'm startled by a tentative touch on my shoulder. It's the scribe, who instantly, apologetically, snatches his hand away. 'Sorry,' he says, and this surprises me even more than his touch does. No one's ever touched me so gently before, except for Euterpe. And no one's ever apologized to me.

'I'm Quartus.' He solemnly splays his hand over his heart and dips his head. Behind him, there's no one at his table. The woman and baby are gone. 'What's your name?'

'No name,' I say. 'Just Pusus.'

'Of course,' he says. 'But you're from Helicon?'

I nod. Behind me, Opitria is droning on from the book. Focaria's still making her read until she hears a question she likes.

'Will I sell my cargo?' sighs Opitria.

'No.'

'Will I open a workshop?'

'Nope.'

'Focaria, please . . .' says Opitria.

'Keep reading,' says Focaria. 'What else have you got to do?'

Quartus the scribe touches me again. 'Do you know the girls who work there? At Helicon?' He keeps saying the name, as if afraid I won't understand. I nod again. I shouldn't have answered his first question. I'm not supposed to talk to anybody.

'Do you know the girl they call Thalia?' He peers closely at me. 'Short? Dark like you? Glossy hair?' He makes nervous gestures in the air with his ink-stained fingers.

'I know her!' I say, excited that he somehow knows her, too. This is breaking the rules, but Focaria won't notice. She's too distracted.

The scribe edges closer and lowers his voice. 'Does she ever mention me?' He splays his hand across his chest again. '*Quartus*,' he repeats. 'I'm a *scribe*.'

'Read that last one again,' Focaria says sharply behind me.

'Will I ever see my homeland again?' reads Opitria.

'That's the one,' says Focaria, and Opitria, relieved, says, 'All right then, pick a number between one and ten.'

'Seven,' says Focaria without hesitation, and the scribe touches me again. I edge away from him, deeper into the booth.

'I'm not supposed to talk to anyone,' I say.

'I'm sorry,' Quartus says. 'Could you tell her . . . tell Thalia, I mean . . . tell her that Quartus is thinking of her?'

I edge up behind Focaria. Across the table, Opitria purses her bright lips and lifts her eyes to the threadbare canvas roof of the booth, then she licks her thumb and forefinger and slowly turns the crackling leaves of her book until she gets to the page she wants. It's very dramatic, another demonstration of the power of words. I stubbornly ignore the scribe hovering anxiously behind me and watch over Focaria's shoulder instead as the fortune teller runs her finger down the page, then lifts her hollow, kohl-rimmed eyes to the cook.

'You will see your homeland,' Opitria says, 'and so will your child.'

Focaria gasps, and so do I. Focaria has a *child*? Has she lied to me about who I am?

'Are you serious?' Focaria whispers.

'That's what it says.' Opitria lifts her plucked eyebrows, and her eyes flicker in my direction for an instant.

'You added it up wrong,' Focaria says. 'Do it again.'

Opitria sighs and goes through the motions again, turning the crackling leaves, running her finger down the page. Then she reads the same answer.

'You will see your homeland. So will your child.'

'My child?' Focaria sounds almost as if she wants to laugh. 'My child is dead.'

Over her head, I stare at Opitria. She ignores me.

'It says what it says.' She closes the book with a thump. 'I don't write the answers.'

Focaria seethes for a moment, then fishes out another coin.

'Sell me a curse,' she says curtly.

'Against . . . ?'

99

'You know who,' Focaria says, and the fortune teller takes the coin, then writes something out on a strip of papyrus. Focaria snatches the strip and stuffs it inside her dress. Then she stands abruptly and recoils when she sees me standing so close.

'Move,' she says, pushing me out of the booth. Quartus ducks back behind his partition, but he tugs at my arm as I start to follow Focaria up the aisle again.

'Remember!' he whispers. 'Tell Thalia that Quartus is thinking of her!'

'I said *move*.' Focaria nearly yanks me off my feet by the basket strap. At the steps she stops short and draws a deep breath. Looking up at her, I can see her jaw working. I know I shouldn't speak, but I can't help myself.

'You have a child?' I say.

I've seen Focaria angry many times, but I've never seen her face like this. She looks hollowed-out. She opens her mouth to speak, and I cringe, expecting a curse or a blow or both, but she works her lips for a moment before she whispers, 'Yes.'

Then she looks down at me and says, 'No.'

Before she can say anything else, there's a sharp cry of pain from below, then the roar of the crowd. Both of us turn to look toward the racket. On the stage, the slave dealer is hopping about on one foot and waving his hand in the air. Sold and unlocked from her shackles, the little Syrian girl has apparently kicked him in the shins and bitten him between his thumb and forefinger. She springs, still naked, into the crowd, which scatters out of her way. She lands on her feet while the dealer is still hobbling toward the edge of the stage, and she charges up the steps two at a time, shoving people aside. Every gaze swivels to watch her rise through the rows of booths, every voice lets out an involuntary cry. The eyes of every slave on the stage rise with the girl, up through the theatre.

As she runs, she rips the placard from around her neck and sends it sailing. Some in the crowd laugh at the sight of it spinning. The girl comes straight toward Focaria and me, and her fierce gaze rises to meet ours. I'm paralyzed, but Focaria throws her arm across me and forces me back. As the girl passes, I glimpse a look of rage and determination that a lifetime has not dimmed in my imagination.

Focaria and I turn to watch her pelting up the steps into the empty seats. A vendor makes a lunge for her, and she ducks him, leaving him sprawling painfully across hard stone.

'Make way!'

We turn again, and the slave dealer is making surprisingly good progress up the steps, taking them two at a time. His face, too, is a mask of rage. Watching him come, I edge behind Focaria again. But the instant before he reaches us, she yanks me by the strap of my basket directly into his path. Man and boy collide, and I land painfully on my hip, spilling the basket, apples rolling everywhere, down the steps and underfoot. The dealer curses as he rises, blood oozing from his scraped knee. Focaria hauls me out of his reach and kicks me.

'Clumsy boy!' she shouts.

But the man is already charging up the steps again after the girl. Focaria hauls me to my feet and hisses, 'Stand still', as she collects the apples. Up above, I see the girl nearing the top of the theatre, her arms and legs pumping, her narrow backside working, the whitened soles of her feet flashing. The man is still a couple of rows below her, grunting with the effort. The roaring of the crowd fills the theatre like a tide, and in it I hear laughter and jeering and catcalls and even some mocking encouragement for the girl. Focaria's hand falls on my shoulder, and I'm afraid she's going to make me look away, but she's just steadying herself, watching the girl and the man with a look of almost predatory zeal.

At the top of the theatre, the girl leaps as high as she can and catches the lip of the back wall with the tips of her fingers. The crowd inhales sharply, as one person. She wriggles up and over the edge, and the crowd breathes out again. There's even a smattering of applause.

The slave dealer leaps, grabs the edge, and, with a great deal more effort than the girl, hauls himself up and over. The crowd falls silent.

'Is she—?' I say, and Focaria shakes me hard.

'Shh,' she hisses, and for a moment there's no sound from above and nothing to see, just the noonday sun pouring into the theatre upon all the upturned faces and hammering the bleached hillside where, out of sight, some sort of struggle is happening.

Suddenly the slave dealer reappears at the top of the wall, crouching and holding his arms over his head. At the same time the girl reappears higher up the hill, flinging stones with unerring aim at the slave dealer, as fast as she can snatch them off the ground. The stones thump against his leg, his arm, his shoulder, then rattle against the empty seats below. The crowd starts to laugh and jeer, and the man looks back at us and snarls something, lowering his arms for a moment. Just then, a perfectly aimed stone clips him hard on the side of his head, and he topples from the wall, landing with a meaty thump on the hard surface of the top row. The crowd groans and laughs at the same time, and then someone shouts, 'There she goes!'

The girl sprints away up the hillside without looking back. The crowd roars out its gleeful appreciation – for the entertainment, if not for the escape – while a couple of men hustle up the steps to assist the dealer. The girl passes the ruined temple near the hilltop, and Focaria starts to drag me away down the steps. As the crowd babbles excitedly around us, I look back one last time and see the distant girl, scrambling on her hands and feet through the scrub.

Focaria glances back for the slave dealer, and we see him stumbling down the steps propped up between the two men. Blood streams from his temple, and he's raging and spitting. Focaria drags me up the aisle, away from the steps, and she puts me in front of her and turns her back as the dealer passes, cursing incoherently. We have stopped before a booth where a man is selling live hares out of little wooden cages, five or six of them stuffed in each cage. My heart is still hammering, and even Focaria is breathing hard. She draws a deep breath and tells the man she wants six of them.

'Alive or dead?' asks the man, opening the lid of one of the cages.

'Alive.' Focaria's hand trembles as she puts the coins on the man's little table. Then, as the man hands her one quivering hare after another, she snaps each one's neck with a single twist. I watch, amazed but not horrified – I've seen her kill chickens before by slicing their necks. With the first hare, her whole face contorts as if the little beast has done her a personal injury, but she grimaces a little less as she kills the second one, then a little less with the third, and by time she's placing the sixth limp hare in the basket on my back, her face is calm again, and her hands are steady.

As we pass out of the theatre, the crowd has returned to its normal rumble. The slave dealer is limping along the stage, driving his remaining slaves ahead of him with lashes of his quirt, as if the girl's escape was their fault. They hunch their shoulders and shuffle as fast as they can. Then Focaria and I are back in the theatre's garden. She marches ahead of me up the path between the trees, kicking palm fronds out of her way. I'm full of questions, of course, but I can tell from her furious pace and the set of her shoulders that I shouldn't ask her again about her child. I can't see them, but I'm aware of the boys watching us from behind the bushes and the columns. Clutching the straps of my laden basket, I trot to catch up to Focaria.

'Where will she go?' I say.

Without breaking stride, Focaria says, 'Who?'

'The girl. Where will she go?'

Focaria stops and turns.

'Don't you ever do that,' she says.

'Do what?' I say, though I know what.

'Don't you ever run.'

'But the girl—'

'She'll be dead before nightfall,' Focaria says. 'Or she'll wish she was.'

'You ran,' I say.

'To my eternal regret.' She yanks at the iron collar round her neck.

The boys in the bushes around us laugh softly at our little scene, making me cringe. Focaria ignores them.

'You're not strong enough,' she says, 'or fast enough, or smart enough. If you want to live, you'll do as you're told.'

I meet her gaze, aware of the snickering from the bushes and the shadows of the colonnade.

'Well, do you?' she says. 'Want to live?'

I nod.

Focaria's lip twists in her bitter smile, and without saying another word, she plunges through the gap in the wall and into the passage that leads to the street. The unseen boys start to murmur and catcall – 'Who's your father, wolf boy?' – and I hear the crunch of feet on stony ground, the rustle of leaves as they come closer. To the rising laughter of the invisible boys, I fly down the passage after Focaria, the basket bouncing on my back.

For a long time, I don't leave the garden without Focaria, except for fetching water. Still, I can see she's preparing me to go out alone, and soon I'm making all the transactions with our coin purse, while she simply stands back and makes sure I'm not being cheated. Audo, meanwhile, takes me into the garden several mornings in a row and teaches me a few bits of self-defence, in case the street boys accost me. As Euterpe watches with alarm, he shows me how to wriggle out of a grip, how to watch an opponent's hands and feet and eyes, and how to hit someone where it will hurt him the most.

'Throat, balls, knees,' he tells me in his phlegmy rasp. 'If you can't reach his throat, punch him in the balls or kick him in the knees. Then run like fuck.'

'How's he supposed to do all that with a full basket on his back?' Focaria calls out from the kitchen doorway. 'Maybe you should give him a knife.'

Euterpe cries, 'No!' and presses her hand over her mouth, but Audo hasn't noticed. For a moment, he actually seems to be considering it.

'No,' he says at last. 'They'd just take it from him and cut his throat.' He balls his fist and makes a feint at me, and when I cringe, he laughs.

'There's no fight in the little cunt-licker,' he says, calling me the worst thing he can think of, and lumbers away.

But on my own, in the garden, I practise throwing stones. I know I may never be able to fling them with the savage accuracy of the Syrian girl, but I can get better with practice. To start with, I draw a circle with a piece of charcoal on the garden wall, then I collect a fistful of stones and practise until my arm is sore or Focaria calls me. If the irregular *chock chock* of stone against crumbling plaster draws her attention, she doesn't mention it. Over the course of a week, I start throwing faster and moving farther away until I can put the stones inside the circle nearly as fast as I can pluck them out of my palm. There are a limited number of stones in the garden, so I keep collecting the same ones and throwing them again. When I'm not using them, I keep them in a little heap behind the latrine, where no one else ever goes. As I get better and faster, I set sticks of firewood upright in the dirt and fling stones at them from further and further away, until I'm knocking over more sticks than not. I try hitting the chicken, the rooster, and stray cats that slink through the garden, until they learn to avoid me.

One day I think about aiming at the birds that strut along the wall or the eaves of the tavern, but I hesitate. For one thing, I can't be flinging rocks over the wall into the street. For another, I doubt I could knock one of the darting swifts or even one of the slowly drifting seagulls out of the sky. Then I find myself standing sideways to a little brown ball of feathers on the roof of the kitchen, with a stone in my fist and my arm cocked. The sparrow sits trustingly on the roof, swivelling its head, watching me with one eye and then the other. I can't miss at this distance. I could stun the sparrow or even kill it, dropping it into the dirt outside the kitchen door.

But I can't do it. Ever since Euterpe told me his story, Sparrow has been my brother, my secret namesake. I am Sparrow and Sparrow is me, and together we are not very good at any one thing, but just good enough at everything to survive. And ever since I saw Sparrow in a cage in the theatre market, I know that he, too, can be a slave, just like me. Seeing him caged made me sad, but now, in the tavern garden, as the uncaged Sparrow and the caged boy regard each other across the length of a stone's throw, it also gives me hope. If Sparrow can be both caged and free, then maybe so can I.

As if to warn my brother not to trust me, I toss the stone under-handed onto the roof, away from him. As the rock clatters down the tiles and into the dirt, Sparrow erupts into flight, his wings a blur as he speeds away over my head and out of sight.

Soon I have an opportunity to demonstrate my skill with a stone. The idle boys on the corner have begun to take note of me trotting in Focaria's wake, sweating under a bulging basket of laundry or bread or fruit. Their headquarters is a cookshop where they spill onto the pavement and sprawl on the benches, casting their eyes up and down the passing women and girls, joking and laughing to disguise their avid appraisal of vulnerable passers-by. Three of them in particular begin to watch me like cats, but at first they leave me alone, because Focaria is as formidable on the street as she is in the tavern kitchen. Even so, I make sure to slip a handful of stones inside the belt of my tunic every morning before we leave the garden.

Now the three boys start to separate from the crowd at the corner when they see us coming, and for a couple of days they shadow us on the other side of the street. On the third day, one of them, a pale, spotty kid with tangled hair the colour of straw, makes eye contact with me and puckers his lips in my direction. On the fourth day, we're coming home from the butcher and I'm trotting after Focaria with a basketful of coiled sausage, and one of the boys slips across the street and insinuates himself onto the narrow pavement ahead of me, but behind Focaria. She doesn't notice him and sails on into in the crowd. The boy slows, forcing me to slow down, too. Without turning round I know the second boy is treading right behind me, close enough to smell the sausage and maybe even to help himself to a coil or two. Then, out of the corner of my eye I see the third boy, the spotty one with straw hair, smirking his way through the traffic in the street. Now I'm nearly treading on the heels of the boy ahead of me, and I can't even see Focaria in the crowd. My heart is pounding, thinking of what the boys are going to do me, thinking of what Audo is going to do to me if I lose a whole basket of sausage. Then I think of the Syrian girl, charging up the steps wearing only her skin, chased by a man three times her size, and I put my hands up and shove the boy ahead of me, hard.

He's not expecting it, and he falls to his knees, crying out in pain. At the same I stop short, and the boy behind runs into me – 'Hey!' – and recoils instinctively. I turn as quickly as I can with the basket on my back, sending a couple of sausages spinning into the street. I think of Audo – *throat, balls, knees* – and punch him as hard as I can in the throat. He looks more surprised than hurt, and I turn to face the third boy, Straw Hair, as he hesitates in the street. While he's still thinking, I pull a stone out of my belt and plant it right between his eyes. He doesn't fall, but shouts, 'Oh, fuck!' so loud that nearly everyone around us turns to look. The boy to my left is clutching his throat with one hand and slapping at me with the other, so I punch him again, this time in the balls, and he gasps and doubles over. The first boy is already hobbling away with two bloodied knees, but I hit him anyway with another stone in the back of his head. Now Straw Hair is marching toward me, gripping the stone I hit him with, but as he cocks his arm to hurl it back at me, Focaria grasps his wrist from behind and jerks his arm down between his shoulder blades.

The boy howls and drops the stone, and Focaria swings him staggering across the street, delivering a ferocious kick to his backside. Clutching their bruises and cursing us, the boys scarper into the crowd while shopkeepers and passers-by laugh and catcall. My heart is pounding and I'm shaking, but I can't help laughing, too. Focaria picks the two coils of sausage off the street and slaps them against her skirt. Then she takes the strap of the basket and looks down at me.

'You're ready to go out on your own,' she says.

The following morning, Focaria sends me by myself to Renatus the baker. I've been with her to the bakery before, but she's always had me wait in his yard, where he can't see me, while she enters his shopfront to buy the bread.

'Let's see if he short-changes you,' she says, 'like he always short-changes me.'

'Why does he short-change you?' I ask.

'He doesn't approve of us,' she says, helping me on with the basket. 'I don't think he's ever seen you, so maybe he won't know who he's selling bread to.'

She hangs her little leather coin purse by a string round my neck and under my tunic. She makes me repeat how many loaves of each kind of bread she wants and how much to pay for each loaf, and she asks me to tell her how much that comes to. Once again, she represses her surprise that I've worked it out before she's even finished the question. She leads me across the garden, hauls open the door, and deposits me, alone, on the street.

'Do you have your stones?' she says, and I pat the little bulge under my belt.

'Keep to the wall.' She turns me in the baker's direction. 'Don't talk to anybody.'

After my victory the day before, I am more excited than afraid. Being sent out alone on the business of his Dominus is the most liberty a slave ever enjoys. As I pass the fountain on the other side of the street, I want the women there to notice me, the tavern boy – the wolf cub, little Mouse – running an errand on his own. But Afra is holding court as usual, making the other women hoot and laugh, Lucilia most of all. Tacita, as always, stands apart with her buckets and her yoke, staring across the street at Priscianus's shop. I wave to her when I cross her line of sight, but she looks away.

Hugging the wall to my left, I keep my head down, with one eye on the giants all around who aren't keeping an eye on me, and the other on the pavement. The street is a map of itself, signposted by sawdust crushed into the sidewalk outside the carpenter's shop, by the sharp tattoo of the tinsmith's hammer, by the meaty reek and cleaver thump of the butcher. I pass through the shadows of balconies and canvas awnings and into the steep sunlight again, under the narrow ribbon of blue sky. I can tell where I am by the mules tethered to holes drilled through the kerbstone, by the cookshop benches full of belching loafers, by the pictures above shop doorways – a set of keys over the locksmith, a hammer and chisel over the stonemason, a goat over the dairy. Over some of the shops I can still see the faint images of Mercury or Minerva, still secretly dear to tradesmen, and on the wall above a street altar that has been repainted by Christians, twelve of the old gods still bleed through the whitewash over the picture of Christ, who raises two fingers in benediction. I sail

109

through the tangy haze of urine and rhythmic song issuing from the fuller's shop, where I hear Nazarius laughing at one of his own jokes, while across the street his son fights to keep his eyes open and avoid the schoolmaster's stick.

I come to a cross street and, as instructed by Focaria, I look both ways and wait as a man on horseback passes one way and two men carrying a rolled-up carpet pass in the other. Across the intersection, the boys around the cookshop notice me and begin to taunt their three mates, who sit shoulder to shoulder on the bench, glowering at me. Straw Hair has a purple bulge in the middle of his forehead, and he spits in my direction. The two boys on either side talk past him, each urging the other to take his revenge. As I wait to cross the street, I put my hand inside my belt and close my fingers round a stone. But luckily for all of us, we're distracted by the city's crier, who sets his feet in the middle of the intersection and draws a breath.

'ATTENtion please! A reWARD for the reTURN of a FUgitive slave. A SYRian girl, TWELVE years of age . . .'

I almost laugh out loud. It's been two weeks, and they still haven't caught her. The crumbling old temple on the hill above the theatre gleams in the sunlight. Is she still up there, or has she escaped into the countryside, naked, feet dusted with chalk, living off berries and rainwater? I wonder if I'll ever learn what happened to her.

I never do. I keep telling you, reader, this isn't that kind of story.

Now the boys on the corner are catcalling the crier, who ignores them and declaims even louder – 'FIFty denarii for her SAFE return, UNharmed and INtact' – and I take the opportunity to cross the street unnoticed. I hug the wall for another block, trailing my fingers over the plaster, stepping over a sleeping dog, scooting past a slave stealing a nap in a doorway. Ahead of me a shopkeeper splashes his pavement with a bucket of water, so I slip into the street, where I fall in behind a slave carrying a bundle of firewood on his back, following in his wake as people clear out of his way. Only when I smell baking bread do I slip back to the pavement and into the establishment of Renatus the baker.

Just inside the archway I step to one side and hide for a moment. The yard is still half in shadow, and at the centre of it, a swaybacked mule yoked to a beam crosses back and forth across the meridian as it treads in an endless circle around a rumbling, hourglass millstone. A slave pours wheat from a bag into the top of the millstone, ducking each time the beam comes round. A second slave squats below and collects the flour in another bag, the beam passing again and again over his head. A fine white dust glitters in the sunlight, tickling the back of my nostrils and making me sneeze. The man on the bottom is coated in it, his face a white mask, his hair powdered like an actor's wig. The grating of stone against stone is punctuated by the sighing and blowing of the mule, and the circular track is littered with pungent droppings. As I watch, the slave on top puts down his bag, picks up a short leather whip, and lashes the inside hindquarter of the mule. The beast brays and trots a little faster. It lets out a stream of piss, tracing a dark, steaming arc along a quadrant of his circuit.

The stink of urine drives me from my hiding place and deeper into the yard, where a row of men at a long table are slapping dough into round loaves. Here the warmth of baking bread is stronger than the smell of dust and mule. At the back of the yard a man, his bare chest streaming with sweat, slides loaves out of a heat-shimmering oven with a long-handled peel. Another bare-chested man takes each hot loaf in his bare hands and raps the edge of it sharply against the side of the oven to shake off the ash, then places it in a wooden rack. For some reason, Renatus doesn't sell his bread from a shopfront on the street, but requires his customers to pass through his yard and enter a little room off to the side. It's as if he wants them to see the effort involved. Unlike the workers in Nazarius's fullery, the baker's slaves are silent. There is no conversation or laughter or singing. Even Audo doesn't enforce silence to this degree when he assembles the wolves.

I pass through a doorway into a dim, low-ceilinged room lined with shelves stacked with freshly baked loaves. The smell of warm bread is stifling. Behind the counter is Renatus, a man so wizened and bony that I wonder if he's ever sampled his own wares, or if he just lives off the flour he breathes every day. As I come in, he's coughing drily into his fist, and he turns to me behind the counter. He is a Christian, so Focaria has instructed me to great him with, 'Peace of Dominus.'

'Peace of Dominus,' he replies, barely moving his lips.

I shrug off the wicker basket and clutch the edge of the counter, feeling the flour dust under my fingers. Another figure I hadn't noticed turns toward me out of the gloom behind the counter. It's the baker's sister, Balbina, whom I know from the fountain. Even in the twilight of the room, I can see the resemblance. He's taller than she is, but they're both grey-skinned and hollow-chested, and she watches me with the same heavy-lidded gaze.

'Peace of Dominus,' I say to her.

'Pusus,' she says, nodding. She shares a glance with her brother, and under her breath, she says, 'Helicon.' Then she disappears through another door at the end of the counter.

'Focaria sent me,' I say to the baker, since his sister has already given me away.

'I know where you're from.' Again, his lips barely move.

I repeat Focaria's order, so many loaves of twice-ground fresh bread for the paying customers, so many loaves of coarse, day-old bread for the wolves, Focaria, and me. Renatus says nothing, but only stares at me from under his heavy eyelids. Maybe he hasn't heard me, so I start to repeat the order. But then he turns and starts plucking loaves from the shelves, making one pile for the fresh bread, another for the day old. I stand on tiptoe to reach for a loaf, and Renatus slaps my hand.

'Not yet.' He pauses to cough into his fist, and when he is done, he says hoarsely, 'Money first.' Then he turns back to the shelves for more bread.

I silently count the loaves as he stacks them, and I multiply in my head the number in each stack by the price of each grade of bread. I lift the leather purse out of my collar and spill a handful of coins on the countertop. Renatus watches with eyes half shut as I make three little stacks of coins in the correct amount and then push them in his direction, as far as I can reach. The rest I scoop back into the purse. But the baker doesn't take the coins. He just stares at me and slowly taps the countertop with his bony finger.

'Isn't that enough?' I say.

Renatus says nothing and taps the countertop again, more slowly. I know I'm right, but what can I do? I can't leave without the bread, or Focaria or Audo, or both, will beat me. I lift out the purse and spill a few more coins on the countertop. Renatus taps again. I spill some more. He keeps tapping until I empty the purse. Then, scooping the coins out of sight, he pushes the stacks of bread toward me and stands back, and he watches as I pluck them off the countertop and put them in the basket as quickly as I can, my hands shaking.

'What do you mean he took all the money?' Focaria says. 'I gave you twice as much as you needed.'

I stand in the kitchen clutching the basket full of warm bread in front of me. I'm stammering because I know this will be blamed on me, but somehow I manage to get across that Renatus wouldn't let me leave with the bread until I emptied the purse. Focaria storms around the table. I wheel to keep the basket between us, but she ducks through the door and into the garden.

'Audo!' she shouts.

A few moments later, I'm running in Audo's wake, back up the street to the baker's yard. Unlike me, Audo doesn't keep close to the wall but ploughs up the middle of the street like a bull, marching

113

up the ridge between the wagon ruts. Men, women, children, and dogs scatter out of his way. At the intersection, the corner boys fall silent and slack-jawed at his approach, and not one of them even attempts a joke. As we come near to the bakery, Audo stops suddenly, and I blunder into him. He doesn't hit me, but grips the top of my head, tilting my face up so that I'm gazing past the bulge of his belly at his black eyes.

'How many loaves did you buy?' he asks, and I tell him. 'How much was each loaf?' and I tell him. 'How much does that come to?' and I tell him. 'How much did he take?' and I tell him that, too. He lets go of my head and we start again. Then he stops and looks down at me.

'You're certain?' he rasps.

I nod.

All the slaves who scarcely noticed me before now stop and turn to watch Audo stumping through the baker's yard. Balbina, holding a blackened loaf, is scolding one of the sweaty men at the oven, but she too pauses to watch Audo pass. Even the mule at the millstone seems to hesitate in its circuit. Audo ignores them all and stoops through the doorway without breaking stride, with me at his heels. Renatus is handing change to a woman as she lifts fresh loaves into her shoulder bag. She is smiling and laughing, and, to my astonishment, so is Renatus.

Audo looms over the counter, cutting the laughter short. The woman glances up at him and shoves one more loaf into her bag. 'Peace of God,' she mutters to Renatus, then hustles around Audo and out the door.

'Peace of God,' the baker says, and he turns slowly to the larger man. His mouth tightens, his eyelids slide halfway down.

'How many loaves did you sell Pusus?' Audo says. No peace of God for him.

'Your usual order.' Renatus answers Audo more quickly than he answered me.

'How much did you charge him?'

Taking his time, Renatus reaches under the counter and produces an abacus. He starts to flick the little bronze beads up and down the grooves. In the doorway at the end of the counter, Balbina appears, still holding the blackened loaf, but she does not come in. So many loaves, Renatus says, at such and such a price for fresh, such and such a price for day old. Then he turns the abacus around for Audo and lifts his leaden gaze to him.

Audo doesn't even look at the abacus. 'Pusus says you took twice that.'

'He's mistaken,' says the baker. 'I charged the usual amount.'

'Pusus says you took all the money in my purse.'

Renatus turns his head, almost but not quite looking at his sister outside the other doorway, then he slowly swivels his heavy-lidded gaze at me, where I'm hiding behind Audo.

'I don't think that . . . boy knows how much was in the purse,' Renatus says. 'Either that, or he's cheating you.'

Audo and the baker stare at each other. Balbina edges to one side outside the doorway, so that she's half obscured by the jamb. Above the rumble of the millstone in the yard, I can hear Audo breathing. He reaches back and tugs me by the shoulder up to the counter. He looks down at me and squeezes my shoulder just hard enough to let me know how much he could hurt me.

'Are you cheating me?' he says.

My throat is very dry, but I manage to say, 'No.'

Audo lifts his chin at Renatus.

'Is he telling the truth?' he says to me.

I look from Audo to the abacus, then up at Renatus. I glance sideways at Balbina, and I can only see one of her eyes, as she peers around the doorjamb. Then I look back up at Audo. I can feel the grit of flour dust between my eyes and my eyelids.

'No,' I whisper.

With the tips of his fingers against my chest, Audo pushes me slowly back toward the door. Then, with one hand, he sweeps the abacus off the counter. The board clatters against the floor, the beads rattle all over the room. With his other hand, he drags Renatus across the counter by the front of his tunic. I press my back against the wall just inside the door. The baker cries out as Audo slams him to the countertop, then gasps as Audo shoves his hand up the man's tunic and grabs him by the testicles.

'Tell me the truth,' Audo says.

Renatus wants to curl up in agony, but Audo's hand on his chest has him pinned to the counter. Balbina is nowhere to be seen.

'I raised the price,' the baker gasps.

'Why?'

Renatus whimpers something. His eyes are glazing over. Audo loosens his grip on the man's balls, but he keeps his other hand on his chest.

'You sent . . .' Renatus pants, 'you sent . . .'

'I sent what?' growls Audo.

'*Him,*' says Renatus. He points his shaking finger in my direction.

Audo turns and looks at me. He leans over Renatus.

'What's wrong with him?'

Even against the pressure of Audo's hand, Renatus rears up and hisses in his face, 'He's a *catamite.*'

Audo slams him back down on the counter, but he takes his other hand out from under the tunic and points his finger between the baker's eyes.

'No,' says Audo. 'He's not.'

He digs his fingers into Renatus's jaw and jerks his head to look at me. I'm trembling by the doorway, ready to bolt.

'I'll tell you what he is.' Audo squeezes the side of the baker's face against the counter. 'When you see him, you're seeing me. When you deal with him, you're dealing with me.' He jerks Renatus's face to look up at him. 'When you cheat that boy, you're

116

cheating me.' He slaps the baker's face, but not as hard as he could. 'Do you understand?'

Renatus pants under the pressure of Audo's hand on his chest, gazing up with pure rage. But after a moment, he slides his gaze away and nods.

'What's that?' says Audo. 'I didn't hear you.'

'Yes,' gasps Renatus. 'I understand.'

Audo lifts his hand, and Renatus, groaning, rolls away and falls behind the counter. Balbina rushes in from the other doorway, bent double. I hear Renatus having a coughing fit, and his sister murmuring to him. Audo turns to me and says, 'How much does he owe us?'

I tell him, and Audo grunts. After a moment Renatus rises like a revenant from behind the counter, leaning heavily on his sister, who keeps her eyes down. Still coughing, his hands shaking, Renatus pushes a little pile of coins toward Audo, who scoops them up without counting. He turns away from the counter and hands me the coins, and I put them with shaking hands back into the purse. Audo picks up one of the loose beads from the abacus from off the countertop.

'I'm sorry about your abacus.' He rolls the bead between his fingers. 'Come by Helicon sometime, and I'll stand you a cup of wine.' He smiles. 'Your sister, too. She looks like she could do with a drink.'

Then he lumbers toward the door, waving me ahead of him. Half a dozen slaves who were watching through the doorway scatter all at once like roaches. Audo stoops to follow me into the yard.

'There will be a judgement,' Renatus calls out, and Audo turns. The baker is propped against his sister, one arm round her shoulders. He coughs, once, twice.

'Your enterprise is sinful,' he says, his voice quavering, 'and your Dominus knows it. He may think his family doesn't still stink of the tannery, but it does. You can tell him I said so.'

Audo says nothing. He just rolls the bead between his fingers.

'On the Day of Wrath,' Renatus says, raising his voice, 'he and his whores will hang by their hair over a lake of flaming shit. And you . . .' he adds, spittle flying, 'you'll hang by your heels with your head in it. And that one . . .' He points a shaking finger at me. 'That one will fall from a cliff onto sharp rocks . . .' He's shaking all over now. 'For all *eternity!*' he shouts.

Audo sighs, and I look up at him. *What's a cliff?* I want to ask him, but he's pursing his lips at the little bronze bead he's rolling between his fingers.

'Could be,' he says. He lifts his gaze to Renatus and, with a deft flick of thumb and middle finger, hits the baker between the eyes with the bead. Renatus staggers and claps his hand to his forehead. His sister wraps herself round his waist to keep him from falling over.

'But until then,' Audo says, 'you're going to keep selling us your fucking bread.'

He turns and lumbers away. I glance back at Renatus and his sister swaying together. Just before I turn away, Balbina lifts her heavy-lidded eyes and fixes her fierce gaze on me.

Out on the street again, I run as fast as a lashed mule to keep up with Audo. He looks back once to make sure I'm there, and that emboldens me.

'Audo,' I ask, breathlessly, 'what's a catamite?'

But he doesn't answer, and we tumble home down the street, a rolling boulder with a pebble in its wake.

Now the whole street understood that I operated under the authority of Audo, and not just the tavern's sharp-tongued cook. I won't say that I was safer. I was still a slave, still a child, still subject to beatings from Audo, and occasionally from Focaria. There was still the danger of injury or death from dogs, the wheels of carts and wagons, and the hooves of mules and horses, who didn't care whose slave I was. But even so, shopkeepers began to treat me with wary cordiality, and even the boys on the corner kept their distance.

Now whenever I come into the baker's yard, Renatus steps away from the counter, and Balbina takes his place to accept Helicon's filthy money. At first, she is scrupulously polite, never saying a word more than she needs to, watching me throughout the entire transaction like a cat watching another cat, perfectly still but intensely alert. If she had a tail, it would be lashing back and forth. Over time, our exchanges become more relaxed, and one day she says to me, 'Are you a Christian, Pusus?'

According to Euterpe, everybody is a Christian now, by order of the emperor, but I'm not sure what that means. 'I don't know,' I say.

To my surprise, she reaches across the counter and lays her chill, bony hand on mine. 'Do you want to be?'

Apart from Euterpe and sometimes one of the other wolves, no one touches me except to hurt me or push me out of the way. I'm not sure why she's doing it. Should I be afraid? Should I pull my hand back? I don't know what she wants me to say.

'God loves everyone, both slave and free.' Her touch is cool and dry. 'We're all slaves to our sins.' The liver-spotted skin on the back of her hand stretches tight over her knuckles. 'His Son died to free you from *all* your sins, even the foulest ones.'

Apart from stealing food from Focaria, which she expects everyone to do, I'm not sure what my foulest sins are. I try to slip my hand out from under Balbina's, but she clutches me, not tightly, though it's enough to hang on.

'You could be clean again, Pusus,' she says, her eyes bright. 'All you have to do is ask Him for His forgiveness.'

'I have to go.' I tug my hand away and shrug on the basket.

'I pray for you, Pusus,' she says.

'Peace of God,' I say as I turn and hurry out the door, more puzzled than anything else.

Nazarius, on the other hand, has always been friendly to me, and every time I come to his shop, we banter like a pair of comedians.

'What's your name today?' he asks me as he takes the basket full of dirty laundry off my shoulders. 'Pusus? Mouse? Little Brother? Who are you this time?'

'Antiochus,' I announce.

'Your worship!' He lifts me onto a stool and offers me a little watered wine in a wooden cup. 'A libation for the king. Don't tell your mother.'

'I don't have a mother.'

'Every pusus has a mother,' he says, stripping the dirty laundry out of the basket.

'I don't.'

'Who's Focaria then?'

'Not my mother.' I hand him the empty cup. 'I don't know my father, either.'

'Neither do I!' Nazarius says heartily. He starts layering the tavern's clean linens into the basket. 'But you see that boy over there?'

He lifts his beard to the school across the street, where Lutatius is giggling with a couple of other students in the back row and not paying attention to the droning schoolmaster. Nazarius can't help himself. He points out his son nearly every time I come to the fullery.

'I started where you are, Antiochus,' Nazarius says, 'and now someday my boy is going to be an aedile.'

Who knows if that turned out to be true? From his father's shop, Lutatius doesn't seem any different from the other useless boys I fend off with stones. In fact, he doesn't seem all that different from me, or from any of the other slaves I see in the street. Now that I travel alone, this has become one of my greatest sources of fascination – who is a slave and who isn't. With a few people it's obvious – Focaria wears an iron collar, so she's a slave. Men shackled to a single chain by their necks and marched up the street, they are slaves. But Tacita doesn't wear a collar, and she's a slave, because Focaria told me so. I don't wear a collar, either, and I'm a slave. All five of the wolves do the same work, whatever that is, but Melpomene is not a slave and the others are. Sometimes I see Renatus working bare-chested at his oven, with his ribs practically poking through his skin, while a slave waits on customers at the counter. If Renatus is working harder than the man at the counter, then who's the slave? Can you be a slave sometimes and not a slave at other times? The mule yoked to the millstone, lashed endlessly in the same circle, is it a slave? The man carrying firewood on his back, is he a beast?

After Euterpe's stories, I used to think that birds could not be slaves. But then I saw them for sale in cages in the theatre, and now I see them everywhere on the street – colourful goldfinches or dull little nightingales hung up in the windows of houses or the doorways of shops, where they chatter all day and keep their masters company. Or I see shockingly green, hook-nosed parrots, uncaged but chained to a perch, squawking rude words at passers-by. Now and then a parrot tests its chain, beating its wings in a pointless frenzy, rising just so high but no higher. Then after this fury of screeching and feathers, it subsides to its perch and curses you for watching it. This is the greatest mystery of all: even a bird can be a slave, but even in its cage, it sings. Early in the morning, when the street is just stirring, the free birds fill the air with song, and then, as their masters and mistresses hang them in windows or doorways, the caged birds answer. They sing together, call and response, like the men treading in piss in the fullery.

This must be one of Euterpe's philosophical paradoxes. Balbina tells me she's a slave to her sins, so she's both free and not free. She says I can be free of my sins if I ask God for forgiveness, so I can be a slave and free at the same time. I have seen Sparrow in a cage, and he has watched me walking free in the street. My cage

121

is the garden, and I've watched Sparrow flying free over my head. If I am Sparrow, and Sparrow is me, is it possible that someday he will watch from his cage as I fly straight up into the blue, getting smaller and smaller, shrinking from the outline of a bird to a pair of wings to a squiggle to a dot, until I vanish?

One morning when I'm coming back from Nazarius with a basket full of clean laundry, I find Tacita alone at the fountain, filling her buckets. I haven't tried to talk to her since the morning I gave her the pear, but Audo is away from Helicon on some errand, and only Focaria is expecting me back. So I stop at the fountain. Perhaps Tacita can explain these things to me. She's a slave, like I am. Maybe she knows where she comes from, maybe she doesn't. Maybe we have that in common.

As I come up to the fountain, Tacita glances at me without expression, then turns to her task. I slip the basket off and prop it carefully against the wall, and I stand across the fountain from her as she fills a bucket.

'Tacita,' I say. 'Do you remember me?'

She says nothing. She sets the full bucket down and lifts the other one under the spout.

'I'm Mouse.' Maybe she can't hear me over the splashing of the water, so I raise my voice. 'You showed me how to use the yoke, and I gave you a pear. Do you remember?'

She says nothing, but only steps away from the fountain, setting the bucket near the yoke. I grab the other bucket with both hands, and she starts, as if afraid I'm going to run away with it. But I lug it to the other end of the yoke and set it down.

'Why won't you talk to me?' I say.

Tacita stares at the pavement just beyond her toes for a moment, then lifts her gaze and beckons me. I walk up to her, and she stops me with a hand on my shoulder. She glances across the street at the oil merchant's shop, where Priscianus has his back turned. Then she kneels, so that we're nose to nose. Her eyes are nearly as pale as her skin, only the faintest blue. She tilts her face back and opens her mouth wide. I'm not sure what she wants me to see until she points into her open mouth. Between the rows of her teeth, she has no tongue, only a scarred red stump where it used to be.

I flinch, but she grabs my chin and makes me look. Her sour breath washes over me. Then she closes her mouth and releases me. She holds her finger up again. *Attend.* Her gaze flicks across the street toward Priscianus, then she rolls her eyes to indicate the presence of Afra in the house over her shoulder. Then she gently pinches my lips shut with her fingers, and slowly shakes her head. *Tools don't talk back*, Focaria always says. *Tools don't ask questions.*

Tacita lifts her eyebrows. *Do you understand?* I nod. She stands, turns me around, and gives me a gentle push. I go back to my basket, slip into the straps, and hoist it onto my back. When I turn around, she's well along up the street, her hips moving, her buckets swaying without spilling. Across the street, Priscianus is watching her go. His unreadable gaze shifts to me for a moment, then he looks away.

By the time I reach the garden door, my heart is racing and my ears are ringing, as if Tacita has slapped me. Since Audo is out, the door is unlatched, so I just push it open, carry the basket inside, and push it almost shut, but not quite. I let the weight of the basket tug me back until I'm sitting on my haunches in the dirt. The chicken struts out of the garden, regards me with one yellow eye, and struts away. I want to call out to Focaria, but what would I tell her? If I tell her what Tacita just showed me, she'll just say, *Well, what have I been telling you?* I wish Euterpe were here, so I could ask her about it. She would know what to say. Did Tacita's parents do that to her? Why would they do such a thing? Or is Tacita like me, parentless, and it was her Dominus, Priscianus, who cut out her tongue? Or was it her Domina, Afra? Why would *she* do such a thing?

I slip out of the straps and stand, leaving the basket propped against the wall. I run to the water tank, but there is no one there, not even Clio taking a nap. I run from point to point in the garden, to all the hiding places, but no one is here. Then, from the kitchen, I hear low laughter and the murmur of voices. I run to the door, but at the last instant I stop short. Someone is whispering in the shadows, and someone else whispers back. I sink to my knees and peer round the edge of the doorway into the gloom. Through the legs of the table, in the far corner of the kitchen where I sleep, I see Focaria and Euterpe seated against the wall with their arms wrapped around each other. They are kissing each other, not the way that Euterpe kisses me, on the cheek or the forehead, but open-mouthed, touching their tongues together. Focaria has her hand inside Euterpe's gown, on her breast, and Euterpe has her hand up Focaria's skirt. The cook's bared leg is trembling. They shift, and their mouths slide apart. Euterpe presses her lips to Focaria's throat, while her hand works more vigorously between Focaria's legs.

'Quickly.' Focaria is panting into Euterpe's ear. 'He'll be back soon.'

Then I hear a heavy crunch against the pavement and the clearing of a throat just outside the garden door. It's Audo.

In this moment, I receive a flash of light like Saul on the road to Damascus. I don't know what the two women are doing, but I know that they don't want anyone else to see them. I also know that if Audo catches them at it, he'll hurt them both.

I leap to my feet. The women in the kitchen do not hear me, but only clutch each other even tighter. Across the garden the door starts to scrape open. I dash to the basket I left propped against the wall. Just before Audo appears, I kick it over, spilling half the laundry into the dirt.

'Who left the door ajar?' shouts Audo as he comes in.

'I did!' I shout back, frantically slapping the dust off a dishevelled gown.

Audo stops with his hand on the door, looming over me. 'What
have you done?' he rasps.

'I'm sorry!' I cry, as loud as I can. I jump to my feet and shake
out the gown. 'It was an accident! I was trying to bolt the door
but I couldn't reach it and I knocked the basket over . . .'

Audo is rolling his knuckles, making his eagle writhe.

'There you are, Little One!'

Suddenly Euterpe is stooping beside me, brushing off a sheet
and shaking it out. She's breathless and flushed, and she beams up
hopefully at Audo. 'No harm done,' she says brightly. 'It's just a
little dirt.'

Audo narrows his eyes at the two of us, but he doesn't hit us,
yet. He slams the door behind him and bolts it, but before he
can speak or swing his fist, Focaria is calling him from the
kitchen.

'Audo!' She stands in the doorway with her arms crossed. 'I need
money. For fish.'

Now Audo has the three of us to deal with at once, and it's too
much for him. He lumbers around Euterpe and me, limiting himself
to a slap to the back of my head and a swat to Euterpe's backside.
Then he disappears through the archway into the tavern.

Euterpe sighs and lets her shoulders slump. She looks back at
Focaria, who says to me, 'Pusus, I need you,' then steps back into
the kitchen.

Euterpe stuffs the sheet without folding it into the basket, then
she takes the gown I am wringing between my hands and stuffs it
in, too. She holds my face in both hands and gives me a long, firm
kiss on my forehead. Then, without saying anything, she picks up
the basket of laundry and disappears into the tavern.

In the kitchen, Focaria grabs me by the shoulders and says, 'What
did you see?'

'Nothing,' I say.

'And if you did see anything, who would you tell?'

I lift my fingers to my face the way Tacita did and pinch my lips shut.

Reader, I grew older. I can't tell you exactly how old, because I have no way of knowing when I was born. The milestones of my life weren't months or years. I was never six or eight or ten. Instead, I was old enough to sweep the kitchen floor, I was old enough to fetch firewood from the garden, I was old enough to carry water in from the fountain. I was old enough to ferry laundry to the fuller, to haggle with fishermen for the day's catch, to fetch back day-old bread from sullen Renatus. That's how old I was.

Then one day I'm old enough to work in the tavern itself. Coming back from the butcher with a basket full of sausages, I push through the garden door and hear Euterpe and Focaria locked in one of their arguments about me. Usually on these occasions they stand toe to toe and hiss under their breath, so that I can't hear what they're saying. But today they're in the kitchen, and they aren't expecting me back so soon. And instead of having locked themselves in one of their furtive embraces, today they are arguing loud enough for me to hear them, even across the garden.

'He's too *young*,' I hear Euterpe say.

'He's in the street already,' Focaria says. 'On his own. Every day.' I can hear the rapid tattoo of her knife as she dices vegetables.

'Men carry *knives* in the tavern,' Euterpe says.

'Men carry knives in the street.' *Tap tap tap tap tap.*

'He's too small. Wait until he's a little taller.'

'Small's good,' Focaria says, *tap tap tap.* 'They won't notice him.'

'You know what will happen next. Audo will have him working upstairs.'

Tap tap tap . . . Focaria stops. By now I'm just outside the kitchen door.

'What are you scared of?' She has lowered her voice.

'You know what I'm scared of.' Euterpe lowers her voice as well.

'Then you know there's nothing we can do about it.'

'But there is.'

'Don't say it.'

'We could run.'

'*Keep your voice down.*'

'You did it.'

'And look what happened!' Focaria is suddenly furious. 'Do you want to wear one of *these* for the rest of your life? And that's if you're *lucky.*'

'We could—'

'We could *what?*'

There's a pause. With the basketful of meat dragging on my shoulders, I rest my forehead against the wall. I can picture them, just on the other side. They have moved around the table to stand nose to nose, like wrestlers squaring off. Though I don't really understand it myself yet, each of them knows that neither of them will ever win one of these arguments. The choices they're arguing about aren't up to us. The pot Focaria's always comparing me to might as well decide to run away with the broom.

'What do you think the three of us would look like, on the run?'

I picture Focaria taking Euterpe's hands.

'What would we tell people? That we're sisters? That he's your son? Or mine? Who's going to believe that?'

Euterpe says nothing.

'You need to tell him what's what,' Focaria says, and then her voice drops so low that I can't hear it anymore. I tiptoe back from the wall and stamp my feet loudly in the dirt.

'Sausage!' I shout cheerfully, and I sail into the kitchen as if I haven't heard a thing.

They have already sprung apart to opposite sides of the table. Focaria glowers at the turnip she's murdering. The blade of her knife is a blur. *Taptaptaptaptaptaptaptaptap*. Euterpe looks stricken, but she makes herself brighten at the sight of me. I shrug off the basket and start stacking coils of sausage on the table, chattering about the three-legged cat I saw in the street, about what the women said at the fountain today, about the joke Nazarius told me.

'Listen.' Focaria interrupts me, still chopping. 'Audo wants you to start working in the tavern.'

I look from her to Euterpe. They are avoiding each other's gaze.

'I'm not working in the kitchen anymore?'

'Yes, you're still working in the kitchen, but you're also working in the tavern.' *Tap tap tap tap tap.* 'Starting tonight.'

Focaria looks up at Euterpe, but the wolf is gazing out the door, as if expecting someone. The cook puts down the knife and rests her hands on either side of the diced turnip.

'Anything you'd like to tell him?' she says.

Euterpe turns slowly toward me. She has scrubbed away last night's mask of make-up, and it's almost as if I'm looking at her naked.

'Listen to Focaria,' she says. 'Do what she tells you to.' Then she kisses me on my forehead and slips out the door.

Later that morning, for the first time, Focaria takes me through the arch where I have never been allowed to go before, into the empty tavern. It's a long room with low beams overhead, a tiled floor worn through in places down to the cement underneath, and walls of faded blue plaster with red trim. There's no graffiti in the main room – which I will later learn is unusual for a tavern – because Audo forbids it. A few small, round wooden tables with low stools around them crowd the narrow space, the tabletops sticky and gouged, the stools wobbly. Along the outer wall the room is open to the street through two wide doorways, which are shuttered this time of day.

Along the inner wall of the room is a long masonry counter with four holes in the top. Three of them open into clay pots for cold food – cheese, bread, olives, figs, hard-boiled eggs – and one of them into a brass cistern for the hot food Focaria prepares every day – stews, kebabs, grilled sausages. Under the counter is a little firebox to heat the cistern. Shelves hold rows of cups and bowls and spoons, and there's a grimy wooden bucket where Audo leaves the dirty ones for me to scrub every night.

We crouch behind the counter, and Focaria instructs me with her usual brevity.

'Light the firebox at noon and keep it lit, but not as hot as the one in the kitchen. Enough to keep the cistern warm, but not enough to make it boil.'

'What's this?' I reach under the counter for a little wooden box with a locked lid and a slit in the top. Focaria swats my hand away.

'That's the coin box,' she says. 'You don't touch that.'

The main room of the tavern smells of smoky lamps, spilt wine, and stewed fish, with an ineradicable hint of piss and vomit. On the low ceiling, above the unlit lamps along the walls, are blackened semicircles. Along the far end of the room, above a wooden bench, a series of paintings show figures in pairs grappling with each other, but with the shutters closed it's too dim for me to see what they're doing. Focaria taps the back of my head – 'Pay attention' – and leads me through a doorway in the inside corner of the far wall. Straight ahead is another room with no access to the street, only narrow, barred windows like horizontal slits up along the ceiling. A long wooden table with a bench on either side nearly fills the room. Focaria leans against the wall next to another doorway, which opens at right angles to the door from the main room.

'Sometimes you'll wait on table in here,' she says.

'What's it for?' I say. The room has a dry, stuffy odour. The scent of piss is stronger here.

'Private parties,' says Focaria. 'We get collegia in here sometimes.'

'What's a collegia?'

'Groups of men in the same business. All the tanners in town. The gravediggers. The ragpickers. They hire the room for their monthly meetings. Well, they start with a meeting, but they always end up getting drunk.'

I look up at her, as if to say, how is that different from what happens in the main room?

'They don't fight as often,' she said. 'Or at least they don't pull knives on each other.'

'The bakers, too?' I said. 'They come and get drunk?'

'Not the bakers. Renatus won't let them meet here,' Focaria says. 'Some of the others have stopped coming, too.'

'Why?'

'The church,' says Focaria. 'It doesn't like what goes on up there.' She lifts her chin toward the other doorway. I peer past her into a narrow, unlit staircase with blotched and peeling plaster, where scalloped wooden steps rise into darkness.

'What's up there?' I ask, though I already know the answer.

'The wolves,' says Focaria. 'That's where they live.'

At this hour, I know the wolves are at the baths, so I ask, 'Can I go up?' But I already know the answer to that, too.

'No.' She lays her hand on my shoulder. 'Audo says not.'

I peer into the dark at the top of the stairs. 'Focaria,' I say, 'what do they do up there?'

She says nothing for a moment, then draws me back into the tavern. 'Stand here.' She places me in the middle of the room facing the dim pictures, then she opens one of the shutters to the street, just enough to cast a little light along the wall.

'There,' she says. 'That's what they do.'

In the dusty light from the street, the pictures resolve into six panels. Each shows a man and woman on a couch, without any clothing, grappling with each other like wrestlers. All the way across

130

the top, just under the ceiling, is a sentence in Greek, which Euterpe will later read to me: 'Sing to me, Muses of Helicon, who are divine, everywhere, and all-knowing.' Each panel is numbered, which I know because Euterpe has taught me how to read written numerals up to ten. Each panel also has a Greek word below it, which is the name of each Muse. The sixth panel is for a wolf named Calliope, who died or was sold, I never learned which, and who was never replaced. In several panels the man has a large red penis that sticks straight out from between his legs. In one panel the man is on his back and the woman rides him like a horseman. In another the woman is kneeling beside the couch and putting her mouth over the end of the man's penis. In another the woman is on her back and the man is lying between her legs, which wave in the air like a pair of oars.

'Do you know what they're doing?' Focaria is silhouetted against the light from the street.

I've seen dogs humping in the street – until some annoyed shopkeeper douses them with a bucket of water – but I can't imagine it's the same thing. I suspect that the figures are doing something like what Focaria and Euterpe do in a corner of the kitchen or behind the water tank when they don't think anyone can see them, but I also suspect that neither of them wants me to know that. So I look up at Focaria and say, 'No.'

She watches me as if making up her mind whether to believe me. Then she closes and latches the shutter, and the pictures fade into the shadows again.

'Well,' she says, 'you'll figure it out.'

I spent a few days trotting at Focaria's heels, helping her carry pots of stew, platters of bread and cheese, and plates of sausage into the main room. I had already been washing the dirty bowls and spoons and cups in a bucket, and now it became my job to collect them from punters and carry them back to the kitchen, then carry the clean ones back inside, crouching under Audo's legs to stack them under the counter. When Focaria decided that I wouldn't drop or spill or break anything – when she realized that not only would I not make more work for her, but I might actually make less – she started to send me into the tavern on my own.

During the afternoon, after Audo opened the shutters, the main room was sleepy and hot. The wolves were upstairs, back from the baths, waiting for their first customers. A few solitary drinkers hunched in the shadows, away from the light slanting through the doorways. Standing at the border between the harbour and the city, the tavern attracted punters from both sides. On the same afternoon I might see a lonely African seaman between ships, a slave stretching an errand for his Domina to sneak a quick drink for himself, a Persian merchant trying to drum up conversation in an accent no one could understand.

As the sun descended behind the mountain across the harbour and the street outside fell into shadow, Audo stumped round with a taper and lit the lamps. By the time the sun went down, the tavern was filled with a wavering yellow light, and more men filtered in from the darkened street. The noisy ones sprawled round the little tables to laugh and dice and talk too loud. To discourage cheating and its ensuing violence, Audo had nailed a pair of loaded dice to the front of the counter, right at my eye level. One of them had a bloody thumbprint on it. After a few cups of wine, some of the men would start to sing together, the choruses ragged, the words slurred, and their tuneless clamour spilled out into the night, drawing more punters from the harbour. Quieter drinkers murmured together in knots of two or three, standing on the pavement or slouching shoulder to shoulder on the benches outside. Solitary drinkers wandered in and out, flitting from one conversation to another or silently watching a game of knucklebones over the shoulders of the players.

Some of the regular punters I knew from the street. Nazarius visited nearly every night and held forth with the same group of mates, telling funny stories about his customers or his slaves that held them rapt until they erupted with laughter. Rufus the fishing captain came once a week with his entire crew, who took up one end of the room as if defying anyone else to take it from them. Musa, the pop-eyed moneylender who shared a booth with the fortune teller Opitria and the scribe Quartus in the old theatre, came in the company of his intimidating slave, Deodatus. The moneylender sat apart from the other punters, which was just as well because he was silently flatulent and apparently ate nothing but garlic. He sat in his cloud of stink and drank cup after cup of the pricier wine until his eyes clouded over. Meanwhile, Deodatus either drank the watered stuff or stayed sober, in order to escort his malodorous master home in the dark.

Renatus never came, of course, and neither did Tullus the carpenter, who had named his daughters Perpetua and Felicitas (I later learned) after Christian martyrs. There were other regulars I saw only in the tavern. There was a man whose arms were sleeved in tattoos, a slave in a loincloth whose back was cross-hatched with old scars and who snuck in just before we closed, and, now and then, slumming posh boys who always came in pairs, tiptoed up to the counter as if stepping through shit, and then sipped their wine huddled in a corner away from everyone else, daring each other to go upstairs. They never did. Then there was Brutus, the carter I had seen my first day on the street, his wagon full of firewood. I'd seen him since with his wagon-for-hire, hauling a cargo of amphorae or a consignment of slaves, wearing his ragged straw hat and leading his old mule, Potiscus, with his fingers through the bridle. He came into the tavern at night without his hat, and he always drank by himself in a corner, stretching his longs legs out in front of him and staring into the middle distance as if working something out. He was

133

a big man, but graceful, and more than once I saw him lift his cup only an instant before his table was overturned by a pair of brawlers. He'd calmly sip his wine as Audo heaved the brawlers into the street.

'I like quiet,' Audo said, and most of the time he perched behind the counter like a massive household god, his backside spreading over a stool that was just the right height for him to slide on or off without having to raise or lower his bulk. He dispensed stew by dipping a wooden bowl into the heated cistern, dropping a spoon into it, and licking his fingers clean as the punter carried it away. Wine he dispensed from small amphorae suspended on their sides in hemp netting over his head – an arrangement of his own design – so that all he had to do to fill a cup was raise his meaty arms over his head and flip a spigot. The amphorae were arranged from left to right, from the cheap plonk that left a hangover the next day to the more expensive stuff. He spent all afternoon pushing food and drink with one hand and palming coins with the other, sometimes testing them with his teeth before slipping them into the clinking coin box under the counter.

Here, in this room full of smoky lamplight and the subterranean rumble of deep voices, I continued my education in the ways of men. I learned that most men, at least in groups, at least under the influence of drink, were just like that first man, the one who had attacked Focaria in the kitchen. It didn't matter who they were during the day – a leathery fisherman, a brooding slave, a glad-handing shopkeeper – by the end of the evening they were all the same: loud, mercurial, and unsteady on their feet. They all smelled of sweat and wine. They were all prone to sudden laughter and sudden violence, often at the same time. I learned how easily a joke could lead to an insult, an insult to a shove, a shove to a blow, a blow to overturned tables and drawn knives. Sometimes Audo let these squalls blow themselves out, but he knew when to slide off his stool and swing surprisingly swiftly round the end of the counter to jerk two men apart. Sometimes he just shook them like a pair of puppies, sometimes he cracked their heads together, sometimes he broke a finger or cut one with his knife. In the silence that followed, the two men stumbled or crawled into the street while Audo lumbered slowly back behind the counter and lowered himself onto his stool.

Sometimes, though, he did nothing at all. One night a slave tracker caught a runaway in the tavern, and the punters merely looked on as if watching two dogs fighting in the street. The slave was passing as a freedman from another town, and he was boring two other men at his table with a long and drunken story when the tracker, a lanky man with hollow eyes, marched out of the street and into the lamplight, hooked his arm round the slave's neck, and jerked him up off his stool. The table overturned, the other men recoiled. Audo heaved himself up with a grunt. I backed into a corner with a pitcher of wine clutched to my chest. By now the tracker had flung the runaway face first on the hard floor, pinning him down with a knee in the middle of his back.

'This man is a runaway,' announced the tracker, panting a little. 'The property of Sextus Cresceus of Ilici.'

'Not true!' groaned the pinned man. 'I'm a freedman!' The tracker punched the man in the back of the head, breaking his nose against the floor. The crack made everyone jump. I sloshed a little wine from the pitcher.

'I have a warrant,' said the tracker. 'In my tunic.' He looked up at Audo. 'I can show you the scar inside his thigh.'

Everyone turned to Audo. After a glowering moment, he grunted and settled himself back onto his stool.

'Right,' said the tracker, and he yanked the bleeding man to his feet, pinned one arm behind his back, and marched him, stumbling, into the dark. The men who had been sitting with the runaway righted the table and the stools and returned to drinking. One of them signalled to me for the pitcher.

'Mind the blood,' he said. From behind the counter, Audo tossed me a rag to wipe it up.

In time, I learned to move through this room the way I'd learned to move through the street. I did my best to remain unseen, to scurry along the wall or under the lee of the counter, to dodge under elbows or around backsides. If a punter noticed me at all, it was to make a joke, or pinch me, or slap my ass for the amusement of his mates. When Audo sent me round to retrieve empty cups and bowls, one of them might trip me so that the empties clattered across the floor. Another might hold his cup up high and make me jump for it. One night, I reached between two men and snatched a cup that still had a drop of wine in the bottom, and one of the men grabbed my wrist and twisted it so hard I cried out, catching the attention of the room. Audo shifted off his stool, but it was Brutus the carter who came to my rescue.

'Don't,' he said, stepping up to the table.

The man locked eyes with Brutus, and all around us, the room fell silent. The only sound was my whimpering as I tried not to cry. Across the room, Musa lifted his bleary eyes from his cup. He looked puzzled, as if he were trying to work out where he was, and his bodyguard, Deodatus, sat up straight, getting ready to hustle his master away if violence erupted. Audo, still standing, made no move to come round the counter.

The man who had me painfully in his grip kept his eyes on Brutus. With his other hand, he slowly lifted the cup and drained the dregs of the wine he'd paid for, then just as slowly lowered it to the table. At last he released my wrist – I gasped – and handed me the cup. I took it between two trembling hands. Then the man slowly rose to his feet, scraping the stool against the floor. The crowd around us shrank toward the walls, every man tensing for shouts and blows and knives. Across the room, Musa and Deodatus were already gone. Brutus lifted his chin and set his feet. But then the man turned slowly away, walked straight out the door, and disappeared into the dark.

'Back to work, Mouse,' Brutus said. The crowd contracted around us again, and the room resumed its roar. I carried the bruise for a week, but from then on, I was careful to grab only those cups that were bone dry. A slave, says the philosopher Epictetus, never makes the same mistake twice. Epictetus had been a slave himself, so he knew what he was talking about.

One night I worked a private party in the other room, a meeting of the fullers' collegium, presided over by Nazarius. At the start of the evening, he was the same Nazarius who ruffled my hair and winked at me when I brought him Helicon's laundry. He began the meeting by intoning a Christian prayer and then splashing a cupful of wine on the floor as a generous libation to Minerva, the old god who was still dear to the fullers. Having hedged their bets, the laundrymen proceeded to drink and complain about their taxes, drink and vote to support a candidate for the curia, drink and take up a collection to pay for the burial of a recently deceased member. The collegium was paying for the wine, so the fullers drank more than they would have if they were each paying by the cup in the main room. All the while I raced between the kitchen and the party with skewers of grilled sausage, loaves of bread, and pitchers of wine.

There is something about men drinking together in a small space that raises the pressure of their hilarity. Here were men in their element, men without women, men without children, men distilled. I didn't count as a child – I was a slave. Late in the evening, Nazarius himself lifted me onto the table and made me drain a cup of wine, then tried to teach me an obscene song. When I stumbled over the words, he made me drink another cup, while the fullers pounded the table and chanted, 'Drink! Drink! Drink!' At first I thought he was still teasing me, the way we joked together when I dropped off laundry, but the light in his eye wasn't

137

as merry as it was in his shop. He forced a third cup down my throat, and I gasped and swallowed and coughed wine through my nose. My head brushed the ceiling, my eyes stung from the lamp smoke, and I swayed over the flushed faces round the table, over their rolling eyes and red, spittle-spraying mouths. When I finally staggered back into the main room, Audo took one look at me, then lifted me round the waist and carried me, limp as an empty sack, through the arch and into the garden. To my surprise, he didn't beat me, but only flung me headlong into the dark, where I woke up at cockcrow with a splitting headache and the smell of my own piss. Focaria, however, who had been routed out of the kitchen to wait upon the party in my absence, striped my backside with a leather strap.

And so, night by night, blow by blow, bruise by bruise, I taught myself to be a proper Mouse in the tavern. I learned how to anticipate a fist coming, how to dodge a kick. When a man stuck out his leg to trip me, I learned how to skip over his ankle and not spill a drop from my pitcher of wine, earning a hearty cheer from all the other men. Now when they lifted me onto the tabletop to sing, I knew the words, even if I didn't yet know what all of them meant, and I learned how obscenity from the lips of a child could make a roomful of men roar with laughter. I learned how to wink at a pinch, I learned how to wriggle free of a wandering hand up my tunic. I learned how to circle wide of two men shouting and spitting at each other, I learned how to dash in and snatch bowls and cups out of harm's way at the last moment. I learned how to make myself scarce when tables were overturned and knives came out, and I learned how much blood could pulse across the floor from a man's body, even as everyone else was still laughing and singing.

And yet I still didn't know what happened on the second floor, where the wolves worked. Every night I watched men stare at the paintings on the wall, watched them slide coins across the counter to Audo without taking any wine or food, watched them disappear up the stairs I wasn't allowed to climb. During the day the paintings seemed dull, but at night, through some trick of the sign painter's primitive craft, the images seemed to leap out in the lamplight. Yet no matter what the man in each painting was doing or having done to him, no matter what pitch of ecstasy he was meant to be reaching, each face had the same vacant expression, like someone daydreaming while performing a rote task, or like Brutus staring into the distance over his cup of wine. Some time later, Melpomene explained this to me.

'It's so a punter can imagine it's himself in the picture,' she said. The faces of the wolves were all half turned away, and Melpomene said that was by design as well. 'It saves having to repaint it if one of us is replaced.'

Melpomene also told me that within memory – not hers, but when Audo had been a young man – wolves used to work in the tavern itself, serving wine and food, flirting with punters, leading them upstairs. But under the Emperor Theodosius more people had become Christian, forcing Helicon to become more discreet about its business. One by one, she told me, the church was forcing any taverns that offered the services of wolves to shut down. Helicon was exempt so far, because the brother of Granatus, our Dominus, was the local bishop. He wouldn't shut us down, she told me, because the profits from Helicon were helping to pay for the construction of his new church and baptistery.

But the bishop did require the tavern to conduct its business with discretion. For as long as she had worked at Helicon, Melpomene said, wolves were not permitted to leave the upper floor when they were working. They were allowed to come down into the garden only when the tavern was shuttered and no one could see them from the street, and they were allowed on the street only for their regular trips to the baths – what Euterpe called the Parade of the Wolves – and only if they wore their mantles.

It was slightly different for Melpomene, because she was a freed-woman. As long as she wore her mantle, she could go abroad alone in the street and run her own errands. Not so many years ago, she told me, only respectable women covered their heads, and wolves walked around bareheaded and half naked. But now the church had begun to insist that wolves cover themselves, so as not to tempt men in the street.

'Some wolves still work under the aqueduct,' she told me, 'but they don't live long. We have it better because we work inside, with the bishop's permission. But we have to be careful about it.'

Only Melpomene herself, as the unofficial representative of the wolves, ever broke the rules, coming down into the main room with her gown only loosely wrapped to tell Audo that Clio needed more water, that Euterpe's punter had passed out on the floor, that Urania's chamber pot needed emptying. Audo didn't have the authority over her that he had over the other wolves, but even so, she tested his patience every time she appeared. She acknowledged the gazes and catcalls of the punters like a visiting dignitary, saying nothing but bestowing a smile or a glance or a wink. Just before Audo was about to boil over, she turned with a twirl of her gown, flashed a thigh or a breast, and sailed up the stairs again like a queen.

Then, to the mocking commentary of the punters – 'Your Domina's calling!' 'Your wives need you!' – Audo would slide off his stool and mount the creaking stairs with a plate of food or a pitcher of wine – the wolves got the watered stuff – and come back down again clutching a sloshing chamber pot, which he handed to me to empty. At night, I simply carried the stinking pot into the latrine and dumped it, but when it was still daylight, I had a chance to inspect the contents. There was always piss in the pot, sometimes a turd, but often there was also blood and swirls of what looked like milk. This only deepened the mystery of what happened on the second floor.

Whenever he heard trouble upstairs, Audo slid off his stool without being summoned and squeezed himself up the stairway, taking the steps two at a time if it sounded bad. The uproar of the tavern dimmed as the punters and I breathlessly listened to his heavy tread and the rumble of his voice through the ceiling. There might be shouting, there might be the thump of blows. Then a punter might run down the stairs, or he might tumble down, ass over tit, with a little help from Audo. The punter might be bleeding from Audo's knife or clutching a broken wrist, and he'd run for his life up the street as Audo burst from the stairs, red-faced and roaring his worst insult – 'Cunt-licker!' – after the man.

Sometimes, early in the afternoon or late at night when the main room of the tavern was quieter, I heard rhythmic thumping through the ceiling, like someone stamping on the floor right above my head. The thumping would slow and speed up and slow and speed up again, until it ended in a flurry and, sometimes, a strangled groan. I looked to see if Audo heard it, too, but late in the evening he was usually drunk and half asleep behind the counter, his cheek bunched up against his palm. I could hear the voices of the wolves sometimes, too, through the ceiling or wafting down the stairway – Melpomene moaning theatrically, Thalia chirping like a bird, Euterpe gasping a man's name. The pictures across the room were no help at all. There was nothing in those stiff figures and blank and averted faces that indicated thumping or groaning, no hint that anything those men and women were doing might generate chamber pots full of blood and milk.

I watched the punters for a clue. Not everyone went upstairs, but many of them did. Priscianus the oil merchant went upstairs once a week and left as soon as he came down. Several times a week, Nazarius peeled off from the bonhomie of his friends, slapped his coins on the counter, and heartily announced the name of a wolf.

'Euterpe!' he declared as Audo scooped the coins out of sight.

'Take your pick,' Audo said. 'Leave your knife.'

141

Knives were not allowed upstairs. After offering his, handle first, to Audo, Nazarius bounded up the steps two at a time.

Musa the moneylender went up every couple of weeks, after fortifying himself with several cups of Audo's strongest wine. Sometimes he paid for Deodatus, too, but sometimes he went up alone, while his slave stretched his legs out in a corner, folded his hands in his lap, and tipped his head back for a nap. Trailing his cloud of garlic, Musa climbed the steps more deliberately, perhaps because he was drunk, perhaps to marshal his strength. Once a week, Brutus the carter drained his cup, pushed himself to his feet with a sigh, and silently palmed a coin across the counter to Audo on his way to the stairs, all without breaking stride.

Quartus the scribe came into Helicon nearly every night, but he didn't have the money to go upstairs very often. Most evenings he sat on the bench near the door to the stairway, nursing the one cup of watered wine he could afford and watching other men go up and come down. If he heard one of them say Thalia's name, he stiffened as if in pain and watched anxiously as the man mounted the stairs. Then he sat with his head in his hands, looking miserable until the man came down again. Once every other week or so, he nervously sifted the coins in his palm, then sprang up suddenly and approached the counter.

'Is Thalia with someone?' he asked tremulously. 'Right now?'

'How would I know?' Audo tapped the counter. 'Pay and go look. Leave your knife.'

Rich and poor, old and young, slave and free, each went upstairs in his own way – springing up the steps, creeping furtively, alone or laughing with another punter – and yet they all returned the same man. Sailor or tradesman or banker or scribe, when a punter came down the stairs, his eyes were heavy-lidded, his limbs were looser, his mouth was slack. He looked the way I felt when I woke up in the morning, but he usually wasn't upstairs long enough to sleep, not even for a short nap. His gaze distant or dulled, each man sighed and adjusted himself under his tunic, and he might even yawn as stepped into the street, staggering into the dark back to his wife or his ship or his master's house.

Perhaps it surprises you, reader, that even after several years in the tavern, I still didn't understand what was happening upstairs. Looking back, it surprises even me. As I've said, I'd seen one dog humping another in the street, I'd seen the rooster trying to mount the chicken in the garden, I'd heard cats in heat yowling in the middle of the night. More than once I'd glimpsed Euterpe and Focaria in each other's arms – sometimes vigorous, sometimes just caressing each other's faces. I even began to wake some mornings with an erect penis, from a dream of one of the carpenter's sly, giggling daughters at the fountain, or of the gleaming limbs of the fisherman's boy in the rigging of his father's ship, the one who taunted me as a wolf and asked me if I knew my father. I was too young yet to know what the dreams meant, or to produce a nocturnal emission, but I awoke in my dark corner of the kitchen with my heart racing and my breath ragged. Was this what the men felt who looked at the paintings in the tavern? What did they do when they went upstairs? What did they see?

In my dreams of the carpenter's daughter or the fisherman's boy, I never did anything with them, just gazed with a nauseous longing at the curve of the daughter's shoulder or the curl of the boy's upper lip. I had yet to learn that that the mere thought of beauty was not enough to bring men to release. I had yet to learn that a man's longing for release was inextricably linked with his need to dominate, to penetrate, to humiliate. I had yet to learn that the one pleasure in the world a man most desired was the same one he most feared and despised. And I had yet to learn that the only thing a man desired, feared, and despised more than the moment of ecstasy itself was the woman or the boy who gave it to him.

*   *   *

143

The first time I ever went upstairs was Clio's last night in the tavern.

Early in the evening, the main room of Helicon is quiet. Rain had fallen earlier, a sudden squall off the sea, and the pavement steams in the street just beyond the lamplight. A salty breeze blows through the open arches, flaring the lamps and making shadows dance. A punter leans against the counter and takes his time about choosing his wine while Audo drums his thick fingers. Other punters lean in the doorways or talk in the street, taking advantage of the breeze as they sip their wine. Neither Nazarius nor Brutus is here tonight, but Quartus, Musa, and Deodatus share a table. Musa is deep in his cups already, swaying on his stool, and Quartus's attempts to engage Deodatus in conversation are answered by monosyllables. Three more men hunch round another table, throwing knuckle-bones. For once, the tavern is quiet, and the rattle of the cup isn't drowned out by talk or singing. One of the men calls his throws in a low murmur.

'Venus.' The cup rattles. 'Vulture.' Again. 'Dog.'

I'm standing on a stool, carefully pouring an iron pot of fresh stew into the cistern in the countertop, when a woman screams upstairs. I drop the pot, but it's already empty, and it rings against the tiles without spilling any stew. I freeze and look immediately at Audo. Every man in the room stops and lifts his eyes to the ceiling. The knucklebones rattle into silence against the tabletop, and even the breeze shaking the lamplight seems to hold its breath. But Audo is already squeezing up the stairway, the steps groaning under him. The screaming, which stopped for a moment, begins again at a higher pitch, and now other women are shouting, all the wolves at once. Among them I hear Euterpe's voice, calling sharply for Audo.

Quartus has leaped to his feet, overturning his stool. His eyes are wide, and he's clutching his head with both hands as if to keep the top of it from flying off. Deodatus has already hustled Musa out the door and into the street, the two of them disappearing into the dark. The other punters murmur and cast glances at the stairway. A couple of them laugh. The man at the counter helps himself to a cup of wine from one of the amphorae overhead, from the expensive end of the netting. He catches me watching, winks, and carries his cup into the street. I wrap my arms around the iron pot and inch backwards toward the door to the garden. I've heard screams before – the man beyond the garden door – and I've even heard screams from upstairs. But nothing like this. The voice keeps climbing to a higher and higher pitch, like a cat in pain. The other women's shouts are hoarser, angrier. A man's voice rises above them all, shouting incoherently.

But it's not Audo. For once he doesn't bellow or roar. All we hear is his heavy tread across the floor above. Then, as several women scream at once, we hear a sharp crack which makes every man in the tavern flinch. Quartus staggers as if someone has slapped him. I drop the pot again, and it spins, ringing, on the floor. Now a man is screaming at nearly the same high pitch as the woman, and above our lifted faces, we follow the thumps across the floor above.

'Get back in your cells!' Audo shouts, and as the pot spins to a stop, our gazes swivel in unison toward the door to the stairs, which funnels the man's shrieks into the main room. Then we hear him tumbling down the steps until he spills through, making Quartus dance out of his way. He sprawls across the floor not far from where I stand paralyzed, the iron pot at my feet.

Audo squeezes out of the stairs behind him and stomps the man in his ribs. There's another crack, and everyone, especially me, jumps back. Quartus backs into the bench along the wall and sits down hard, his hands splayed to either side. The man on the floor contracts into a ball and keens like a dog. He holds up a trembling arm, and I see his elbow bent back the wrong way.

'Please,' he whimpers.

Audo stands over him, breathing hard, but he does not kick the man again.

145

'Get this cunt-licker out of here,' he rumbles, to no one in particular. A couple of punters glance at each other, then stoop to the groaning man and lift him to his feet. One of them grabs the man by his twisted arm, and he shrieks again. A moment later, the two men have dragged the broken man into the street, beyond the lamplight.

'Pick up the pot,' Audo says, and I realize he's talking to me.

'Is it Thalia?' whispers Quartus, awkwardly pushing himself up from the bench.

Audo ignores him, and instead glares round the room at the remaining men, who reflexively turn away and pretend to resume their drinking and conversation. The men who are gaming stare at each other, then one of them scoops the knucklebones off the tabletop and drops them, one by one, into the cup.

'Get Focaria,' Audo says to me. 'Tell her to bring needle and thread.' Then he squeezes up the stairs again.

A moment later, Focaria is hurrying out of the kitchen with her sewing kit as I trot at her heels and breathlessly try to tell her what I just heard. Quartus plucks at her skirt as she passes him, and she slaps his hand away. At the bottom of the steps, she stops long enough to snap at me, 'Go fetch water.'

'Water?'

'Bring a bucket upstairs,' she says. 'Hurry.'

I dash back into the darkness of the garden, fill one of the buckets at the tank, and lug it into the tavern. A couple more men are helping themselves to wine from the amphorae over the untended counter, pausing only as I trot past with the sloshing bucket. Quartus trembles at the bottom of the stairway with one foot on the bottom step, and as I nudge past him and start climbing, he tugs at the back of my tunic and hisses, 'Tell me if it's Thalia. Tell her I'm here.'

Halfway up I pause to get both hands under the handle of the bucket. At the top of the stairs lamplight illuminates a plastered

146

wall, and as I start up again, I hear the wolves talking all at once. Someone is cursing, someone is chattering nervously. Someone is making great, wet, gulping sobs. My arms tremble under the weight of the bucket.

'Hold still, dammit,' Focaria says, in a tone of voice I know well.

'It could be worse,' Thalia is saying, her voice trembling. 'It's not so bad.'

'Water!' erupts Audo. 'Where's that fucking Pusus?'

'Here!' At the top of the stairs I turn round to catch my first sight of the home of the wolves. My first impression is of heat and musk. There's no breeze up here, and the air is smoky, humid, and close, smelling of chamber pot. A rough-plastered hallway runs back over the length of the tavern below, and lamps burn in sconces under the low ceiling, bright points in a yellow haze of incense, sweat, sex, and oily smoke. Audo doesn't like graffiti, but here and there, etched into the oily gleam of the walls, are crudely lettered names, stick figures with giant cocks, bulging women's thighs and gaping cunts. Along the hall are six curtained doorways, three on each side, and all but one of the curtains has been pulled aside. Urania stands naked in the first doorway on my right, her eyes wide, her bony shoulders hunched, arms clutched over her stomach. Behind her a naked fat man peers down the hall over her shoulder, his balled-up tunic clutched under his belly over his genitals. Across from her Melpomene has pulled her white gown over her shoulders but leaves it hanging open as she leans in her doorway. In the cell behind her, a man lies naked on her cot with his hands behind his head and his damp penis limp against his thigh. He sighs as I pass.

'Hold her down,' barks Focaria, from the end of the hall. 'I can't work if she keeps fighting it.'

'Pusus!' Audo's voice roars out of the same room.

I trot faster, splashing the wooden floor. Euterpe appears out of the last doorway on the left, clutching her red gown at her throat. She reaches for me and guides me by the shoulders into Clio's cell.

147

Audo fills the far corner of the little cell, glowering over the bed but doing nothing. Thalia sits at the head of the bed with her arms and legs wrapped around Clio, who leans back against her. Blood is pouring from a slash across Clio's face, which starts below her eye and parts her upper lip like the halves of a worm. Focaria crouches beside the bed, trying to thread a needle in the flaring light of a lamp on the little table next to the bed. A bloody cloth lies crumpled on the floor beside her.

'It's all right, it's all right, it's all right,' Thalia murmurs over and over again into Clio's ear, clutching her across the clavicle with one hand and clasping her forehead with the other. Clio is gasping and blowing bloody bubbles through the slash in her lip. I glimpse her gum and a couple of teeth. Blood pools in her lower lip and runs down her chin, soaking the front of her gown.

'Where's that water?' Focaria has threaded the needle, and she jabs it into the thin mattress of Clio's cot.

'Right behind you.' Euterpe grips my shoulders and guides me forward. Audo takes the bucket and swings it to the floor next to the bed. Focaria soaks the bloody cloth in the water, wrings it out, then soaks it again and dabs at Clio's cut. Clio writhes and cries out.

'Hold her!' shouts Focaria, and Thalia squeezes her eyes shut and tightens her arms and legs around Clio. Audo is flexing his fists, first one and then the other, and I can see that he wants to hit somebody. Maybe Clio, maybe Focaria, maybe everybody. Euterpe tries to push me out of the cell.

'Go downstairs, Mouse,' she says, but just as Audo lifts himself on his toes and balls both fists at once, I duck under her arm and say, 'They're stealing wine downstairs.'

Audo swings his black gaze in my direction.

'They're helping themselves to stew, too,' I say, and as Euterpe yanks me into the corner, Audo shoulders through the doorway and down the hall. I pull free from Euterpe to watch him go.

Urania and Melpomene instantly retreat into their cells, but around the horizon of Audo's backside I see Quartus peeking round from the top of the stairway.

'Move!' bellows Audo, and Quartus disappears, hammering down the steps just ahead of Audo. A moment later we hear Audo thundering – 'You fucking thieves!' – first in the tavern and then in the street. We hear men shouting back and laughing, their voices dwindling as they scatter like crows into the night. For a moment only one voice remains, Quartus crying Thalia's name, over and over, until he's silenced suddenly by Audo roaring, 'Fuck off, you little cunt-licker!'

But I'm scarcely paying attention, because I'm back in the cell with Euterpe's arms around my shoulders, watching as Focaria rapidly hooks the needle across the slash in Clio's face and draws the two sides together. Clio is still shuddering and gasping, but she has stopped screaming. Thalia holds on to her for dear life and whispers urgently in her ear. I can't make it out at first, but as the clamour in the street dies away, I can hear Thalia saying over and over again, 'You're alive, you're alive, you're alive, you're alive . . .'

No one else speaks until Focaria is finished and ties off the thread in a tiny knot under Clio's eye. She bends close to Clio as if to kiss her and bites off the excess thread. The stitches are a red centipede across Clio's pale cheek, and her upper lip is tugged up and to the side like a harelip. The scar is still leaking blood, but not as much as before. The room is full of the smell of it, though. It's like the smell of the butcher's shop, or the old iron pot when I'm scrubbing it.

Thalia relaxes her grip but doesn't let go, and she looks tearfully up at Euterpe. I look up at her too. Her eyes are glistening, but her face is stern. Focaria wrings out the bloody cloth in the bucket and then dabs at Clio's face again, wiping away the last oozes of blood. Clio stiffens, but she does not cry out. Then Focaria stands. She drops the cloth into the bucket and stretches, arching her stiffened back. She turns. She and Euterpe share a quick, silent look, and I can almost tell what they're saying.

It wasn't you, Focaria seems to say.

It could have been, Euterpe seems to reply.

Then Focaria looks at me. 'Take the bucket away and empty it in the garden.'

I slip out of Euterpe's arms. I lift the bucket with both hands and heft it through the doorway.

'I'll stay with her,' I hear Thalia say, and Focaria and Euterpe follow me into the hall. Urania's curtain is drawn, but Melpomene has reappeared in her doorway, her gown belted now. I stop in front of her to set the bucket down and adjust my grip. The man in her cell is gone. Over my head she says, 'How bad is it?'

Euterpe shakes her head without speaking. Focaria draws a finger across her own face.

'Here to here,' she says. 'She's lucky he didn't catch her in the eye.'

'Hm,' says Melpomene. 'Looks like we're getting a new Clio.'

Euterpe gasps. Focaria grunts and shoulders her way past her.

'Hurry up with the bucket,' she says as she disappears down the stairs. I don't move, watching as Euterpe and Melpomene square off.

'Keep your voice down,' Euterpe hisses. 'She can hear you.'

'It's the truth,' Melpomene insists, but she lowers her voice.

'You can't wait till tomorrow?' Euterpe is as angry as I have ever seen her. So angry that she isn't even aware that I'm standing there, listening. 'You have to talk about this now, tonight?'

'I'm just talking sense,' Melpomene says. 'They'll have to sell her, and they won't get much. But it's an opportunity.'

'Don't . . .' warns Euterpe.

'Well, it is.' Melpomene widens her eyes. 'She's the least popular, she lowers the tone. We'll be better off without her. She'll be better off under the arches.' She pauses. 'You know I'm right.'

Euterpe's rage steams off her, thickening the yellow fug of the hallway. She cannot speak.

'Maybe she could work in the kitchen,' I pipe up, 'with me and Focaria.'

Melpomene lifts her eyebrows at me, as if surprised to see me there. Euterpe, eyes wide, nostrils flaring, slaps me hard, making my head snap, making my cheek burn, making my eyes sting with tears. She has never hit me before.

'You heard Focaria.' She looks as if she hates me and has always hated me. 'Take the fucking bucket downstairs.'

Then she turns into her own cell and violently yanks the curtain shut. Melpomene looks down the hallway over my head and says, 'No more work tonight. That idiot Audo has chased all the punters away.'

She sighs and pulls her curtain shut. My cheek still stinging, I lift the bucket and stump down the stairs, one leaden step at a time. By time I reach the bottom, I am no longer crying.

When the wolves gather in the morning for their daily parade to the baths, Clio is not with them. Thalia, Urania, and Melpomene whisper together in the garden as they wait for Audo, while Focaria watches silently from the kitchen door with her arms crossed. Euterpe stands apart, clutching her mantle tight around her throat, staring at nothing. I avoid her, and instead I fetch water from the tank so I can scrub the floor in the empty tavern. As I pass with my bucket, Euterpe's gaze focuses, and she reaches for me. I keep my head down, but she clutches my shoulder, takes the bucket, and sets it aside. She falls to her knees, the mantle bunching around her, and wraps her arms around me. I hunch my shoulders.

'I'm so sorry, Little One,' she says. 'Please forgive me.'

She holds me at arm's length and peers at me with moist eyes. I look at Focaria. She shrugs, as if to say, *Don't look at me, I didn't hit you.* At last I bury my face in Euterpe's warm neck. She holds me tight. 'I'm sorry, I'm sorry, I'm sorry,' she murmurs in my ear.

'What's going to happen to Clio?' I mumble. Euterpe squeezes me tighter and says, 'I don't know.'

'Where's "under the arches"?' I say, and Euterpe unfolds her arms and looks at me.

'Last night,' I say, 'Melpomene said Clio belonged under the arches.'

Melpomene hears her name and looks in our direction, and Euterpe tugs me a little further away.

'Some wolves work on the street and they don't have a place to live,' she whispers, 'so they sleep together under the aqueduct.'

'What's an aqueduct?'

'It's . . . like a bridge. A bridge that carries water into the city.'

'Is it a bad place?' I say, but just then Audo comes into the garden and pulls back the bolt on the door. Euterpe kisses me, rises, and joins the others. Audo opens the door.

'Melpomene,' he rumbles, 'you're in charge today.'

Thalia and Urania exchange a glance. Euterpe widens her eyes at Audo, who waits with his hand on the open door. Melpomene lifts her chin and straightens her shoulders. 'Line up, ladies,' she says.

Thalia moves through the door with Urania right behind her, their mantles trailing in the dirt, but Euterpe hangs back.

'Will Clio be here when we get back?' she says to Audo.

'Shut up,' he says.

Euterpe waits a moment longer, testing his patience. Melpomene puts her hands on Euterpe's shoulders from behind. Euterpe twitches them off and raises her hood as she marches out the door. Melpomene follows, and Audo shuts and bolts the door. He looks at me.

'When you're done in the main room,' he says, 'bring the bucket upstairs.' Then he lumbers through the arch and back into the tavern.

I turn to Focaria, but she has already disappeared into the kitchen. I carry the water into the tavern, where Audo is unlatching one of the shutters to let someone in. Against the glare from the sunlit street, I can't tell who it is at first.

'This better be important,' Calidus says abruptly. No 'peace of God' this morning. 'I'm supposed to be in court right now.'

'Your Honour,' mutters Audo, latching the shutter again. 'One of the girls was cut last night.'

Calidus sighs, the sort of noise you make when you've spilled food on yourself or broken a pot.

'How did that happen?' he says.

Audo hovers over the young man, explaining in a low murmur, trying without touching him to usher him across the room toward the stairs. But the young Dominus won't be hurried.

'Why did he have a knife?'

'Everybody carries a knife, Your Honour.'

'I thought we'd agreed.' Calidus holds up his hand. 'Everybody leaves his knife with you before going upstairs.'

'Your Honour,' murmurs Audo.

'No knives upstairs!'

'Your Honour.'

'That's the policy, Audo!'

'Your Honour.'

'This is what happens when you *don't enforce the rules.*'

'Your Honour.' Audo is almost touching him, urging him toward the stairs. Calidus waves him away, nearly striking him.

'Enough. Let's see how bad it is.'

I kneel next to the bucket and press the brush into the floor with both hands. But instead of scrubbing, I listen to the light tread of Calidus and the ponderous one of Audo across the floor above. I can't tell what they're saying, but I hear Calidus speaking more quickly the angrier he gets, his voice rising in pitch, and I hear Audo's low, placating rumble. The one voice I don't hear is Clio's.

I already understand that she has nothing to contribute to this conversation. Whatever she thinks isn't important. Even though I still don't understand exactly what the wolves do upstairs with men, I already know that a wolf with a red centipede scar and an artificial harelip is no longer fit to be a wolf.

Calidus's voice continues as footsteps start back down the hallway above. The voice of the young Dominus swells down the stairway, and then emerges like a trumpet blast into the tavern. I dip my brush into the water and make a show of scrubbing, but it doesn't matter. Calidus doesn't even notice me.

'Perhaps *you'd* like to explain to my *father*,' he's shouting, 'why the revenue from this place is about to drop by *twenty per cent*.'

The room is dim with the shutters closed, but I can see a vein bulging in his forehead. Clio slouches into the tavern after him, Audo looming behind her. I keep scrubbing as quietly as I can.

'And perhaps *you'd* like to explain to my uncle the *bishop*,' Calidus rages, 'why my father's contribution to his new *baptistery* is going to *shrink* for the foreseeable future.'

'Your Honour,' says Audo.

Clio lowers her head and huddles against the wall under one of the paintings, a picture of a lithe, dark girl straddling a man. It looks nothing like her. But then she doesn't look like herself anymore, either. She is no longer wearing her bloodstained blue gown, but a burlap shift that hangs to her calves. Her hair is tied back tight like Focaria's. Her face is round and pale, but even in the shadowed room, I can see that the flesh around her scar is bruised black and green, and that the stitching pulls her whole expression out of true. She's a broken pot, clumsily reglued. She holds a bundle tied up in a cloth against her belly. She is not wearing shoes or make-up. She's looking in my direction, but she does not see me, or the room, or anything. Her gaze is set in what a soldier of my future acquaintance will call *the horizon stare*.

'Do you understand, you massive ape, what I'm telling you?'

154

Calidus thrusts his finger right under the nose of the larger man, who glowers at the floor. Calidus turns away and sighs theatrically.

'Your Honour . . .' says Audo, and Calidus holds up his finger again for silence. He draws a deep breath.

'This is not my father's only enterprise.' Calidus speaks slowly and distinctly, as if to an idiot or a foreigner. 'But it is an important one. I don't expect a brute like you to understand the subtleties of cash flow, but I *do* expect you to understand that whenever your weekly profit diminishes, we have to make it up *somewhere else.*'

'Your Honour.' As Audo endures this, Clio sinks slowly to the bench along the wall. Without turning away from Calidus, Audo reaches back and hauls her to her feet again.

'Can you *possibly* understand that?' Calidus has not even noticed. 'Someone *else* has to make *more* because *you* are not making *enough.*'

'Your Honour,' murmurs Audo, and Calidus strikes him with the back of his hand.

'Quit saying that!' he shouts. 'You sound like a fucking parrot!'

Audo, who has certainly been hit harder in his day, holds his head to one side and breathes deeply through his nose. Calidus watches him, wide-eyed and panting. He cannot help noticing that Audo is balling one fist and then the other, and he steps back. Then he turns so that Audo cannot see him rub the back of his hand. Audo raises his own hand to a spot of blood on his face, where one of Calidus's rings has cut him.

I'm still moving the brush, but as slowly as I can. Audo catches me watching him, and I drop my eyes to the floor and start furiously scrubbing. For a moment the rasp of my brush is the only sound in the room. Calidus, still rubbing his hand, looks down at me.

'Who are you?' he says.

I look up, pressing the bristles of the brush into the worn tiles. 'Pusus,' I squeak.

'I can see that,' he says. 'What's your *name*?'

'Pusus,' I say again. I don't want Dominus to know my name.

'Idiot,' sighs Calidus, turning away. 'I suppose I'm paying to feed him, too.' He glances at Audo, who is still balling his fists. Calidus edges toward the shutter. 'Take her to the theatre,' he says, unlatching the shutter. 'Get what you can for her.'

Audo grabs Clio by the upper arm and pulls her forward.

'Shall I buy another Clio?' he says.

Calidus pauses in the glare from the street. 'No,' he says, without looking round. 'Not until you hear from me.'

'We'll be down a wolf,' Audo says, pulling Clio toward the door.

'Well, you should have thought of that,' says Calidus, impatient to leave, 'before you let someone take a knife upstairs.'

'What about the mattress?' Audo says.

'What about the mattress?'

'It's bloody. I'll have to buy a new one.'

'Flip it over,' Calidus says. 'No one will notice.'

'You could . . .' says Clio in a small voice, tightened by pain and distorted by the hitch in her upper lip. The two men turn to her in surprise.

'You could flip me over, too.' She lowers her eyes to the floor. 'Some of them already do. They don't have to see my face.'

Calidus stares at her in astonishment. Audo tightens his grip on her upper arm, adding to her pain. But Clio speaks again.

'Please don't sell me, Dominus.' She lifts her eyes to Calidus. She already knows that beseeching Audo will not do her any good. 'I don't want to go under the arches . . .'

Her voice catches on the last word, and she falls silent as Calidus steps up to her. She watches him like she'd watch a dog which may or may not bite her.

'What's your name?' says Calidus.

'Clio.'

'No, your *name*,' says Calidus, close enough to kiss her.

'Silvia.' I can barely hear her.

'Well, Silvia,' says Calidus, 'silence is a woman's glory. Have you heard that before?'

Clio lifts her scarred lip to speak, then understands she's not supposed to. She shakes her head.

'No reason you should,' Calidus says. 'It's from Aristotle, you stupid cow.' He looks up at Audo. 'Perhaps if someone had told her that *before*,' he says, 'we wouldn't *be* in this situation.'

As he says 'this situation', he waves his hand in front of Clio's face. Audo dips his head. 'Your Honour,' he whispers. Clio closes her eyes.

'Like I say, get what you can from the dealer.' Calidus steps out into the sunlight. 'If you can't do this job, Audo, I will find someone who can.'

Then he's gone, leaving the shutter wide open. Across the street a beggar is sunning himself against the wall, and he stirs as Calidus passes, pointlessly thrusting a three-fingered hand in his direction. Through the doorway I can hear the sounds of the street – the rattle of a distant cart, someone hammering, the cries of gulls. Inside the tavern it is silent. I am very still on my knees, my hands gripping the brush without moving it. Then Audo is standing over me. He's still clutching Clio tightly by the upper arm. She's staring again at the horizon only she can see.

'Leave that,' he says. 'Go upstairs and scrub the floor in her cell.'

I glance at Clio. She doesn't look at me. She has already gone to wherever it is she is going to go. Maybe it will be worse than Helicon, maybe not. Looking back, it occurred to me that I should have asked her if she had any messages for the other wolves, that I should at least have said goodbye. But a moment later, it's too late. Audo has hauled her out the door and closed the shutter after them.

'Latch it,' he says to me from the street.

*   *   *

The hall upstairs is in a kind of twilight during the day. The only light comes from the little barred windows up near the ceiling of each cell, and the unstirring air smells of dried sweat, empty chamber pots, and last night's perfumes and incense. Without the gleam of lamplight in the oily walls, the graffiti is easier to see: a spurting penis, a round face with mouth open and eyes squeezed shut in ecstasy, the same Christian chi-rho symbol Renatus stamps into his loaves. One of Rufus's fishermen has etched a ship into the wall – a sideways crescent, a stick for a mast, and a triangular sail.

I carry the bucket before me with the brush bobbing in the water, a twiggy-limbed, knock-kneed boy treading as softly as he can. This is the first time I have ever been alone in an empty building, an unusual experience for a slave. The curtains of each cell are pulled aside, except for the one on the end, across from Clio's. This used to be the cell of Calliope, who died or was sold and was never replaced. As I turn into Clio's empty room, Calliope's curtain sways slightly from my passage, which spooks me a bit. I know I'm the only one here, but what if I'm not? What if someone lunges through the curtain when there's no one to hear my cries? When Euterpe isn't around, Focaria sometimes takes malicious pleasure in telling me stories of angry ghosts, maybe to make me behave without having to hit me, maybe just for the fun of it. My heart rattling in my bony chest, I set the bucket down. If Focaria could see me right now, she'd laugh. If Audo catches me malingering because I'm scared, he'll beat me. So I draw a deep breath and yank the curtain aside. There's no one there, just an empty cell like the others, with a bed, a table and a stool, and a chamber pot. I let my breath out, feeling foolish, then I turn into Clio's cell and back to the job at hand.

Except for the bloodstains on the floor and the wall, there is little to show that Clio was ever here. The cot and the mattress remain, along with the graffiti on the wall next to the bed, within easy reach of a man lying on the mattress. On the little wooden

158

table next to the bed are an unlit lamp, a battered ewer and a basin, a jar of olive oil, a tin cup, a lead spoon, and a wooden bowl, still crusted with the remains of Clio's last meal. Her empty chamber pot is in the corner, turned upside down to dull the smell. Hammered into the wall next to the door are three wooden pegs. A blue gown hangs from one of the pegs, and from another hangs the limp mantle Clio wore to the baths. Her bloodstained gown has no doubt been burnt already by Audo or Focaria, and the burlap shift she was wearing when I saw her downstairs was probably the only other article of clothing she had.

I drag the cot to the opposite side of the cell, and I kneel beside the bucket and pluck out the brush. The bloodstains have dried deep in the grain of the floorboards and won't lift no matter how hard I scrub, and when I try to clean the dried splashes of blood on the wall, the graffitied plaster starts to flake away, so I give up and push the cot back into place. The scrape of its legs against the floorboards seems too loud but dies away quickly. There's a black bloodstain on the mattress up near where Clio's head had been, dry now and stiff to the touch. Remembering what Calidus said downstairs, I flip the mattress over – easily, because it's filled with nothing more than rustling straw – only to discover another stiff, dark stain on that side, too. I sigh again and put my hands on my hips. When Audo comes back, he'll beat me for sure, as if the stains are my fault. But what can I do?

Then I remember the bed across the hall, in Calliope's old cell. I'm in luck. That mattress has a stain on it, too, but only on one side, and it doesn't smell any worse than the one in Clio's room. So I drag it hissing across the floorboards into Clio's cell and switch the mattresses, putting the new one stain-side down on the cot. Then I drag Clio's mattress across into the empty cell and heave it onto the bed. Maybe now Audo won't notice the blood I couldn't get out of the floor or the wall. I'm so pleased with myself, I let myself sit down on the bed in Calliope's cell. A few steps from me is a wooden table with a three-legged stool under it, but unlike Clio's table, it's cluttered with little pots and jars, and some other things I don't recognize. There's still no sound from the tavern below – the wolves won't be back from the baths for a while, and Audo may be gone even longer – so I push myself up from the cot and go to the table.

The pots and jars are arranged in a semicircle, in the middle of which is a little metal tray cluttered with tiny, delicate tools. These are the shared grooming implements of the wolves, and this empty cell serves as their dressing room, where they take turns applying make-up, perfumes, and oils at the start of the evening. Melpomene has her own toiletries, which she doesn't share, and a set of spotless silver tools. The tools in this cell are cheaper, made of tin, lead, or bone. I pick up each one and turn it in my fingers, trying to guess what it's for, but I won't really know until I start to use them myself – a stiff pair of tweezers, a razor, a tiny lead spoon for ear wax, an ivory comb with a missing tooth, a pumice stone, little brushes with clotted bristles, an assortment of hairpins made of bone or wood. A hairbrush with different coloured hairs stuck in its bristles sits to one side.

I glance back at the doorway. The tavern is still silent, so I start at one end of the crescent of jars and lift the stopper of each one, sniffing the contents, or rubbing a little between my dirty fingers. Some are oily, some are just wet. Some smell sweet, like flowers, some musky. Some of them smell like Euterpe does when she comes down in the morning, some smell more like Thalia or Urania. I touch one perfume with my finger to the tip of my tongue, but it's horribly bitter, and I try to spit the taste away. Some pots are full of paints that are tacky to the touch, and one is half full of a sticky black powder that stains my fingertips. It's the only thing I recognize – it's the stuff Euterpe uses around her eyes. It smears and spreads when I try to rub it off, so I get up and go to the bucket across the hall and wash it off in the water.

As I start to pull the curtain back across the doorway of Calliope's cell, one more thing catches my eye, something I hadn't noticed before: a round, flat metal pan hanging by a long, thin handle from a hook above the table. I go back into the cell and lift the thing carefully by the handle with both hands. It's heavy and made of brass, which is dull and slippery and splotched with verdigris. There's an image etched into the greenish surface of the pan, but I can't make it out, so I carry it to the little window and angle the pan in the light until I can see that the etching shows a naked boy being carried on the back of a giant bird. It's not like any bird I've ever seen, not like the swift or the rooster or the sparrow. It's larger than the boy, with wide, powerful wings, huge talons, a sharp beak, and a fierce look in its eye. The boy clings to its back for dear life, but his expression is so dim under the mould that I can't tell if it's fear or excitement or something else. I step up on the stiff mattress of the cot to get the ungainly pan closer to the light from the window, and in my unsteady grip, the slippery handle twists and the pan flips over. For the first time in my life, I see my face. It's a mirror.

I know what I'm looking at the moment I see it. I have glimpsed my reflection in water before – in the trembling surface of the fountain, in the sloshing surface of the bucket, in the dirty sheen of a puddle – but each time the light has been behind me, so that I can't make out my features, only the narrow silhouette of my head, the way my ears stick out, the unruly spikes of my hair. For all I know, that's how everyone else sees me – just a boy with wide ears and spiky hair and no face. Until this moment in my young life, it had never occurred to me to wonder what I look like, and yet, now, suddenly, by accident, here I am.

At first it's like looking at someone else. I'm more familiar with the humblest slave in the fuller's yard or the most anonymous fisherman's boy on the quayside than I am with the face I'm looking at now. He's a stranger, and yet he reflects my own confusion and curiosity back at me. If I widen my eyes and recoil from the sight of him, he does the same. If I angle the mirror and try to hide from his gaze, he tries to hide from mine. If I gasp, he gasps. If I blink, he blinks.

After a moment, I can't stand it anymore, and I flip the mirror over, back to the worn image of the boy and the eagle. I'm breathless, and my heart is rattling against my ribs even harder than it did when I thought someone was lying in wait for me behind the curtain. Someone was, it turns out, and now I've seen his face. I look round the narrow cell, but it's the same as it was before, empty, close, musty. No one stirs downstairs in the tavern. There are no sounds from the street, not even the tread of passing feet or the crying of gulls from the harbour. Everything is as it was a moment ago.

Except for this. I turn the mirror back over and, gripping the handle by both hands, I move it close to my face, until my nose is almost touching the surface, almost touching the nose of the other boy. He has brown eyes with fine lashes above and below. His thick black hair is ragged and spiky – Focaria trims it with a pair of blunt scissors – and he has a low, smooth forehead and thick eyebrows. His ears stick out a bit, but not too much, and his nose is long and a bit pointed. His lips are thin, but his mouth is wide, and his face narrows to a chin in perfect alignment with the tip of his nose. I won't know the word for years yet, but his face is symmetrical.

I smile at him, and he smiles back, keeping his lips together, without showing any teeth. The ends of his mouth reach nearly to the edges of his narrow face, dimpling his cheeks on either side. The sight makes me laugh, and now I see his teeth, which are (in retrospect, against the odds) straight and white and all there. He's a good-looking boy. If I saw him on the street, I'd want to know him better. If I knew how to draw, I'd etch his face on every wall in town.

Then, of course, I lose myself, as I was bound to, and I bare my teeth and stick out my tongue and tug my mouth to one side with a finger. I cross my eyes and pout and growl and grimace and laugh and shout. The clamour of my delight bounces off the oily walls of the cell, it fills the narrow hall, and, for all I know, it echoes down the stairs through the shutters of the empty tavern and into the street. I want to take this boy into the garden and show him to Focaria or Euterpe. I want to carry him up the street and introduce him to the women at the fountain, to the boys on the street corner. I want to pass him before Musa the moneylender and Quartus the scribe, I want Opitria the soothsayer to take a good look at him and tell me his future. I want to bring him to Nazarius, who will wink at him, and I want to show him to surly old Renatus and ask him, how could you hate a face like that?

Then the silence closes in again. I have stopped shouting, and I don't even realize it until I see that he has stopped shouting, too. All we do is stare at each other for a long time, looking deep into each other's eyes. I'm trying to guess what he's thinking, and I can see he's trying to do the same with me. I can know what Euterpe's thinking when I look at her, I can see Focaria's anger, I can tell when Audo is getting ready to hit me, but I cannot see anything more in the face in the mirror than a boy who is as mystified and excited as I am.

Then I hear a single, discrete, high-pitched sound, very close, just above my head. A chirp. I break away from the gaze of the boy in the mirror and I see a tiny bird sitting in the window, resting on the crumbling brickwork between two of the bars. The bird is silhouetted against the light, but I can tell it's a sparrow, and I think I can even see the gleam of its eyes as its head turns this way and that, watching me. I twist the mirror toward him.

'Look,' I say, as quietly as I can. I don't want to scare him away. 'It's you.' I hold the mirror out at arm's length, so that we can all three see each other, the sparrow and the boy and me, all at once. 'It's us,' I say.

Then there are voices from the street, two men talking just outside. One of them rattles the shutter of the tavern and, finding it latched, curses. The sparrow bursts into flight and disappears from the window and the mirror at the same instant. The boy in the mirror slides away as I jump down off the cot and carefully hang it by its handle on the hook above the table. The wolves will be back soon, but I wait until I hear the men's voices dwindle in the heat of the morning. I draw the curtain behind me as I leave the cell, then I pick up the bucket and carry it down into the empty tavern.

The wolves come back from the baths before Audo returns, alone, from the theatre. Urania and Thalia are already acting as if nothing has happened, whispering and laughing together as they come through the door into the garden. Urania is back to surveying the world from the heights, her eyes heavy-lidded, her mouth pursed at some private joke, but Thalia's vivacity seems a little more strenuous than usual. Her laughter is louder, her smile is stretched tighter. Melpomene, meanwhile, holds herself even more erect than usual, chin lifted, shoulders back. Her lips are pursed with the banked satisfaction of a cat after it has devoured something when you weren't looking. It is the look of a victor trying not to show it. Only in Euterpe's face do I see the events of last night. She comes through the door with the others, but it's as if she is walking alone, her gaze fixed on something no one else can see.

I have only just come back into the garden myself a few moments before, bursting with the revelation of the mirror, overflowing with my need to tell someone, everyone, that I have seen myself for the first time. I pour the scrub water from the bucket into the watering can, and as Focaria lets the wolves in through the garden door, I am practically skipping between the rows of herbs and vegetables, sprinkling the thyme and turnips, the oregano and onions, with the last, pinkish traces of Clio's blood.

'Is Audo back?' asks Euterpe, and when Focaria shakes her head, Thalia and Urania simultaneously sink down against the wall of the tavern, wrapping their mantles around them. Even Euterpe lets her shoulders loosen. No matter what else they might be feeling, the remaining wolves are briefly at liberty.

'Can you give us something to eat?' asks Urania.

Melpomene, who is bolting the door, scowls. But Focaria nods and steps back into the kitchen.

No one pays any attention to me. I want to tell Euterpe what I've seen upstairs, but I realize she won't want to hear it right now. Against the wall, Thalia and Urania tilt their faces to the sun, waiting for whatever scraps Focaria is willing to give them. I return to the bucket, which I left near the door, and as I refill the watering can with the last of the water, I look up at Melpomene, a few steps away. She's looking round the garden as if she's considering buying the place.

'I finished cleaning upstairs,' I tell her. 'I got most of the blood out of the floor. I scrubbed as hard as I could.'

There's that slight, theatrical pause before she looks down at me, wide-eyed, as if she's pretending to be surprised to see me there.

'I flipped over the mattress, too,' I say. 'You can't see anything now.'

'Good,' she says.

'I cleaned the wall, too,' I say, though I don't tell her about the plaster coming off in the brush. 'I got most of it.'

Euterpe turns to me slowly, as if waking up. Focaria comes out of the kitchen with a bowl of bread and cheese. She hands some of each to Thalia and Urania.

'And I saw myself!' In the absence of Audo, my excitement rises to the surface. 'In a piece of metal!'

'You did what?' Euterpe waves away Focaria's food.

Melpomene's eyes widen. 'Did you go in my room?'

'No!' I feel my face get hot. 'I went in that room across from Clio's. The one with the table with the jars on it. There was a . . . metal thing, hanging on the wall.'

Melpomene stands very still, back erect, hands pressed together. She looks as if she is about to declaim a poem. 'It's called a mirror,' she says.

'What were you doing in there?' Euterpe edges between Melpomene and me.

'I saw myself!' I say to both of them, wishing it would please them as much as it pleases me.

'You shouldn't go in there,' Euterpe says, but at the same moment Melpomene says, 'Did you like what you saw?'

I look past Euterpe to Melpomene.

'Is that what I look like?' I say to her. 'In the mirror?'

'Yes,' says Melpomene. 'You're a pretty boy.'

'Don't!' Euterpe's voice is so sharp, it silences Urania and Thalia whispering along the wall. It even makes Focaria start.

'It's true.' Melpomene levels her gaze at Euterpe. 'He is a pretty boy.'

'Don't tell him that!' Euterpe places herself between Melpomene and me.

'Why shouldn't he know it?' says Melpomene.

'Leave him out of it,' Euterpe starts to say. Then someone hammers on the door, and every one of us jumps, except Melpomene.

'Focaria!' It's Audo. 'Open up.'

Thalia springs to her feet and dashes through the arch into the tavern. Urania snatches another fistful of bread from Focaria and follows her. Focaria hands me the bowl and says, 'Put that in the kitchen,' and heads for the door. Melpomene and Euterpe do not move.

In the stifling kitchen, I stuff a fistful of bread and a couple of pieces of cheese into my mouth. I hear the grating slide of the bolt, the scrape of the door opening. Then I hear it slam again, and the bolt sliding shut.

'Clio?' I hear Euterpe say.

'Gone,' says Audo.

166

'So,' says Melpomene, 'I have an idea . . .'

'What?' Audo says. I peer out the kitchen door, still chewing.

They make up a little triangle, Melpomene and Euterpe facing off, while Audo looms over them, looking from one to the other. I can't hear what they're saying at first. Focaria strides toward the kitchen and shoos me inside, but I wave her off and keep watching.

Euterpe raises her voice. 'The punters won't want him up there.' She's glaring at Melpomene, but she's speaking to Audo. 'The punters won't want a boy hanging about upstairs.'

'They won't even notice him.' Melpomene's face is the mask of reason. 'They barely notice him now.'

Audo scowls, which is what he does when he wants you to believe he's thinking.

'He'll get hurt . . .' Euterpe says, but Melpomene addresses Audo directly.

'He'll be safer upstairs,' she says. 'The punters have other things on their minds. They won't even know he's there.'

'Why are you doing this?' Euterpe says.

'He's not your plaything, Euterpe,' Melpomene says. 'He's here to work, just like the rest of us.'

Audo is balling his fists, one after the other. He's getting bored. Melpomene lays her hand on his arm.

'Aren't you tired of running up and down the stairs, Audo?' she says. 'Let Pusus do it. He can bring us water and carry away the chamber pots. You're better off at the counter, where you can keep an eye on things.'

'What if we have another night like last night?' Euterpe moves closer to Audo, but she doesn't touch him.

'Then you're still right downstairs, aren't you, Audo?' Melpomene squeezes his bicep. She looks wide-eyed at Euterpe. 'He's no further away than he was last night.'

Audo grunts, deep in his throat.

'He's not *ready*,' Euterpe insists.

'I think he is.' Melpomene looks right at me, across the garden. 'Aren't you, Antiochus?'

In the doorway, I catch my breath. I didn't think they knew I was there, but Melpomene did, of course, all along. Audo narrows his black gaze at me. Euterpe turns to me bleakly.

'Don't you want to be our helper?' Melpomene smiles at me across the garden. 'Don't you want to be a big boy?'

My heart is racing. I'm frightened by the idea of working upstairs, because it's where Clio was cut, but I've seen things just as bad, many times, downstairs in the tavern. I also know that Euterpe loves me and that Melpomene does not, but I'm excited by the idea of working upstairs, with the wolves. I can't work out why Melpomene, of all people, wants me to, and why Euterpe, who has schooled me in curiosity, does not.

'Yes,' I say.

Euterpe stares into the dirt at her feet, her shoulders slumped, her hands dangling from the sleeves of her mantle. She's always seemed big to me, the woman who used to carry me on her hip, who still folds me in her arms. But now she seems diminished and frail, and I'm afraid that if I crossed the garden to her at this moment, she would be smaller than I am.

'It's settled.' Melpomene slips her hand inside Audo's arm and steers him toward the arch. 'Everybody wins,' she says as they disappear into the tavern.

Euterpe is dry-eyed, but she looks older than she ever has before. She turns toward the kitchen, but she's not looking at me, she's looking past me at Focaria.

'You could have said something,' Euterpe says.

'What?' says Focaria.

'That you need him in the kitchen. That you need him to help with the shopping.'

'What I want doesn't matter,' says Focaria. 'What you want

doesn't matter. What he wants . . .' She lays her hand, almost gently, on my shoulder. 'This was always going to happen.'

Her hand slides away, and I hear her step back into the kitchen. A moment later, I hear the *snick snick snick* of her knife. I stare at Euterpe, too ashamed to speak. I feel as if I've betrayed her. She makes herself smile and holds her hand out.

'Little One,' she says. 'Come here.'

It has been a long time since Euterpe and I have sat together in the garden. I'm often out on the street before she rises in the morning, off to do the tavern's shopping. And perhaps I've seen too much, in the street, on the docks, in the theatre, in Helicon itself, for her stories and fables to enthral me the way they used to. And I'm growing – I'm too big for her to hold on her lap any longer. So we sit one last time in our old spot by the water tank, in the narrowing wedge of shadow as the morning sun climbs toward noon and the meridian creeps back across the garden.

We sit with our legs crossed, knees close but not quite touching. My knees are callused from kneeling each day to scrape ash out of the oven or scrub the tavern floor. The mantle Euterpe wears in the street is pulled tight over her knees. On those rare occasions when we do have time together, she never hesitates but launches into a lesson as soon as we're settled, drawing from all the stories that her father, the doomed priest, taught her. But today she gazes at me without speaking, as if hoping I'll take a turn for once and tell *her* a story instead. Just to break the silence, I speak.

'Why did Focaria say that this was always going to happen?'

'All she means,' Euterpe says, 'is that sooner or later you were bound to work upstairs.'

'Like you do?'

'No,' she says, 'not like me. Not like us.'

'Why won't you tell me what you do?'

Euterpe leans forward and takes my hands.

169

'You're going to find out,' she says. 'And you need to know something.'

I've never been frightened by her gaze, but now I wish I could look away. She grips my hands tighter.

'Listen to me. Are you listening?'

I nod.

'Whatever you see me doing with the punters upstairs, whatever you hear, it's not real. It doesn't mean anything. It's just a game. Do you understand?'

'I guess.' For the first time in my life, I wish she would let go of me.

'It's not something I want to do. It's my work. You have to fetch water and buy bread and sweep the floor and carry laundry to the fuller. Well, I have to work, too. I have to do what Audo tells me to, just like you.'

'If it's work,' I say, 'then how can it be a game?' I can't imagine how being tickled by Thalia is like scrubbing the tavern floor. I can't imagine playing a game with Audo.

'When I say it's a game,' Euterpe says, 'I don't mean it's a game, I mean, it's not . . . it's not real. What I do with the punters, I'm just pretending. I'm performing.' She squeezes my hands and tries to meet my shifting eyes. 'Do you know what I mean?'

I can't bear her gaze for much longer. I can see Focaria watching us from the kitchen door.

'Focaria needs me,' I say. 'I have to bring the water in.'

'I know, Little One.' Euterpe won't let go. 'Just one moment more, please.' She tries to smile. 'Have I ever told you the story of the monkey and his two mothers?'

'I haven't got time for a story.' I glance at the kitchen door again, but Focaria has gone back inside.

'It's a short one,' she says. 'I'll tell it quickly.' She squeezes my hands even tighter. 'A little monkey has two mothers. One smothers him with kisses and embraces. She suffocates him, she makes him weak.'

The pressure of her hands, of her gaze, is too much. The urge to pull free from her is almost irresistible.

'But his other mother,' she says, trying to smile again, 'she ignores him. She leaves him alone and makes him find his own food, his own place to sleep.' She lets go of one of my hands, lays her trembling hand on the side of my face. 'She says she does it to make him stronger. Which mother should he listen to?'

I pull my hand free. 'I have to go.' I push myself to my feet.

Euterpe stands too, but clumsily, tangling herself in her mantle. 'Do whatever Focaria tells you to,' she says.

'I always do.'

'I know, but especially now.'

I try to step past her, but she catches my arm.

'If anyone ever tries to hurt you,' she says quickly, her voice low, 'if Audo tries to hurt you, come to me. I'll take you away.'

I look at her, utterly bewildered. If anyone tries to *hurt* me? Everybody tries to hurt me, all the time. Especially Audo. And does she mean, *away*? Where would we go?

'You'll know what I mean when it happens,' Euterpe whispers. 'And when it does, come to me, and we'll run away. I promise.'

One more time, she holds me, wrapping her arms round me. Her breath is hot in my ear. I can feel her tears on my cheek.

'I love you, Little One,' she says. 'I'll always be your mother. Don't forget.'

Then she releases me, as if she's casting a bird into flight from between her two hands. A moment later, she has disappeared into the tavern.

II

R eader, I know you know where this is going. Please believe me when I tell you that I didn't see it coming myself until it happened. Even after it did, I didn't really understand. It's taken me a lifetime to work that out. I've spent my whole life not knowing *who* I am, but now, at the very end of it, I know *what* I am. I may not know my parents, but I know my ancestry. Euterpe told me to remember that Romulus and Remus were born of a princess and a god. But as usual, she told me only part of the story, the version she thought was suitable for a child. Which is to say, she didn't tell me the truth. I have since discovered the real story in the histories of Livy, in the very library where I write these words now.

The truth is that Mars raped Rhea; that the wolf that raised Rhea's children was really just a whore, like Euterpe; that Romulus and Remus were bastards who grew up to be thieves and bandits; that Romulus murdered Remus and then named the city they founded after himself; that the descendants of Romulus peopled their city by inviting in more bandits and murderers who were unwanted in their own cities; that these same bandits and murderers peopled their little criminal empire by kidnapping the women of a neighbouring tribe and raping them in turn, the way Mars raped Rhea; that the children of these rapes proceeded to found a republic based upon the methodical rape and enslavement of their nearest neighbours, and then the cities beyond them, and the cities beyond them, until at last they had the whole of Italia; that they then made an empire by conquering their way around the rim of the sea, killing or enslaving everyone they came upon and eventually making everyone they conquered complicit in their own enslavement by turning them into Romans, too.

Centuries before I arrived in Britannia, a British chieftain stood with his kingdom in flames and a legionary's sword at his throat, and he said that the Romans created a wasteland and called it a peace. The entire empire is a mosaic of rape and murder and bastardy and forced labour, of which I am only one insignificant, dull-coloured fragment, off to the side, at the very edge. Insignificant, perhaps, but also representative. I, too, am a product of rape, murder, bastardy, and forced labour. I am the empire in a nutshell.

For a brief time in my life, after I started to work upstairs in the tavern, and while I was still able to go abroad in the city, I saw my world from both above and below, in its broadest outlines and its most intimate details.

Whenever I go to the old theatre, I snatch an apple when the grocer isn't looking and carry it up the steps to the highest row of seats, where I sit in the sunlight and eat my pilfered fruit with Carthago Nova laid out at my feet. Over my right shoulder, above the theatre, is the abandoned temple of Asclepius, the old god of healing, defaced by angry Christians and inhabited by feral cats. Beyond the theatre below is a grid of narrow streets and red roofs, and rising among them on the far side, under another hill, is the creamy dome of the caldarium at the baths, wisping grey smoke from its chimneys. To the right, within the square of the forum, tiny men in white togas strut aimlessly like baby chicks. Further to the right rises the half-finished dome of the bishop's new Christian church, a broken cup encrusted with scaffolding, and the eight-sided cupola of his new baptistery, both of them crawling with workmen like ants. All around the city are pale, dry hills like

176

the crust of a pie, and in the distance, rumpled red mountains with hollows full of blue shadow, holding up the vault of the sky. Between the city and the mountains to the north is a wide, brackish lake, its dull sheen rippled like a piece of faded grey silk. To the left of the lake, where the nearest mountain looms close over the city, an aqueduct and a bridge cross a shallow stream that runs from the lake down into the harbour. I can't see them from here, but under the dripping arches of the aqueduct live the cheapest wolves – the fornicators, who specialize in sucking cock and doing it standing up. To my left ships and fishing boats cluster along the quay while tiny men shift tiny barrels and bales in and out of long warehouses.

As a boy I knew nothing of the city's history, but since then I have learned from Livy and the Greek historian Polybius that Carthago Nova was founded by the Carthaginians hundreds of years before I was born. They gave it the same name as their capital across the sea in Africa – Qart-hadast in their language, which means 'new city'. For many years the Carthaginians fought the Romans for supremacy of the whole world, and when a Roman general named Publius Cornelius Scipio Africanus captured the Spanish Carthago, he renamed it Carthago Nova, to distinguish it from the original Carthago in Africa. So now its name was New New City, but then the Romans have always had a weakness for prosaic superfluity. Two generations later, Scipio Aemilianus, the adoptive grandson of Scipio Africanus, erased the old, African Carthago from history, burning it to the ground, slaughtering most of its people and selling the rest into slavery. Wasteland, peace.

Apple devoured, I plunge from my sparrow's eye view into the intimate life of the tavern. I'm alone upstairs every day now while the wolves are at the baths. I strip the dirty sheets off their beds, rinse their chamber pots, scrub the sticky stains off their floors. I tidy the make-up table in the empty cell and steal a glance at myself in the dusky mirror, still me and not me at the same time. I poke through their cells, where I find their hoarded treasures under a loose floorboard or in a hole in the plaster. Urania has a little brass goddess whose face she's rubbed away. Thalia has a medallion embossed with the chi-rho. Euterpe has no talismans or charms, only a cache of tip money tied up in a handkerchief, but when I pull her bed away from the wall, I find she has scrawled words on the plaster, though I don't know what they say. In Melpomene's cell I'm careful not to touch her little silver implements, her gleaming mirror, her brushes and pots of paint, because every day she counts everything she owns just before she leaves for the baths and counts everything again just as soon as she gets back.

Then it's past noon, and at Audo's nod I unlatch the shutters and let in the first punters of the day. Some I know from the street, some are sailors or farmers or itinerant labourers whom I've never seen before and will never see again. Some know the tavern by word of mouth or from previous visits, but some are first-timers drawn by the silent tintinnabulum that hangs from the awning outside. This is an erect brass penis as long as my forearm with a pair of wings sprouting from its shaft, a crooked tail like a cat's, and another, smaller penis sticking up from between a pair of dog's legs. Little bells hang from its foreskin, its paws, and the tips of its wings, but none of the bells have clappers any longer. Men tap it or flick it or jokingly stroke it with their fingers when they come in, and newcomers are surprised when it doesn't make a sound. The clappers have either fallen out, or Audo's pulled them out. Later, Melpomene will tell me that tintinnabula used to hang from all sorts of places for good luck, in front of houses and shops and workshops, not just lubricious taverns like Helicon. But in recent years, she says, the Christians have pulled them all down. Ours remains to announce the tavern's business, but silently. Depending on your point of view, it's either an invitation or a warning.

As the sun goes down behind the mountain across the harbour, I haul a stool round the room and stand on it to light each lamp with a burning taper. From then on, I'm back and forth from the kitchen all night long, ferrying pots of stew, platters of bread, coils of sausage. Most of the punters ignore me or don't even see me, but just in case, I smile, I laugh, I joke. I mug at their wisecracks, I roll my eyes behind their backs to the hilarity of their mates, I join in on a verse or two of every filthy song they sing. I make myself amenable, indispensable, and unnoticeable.

But now I am a Mouse for the entire tavern, upstairs as well as down. I am a pan-Helicon pusus. I have been working since dawn, but only after we open do I participate in the real work of the tavern. Only then do the anonymous paintings on the wall downstairs come alive for me, wearing the actual flesh and faces of the women I know.

At the start of my first night upstairs, Audo threatens me with the worst beating I've ever had if I go into any of the cells when a punter's inside. I'm not even supposed to look, he tells me, slapping the back of my head for emphasis.

'Nobody wants to see you when they're fucking,' he rumbles.

And so I carry water, wine, and food up the creaking stairs, and I come down again with sloshing chamber pots. I slip silently along the upstairs hall through the yellow fug of lamp smoke and incense and musk. At first I don't see much, because I have the fear of Audo in me, and because each wolf keeps her threadbare curtain drawn when she's with a punter. But I hear every sound you can imagine before I learn what they're actually doing. The men who sing and laugh full-throated downstairs, who whisper and shout at each other, who tell stories and jokes and lies in an endless torrent of words – upstairs these same men groan wordlessly like animals, they moan and sigh like girls, they whimper like children in pain, begging for release. Downstairs I hear the rattle of knucklebones against tabletops, the sudden scrape of a stool's legs against the floor, the stamp of feet keeping time with a song. Upstairs I hear the dull, rhythmic slap of flesh against flesh, the frantic creaking of a cot, the harsh, urgent grunting of a man hard at work in pursuit of his own pleasure, and then his strangled cry when he catches it.

I hear the wolves, too. The sound of their pleasure, if that's what it is, lasts only as long as the punter's, stopping abruptly as soon as the man is finished. Then while he lies there panting or sighing or scraping his name into the wall, I hear the wolf behind the curtain moving about her cell. I hear the splash of water as she washes, I hear the trickle of urination, I hear her expectorate into the chamber pot. Now and then there's a genuine cry from one of the wolves, but it's usually a cry of pain. Then the whole floor is suddenly quiet, and each of the other wolves peeks through her curtain to see if her sister needs help. But apart from the time a punter cut Clio, the wolf usually modulates her pain and forces it into a laugh or a joke, like a high-wire walker regaining her balance. A wolf knows no one is coming to help her, so she learns to roll with the punches. Literally.

When she's working, each wolf has her own, distinctive song. Thalia chirps rhythmically, timing her cries to match the man's, becoming faster and higher in pitch until she's almost keening. Urania, on the other hand, is as taciturn in her cell as she is in the garden, but she's popular nevertheless with those punters who are excited by her silent, teeth-grinding intensity. Through her curtain I mostly hear the rhythmic creaking of the cot and the grunting of the man, and only occasionally Urania herself, panting like a runner who is conserving her energy.

Melpomene's the most theatrically vocal of the wolves, and the least believable, at least to my ears. But such is the credulity of men in a brothel, the punters are excited by her artificial enthusiasm. She makes a point of learning the name of each man, and she makes sure to call it out, repeatedly, enthusiastically, as if in ecstasy. She laughs, she moans, she sings, she screams. She has a

180

repertoire that would put an actor to shame. She says the filthiest things imaginable, and she plays each man like a harp: *Please, Marcus! It's too big, Marcus! Don't hurt me, Marcus! Deeper, Marcus! That was wonderful, Marcus! Marcus, you're the best!*

The only wolf it unsettles me to hear is Euterpe. Perhaps because she so desperately insists that what she does is only a performance, the fact that she sounds so good at it confuses me, and hurts me. I won't know for years yet what a martyr is, but somehow, even before I did, I wanted her to sound martyred. Too often she sounds, through the curtain, just like she does when she's cuddling me in the garden – warm, affectionate, maternal. Hesitating in the hall outside her cell, I am alarmed to hear her say to a punter some of the same things she says to me when she's teaching me to count in the garden, or singing to me, or asking me to provide the lesson of a fable. *That's good*, she murmurs to the man in the voice I love, *you're almost there. You're doing it. You make me so happy.* Hearing her say these things is like a knife to my heart. Is she telling the punter the truth? Or has she been performing for me, too?

Per Audo's instructions, I never enter a cell when a wolf is working. I leave her wine or food just outside the curtain, or take away the chamber pot she has left out for me. When a wolf isn't working, she pulls her curtain open, to let punters know she's available and to stir the air a little. Then I might go in and let Thalia teach me how to make fart sounds with my hand under my arm, or stand by while Urania gobbles the sausage I've stolen for her from the kitchen, or wait attendance on Melpomene as she touches up her face and hair and fans herself in the heat. Sometimes Euterpe holds me and pets me and calls me her Little One, but in her cell, dishevelled and sweaty, she doesn't smell or feel the way she does in the garden. It's not the same anymore, and we both know it. But she pretends that nothing has changed, and so do I. Now we are both performing.

It isn't long, though, before my curiosity overtakes my fear of Audo and I start to watch. The curtains over the doorways are threadbare, except for Melpomene's, and sometimes a wolf doesn't close it all the way, leaving a gap through which I can see what's happening inside. As I pad silently along the hall with a sweating pitcher of water or a stinking chamber pot, I pause to watch the wolves at their labours in the steady lamplight in each cell. I learn what the different sounds signify – the slap of belly against belly or belly against backside, the frantic drumming of the end of a cot against a wall, the moist, masticating smack of a cock being sucked. I watch Melpomene at work under a man, singing his praises, I watch Thalia as she chirps like a bird, I watch Urania riding a man as if she's riding a bucking horse, clenching him with her knees and swaying her arms.

I see the punters in all the variety of their nakedness. I see firm young flesh and sagging ageing flesh, I see bony ribcages and shuddering bellies and writhing tattoos. I see pimples and warts and birthmarks and moles, I see old scars and recent burns and varicose veins and bulging goitres. I see men with missing fingers, missing toes, missing ears, missing eyes. I see black men and brown men and white men, I see dirty yellow hair and shiny bald spots and tight black braids, I see leathery backsides and fish-pale buttocks and scaly, callused feet. I see the fine web of wrinkles on the sun-baked nape of a fisherman's neck. I see the crosshatched welts on a young slave's back. I see an old man's pendulous testicles, swinging like the clappers of a bell.

But I'm not watching animals. I'm watching men, some of whom I know. Rufus the fishing captain comes to Helicon several times a week to drink, and once a month he treats the crews of his boat, free and slave alike, to a visit upstairs. Audo likes these evenings, because Rufus enforces discipline himself if one of his crew gets too drunk or too violent. This allows Audo to stay behind the bar and get more drunk than usual, and so he gives the Rufus and his men a wholesale rate. Rufus pays for the whole evening in advance and then lets his men all go ahead of him. He passes the time while he's waiting by drinking with Audo at the counter, the two of them talking in low voices. It's the only time I ever hear Audo laugh, a deep, liquid, guttural sound that makes his shoulders shake.

Meanwhile, the fishermen take over the second floor for the entire evening, going up in shifts until each one has had a go. By the end of the evening, the whole tavern smells of fish. It's even more work than usual for the wolves, of course, but they do everything they can to make each visit go quickly. Even Melpomene works faster than usual, not bothering to sing the praises of each man so enthusiastically. I'm busier than usual, too, because there are no lulls, just a steady stream of water going up, and a steady stream of chamber pots coming down. All night, all four cells are full of grunting fishermen, fucking almost in unison, and it doesn't quiet down until Rufus himself comes up the stairs. By then, the rest of the fisherman have all wandered back to the harbour, and Rufus finishes quickly with one of the exhausted wolves, fucking with the methodical efficiency of a man who eats to fill his belly, with no interest in savouring the meal.

Musa the banker usually sends his slave up first, and after Deodatus has finished and made sure the upstairs is safe for his Dominus, Musa mounts the stairs slowly, marshalling his strength, passing gas. The wolves call him Garlic Farter. He prefers a younger wolf, usually Urania, which is just as well, because she has to do most of the work. Musa is plump and easily winded, and he doesn't fuck with the animal urgency of the fishermen. Instead he gets sweaty and red-faced, stopping often to catch his breath or wait for Urania to coax his drooping erection back to life with her hand or her mouth. His buttocks shudder, his girlish breasts jiggle, his upper arms wobble. When he finishes, his whole body sags over the cot, his belly trembling like a pudding, his cock wilting. Meanwhile Urania pries herself from under him and gives him a tight smile, which disappears the instant she turns away and squats over the chamber pot.

Priscianus the oil merchant goes upstairs once or twice a week, but all he ever wants is to be fellated, usually by Melpomene, who moans as if his cock were coated with honey. He ignores her theatrical appreciation, though, and only stares at the flare of the lamp over her shoulder, or lifts his eyes to the ceiling as if trying to remember someone's name. He winces when he comes, as though she's just extracted a thorn from his foot. Then he pays her, swishes through the curtain, and hurries down the stairs. Melpomene, who knows I might be watching, yanks the curtain shut before she deposits her coins into her hiding place.

Brutus the carter, on the other hand, favours Euterpe, stooping his head to pass through the low doorway of her cell, where he rattles her cot and grunts in her ear until he's finished. Then, to my surprise, Brutus – who barely has a word to say to anyone in the street or the tavern downstairs – sits on the floor next to her bed with his long legs stretched out and crossed at the ankles, and talks to her in a low murmur. I can't hear what he says, but sometimes he makes her laugh.

Lovesick Quartus can only afford Thalia every other week or so, but even so he spends much of his precious time with his beloved loudly declaiming a poem which he says he's written specially for her, the gist of which is usually that Quartus thinks he shouldn't have to pay.

'Do mares demand gifts from stallions?' he says, striking a pose in the middle of her cell while Thalia watches from the bed and tries not to laugh. 'Do cows solicit their bulls? Must a ram court ewes with offerings?'

Later, Euterpe tells me the poem was actually written by an old Roman named Ovid. Mostly what Quartus wants to do, though, is just talk, and Thalia's perfectly happy to let him do it, too, since this makes him the easiest punter she's ever had. It's as if he's saved up all the clichés and platitudes he's heard writing other people's letters all week long, in order to spill them into Thalia's lap: *You're the most beautiful girl I've ever seen. I want you more than life itself. I know you're not like the others. My darling*, he says. *My dearest*, he says. *My little bird.* Thalia says nothing as she strokes his hair and tries not to yawn. Quartus always ends in a passionate whisper, as if afraid someone else is listening – and I usually am. *I'm saving my money to buy you*, he tells her, *and then we can be together, forever. You'll be mine, then*, he says, *and you'll never have to let another man touch you as long as you live. I'll take care of you forever*, he says, *and you'll be mine, you'll be mine, you'll be mine . . .* Thalia finishes him with her hand, and Quartus, forlorn and satisfied in equal measure, hurries down the stairs, almost in tears. Unlike Thalia's other punters, he never tips her.

'My gift is my poetry,' he whispers to her while she yawns with her head propped up on her fist. 'Gold, jewellery, perfume,' he says, his eyes shining, 'all that perishes. But your fame will be *immortal*!'

And yet, as different as the punters are, there's one way in which they are all the same. More than once, I've glimpsed Focaria and Euterpe alone together in mutual embrace, in a dark corner of the kitchen or behind the water tank. They kiss and caress, they look at each other, they *see* each other. But upstairs I never see a man caress a wolf, and I never see them kiss. The punters are all variations on the same man, greedy and joyless and quick, taking his pleasure the way a stray cat quickly devours whatever it finds on the street, afraid it'll be snatched away at any moment. He grapples the wolf like an animal pinning down its prey, roughly turning or twisting her to his own advantage. He holds her down, he pushes her legs apart, he digs his fingers into her flesh.

Then, usually in less time than it takes me to eat a piece of bread, it's finished – for the punter, anyway, if not for the wolf, whose work isn't necessarily over. Sometimes the man wants to talk afterward, and from behind the curtain I hear him complain to the

185

wolf that his children won't obey him, that his wife won't let him touch her, that his Domina beats him, that his taxes are too high, that his business partner cheats him, that his Dominus tries to fuck him when he's drunk, that his slaves don't like him, that nobody understands him. Slave or free man or freedman, each punter empties himself into the wolf, one way or the other, and each wolf responds in her own way. Here's where they earn a tip, if the punter is inclined to give one. Melpomene sighs sympathetically and tells him, 'You poor man.' Thalia coos like a dove and strokes his forehead. Urania lets him fuck her again if he'll stop talking. Euterpe reassures the punter that his children revere him, that his wife loves him, and that, yes, the Emperor's taxes *are* too high.

Then at last a man is ready to leave, and especially if it's someone I know from the street, I slip into one of the empty cells at the end of the hall until he's down the stairs. I'm the same boy on the street I always was, the tavern boy who buys fish and apples and hares, but if I've passed a man on the stairs or in the hallway of the tavern at night, there's something different now in the way he does business with me during the day. His jokes are a little more laboured, he won't meet my eye, his smile is a little more fixed. I can see he's trying to pretend that the boy he deals with in the daylight is not the same boy he ignores in the tavern at night.

Long after I've glimpsed the others, I still haven't seen Nazarius in the act. He goes upstairs several times a week, and he doesn't seem to prefer any particular wolf over the others, frequenting each of them in turn. And yet when he enters a wolf's cell, Nazarius is the one who yanks the curtain shut, not her, and he adjusts it carefully so that there are no gaps for me to see through. Then he blows out the lamp. Strangely, the wolves don't utter a word or make a sound the way they do with the other punters, not even Melpomene. Only Nazarius speaks, and he's so quiet I have to lean close to the curtain – careful not to disturb it – in order to hear him. Over the urgent slap of flesh against flesh, I hear him muttering through gritted teeth, cursing the wolf and calling her by the name of an animal. *Lazy cow. Useless pig. Thieving dog. I'll show you*, he hisses. *I'll teach you to steal from me. I'll teach you to lie to me. I'll teach you to talk back to me. I'll teach you . . .*

Because I haven't seen him, and he hasn't seen me seeing him, he's still jolly with me in his shop during the day. He still ruffles my hair, still makes the same jokes, still sings the praises of his useless son. He gaily drags the wolves' stained gowns and sheets out of the basket, as if he has no idea what the stains are or who put them there. With Nazarius, it's not that I'm a different boy than the one who haunts the second floor of the tavern. It's that the man in the shop is not the same man I hear behind the curtain.

I finally see him one night, by accident. I carry a brimming pitcher of water up the stairs and into the hall. Melpomene, Thalia, and Urania are each with a punter, and the punters are all groaning louder than usual, as if excited by hearing the other men. It's almost a competition. But I hear nothing from Euterpe's cell, so when I see her curtain is still partly open, I assume she's alone and I walk in with the pitcher, ready to steal a few minutes with her while she has a drink and dabs under her arms with a wet cloth. But Nazarius has simply forgotten to pull the curtain all the way across, and because he's quieter than the other groaning men, I don't hear him. The lamp is out, the way he likes it, but enough light spills into the cell from the hall for me to see them both, instantly. They're not on the cot, they're on the floor. Euterpe is on her hands and knees, and Nazarius is squatting behind her. He has hooked his middle fingers in the corners of her mouth like a bridle. With each thrust, he jerks her head back, and with each thrust, he grunts, *dirty slave, dirty slave, dirty slave . . .*

I nearly stumble over my own feet, splashing water from the pitcher to the floor. Nazarius looks straight at me, but his eyes are as glazed as a blind man's. *Slave . . . slave . . . slave*, he gasps, spittle catching in his beard.

But Euterpe sees me. Her lips are stretched into a rictus – her teeth involuntarily bared, her head jerking – and she can't speak. But our eyes meet, and I can see what she's thinking. As clearly as if she were speaking aloud, I hear her voice in my head, humiliated and hurt and angry all at once.

Get out, she says.

I jump back as if she's struck me. Holding the sloshing pitcher with one trembling hand, I yank the curtain all the way across with the other. Then I duck into the empty cell, set the pitcher down, and close the curtain. I sit on the bed, clutching my knees until my heart slows. Down the hall, a man climaxes, shouting wordlessly as Melpomene cheers him on. Then, as if his pleasure were a cough or a sneeze, the other two men catch it, and they call out, too. One of them even laughs.

But not Nazarius. Not a sound comes from Euterpe's cell. Finally I hear the rustle of her curtain, and I hear footsteps moving away down the hall. I rise from the bed and peek through the curtain. Euterpe's curtain is still closed, but I see the sloping shoulders of Nazarius as he turns out of the hallway to descend the stairs. I count to ten under my breath to give him time to reach the bottom, then I slip out of the cell with the pitcher and hover just outside Euterpe's curtain. Her lamp is still out. Up the hall, men and wolves are talking and moving about. But Euterpe's cell is still silent. As quietly as I can, I set the pitcher on the floor and give her curtain a tug, just enough to rattle the curtain rings.

'Water,' I whisper. I don't wait for an answer. I hurry downstairs, slip through the noisy tavern behind the bar, and into the garden.

I don't see Euterpe again until the following morning, when I'm carrying water in from the fountain. She's up earlier than usual, and as I come in from the street with the yoke pressed across my shoulders, she's standing in the kitchen doorway with Focaria, their heads together in urgent conversation. Focaria sees me and falls silent, and Euterpe turns. I avoid her gaze and trudge to the tank in the corner of the garden. I'm aware of her coming toward me as I squat to lower the yoke, but I ignore her as I lift the lid of the tank and stand on tiptoe to empty the first bucket. When I turn to pick up the second bucket, she's only a few paces away, her hands clutching her gown tight at her throat.

'It's a game,' she says.

'I know.' I lift the other bucket onto my shoulder, stand on tiptoe, and heave it in all at once, splashing more than usual.

'He doesn't hurt me.' She steps closer. I put the bucket down and hunch my shoulders, as if Audo's about to hit me.

'I know.' I stare at her feet.

'Don't be angry.' She touches me lightly, and I stiffen. She pulls her hand away.

'I'm not.' I'm still staring at her painted toes.

'Look at me.' Her voice is stern. She almost sounds like Focaria. I lift my gaze as far as her knees, so she grips my chin between her fingers and forces my head up until I'm looking into her eyes. I catch my breath – is this what it feels like when he clutches her?

'I know you watch,' she says. 'You've seen me with punters before.'

I say nothing. I tug my chin out of her grasp. But I don't look away, and neither does she. She looks tired. For the first time in my memory, I'm not looking at Euterpe, the woman who holds me in her arms and sings to me and tells me stories, the woman who gave me my names, the woman who taught me nearly everything I know about the world beyond the garden. I'm looking at an exhausted woman with slack skin under last night's smudged make-up, a woman in a flimsy, wrinkled, dirty gown, a woman with her hair pressed down on one side where she slept on it. I'm looking at a wolf.

It's as if the ground has opened up between us. It's all I can do not to fall into the gap. Suddenly Euterpe kneels heavily before me, her gown revealing more of her, perhaps, than she wants me to see right now. I can smell her morning odour, of sweat and sex and stale perfume. Her smell never bothered me before. She smelled like a mother to me. But now she smells like the dusty, shit-dappled street, like the sewer reek of the sea along the quay, like the tang of urine from the fullery. She smells like all the men who have had her.

Through her weariness, through her mask of paint and grease and kohl, I can see her tenderness struggling to rise to the surface. I can see the force of will behind it, and I see that it still matters to her what I think. But she doesn't take my face between her hands. She doesn't touch me the way she used to.

'No matter what you see,' she whispers. 'No matter what you think of me . . .'

Can she see me struggling to believe her? Or can she only see how close I am to running away? Is that why her voice is shaking? At the far end of my life, sitting at this desk in this crumbling library, with this pen in my hands, it shames me, reader, to put the words on papyrus: can Euterpe see how much she disgusted me?

Behind her, Focaria watches from the shadow of the kitchen doorway. Her face is blank. It's as if she, too, is watching from behind a mask.

'No matter what,' Euterpe says, 'I'll always love you.'

'I know,' I say.

We're close enough to breathe on each other. Then, just at the moment when she used to embrace me, she stands instead, pushing herself up with a grunt. She hurries back through the garden to the tavern, her head down. She passes Focaria without a glance and disappears through the arch. Focaria watches her go, looks at me, then turns away into the darkness of the kitchen.

*　*　*

190

Later that morning, I carry the laundry to Nazarius. I'm not sure he saw me last night, but I'm not looking forward to finding out. I'm wishing I was as invisible in the street during the day as I am in the tavern during the night. Do these people around me all know what I know now, or am I the only one? Are the separate halves of my secret knowledge – what happens at night versus what happens in the day – are they known by everyone, or am I the only one who has put the halves together, who apprehends the whole secret, all at once? Does Afra know what Priscianus does in the tavern? Can she imagine him with his cock in Melpomene's mouth? Does she ever take it in her mouth, or is that why he visits Melpomene? Does Quartus know how Thalia rolls her eyes when he's reading poetry to her? Does Musa know the wolves call him Garlic Farter?

At Nazarius's shop, there are a couple of women ahead of me, laughing. I don't see the fuller, and for a moment I'm relieved, thinking I won't have to see him at all this morning. Then I hear him laughing, too, and he stands up from behind the counter, joking and winking at the women as he slides across to them one stack and then another of clean, folded laundry. Behind him, I hear the thump of the beaters, the work song of the men treading in place in their tubs. I see the shaft of sun from the skylight limning the arms of the women at the rinsing bath. I could still slip out and wait across the street, under the portico of the school, until Nazarius disappears into the back, and Lucilia comes out to mind the counter.

The laughing women brush by me as if I'm not even there, and I look up. Nazarius is watching me from behind the counter. The laughter has faded from his face. I freeze again, just as I did the night before. I know he knows what I saw. He purses his lips, he narrows his eyes. Just when I think I can't bear it, just when I think I really will turn and run, he smiles broadly again.

'Mouse!' he cries. 'My old friend!' He throws his arms wide. 'What have you brought me this morning?'

Then I'm at the counter, and he's leaning across and helping himself to the stained sheets and gowns from the basket, clicking his tongue in jocular disapproval as he stuffs them out of sight behind the counter.

'What do you people *do* over there?' he says. 'All my hard work ruined.'

When I don't meet his gaze, he snaps his fingers. I flinch, as if he's raised his hand to me. When I look up, he winks and lifts his voice again. 'Lucilia! Front!'

As if out of thin air, his wife appears at the end of the counter. Behind her hovers the girl I saw with her before, her daughter. Lucilia regards her husband warily, while the girl peeks out from behind her mother.

'Look who's here,' Nazarius says. 'Our old friend, Mouse!' He smiles at me again like a cat in the last moment before it pounces. He reaches suddenly over the counter to grab my shoulder. I flinch, but he's only steadying me so he can reach deep into the basket and pull out the last, sour garment. He whisks it behind the counter, then grabs the basket he's filled there and hands it to his wife.

'A little extra effort on these today, my love,' he says. 'They had a busy night last night.'

Lucilia steps close enough to him to take the basket, but no closer. Without looking, she swings it behind her, and the girl takes it and hurries back into the shop. As Lucilia turns away, our gazes meet, and in spite of myself, I imagine her on the floor, on her hands and knees, her husband behind her, his fingers hooked in her mouth. He's calling her *dog, pig, wolf,* and she's begging me with her eyes not to look. Then Lucilia is slipping through the laundry after her daughter.

Meanwhile, Nazarius is stacking our clean, folded laundry onto the counter. Usually he lets me collect it, but today he pulls me close and presses the sheets and gowns into the basket himself, pushing me back on my heels.

192

'You're a lucky boy,' he says. 'If I got to see what you see every night, I'd be walking around like . . .' He stiffens his forearm and clenches his fist. ' . . . all day long.' He ruffles my hair, but harshly, nearly pushing me off my feet.

'Now,' he says, standing up straight, 'what have you got for me?'

I blink at him. 'Your Honour?'

He rubs his fingers together. 'Nothing in this world is free.'

I fumble at the purse round my neck and spill a few coins onto the countertop. Nazarius grabs my wrist and pins it to the counter while he flicks through the coins with his other hand.

'When adults are busy,' he says, under his breath, 'you knock before you come into a room.' He's not laughing. 'Don't you?'

All I can do is nod.

'Of course you do!' He smiles and releases my hand, then he hands back one of the coins. 'Here.' He winks. 'Keep this for yourself.'

I close the coin in my palm. A moment later I'm on the street, without knowing how I got there.

'Lucky boy!' Nazarius calls after me.

I take a few steps until I'm out of sight of the shop. Through the passers-by, I see Lutatius, the fuller's son, across the street under the portico, paying attention to the schoolmaster for once, gamely repeating his lesson along with the other students.

'All of Gaul,' they are chanting, 'is divided into three parts . . .'

Clutching the coin tightly in my palm, I wonder, does Lutatius know what his father does at night? Am I getting a better education than he is? Or will there come a night when Nazarius brings his son with him to the tavern, to teach him what he needs to know to be a man? I open my palm, and look at the coin. Taking it feels like a betrayal, as if I'm profiting from whatever it is Nazarius is doing to the wolves. Someone jostles me and curses, and I start back up the street. Even if I keep the coin, where would I hide it? Focaria knows every inch of the kitchen. She'll accuse me of stealing it from her. I could spend it now, somewhere between the fullery and the tavern, but what would I buy, and where would I keep it? And how would I explain it to Focaria?

Halfway home, I pass a doorway where a blind beggar with a jutting beard holds his shaking palm out and repeats the word 'Please' in a dull rhythm. The shock of my coin hitting his palm convulses him and he nearly drops it, but at the last minute he closes both hands over it, his mouth working, spraying spittle into the sunlight.

'Bless you, Dominus!' he cries. But I'm already gone.

Late that night, I lie awake in my corner of the kitchen, while Focaria sleeps like a dead donkey in the other corner. The moon is full, and the garden beyond the kitchen doorway is glazed with silver light. At last I take my ragged blanket with me and go out into the cooler air. I cross the garden, the damp night-time earth between my toes, and I sit with my back to the water tank, pull up my knees, and wrap the blanket tight around me. I lift my gaze above the sloping roof of the tavern, where the exhausted wolves are asleep, to the black silhouette of the mountain looming over the town beyond the harbour and to the moon itself, full and round and simmering in its own haze like a lamp glowing through the fog. Directly overhead, the sky is crowded with the pinpricks of stars, but near the moon, only two shine brightly enough to be seen, a dusty red one above and a white one like a jewel below. I stare at the moon, and I try to knit the two halves of my world together.

I have lifted the rock and seen the worms writhing underneath. What the punters do with the wolves upstairs turns out to be not much different than Audo beating Focaria, or one of the wolves, or me. It doesn't look much different than men brawling with each other in the street. There's usually less blood involved – except, of course, for Clio – but the spent look on a man's face after a fuck looks just like the spent look on his face when he stands over another man he's just beaten to the ground with his fists. Am I

194

the only one alive who knows this? Am I the only one who moves through both worlds? I float through the street and the tavern as if I truly am Sparrow, as if I can soar above everyone's houses and see in their windows. It's as if I can see everyone with their clothes off – perhaps because I *have* seen many of them with their clothes off. It's as if I can see what no one else in the world but the Christian god or the old gods can see. And if I'm not supposed to know this, why is the world showing it to me?

I can still see Nazarius on his knees, I can still see Euterpe bridled by his fingers like a mule. Does he do this at home, to his wife? Does he use her the way he uses a wolf? No wonder she's wary of him all the time. Then I wonder: is this how I was made? Did my father do this to my mother? Did my father love my mother, as Euterpe swears he must have? Did they look into each other's eyes and stroke each other like Euterpe and Focaria do when they're alone? Or did my father just force my mother to the floor and fuck her? Did he roughly move her limbs about like a doll's? Did he call her by the name of an animal? Did they belong to each other, the way Quartus swears he and Thalia belong to each other, or did she merely belong to him the way a wolf belongs to a punter for a few moments, or the way I belong to Dominus all the time? Am I a child of Euterpe's tenderness, or a child of Nazarius's rage? Or am I just an accident, a child of restlessness and boredom and too much to drink? Will I be like Nazarius when I'm old enough? Will I do this to a woman, too? Is this what it's like to be a man?

And the children that result from this violence – do they know? Every day I see them when I'm on the street. They're even more alien to me than men. Through the open door of a house, I see a boy pulling a tiny wooden cart on a string, or a smiling girl riding in a little wagon pulled by a dog, or a mother changing her baby's diaper and blowing raspberries on its belly, making it squeal with laughter – and I wonder, aren't any of them slaves, like me? Don't any of them have any work to do, the way I do, all day, every day?

Then I wonder, what would that boy and girl think if they saw what I saw, every night? Has either of them ever seen their father groaning between a woman's legs? Will that baby grow up to see its mother held down and ridden like an animal? And if they haven't, how will they learn to do it themselves, when the time comes and they're old enough?

Is it like this everywhere, in every house, every night, or is there something about the tavern itself that changes men? Something in the air of the place, a kind of miasma within its walls that turns men from festive to melancholy to violent and back again in a matter of moments. Does the miasma affect Audo, who lives here, in his cramped cell under the stairs, or is he the source of it, like an old underground fire that's been smouldering for years, filling every room to its walls with his acrid rage? I've never actually seen him with one of the wolves, but I know he goes upstairs in the morning, when I'm out in the garden or in the street. Sometimes when I'm scrubbing the floor in the silent tavern, I hear the rhythmic thumping of a cot over my head, I hear Audo grunting. But I never see him in the act.

And what about Calidus, the young Dominus, who visits at least once a week, sometimes more? He, too, goes upstairs sometimes and wakes a wolf, then comes down looking flushed and breathless, with the same dulled look in his eyes as every other punter. In the time since I first met him, he's gotten a little thicker round the middle, a little fuller in the face, but he's still as perfumed and plucked and manicured as that first day I saw him in the garden. In spite of all that, could he be the secret source of the miasma, and not Audo? After all, we do his bidding, not the other way around.

And what about me? I breathe the miasma every day of my life. It settles on my skin and sinks into the coarse weave of my tunic. It penetrates my lungs and permeates my blood like a poison. I carry the dirty laundry to the fuller, I carry chamber pots of piss and shit and spunk, I move through the humid fug of the second storey all night long, and all day long, I smell of its sweat, its spittle, and its musk. Could I be the source of it? Did I bring some infection with me in my swaddling clothes? Was I that dirty from the start? Was I ever clean? Will I ever be clean again?

I look up from the garden. The bright white star below the moon has already sunk behind the black hump of the mountain. The moon itself is nearly touching the mountain's silhouette, and the dusty red star is twinkling now, as if its eyelid is getting heavy and it's struggling to stay awake. At last I'm feeling sleepy myself, and I shift my stiff legs and stand. Clutching the blanket around me, I go back into the kitchen and lie down across from Focaria, to catch an hour of sleep before the sun comes up.

What do *you* make of all this, reader? If, against the odds, someone is reading this, then the chances are very good that you're a man. And because you're a man, the chances are likewise very good that you've visited a place like Helicon yourself. More than once. Even if you're a woman reading this, the chances are very good that you know a man who has visited a Helicon, more than once. So perhaps you're not surprised by the difference between the two faces each man wears – not tragedy and comedy, like the dramatist's masks, but banker and panting beast, scribe and trembling lover, tradesman and rutting animal. You haven't just seen it, you've lived it. You know what the difference is.

Now, at the end of my life, so do I. But even then, I had a hint of it. I had learned on my own the pleasure that men seek. I'd discovered it myself, with my hand. Late at night, when I know Focaria's asleep, I stare into the dark above me and think of one of the girls on the street, or of the wiry boy from the quay, his limbs and bare chest gleaming as he clings to the rigging and laughs at me. I stroke my stiffened penis and think of one or the other, and sometimes I think of both, stuttering between them, unable to make up my mind, until my pleasure surprises me, short and sharp, before I mean it to. Then I feel sad, and as I stare up into the dark, I wonder if I look just like every other man does afterwards, my eyes dulled, empty, useless.

Is this what makes Priscianus melancholy? Is this what makes Quartus desperate? Is this what makes Musa shed his dignity? Is this what fills Nazarius full of rage? Is this what makes men mad? Is this what made me? Is this what drives the world?

I used to go to Euterpe with all my questions, but I can't ask her about this. Focaria would roll her eyes and laugh at me. Audo would hit me. I suppose Thalia or Urania might explain it to me – they live this, after all, every day of their lives – but now that I spend my mornings working, I don't see them much anymore. Melpomene would probably answer my question, but I don't want to ask her. There's something about the way she looks at me that frightens me.

The one person I know who would tell me, can't. Tacita and I are often the only two slaves at the fountain, and we have our own private language. She lifts her pale eyebrows, as if to say, *And how are you, this morning, Pusus?* I shrug, as if to say, *Not too bad.* Then I lift my eyebrows: *You?* She shrugs, and sometimes she even smiles. We help fill each other's buckets, she lifts the yoke across my shoulders, and we walk together, silently, back up the street with our water, parting before our respective doorways. It isn't much, but it's the only real friendship I have outside of the wolves.

But then Tacita stops coming to the fountain for a few days running, and one morning Afra brings her doorkeeper to fetch the water instead. His presence tamps down the merriment of the other women, even though the slave himself doesn't say a word. He doesn't look at the women, and he doesn't even make eye contact with me. Afra asserts her priority at the fountain, waving her man ahead of everyone instead of letting the other women go first. She holds court as he fills her buckets, but her sharp wit sounds forced today, and so does the laughter of the other women. If Afra turns to glance at her husband's shop across the street – where Priscianus keeps his head down and never looks back – or if she simply falls silent for a moment, the others exchange looks behind her back.

Later that morning, I'm in the old theatre buying pears from a grocer's stall when the sight of Tacita up on stage with a line of slaves on auction stops my breath. As the grocer loads the pears from his barrel into my basket, I stare at her, willing her to pick me out of the crowded market. But she just gazes straight ahead at nothing, the way Clio did the last time I saw her. Her dress is in a puddle round her ankles, and except for the sign hanging from her neck, she's naked, so the little crowd of buyers can get a good look at her. Her coarse yellow hair is undone, frizzing out across her shoulders. She's not shackled or manacled, and she clasps her hands before her, under a little round belly I've never noticed before.

The slave dealer is deep in conversation with a potential buyer, but at this distance, over the racket of the market, I can't hear what either man is saying. The buyer slowly circles her, pursing his lips as he looks her up and down. The slaves on either side, both men, both naked, each steal a look, then look away. The buyer parts her hair to peer at her scalp, then he squats and runs his hands up and down her legs, squeezing her calves and her thighs, manipulating her knees. Tacita's lips tighten. Then the man stands and says something to her, and Tacita unclasps her hands, lifts her arms, and makes fists, flexing her upper arms while the man squeezes her biceps. She lowers her arms, and he says something else to her, but she only stares straight ahead. The man turns to the dealer, and the dealer steps up, grips her by the jaw, and squeezes her mouth open, baring her teeth. He pushes the end of his quirt against the roof of her mouth, propping it open while the buyer peers inside. The man shakes his head at the dealer and starts to turn away, but the dealer catches him by the arm and presses the man's hand to the round bulge of Tacita's belly, holding it there while he talks rapidly.

The grocer taps me on the shoulder and says, 'All done.'

As I count coins into his palm, I ask him, 'Why are they selling Tacita?'

'Who's Tacita?' He tests each coin with his teeth.

'The girl with the yellow hair.' I point at the stage. 'Is she getting too fat? Does she eat too much?'

The grocer leans out of his stall and looks. He starts to laugh.

'Did you hear what Pusus here just said?' He catches the attention of the men in the stalls on either side of him. 'He wants to know if the girl's getting fat.'

Now all three men are laughing. A moment after that, people along the row of stalls are repeating what he said, and the laughter ripples through the crowd until it rises up the crumbling rows of the theatre and fills the whole market. All around, people's heads swivel in my direction, then down at the stage. I can hear some of them saying, 'Kid over there wants to know if she's fat,' and I make myself laugh, too, as if I'm in on the joke.

Then I see Tacita looking straight at me. Somehow she's picked me out of the raucous crowd. Her lips are still pressed together, and she's breathing steadily through her nose. I know she sees me laughing, so I stop. The two men are still haggling in front of her, flashing hand gestures as they negotiate a price.

'Is she getting fat,' the grocer snorts. 'That's a good one.'

Tacita's gaze penetrates me. My throat tightens. As laughter swells through the theatre, we share a long look. Her eyes brim with meaning, but I can't understand everything she's trying to tell me. The only thing I'm certain of is that she's saying goodbye. Then her new Dominus steps in front of her and blocks my view.

'She's not fat.' The grocer lifts his voice to be heard over the hilarity of the crowd, taking pity on me. 'She's going to have a baby, and her Domina doesn't want to raise her husband's bastard.' He lowers his voice. 'Especially since Afra can't give him any children of his own.' He winks at me, but I'm not paying attention.

Why doesn't Tacita run? I think. *Why doesn't she run like the Syrian girl did?* She's young still, she's strong, and she's not shackled at the moment. She's naked, but so was the Syrian girl. Surely she could snatch her dress before she leaped from the stage. She can't speak, but she's strong, even stronger than the girl was. Up on the stage, her new owner has moved to the side, and I try to catch her eye again. *Why don't you run?* I try to tell her.

But Tacita's not looking at me anymore. She's not looking at anyone. The dealer lifts the sign from around her neck, and Tacita bends her knees to pull up her dress. Then her new owner grips her by the arm and leads her away, between the pillars at the back of the stage and out of sight.

'I'll bet she fetched a good price, though,' says one of the tradesman next to the grocer.

'She's a breeder,' says the man on the other side.

'The baby'll be worth something,' says the grocer, and all three men grunt their professional agreement.

The show is over. The hilarity has blown itself out like a squall off the sea, and the theatre returns to its dull oceanic murmur. The dealer on stage is now pitching his other slaves to a dwindling crowd. Before I descend, I stare at the doorway at the back of the stage where Tacita disappeared just now. What would happen, I wonder, if I ran after her, just to say goodbye, just to give her one more pear from the basket on my back? Would her new owner allow me to spend a moment with her? Would Tacita even want me to, or has she already shed her old life like a skin? Of course, Clio disappeared the same way, so it's not the first time I've lost someone without saying goodbye. It won't be the last.

* * *

'What took you so long?' Focaria says as soon as I get back to the kitchen. 'I've got a special errand for you.'

She's scrubbing the kitchen table, which is usually my job. She's leaning into it, too, pressing down on the brush with both hands, making it sizzle across the tabletop.

'Tacita's been sold,' I say. It just bursts out of me.

Usually Focaria simply grunts at the news I bring her from the street, but now she stops scrubbing and looks up.

'What?' she says. 'When?'

'Just now.' I start to unload the pears. 'In the theatre. I saw it.'

'Not on the table,' she says. 'Put the basket in the corner for now.'

Focaria no longer needs to tell me anything twice. I put the pears back into the basket and heft it into the corner. 'She's going to have a baby.'

'Who says?' For once, Focaria looks surprised.

'You could tell.' I hold my hands out in front of my belly, as if I have always understood how the world works.

'Huh.' Focaria stands erect and stretches with her hands in the small of her back. 'That's . . . funny.' She picks up the brush again and starts rasping it against the table. 'That's why I need you to go back out again.'

Now it's my turn to look confused. Focaria says, 'One of the wolves is pregnant.' She almost smiles at my reaction. 'Thalia,' she adds, before I can ask.

'How?' I say, stupidly. I know how.

For once Focaria doesn't roll her eyes or lose her temper. She just presses down harder on the brush. 'I need you to go back to the theatre,' she says over the rasp of the bristles, 'and bring Opitria here. Tell her to bring her kit.'

'Opitria?' Now I'm really confused. Why is Focaria scrubbing the table? Why does she want me to bring the fortune teller here?

'What do I tell her?' I ask.

'Just tell her she's needed at the tavern. She'll know why.' Focaria stops scrubbing and looks at me. 'Now,' she says, and I dash into the garden. At the door, I hear her shouting after me from the kitchen.

'Bring the kit!' she says. 'Don't forget!'

It's unusual for me to be on the street this late in the morning, and it's even more unusual for me to be on the street without the basket. I'm still rattled by the sight of Tacita disappearing for ever, and yet I'm enjoying slipping so easily through the crowd on the pavement, almost like one of the boys from the corner. Not only that, I'm excited in spite of myself, because something unusual is happening, something out of the ordinary routine. I bolt up the alleyway that leads to the theatre, dash between the drooping palms in the garden before any of the boys lurking there can even notice me, and burst into the crowded market. I take the steps two at a time up to the highest row of stalls and slip along the aisle until I'm standing breathless in front of Opitria, just as a customer is taking leave of her. On either side, Musa is pushing at the beads of his abacus while a man across from him chews his lip, and Quartus is furiously writing as an old man mumbles across the table at him.

Opitria's customer brushes by me, and I step up to the table. The fortune teller is scooping his coins into her palm.

'Focaria . . . tavern . . . bring your kit,' I gasp.

Opitria levels her gaunt, kohl-rimmed gaze at me. At the sound of my voice, Quartus looks up.

'Take a breath, Pusus,' Opitria says, slipping the coins out of sight.

'Focaria says,' I gulp, 'Focaria says . . . fetch Opitria . . . bring her back.'

She cocks an eyebrow. 'And bring my kit.'

'Yes!' I say. 'Don't forget, she said.'

Opitria says nothing, but turns to the bookcase behind her, pulls out a leather wallet, and sets it on the table. It's like the wallet that holds Melpomene's make-up implements, but it's longer and bulkier and bound with a strap. Quartus stands up and comes round to the front of Opitria's stall. The old man who was dictating a letter looks up, wondering where he's gone.

'Is one of them . . . ?' Quartus says in a low voice. 'Is it . . . ?'

As I look up at him, confused, Opitria leans over the partition between her stall and the banker's and catches the eye of Deodatus, who sits in the shade at the back.

'Watch my stall,' she says. Deodatus glances at Musa, who, without pausing from his clicking abacus, gives a brisk nod. Deodatus nods to Opitria.

'Who is it?' Quartus is grasping my shoulder, but before I can say anything, Opitria picks up the wallet, pushes him aside, and pushes me ahead of her down the aisle. Quartus snatches at me, and she wheels on him, an old, birdlike woman who only comes up to his shoulder. Quartus recoils. Behind him the old man is peering out of the scribe's stall at all three of us, his mouth agape.

'Which one is it?' Opitria says to me in a low voice. 'Who's going to have a baby?'

'Thalia,' I say, surprised. How does she know?

Standing in the sun outside his stall, Quartus rocks back on his heels as if someone has struck him. Behind him the old man instinctively lifts his hand to steady him.

'Come.' Opitria steers me along the aisle and down the steps. She hangs on to me all the way out of the theatre and through the garden. By time we reach the street, Quartus is right behind us, blundering through the crowd, manhandling people out of his way, leaving little eddies of outrage in his wake. Opitria ignores him, guiding me steadily up the pavement with her claw on my shoulder. He doesn't catch up to us until I'm pushing the garden door open. He dances on his toes in the street, sputtering.

'Who's the . . . ?' he says. 'Does she know who . . . ?'

Opitria pushes me inside, then puts her hand firmly on Quartus's chest, keeping him from following us.

'Of course she doesn't,' she says calmly. 'Don't be an ass.' She gives him a surprisingly forceful shove. 'Go home.' Then she pushes the door closed and, standing on tiptoe, slides the bolt across. Quartus shouts something from the other side, and he starts to pound on the door. But Opitria only takes my shoulder again and says, 'Where?'

'In here,' says Focaria from the kitchen doorway.

The kitchen is humid with steam. Focaria has a pot of water on the boil. To my surprise, all four of the wolves are in here with her. Thalia is sitting on the edge of the table in her loosened gown, with her legs hanging down. She's wide-eyed and breathing hard. On one side of her, Urania is squeezing one of her hands, and on the other, Euterpe is stroking her shoulder. Melpomene stands back, watching keenly from the far corner where I sleep. She's the only wolf who registers the arrival of Opitria, her eyes widening avidly. Focaria and Opitria exchange a nod, and Focaria takes me aside.

'The purse,' she says, holding out her hand. I've been carrying it round my neck all morning, so I lift it off and hand it to Focaria. She plucks a few coins out and gives them to Opitria, who slips them inside her dress. Then she hands Focaria the wallet, and Focaria lays it on the kitchen counter and unties its strap. Outside, Quartus is pounding on the garden door and shouting Thalia's name, but only I seem to notice. Opitria steps up to the table, where Thalia is kicking her legs nervously. From the way her gown is hanging, I can't tell if she has a little belly, like Tacita did. Opitria puts her hands on the girl's knees to still them, then she curls her bony fingers behind Thalia's neck and pulls her head down to murmur in her ear. Urania and Euterpe exchange a glance over her head. Thalia swallows and nods at whatever Opitria is saying to her, then she lies back on the table with her legs dangling off the edge. Melpomene steps up and lays her hands on Thalia's shoulders, and Euterpe gives her a look. But Melpomene glares back at her, and Euterpe looks away.

Outside, Quartus is silenced in mid-shout. There's a thump and a grunt, and I can hear Audo growling at him. Meanwhile, Opitria is at the counter, where the wallet lies open to reveal several thin metal implements. They look like the make-up tools upstairs, but longer and sharper. Some are straight, some are bent, some have hooks on the end. She plucks out three of them and hands them to Focaria, who grasps them in a pair of tongs, turns to the stove, and dips them into the pot of boiling water.

'Does he need to be here?' Opitria says to Euterpe, who is standing by the side of the table, still stroking Thalia's arm. She lifts her chin at me. 'Do you want him to see this?'

Euterpe notices me for the first time. 'Little One,' she says, and tries to smile, but before she can say anything else, Urania has knelt in front of me.

'Mouse,' she says, her eyes wide, her breath smelling of olives. 'I need you to do something for me.'

I nod. My eyes stray to the table, where Thalia is breathing hard, but Urania grabs my hand.

'I want you to take this.' She pulls something out of her gown. 'Go up to the old temple behind the market.' She presses it into my hand, something small and heavy and metal, warmed by her skin. It's the little brass god I've seen in her cell, the one with its face rubbed away.

'Do you know the one I mean?' She catches my gaze. 'The little round temple, on the hill behind the theatre.'

I nod again. Behind her, Focaria uses the tongs to pluck the implements out of the boiling water. Opitria is tearing a piece of cloth into wide strips.

'Set him on the altar there,' says Urania, pressing my fingers

206

around the little god, 'and say a prayer for Thalia. Ask the god to keep her safe. Do you understand?'

I nod. My throat is tight.

'How high can you count, Little One?' Euterpe says from the table.

'A hundred?' I say.

'While you're praying,' she says, 'count to one hundred, slowly, then do it again. Do it ten times.'

'That way the god knows you're serious.' Urania rises and looks down at me. 'Bring him back when you're done, all right?'

I nod. As the boiled implements cool on a cloth, Opitria moves round to the end of the table to stand between Thalia's knees. Focaria moves to the other end of the table, near her head, and she lays her hand along Thalia's jaw.

'Open your mouth,' she says, and when Thalia does, Focaria gently places a thick strip of leather between her teeth. 'Bite down,' she says. Euterpe tightens her grip on Thalia's arm. Melpomene shifts her hands on her shoulders. Urania turns me round and pushes me out the door.

'Run,' she says.

In the garden I hesitate, wondering whether to hide and watch what's going on. They wouldn't know if I went to the temple or not. They're just trying to get rid of me. But the little god is surprisingly heavy in my fist, and I start to worry what will happen to Thalia if I don't go the temple and do as Urania said. I can't unlock the garden door on my own, so I leave through the tavern, pushing the shutter closed after me and dashing past the dangling tintinnabulum round the corner. Quartus is sitting with his back to the garden door, his knees up and his head in his hands, so I streak past him on the other side of the street.

When I reach the theatre again, I slip through the crowd below the stage and out the doorway on the other side. I tuck the little god inside my belt and start to climb the rough, rocky hill along the outer wall. It's so steep I have to scramble on my hands and knees, while small stones and little rivulets of dirt hiss downhill behind me. Near the top I pause to catch my breath. Below me is the half shell of the theatre, the lower rows barnacled with market stalls, the well humming with people like a beehive. Beyond that, I can see the roof and the garden of the tavern. I wonder where Tacita is right now. I wonder what's happening to Thalia.

Then I climb the rest of the way up the hill. I go slowly, wary of the boys who sometimes spend their days up here, but this morning they must be somewhere else. I stare up at the little temple as I climb. The four pillars in front are still erect, but the peaked pediment above them is cracked right down the middle. When I reach the front step I stop, because the little portico behind the pillars is strewn with cats of all sizes and hues, sprawled among the rubble that litters the floor. Some are flattened against the stones, some rest chins on paws and stare heavy-lidded at nothing. Only one cat takes notice of me, a huge, hairy, orange beast with one eye who stares at me from her throne on the largest piece of rubble. I almost turn back, but remembering Thalia, I pull the little god out of my belt, clutch it tightly, and tiptoe through the cats until I pass into the temple, the orange goddess watching me every step of the way.

Inside, the temple smells of dry rot and ash and urine. A shaft of sunlight twinkling with dust falls through an irregular hole in the roof, and in the middle of the gritty floor are the remains of a fire, a heap of ashy sticks in a splash of blackened stone. The painted walls have all been defaced with slogans I can't read, daubed in red. In some places the plaster has been torn right off, baring the roughly mortared bricks behind it. Bits of coloured plaster crunch under my shoes. The statue of Asclepius has been toppled and broken in two, revealing that he isn't a proper statue, but only a hollow one, plaster over a wooden frame. His staff, wound with a serpent, is broken in many pieces, and the god's severed hand lies with its fingers curled around nothing, like a punter miming masturbation. Only his head is solid marble, and it's been propped back on the pedestal against what remains of his feet. His nose is gone, his ears are broken off, and his eyes have been chiselled out.

And yet all along the edge of the pedestal in front of his sightless gaze are the remains of offerings: figurines of brass or wood, bundles of desiccated flowers, plates of withered and blackened fruit, crusts of bread as hard as rock. Melted candles, a couple of burnt-out lamps, an empty cup turned on its side. There are stains of what look like dried blood. Across the front of the pedestal the chi-rho symbol has been daubed in red, but unlike the angry words on the wall, it's been painted with care and a sense of proportion, symmetrically filling the front of the pedestal, obscuring the letters cut into the stone. It's the same as the symbol on Thalia's medallion, the same symbol Renatus stamps on each loaf of bread, and I remember why I'm here. I place Urania's little brass god onto the pedestal, leaning him upright against the cheek of the old god's severed head.

I don't know what prayer to say. I don't know any prayers at all. Do I ask the god to look after Thalia? Should I pray for Tacita, too, or can you only pray for one person at a time? And which god am I praying to? The little brass god with no face? The ruined stone head? The Christian god I can't see, whose symbol is the brightest thing in the temple? Or all three at once? Not knowing what else to do, I step back from the pedestal and start to count, as Euterpe told me to. 'One, two, three . . .' The numbers catch in my throat. I wish I had something to drink, but I swallow against a dry throat and keep going. 'Four, five, six, seven . . .' My voice reverberates off the walls, so I lower it to a whisper. '*Eight, nine, ten . . .*'

When I reach one hundred, I stop and listen. I can't hear any sounds from the city below. The cats outside are silent, and there's not even any wind. I start counting again and the only sound is me, whispering numbers that bounce off the walls and are swallowed by silence. The temple is the quietest place I've ever been, even quieter than the upstairs of the tavern when the wolves are at the baths. I'm alone up there every day now, so it doesn't spook me the way it did the day after Clio was cut. But standing in this empty, echoing, malodorous temple, acutely aware of the open doorway at my back, I think of that first morning, when I wondered if someone was up there with me, behind the curtain of the empty cell. Is there anyone here with me now? I reach one hundred again and stop, and the temple is so silent and still it's as if I was never counting at all. I start again, just moving my lips. I stare hard at the faceless little figurine. I strain to hear any telltale sound, I breathe deeply for any scent that might give something away.

But the higher I count, the more bored and distracted I become. My skin prickles. My ears ring with the silence. My gaze drifts over the defaced and weather-stained walls, the fragments of plaster and stone on the floor, the forlorn little offerings on the pedestal, the beaten head of a beaten god with sightless eyes. I look up at the hole in the ceiling where the sun is streaming through, hoping to see a sparrow or the flash of a swift. But there are no birds, not even a wisp of cloud, just fathomless blue sky. All I smell is the stink of decay.

There's no one here. This place is empty, and it has been for a long time. If there ever was a god here, he's gone now, and the new one, whoever he is, isn't here either. The temple is a dried, empty husk. There's no one here but me, stupidly counting to myself.

I stop. I shift my weight, I scratch myself, I yawn. I'm not expected back until I've counted to one hundred, ten times, but nobody's here to make sure I do it. Nobody needs me to fetch anything or clean anything. For one blessed moment, nobody cares what I do. I scrape the grit away from a patch of floor with my foot, then I sit facing the door with my back against the red chi-rho on the pedestal and my feet stretched out in front of me. From the doorway the orange cat watches me with her one eye. She's the closest thing to a god here at the moment, and without thinking, I snatch up a stone and fling it at her. I'm good, but she's better, gone before the stone reaches the doorway. Instead it taps through the shadow of the porch and lands silently in the sunlit dirt beyond the steps. I laugh, and as my laughter is absorbed in the silence, I tilt my head back against the stone of the pedestal, fold my hands in my lap, and close my eyes. Wherever Tacita is, whatever Opitria is doing to Thalia, nothing I do or say or think in here will make any difference.

I wake with a start. At first I'm alarmed, because I don't know where I am. Then I remember, and I notice the patch of sunlight on the floor has moved. How long have I been asleep? How much trouble am I in? Focaria's fuming, Audo's balling his fists. I scramble up from the floor and brush the grit off the back of my tunic, and I run out the door onto the porch. The glare of the sun stops me short. I hold my hand over my eyes and squint down the hill into the theatre and across the town. Nothing has changed. People still mill like ants in the theatre, the inland lagoon still shines like beaten tin. To my left, a tiny ship under sail drags the V of its wake across the harbour like a blade cutting a piece of silk. The sun hasn't moved very far, but I know I need to go back now.

Halfway down the hill I remember Urania's little brass god, so I run back up and burst breathlessly into the temple again. The slap of my feet rings round the empty room and dies. The head of the sightless god frowns at me, as if he weren't expecting me back so soon. I snatch the brass figurine off the pedestal, stick him in my belt, and dash back out through the porch. The orange cat bares her teeth and hisses at me. I skid down the hill in a little cascade of dust and rolling stones, and I slip through the crowd in the well of theatre. Here I pause to catch my breath, and I see Opitria standing in front of her stall, her hand on the arm of Quartus, who is staring off into space. Even at this distance, I can see his eyes gleaming with tears.

Why is he crying? Has something happened to Thalia? I bolt from the theatre, bouncing off people who shout angrily after me. Then I'm through the garden and ricocheting up the street. With my hand inside my belt, I'm furiously rubbing Urania's brass god and counting as fast as I can, hoping it's not too little, too late. Have I failed her? What have I done? Did she die while I was taking a nap?

I bang against the garden door, but it's unlocked, and I leave it open behind me as I plough through the herbs in the garden and into the kitchen. It's empty. Not even Focaria is here. The fire is glowing in the oven, but there's no longer any water on the boil, and the table is bare and freshly scrubbed. The room smells like blood, a smell I remember from the night Clio was cut. I run back through the garden and into the tavern, still rubbing the god, still counting frantically under my breath. The tavern's empty, too, and I count all the steps up to the top and stop short at the end of the hall. All the curtains but one are pulled open. The wolves are all at the baths. Breathing hard, I tiptoe up the hall. Melpomene's cell is empty, and so is Urania's across the hall, and so is Euterpe's next door. And so, alarmingly, is Thalia's. I fumble the god out of my belt and rub it between both hands. I whisper numbers to it. I pray for the first time in my life, that Thalia isn't dead or sold.

'Pusus.' Focaria's voice cuts through the silence, from the empty cell at the end of the hall, the one across from Clio's old room. It's the only cell with its curtain drawn. I lift the edge of the curtain. Focaria is sitting next to the bed on the little stool from the make-up table, and she's spooning broth from a bowl into the mouth of Thalia, who is propped up at the head of the bed with a sheet pulled all the way up to her chin. Neither of them looks at me, but Focaria says, 'Come in.'

I slip through the curtain without opening it. The cell is dim and close, and it smells strongly of the broth Focaria is feeding Thalia. It also smells of blood, more so than the kitchen did. Still not looking at me, Focaria puts the spoon in the broth, sets the bowl on the floor, and lifts a cup of wine to Thalia's lips. Thalia takes a couple of sips and swallows hard, then tilts her head back against the wall. Her eyes are sunken and her face is drawn, but she's alive. She turns her eyes to me and smiles weakly.

'What have you got there, Little Brother?' she whispers.

I look at Focaria, but she's setting the wine cup on the floor and picking up the bowl again. I hold out the little god.

'Urania,' I say in a trembling voice. 'She sent me to the temple with this . . . the temple on the top of the hill . . . the temple behind the theatre . . .'

'Bring it to me,' Thalia whispers.

I hesitate, but Thalia nods, so I tiptoe around Focaria to the head of the bed. The smell of blood is almost reassuring. I hold the figurine out to Thalia, and she slowly pulls one arm out from under her sheet and takes it, clutching it to her chest like a doll.

'I thought you were a Christian,' Focaria says, dipping the spoon in the broth.

'What can it hurt?' says Thalia. She opens her mouth for the spoon.

Focaria widens her eyes at the girl, and Thalia slurps the broth.

'You sure he won't mind?' says Focaria.

Thalia swallows and says, 'Not today.'

'Who?' I say. 'Audo?'

Focaria rolls her eyes, and Thalia smiles weakly at me.

'God,' she says.

Focaria lifts another spoonful of broth, but Thalia shakes her head.

'Where's the baby?' I say.

Focaria looks at Thalia, and the wolf tips her head back against the wall and closes her eyes. I look around the room. There's no one else here.

'Is it dead?' I say.

'Opitria took it,' Focaria says, setting the bowl aside.

'Where?'

'To the market.' She lifts the wine cup and takes a sip herself. 'To be sold.'

I know she's lying. I was just in the market, and I didn't see a baby. Still, I say, 'Like me.'

'Yes,' Focaria says. 'Like you.' She hands me the cup, and I take a sip of the wine. Audo only lets me drink the watered stuff, and this is undiluted. I make a face as I hand the cup back to Focaria.

'Is he on a ship?' I say. 'The baby?'

Thalia sighs, and Focaria says, 'Yes, Pusus. We'll never see him again.'

'It was a boy?'

Thalia gasps and shifts under her covers. 'It hurts,' she says.

Focaria lays her hand on the girl's forehead. I start to say something, but Focaria gives me a look.

'Can you sleep?' she says to Thalia.

Thalia nods her head and settles further down in the bed. 'I'll try.'

'Let me change the cloth before I go,' Focaria says, and she hands me the bowl of broth and the wine cup. 'Take these to the kitchen.' I hesitate, and she glares at me.

As I turn to go, Thalia says, 'He's better off, Mouse.' She has turned to me on her pillow. I look at Focaria before I speak. She ignores me. 'The baby?' I say.

'He's better off where he is,' Thalia says. 'He'll never suffer.'

I lift the curtain.

'Thank you, Mouse,' she says.

I look back one more time before I let the curtain fall.

'For this,' she says, stroking the head of the little faceless god.

* * *

214

No, reader, Thalia did not die. She has by now, of course, as I write this many years later, but she didn't die when I knew her, though I doubt she lived nearly as long as I have. Audo gave her a week to recover, and she spent it in the cell at the end of the hall, with the curtain drawn. When she wasn't sleeping, she sang to herself in the language of her homeland, in the tongue of the Egyptians. I didn't know what the words meant, but I could tell that the songs were sad, and yet they seemed to make her happy. Euterpe regularly stepped across the hall to see her, and even Melpomene dropped in from time to time. Urania spent as much time in the cell as she could get away with, during the day. Behind the curtain I could hear the two girls whispering and even laughing together, and whenever I brought Thalia a bowl of stew or a cup of wine, I found them in the bed together. Urania sat with her back to the wall and both arms around her friend, while Thalia clutched the little brass god in one hand and her chi-rho medallion in the other. Sometimes Urania whispered a joke at my expense and they'd both laugh. But I didn't mind, and I'd hand the cup to Thalia, who reclined in her friend's arms and drank while Urania stroked her hair and kissed her forehead.

At night, however, Urania was too busy to spend time with her friend, since the other three wolves had to work that much harder to make up for Thalia's absence. When punters asked for her, Audo said she was having her monthlies. By the rules of the tavern, the punters knew not to walk into a cell where the curtain was drawn. Except for Quartus, of course, who knew why Thalia was unavailable and still came every night. Three nights in a row, he paid and came upstairs, where he was intercepted each time by one or more of the other wolves.

'Just let me see her,' he said on the third night, as Euterpe put herself in his path.

'She's having her monthlies,' Urania said, pulling on him from the other side.

'I know that's not true,' he said, trying to pull free.

'What's going on?' came a man's voice from Urania's cell, her punter wondering where she'd got to.

'Thalia!' Quartus hissed, knowing not to raise his voice and draw the attention of Audo. 'I'm here!'

By now Melpomene had abandoned her punter as well to tug at Quartus, who struggled feebly between three naked women. 'Thalia!' he whimpered, until I came up behind him and yanked sharply on his tunic.

'Audo can hear you,' I told him, and he stopped struggling and stepped back. He stood on tiptoe and craned his neck to project his voice.

'Thalia!' he hissed as loud as he dared. 'I love you!'

After that he still came to the tavern every night, but he stayed downstairs and sat in a corner by himself, nursing a cup of wine and glowering at everyone who went upstairs.

Calidus wasn't any happier than Quartus. The tavern was down to three working wolves, and revenue was down by another quarter – down by forty per cent all told, if you counted the lack of Clio. He showed up every day and even a couple of times at night, wanting to know why Thalia wasn't working yet. One morning, I hear Calidus and Audo having words in the empty tavern, the young Dominus's agitated, high-pitched voice spilling into the garden. I stand with the brimming bucket and the scrubbing brush just outside the arch, and Focaria says, 'Go fetch the laundry instead.' But then she recedes into the kitchen, and I stand and listen anyway.

'She drinks the atocium, right?'

'Every week, Your Honour.'

'Then how did this happen?'

'Your Honour.'

'What does she put in it, in the atocium . . . what's her name, Focaria . . . ?'

'Whatever's necessary, Your Honour.'

'Focaria!' Suddenly Calidus is striding through the arch into the garden, and I freeze, clutching the brush. But he doesn't even notice me, and neither does Audo, who lumbers in his wake. Focaria reappears in the kitchen door, holding a knife. I leave the brush floating in the bucket and fill the watering can instead, dribbling water up and down the herbs and vegetables, listening.

'What do you put in it?' Dominus demands. 'The atocium.'

'Rue, Dominus. Dill.' Focaria lowers her eyes, but hangs onto the knife. 'An egg, to make it go down.'

'And that works?'

'Most of the time, Your Honour,' says Audo.

More voices spill out of the tavern, and a moment later, all the wolves except Thalia sail into the garden, wearing their mantles for their trip to the baths. They stop and fall silent when they see Calidus pacing up and down before the kitchen door. Even I stop pretending to water the garden, and we all watch him as he runs his hands over his glossy hair and blows out an impatient sigh like a horse. Audo silently gestures the wolves toward the garden door, but Calidus wheels on them. Now even Audo freezes.

'You girls know not to come with the punters, right?' Calidus says.

It's not clear if the young Dominus actually expects them to answer, and none of the wolves speak.

'You can't conceive if you don't come!' he shouts. 'Am I the only one who understands that?'

Urania lowers her eyes to the dirt. Euterpe exchanges a look with Focaria, who is wearing the blank mask she assumes in front of her masters. Melpomene presses her hands together and glances at Audo as if for permission to speak. Audo smoulders, balling his fists and saying nothing.

'Twenty-five per cent!' cries Dominus, throwing his glance all around the garden, taking us all in. 'Twenty! Five! Per cent! That's how much revenue is down, until, until . . .' He waves his hand toward the second floor.

'Thalia,' says Melpomene.

'Thalia!' shouts Calidus. 'Until *Thalia*, God damn the careless bitch, can go back to work. And yet I'm still paying the same amount to feed you all!' He glares at each of them in turn – Focaria, Audo, Melpomene, Euterpe, Urania – until he comes to me. I stand as still as a hare amid the plants, clutching the sloshing watering can in both hands.

'Even him!' He throws his hand in my direction. 'And what the fuck does he do?'

'Your Honour.' Melpomene approaches him, smiling brightly. Audo stirs, but he doesn't stop her. Calidus looks her up and down.

'What?' he says.

'Your Honour,' she says, dropping her voice, 'if I may . . .' To the astonishment of everyone in the garden, she places her hands familiarly on the young master's arm. To our further astonishment, Calidus lets her do it. Murmuring to him, Melpomene steers him toward the arch, while Audo edges after them. We can't hear what she's saying, but from the shadow of the archway, she turns and gestures into the garden, toward me. Calidus and Audo turn to look at me. Euterpe appears at my side.

'Get your basket, Little One,' she says in a low voice. 'Go fetch the bread.'

'I already got the bread,' I say.

'Get the basket and go.' Euterpe takes the watering can. 'Do it now.'

I've never seen her look so stern. She grips my shoulder and shoves me toward the kitchen door. '*Now.*'

But before I can move, Melpomene has walked away from Calidus and Audo. She's smiling.

'Ladies,' she says, clapping her hands as if shepherding geese. 'Let's go.'

'Pusus.' Audo beckons me from the archway. 'Come here.'

'No,' says Euterpe, stepping in front of me.

'Come, Euterpe.' Melpomene holds out her hand. 'We'll be late.'

'No,' says Euterpe, louder.

'Pusus!' barks Audo. 'Now!'

I start toward the archway, and Euterpe grabs me. But Melpomene steps between us and pries us apart. With one hand she holds Euterpe back, and with the other she pushes me toward the tavern.

'Go on,' she says, smiling down at me. 'It will be all right.'

As I cross the garden, I hear the two women hissing at each other. From the archway, Calidus narrows his eyes at me as if he's never seen me before. Audo holds his hand out and twitches his fat fingers at me.

'Focaria!' cries Euterpe. 'Say something!'

In the final moment of my innocence, I look back. Euterpe is being manhandled through the garden door by Melpomene, while Urania hovers behind them, still staring at the dirt. Focaria stands in the kitchen doorway with the knife hanging from her hand, her mask as blank and impenetrable as I've ever seen it. Audo takes me by the shoulder and pushes me ahead of him, and she steps back into the kitchen.

In the shadowy tavern, Audo jerks me to a stop.

'Have you had a shit this morning?' he says.

I look at Calidus, who is hovering near the shutters.

'Don't look at him.' Audo flicks the back of my head with his finger. 'He doesn't know.'

'Dominus?' I say, looking up at Audo.

'Have you or haven't you?' he says again.

'Yes, Audo.'

'Good.' Audo pushes me ahead of him, toward the stairs.

'Wait,' says Calidus.

Audo grips my shoulder again. Calidus unlatches one of the shutters and opens it halfway, brightening the inside of the tavern. He beckons me, and Audo gives me a shove from behind. The young

Dominus takes me lightly by the shoulder and stands me in the light. He casts his gaze up and down my body and turns me around in place. He lifts my arms and pinches my flesh. He pushes his fingers back through my hair. He brushes my cheeks with the backs of his knuckles. Then he squats in front of me and grips my jaw. I flinch, but he only grasps me tighter. He turns my face from side to side, then tilts my head back and squeezes my mouth open to peer at my teeth.

Please don't sell me. I almost say it out loud, but then I remember how little it mattered to these two men when Clio said it. My heart is pounding. My mouth is dry.

When Calidus lets go of me I lift my hand to rub my sore jaw, and he pushes my hand away. Now he grips my arm with both hands and squeezes my muscles, from shoulder to wrist, then he does the same with my other arm.

'He's strong,' he says, looking up at Audo.

'Your Honour,' says Audo.

Calidus does the same with each of my legs, reaching under my tunic and squeezing my muscles from the top of my thigh to my ankle. I know not to flinch. Then he pushes himself to his feet with a grunt, and he puts his hand on top of my head and tilts my face up to his. He looks into my eyes.

'Melpomene's not wrong.' He looks at Audo. 'I can see it.'

'Please,' I say. It just pops out of me.

Both men look at me, surprised.

'Please don't sell me,' I say.

Calidus laughs, and even Audo laughs, rumbling liquidly in his chest. Calidus squeezes the top of my head.

'Nobody's going to sell you,' he says. 'You're going to make me a lot of money.'

Almost affectionately, he gives me a little push toward Audo, who lifts his eyes to Calidus.

'Unless you'd rather, Your Honour . . .' He gestures at me.

Calidus catches his breath, considers it, then says, 'No, you do it.' He turns and steps into the sunlight, pulling the shutter after him.

'Have fun,' he calls from the street.

Audo is already marching me up the stairs. As I climb he stumps behind me, breathing hard, his fingers splayed against my back as if propping me up. At the top, he takes my shoulder again and pauses to catch his breath. Now that I'm doing the work he used to do, he doesn't climb the stairs as often as he used to. He's gotten used to sitting behind the counter and drinking all night. Then he pushes me along the hallway, past the empty cells and their open curtains. Only the curtain at the end, where Thalia is resting, is drawn, and I glance at it as Audo directs me into the empty cell across the hall, where Clio used to live. I stand in the middle of the cell, not sure what to do with my hands. Audo comes in after me. Out of habit, perhaps, he yanks the curtain shut. He looms over me, breathing heavily, and he tugs at the collar of my tunic.

'Take it off,' he says.

I pull the tunic over my head, and he balls it up and tosses it in the corner. Then, with a massive sigh, he sinks heavily back onto the bed. The straw rustles, the cot creaks under his weight. He gestures in a little circle.

'Turn round.'

So I do, shaking and dry-mouthed, my hands over my crotch. I'm aware of Thalia across the hall, silent, listening. Even after months of hearing what goes on in the cells, of watching punters and wolves in the act, I still have no idea what he wants. That's how stupid I still was. Downstairs I thought they were getting ready to sell me, and now I think he's going to beat me for something I've done but can't remember. He doesn't want anyone to see for some reason, and he wants me naked so that I'll feel each blow. Then it occurs to me that he's going to kill me, and he only made me take my tunic off because he wants to use it again for the next

Pusus and doesn't want my blood all over it. I glance at the curtain, hanging still in the breathless heat of the cell. What if I run? I could be down the stairs and into the street before Audo has levered himself up off the cot. But then I'd be alone in the street, a naked boy with nowhere to go. I stare hard at the curtain, trying to see through it and then through the curtain across the hall. What if I called out to Thalia? But what can she do? He'd only kill her, too.

'Get on your knees,' Audo says. He's sprawled across the bed, his shoulders and the back of his head against the wall, his knees splayed, his massive belly rising and falling. I hesitate. The room is hot, but I'm shuddering as if it were cold. I remember Euterpe, holding me close in the garden, telling me that if Audo tries to hurt me, I should come to her, and we'd run. 'Hurt me how?' I'd said, and she'd said, 'You'll know when it happens.' It's happening now, and Euterpe is nowhere to be found, streets away, at the baths.

'Kneel,' says Audo, more sharply.

I kneel before him, shaking all over, still cupping my penis and balls. Audo pulls back his own tunic. Under the wattles of his sagging belly, I can see his crumpled testicles and his limp, pale penis like the head of an ancient turtle, poking out of a tangle of grey hairs. Slowly it's dawning on me what he wants me to do. I've seen the wolves doing it, I've heard Melpomene moaning as she's doing it, as if she were eating a sweet bun. I look up at Audo's face. This is something wolves do, I want to say. I didn't think boys did it, too.

But Audo has his eyes closed. He has reached between his legs and he's tugging at his penis. As it stiffens and purples, he pulls his foreskin back, and I see a ring of yellowish crust round the tip, just below the slit in its head. With his other hand, he grabs the back of my head and pulls my face down between his legs. He's breathing hard, but I'm scarcely breathing at all. I put my hands on his knees and push back. All I can see is blurry, wrinkled, mottled flesh. The smell is overpowering, like a ripe cheese, plus sweat, plus urine, plus the sour vapour from his backside. I can't help myself: it makes me gag, and I begin to cry. He's going to smother me between his legs, I think. This is how I'm going to die.

Suddenly he lets go of me, and I sit back on my haunches, gasping. Audo's eyes are open now, and he's glowering at me.

'Thalia,' he says, lifting his voice to the girl across the hall. 'Doesn't this little cunt-licker know what to do?'

Thalia says nothing. Perhaps she's asleep.

'Thalia!' shouts Audo. A moment later, her voice, thin and uncertain, floats across the hall, through the two curtains.

'I don't know,' she says.

'Is he an idiot?'

Another pause, then, 'I don't know.'

'Whatever I did, Dominus, I'm sorry.' My eyes and nose are dripping and I wipe them with the back of my hand, desperate to stop. I know that showing weakness only makes it worse. 'I won't do it again.'

'Shut up,' he says. 'Help me up.'

I scramble to my feet, still keenly aware of my nakedness in front of him in that little room. I take his fat hands and haul at him, leaning all the way back on my heels until he's upright. He sways before me for a moment, breathing hard, his eyes dulled. Then, with martial quickness, Audo grabs me round the waist and throws me face down on the cot. When I try to get up, he puts his knee in my back, bearing down on me with all his weight, and in spite of myself, I cry out in pain.

'You'd better not be lying about taking a shit.' He twists my arm up between my shoulder blades. 'I don't want to meet your dinner coming the other way.'

Reader, this is my initiation to the art of love. It feels as if Audo is doing to me what Focaria does when she's boning fish, that he's ripping me open all along my spine, snapping my ribs off one at a time. I sob and scream, but he only presses my face into the stale pillow, and now I can't see, I can't breathe. I burn from the rim of my anus to deep inside me. He is tearing me up. He is murdering me. I am the man bleeding to death beyond the garden door. I am Clio, slashed in the face in this very room. I am the man who cut her, screaming from his broken arm.

Then Audo splits me in two, and I soar away from myself like a bird to perch in the window over the bed. Below me I see a boy pinned under a gross, sweating, red-faced man. The boy has my thin, twitching limbs and my ragged hair, but I can't see his face, only the back of his head being pressed into the pillow by the man's hand, with its blue tattoo of an eagle. In an eruption of wings I burst from the window into the open air, and I hang over the garden. Now I see the overlapping tiles of the roof, I see the top of Focaria's head as she plucks herbs from the garden, I see a slave dipping a bucket at the fountain in the street. I smell the smoke rising from the kitchen chimney and the sour, salty breeze off the harbour, but I can still hear what's happening in the cell below me, I can still hear the quick, rhythmic chuffing of the man and the slap of his belly against the boy's back. So I rise even higher, until all I can hear is the flapping of my wings in the air and all I can feel is the fluttering of my heart, and I hang halfway between the impeccable blue dome of the sky and the red rooftops of the town, laid out below like a map of itself. And there, for the first time, in the beating silence of the air, during an endless moment that lasts for ever and no time at all, I finally become my secret name, my true name. I become Sparrow.

Then Audo groans and sags sideways against the wall, and Sparrow plummets with terrifying speed back down toward the street and into the garden and through the window until he is inside me once more, seeing through my eyes, feeling my pain. I tumble off the cot, gasping for breath, and I scramble into the corner and curl into a trembling, weeping, snotty ball. My anus burns, and the insides of my thighs are damp with bright red blood. I am afraid to look at Audo, so I keep my eyes closed, still enough of a child, even at that moment, to think that if I can't see him, he can't see me. But I hear him panting on the cot, and I crack my eyes to see him wipe the blood off his flaccid penis and then wipe his hand on the mattress. Then he tugs his tunic down again and pushes himself with a grunt up off the cot. I watch him through my tears as he yanks the curtain back.

'One of you needs to teach him what to do,' he rumbles. Then the floorboards creak as he lumbers down the hall. When I hear him descending the stairs, one groaning step at a time, I pull my tunic out of the corner with trembling hands and clutch it to my chest as I huddle against the wall, choking on my own snot. I hear the creak of a floorboard, and I start, violently. But it's only Thalia, standing in the doorway. She's not as gaunt as she was earlier in the week, but she still looks thin and tired. She turns away, but she comes back a moment later with a sloshing washbasin and one of the wolves' menstrual napkins.

'Come,' she says, and carefully, as if she's handling a frightened animal, she tugs my tunic out of my grasp, stands me on my shaking legs, and bathes me over the washbasin, turning the water pink. I flinch from her touch, and I whimper with pain when she washes between my legs. Then she wraps the napkin under and around me, lowers my tunic over my shoulders, and leads me into the cell across the hall, where she has been recovering. There we lie together on the cot, and she cradles me in her arms, stroking my hair and kissing my forehead. 'There, there, Little Brother,' she says. 'There, there.'

She presses my face to her shoulder and rests her chin on the top of my head.

'The first time's the worst,' she whispers. 'But you get used to it.'

* * *

225

In the kitchen, before I can say a word, Focaria holds me at arm's length and just peers into my face. I've stopped crying by now, but she can see the streaks of my tears, she can see my red-rimmed eyes, she can see how stiffly I walk. I want to tell her what has just happened, but I don't have the words. She starts to say something, thinks better of it, starts again.

'It's all just . . . work,' she says at last. 'Everything they make us do, it's just work.'

She watches me, as if waiting for me to say something. But I can't. My throat is too tight to speak. Instead, she puts the wicker basket on me and hangs the purse around my neck.

'Laundry,' she says.

In the street I stumble through the ordinary, daily traffic, but everything around me has changed. The light is harsher, as if I had been seeing only a dim reflection of the world before and now I see it face to face, unveiled. The voices of the women at the fountain are louder, the rumbling crunch of wagon wheels is more grating. The glances of passing men and boys are sharper, as if they know and they're laughing at me. I want to close my eyes, but I can't, so I narrow them against the glare of this brighter, crueller world. My anus burns, my shoulder aches from Audo twisting my arm behind me. The woman's napkin I'm wearing chafes between my legs and feels warm and damp behind, as though I've shat myself. I am raw all over, my skin feels flayed. Everything is painful, as if the tinsmith is tapping on my eardrums, as if the carpenter is sawing off one of my limbs. In spite of the harsh light, I am the brightest thing in the street. I burn like a brand in pitch darkness.

At the fuller's shop, I'm the only customer, and yet Nazarius doesn't see me for a moment. He's staring out the door into the street, absently stroking his beard. Shaking and burning, I stand on the other side of the counter, still unable to speak. Since I saw him with Euterpe, he is neither hearty nor brusque with me, only matter-of-fact. It's almost as if we don't know each other anymore. Then he sees me and beckons me forward without a word, reaching over the counter to turn me round by my shoulder. The instant he touches me, I stiffen and become Sparrow again, floating above myself. No one is singing today, and I hear only the rhythmic slosh of the men in the tubs and the slap of wet laundry being beaten and wrung out. From above I see the women working round the rinsing tub, the sun shining through the skylight and making the droplets sparkle. I wonder what would happen if I plunged into the water. Would they slap me, too, and wring me out? Would I be clean then? Will I ever be clean again?

'Mouse.'

I start, and become myself. Nazarius has come round the counter and is squatting before me. The basket is no longer on my back, but resting, still full of laundry, against the counter. Nazarius is gripping me lightly by the shoulders.

'You're bleeding,' he says.

I make a gulping sob and start to cry. Nazarius turns me round, lifts the hem of my tunic, and sees the bloody napkin.

'Ah,' he says. He glances into the street, then says, 'Come round.' He guides me behind the counter with one hand, lifting the basket with the other. He sets the basket to one side, then stands me in the corner and reaches under my tunic to take off the sodden napkin, which he tosses into the basket. Then he pulls another one from the stack of the tavern's clean laundry and lifts my tunic to wrap it round me. I can smell Nazarius's breath and his sweat, and I stand stiffly as he turns me this way and that. Sparrow hovers at my shoulder the whole time, ready to fly in an instant, but Nazarius, despite his rough hands, is gentle.

'Now sit.' He bends my stiff legs and lowers me into the corner. He lifts the basket and steps into the back. I stare up at the low ceiling of his shop, at the cubbyholes of folded laundry along the wall and under the counter. The unseen traffic in the street is both

227

strange and distinct, like the sounds I used to hear beyond the wall when I never left the garden. Through the noise I clearly hear the schoolmaster dully declaiming and his students parroting back to him in ragged unison.

"'Oh, child of heartbreak!'" sing-songs the schoolmaster.

"'Oh, child of heartbreak,'" mumble the students.

"'If only you could burst the stern decrees of fate!'"

The students repeat it as if the words have no meaning.

Nazarius returns with the empty basket and a cup of wine. He presses my fingers around the cup.

'Drink,' he says, and when I hesitate, he gently tips it against my lips. 'Drink it all,' he says. 'It'll steady you.'

As I force the undiluted wine down my tightened throat, Nazarius stands and starts loading the tavern's clean laundry into the basket. He works his lips silently for a moment. Without looking at me, he says, 'I was a slave, too, once. When I was your age.' He pushes the last folded sheet into the basket, and he squats down next to me.

'I'm going to reach inside your tunic to get the money.' He holds his hands up to show he means no harm. 'That's all I'm going to do.' I nod. He lifts out the little purse and rests it against my chest as he picks out a few coins, then he tightens the drawstring, pulls back the collar of my tunic with a finger, and drops the purse back inside.

'All right?' he says. I nod again. He touches the cup trembling in my hands.

'Finish it,' he says.

I drain the cup and hand it to him, then he stands and pulls me to my feet. He turns me round and slips my arms through the straps of the basket. The weight of the clean laundry tugs me back on my heels, and Nazarius steadies me with his hands lightly on my shoulders. I can hear him breathing behind me. He guides me round the counter, and we stand together in the doorway of his shop, his hand still on my shoulder. Through the traffic passing in the street, we both gaze across the way at his son among the other bored students, his head nodding, his mouth agape. Nazarius squeezes my shoulder, and I want to tear myself away before he speaks, before he tells me one more time about his son, the scholar, the future aedile. But instead Nazarius says, 'He'll never know what we know.'

I look up at the fuller, but he's staring across the street. I'm not even sure he's speaking to me. Lutatius and the other boys are the strangest creatures I have ever seen, more alien to me now than any of the monsters from Euterpe's stories. They may look like me, but they are nothing like me. They are enviable and contemptible all at once. If I ever felt any kinship with them at all, it's gone for ever, because we stand on the opposite sides of an unbridgeable abyss.

'Can you make it back on your own?' Nazarius looks down at me. My anus still burns, but the wine has dulled the pain and made me light-headed as well. I nod. Nazarius lifts his hand from my shoulder.

'Goodbye, Mouse,' he says, and I walk stiff-legged away from his shop, my shoulders hunched under the basket. I can feel his eyes following me until I disappear in the crowd.

At the tavern, the wolves have just returned from the baths. In the absence of Audo, they are lingering in the garden, enjoying a moment in the sun before they have to go upstairs. As I come through the door, all three turn. Euterpe gasps with relief at the sight of me, with the basket full of clean gowns and sheets on my back. Melpomene studies my face. I look away from her and shrug off the basket. Urania takes the laundry from me and carries it inside. When I try to brush past Euterpe to go into the kitchen, she catches me and kneels in the dirt. As she searches my face, her relief dissolves before my eyes. She can't speak for a moment.

'Did he hurt you?' she says at last in a low voice.

What am I supposed to say? It doesn't matter if he hurt me or not. Euterpe embraces me, folding me in her warm, post-bath smell, but I am rigid in her arms.

'We can run,' she whispers, her lips damp against my ear.

That's what you said before, I want to say, *but it's too late now.* She pulls back and looks at me.

'We can run,' she says again, but I know she doesn't mean it. And she knows I know it.

'Nobody's going to run.' Melpomene is standing over us. 'Don't talk nonsense.'

Euterpe looks up, digging her fingers painfully into my shoulders.

'You did this to him,' she says.

'It's for the best,' Melpomene says.

'How dare you!' Euterpe pushes herself to her feet, putting all her weight on my shoulders, nearly driving me to my knees.

Melpomene holds her hands up, but she doesn't step back.

'He'll be one of us,' she says. 'They'll never sell him now.'

'They sold Clio,' Euterpe says, trying to control her voice.

'Well, Clio.' Melpomene makes a face. 'He'll be something special, won't you, Antiochus?' She purses her lips at me, then meets Euterpe's furious gaze again. 'None of the other taverns in town have anything like him. Not anymore.'

Euterpe's breath hisses through her nostrils. Her shoulders are set like Audo's the moment before he swings at someone.

'She's right.' Focaria has come into the garden.

Euterpe holds her finger up. 'Don't.'

'It was always going to happen.' Focaria steps closer.

'He has a lot to learn, of course,' Melpomene says.

'Who's going to teach him?' Euterpe pushes her face close to Melpomene's. 'You?'

'Unless you want to,' Melpomene says.

Euterpe recoils as if Melpomene has slapped her. Focaria comes a step closer.

'You're his teacher,' says Melpomene. 'Aren't you?'

Euterpe is unable to speak. Melpomene touches her on the shoulder, and Euterpe jerks back.

'You can't ask me . . .' she says. 'I can't . . .'

'You don't have to,' murmurs Melpomene. As if calming a frightened animal, she rests her hand on Euterpe's shoulder. This time Euterpe submits, her shoulders slumping.

Focaria takes her by the other arm, but she says nothing.

'You'll always be first in his heart,' Melpomene says. 'That will never change.'

I look up at Euterpe, and I can tell she's not seeing Melpomene or Focaria or even the garden. She has been driven all the way inside herself. Whatever she's seeing is something that happened to her a long time ago, that none of the rest of us can see.

'He needs to know how to protect himself.' Melpomene's voice is low and soothing. 'I can teach him that.'

'If the two of you run, you're dead,' says Focaria, caressing her lover's arm. 'If you stay, he has a chance.'

Euterpe lets out a long, shuddering breath, like someone letting go of something on her deathbed.

'Don't do it here,' she says, without looking at me. 'Take him somewhere else. You can do that.'

'I can.' Melpomene exchanges a look with Focaria. She strokes Euterpe's arm. 'I will.'

Focaria turns Euterpe toward the kitchen, the cook's arm around the waist of the wolf, as if Focaria is holding her upright. Euterpe reaches back for me, but I shy away. Melpomene sees me do it, and she smiles.

'Antiochus,' she says. 'We're going to be such good friends.'

Late in the afternoon, she comes for me. The tavern is already open, and I'm keeping to the outer wall and corners, as far away from Audo as I can get. I collect empties from the light crowd of early drinkers, my back to the counter, my eyes on the floor. I am no longer wearing a napkin, but I still feel pain and damp behind. Audo doesn't speak, but I feel his gaze pressing on me. It's as if all his weight were still on top of me, splitting me open.

'Antiochus.' Melpomene's voice dims the buzz of conversation. It's rare to see a wolf downstairs when the tavern is open, and there she is, sailing through in the mantle she wears to the baths. Every man sits up straighter, every eye follows her. But she's looking only at me, and she stops in the archway to the garden, smiling, her hand extended to me. My first thought is to pretend I haven't heard her, but now every man in the room is looking at me. I'm standing near one of the doors to the street, pinching three empty cups between the fingers of each hand. The last of the day's heat radiates from the pavement behind me. What if I just dropped the cups and ran? How far would I get? Where would I go? What would they do to me after they caught me? How could it be worse than what Audo's already done?

But it's too late for that. Melpomene widens her smile and beckons me. One man winks at me, another swats my backside, making me wince. All the men laugh, including Audo.

'Atta boy,' says one.

'Go get her,' says another.

'Lads.' Melpomene's gaze sweeps the room. She comes to me, grips my shoulder, and marches me into the garden. She steers me into the kitchen, where Focaria is sweating over the stove, frying sausages.

'I'm taking Antiochus out for a while.' Melpomene takes the empty cups from me and sets them on the table. 'Audo needs you to help out inside.'

'Does he,' says Focaria, without turning round from the sizzling pan. 'Who's going to do the cooking, then?'

'Don't worry,' Melpomene says. 'It's all going to work out.'

'Says who?' Focaria turns from the stove, a pair of tongs in one

232

hand and a spatula in the other. 'Are they going to get me another kitchen boy?'

'Things will get better, Focaria, you'll see.' Melpomene gives the cook her brightest smile. 'Do you have a carrot?'

'You'll eat when you're fed.' Focaria turns back to the stove.

'No one's going to eat it,' says Melpomene. 'I'll bring it back.'

Without looking at her, Focaria points the tongs at the counter, at a leafy heap of vegetables she hasn't chopped up yet. Melpomene picks through the carrots, holding up one after another before selecting a fat, yellow one and slipping it inside her mantle. Then she grips me by the shoulder again.

'Come, Antiochus.' She pushes me ahead of her, across the garden, through the door, and into the street.

The sun has descended behind the mountain across the harbour. The city is already in shadow, but the sky is still bright above us. A seagull hangs far overhead, the black undersides of its wings like two eyebrows against the deepening blue. The shops are all shuttered, and only a few people are abroad, hurrying to get to wherever they're going before dark. We meet Brutus, without his cart and mule, striding in the other direction, on his way to the tavern. He pauses and watches us pass, clearly wondering what Melpomene and I are doing on the street at dusk, walking away from where we work. I have never been outside the tavern this late, and I'm afraid. I have heard what can happen on the street at night, and Melpomene has marched me out of the garden before I had time to tuck a few stones into the belt of my tunic. I look up at her, but her face is serene, as if she's taking an afternoon stroll. Doesn't she know that people die out here at night? We pass the trickling fountain and the shuttered shops of Priscianus and the butcher and the carpenter, where shavings lie curled in the street and I can still smell cut wood. Melpomene directs me up the alley toward the old theatre, and for a moment I resist. She tightens her grip and pushes me ahead of her into the dusky garden. It's full of the liquid whirring of insects and the rattling of palm trees in the evening breeze off the harbour. I can hear the whisper of boys, and I instinctively reach for the stones that aren't there in my belt. I look up at Melpomene again, and in the dusk, her eyes are sharp like a cat's on the hunt. A boy steps out from behind a palm tree, directly in our path, and suddenly she's holding a slim, elegant knife – not threateningly, but loosely, casually, rolling the ivory handle between her fingers. She lifts a corner of her lips, and the boy disappears behind the tree again.

Then we're in the market, which is not quite empty. Some of the merchants sleep here in their stalls, and we can see them moving about, throwing canvas over their wares, cooking dinner over braziers, chatting with each other. Sitting on the very top step of the theatre, above them all, is Opitria. Her knees are spread like a man's, and she's eating her bread and cheese out of the lap of her dress. She's the only one in the theatre who sees us, and she watches, chewing slowly, as Melpomene steers me along the foot of the stage and out of the theatre through the other side.

We climb the hill beside the theatre. I scramble on my hands and feet again, but Melpomene remains upright, taking long strides, her eyes fixed on the top of the hill. I think she's taking me to the temple, but near the top, we can see the glow of a fire through the portico and hear the sound of boys laughing inside. I freeze again. She takes me by the shoulder for a moment while she catches her breath, then without speaking, she pushes me past the temple, higher up the hill.

The breeze off the harbour is cooler and stronger up here, pressing Melpomene's mantle between her legs. She grips her skirts tightly in one hand and tugs them to the side, making it easier for her to climb, while keeping her other hand on my shoulder. At last we enter a little thicket of bushes with stiff, leathery leaves, and at the centre of it, carved into a knob of reddish rock, is a bench. She steers me to the bench and sits me down. The gritty stone is still warm from the heat of the day. She sits down beside me.

'Oof,' she sighs, panting from the climb.

I have never seen a landscape painting at this stage of my life, just the pictures of wolves coupling with punters in the tavern, the signs outside shops, and obscene drawings etched on walls, but in retrospect, the view from the bench was like a painting, the town and harbour at twilight, framed by the sharp silhouettes of leaves – the darkening horizon pulled tight between the two massive hills at the harbour mouth, the grid of streets below us filling with gloom and twinkling points of lamplight. A few more lights shine among the boats along the quay, but the water in the harbour and the lagoon beyond is dark. The hills to the north and east are still tinted gold, their folds filling with shadow. More lights shine on the far side of the lake and against the black bulk of the mountain across the harbour, where people live in villas. Above the sharp silhouette of the mountain, the sky is still the pinkish grey of a fish's belly, but overhead, a few stars are already pricking out of the deepening blue.

'I used to bring punters up here,' says Melpomene, 'back when I was living under the arches.'

I look up at her. I don't know what to say to her. I've never spent this much time alone with her before. I don't know why we're here. But I have a question, one that's been bubbling up in my chest since this morning, since Audo expected me to suck his cock, since he threw me on the bed and fucked me.

'Am I a woman now?' I say.

If I asked Euterpe, she'd embrace me and tell me a story, which might or might not answer my question. Focaria would roll her eyes and slap the back of my head and make me wish I'd never asked. Tacita, wherever she is now, wouldn't be able to tell me. I wouldn't even ask Audo. But Melpomene surprises me by thinking about it for a moment.

235

'Before I answer that,' she says, laying her warm hand on my thigh, 'I'm going to do something for you first.'

She slides her hand up under my tunic. Instantly my penis stiffens, and I inhale sharply. No one's ever touched me like this before.

'Whatever you are,' she says, 'you're going to be a wolf.' With a grand rustle of linen, Melpomene stands and shrugs off her mantle. She folds it in half and lays it on the ground, then, her bracelets and the beads of her necklace clicking softly, she kneels on the mantle and parts my knees, sliding both her hands higher up my narrow thighs under my tunic.

'But you're going to have an advantage over the rest of us.' She peers at me out of the dusk. 'The rest of us know how to please a man, but you're going to know what it actually feels like. I'll never know that, and neither will any of the other wolves.'

She slides her hands all the way up and grasps my buttocks, pulling me forward to the edge of the bench. I gasp – it still burns back there – but Melpomene only purses her lips at me.

'Don't be nervous,' she says, folding back the hem of my tunic. 'Maybe the answer to your question is, you're going to be a woman and a man, at the same time.' She smiles up at me. 'That makes you special.'

She takes my stiff little penis between the tips of her fingers, and I squirm.

'I'm not going to hurt you, Mouse,' she says. 'You're going to like it.'

I feel my face get hot as she turns my penis from side to side, peering at it in the dusk. She looks up at me again.

'Are you a Jew?' she says. 'Do you know?'

'I don't know.' My mouth is dry, my heart is beating fast.

'Hm.' Melpomene considers it. 'Well, you could be a Syrian, I suppose. Or even an Egyptian. They all clip their boys in that part of the world.' She sighs, still holding my penis between the tips of her fingers. 'It doesn't matter. The tip of your cock has been nicely trimmed back, but most of the ones you're going to see will have a little sheath over the tip, like this.' She curls her fingers loosely around the tip of my penis, and I gasp again.

'No one's ever done this for you before?' She looks at me. 'One of the boys in the street, maybe? Or a shopkeeper in the back of his shop?'

'No,' I whisper.

'Hm,' she says again, and she lowers her mouth and begins to suck my penis. The only sound is the smacking of her lips and tongue. She doesn't moan for me like she does with a punter. What she's doing feels good, better than when I stroke myself at night. But at the same time, I can still see Audo's blunt, purplish penis only inches from my face, I can still smell the unwashed reek of his groin. I can still feel his crushing weight, I can still feel his hand pressing my face into the smothering pillow, I can still feel the blunt pain of him inside me. The breeze off the harbour tightens the skin of my bare thighs, it rustles the leaves of the bushes. I want to close my eyes, but I'm afraid. I don't know where to look – at the darkening city below? At the merciless stars above? *Lucky boy*, says Nazarius, but I don't feel lucky. *Go get her*, says the man in the tavern, but I'm not getting her, she's getting me. I'm half naked and exposed to the sky, and Melpomene could do anything to me right now. She could hurt me worse than Audo did. She could bite it off. As I feel my own pleasure swelling unstoppably between my legs, I wonder what I look like, but Sparrow is nowhere to be found, and instead I sit with my knees spread and my hands gripping the edge of the seat, looking out of my own eyes at a woman's head bobbing up and down between my legs. I am confused and afraid and excited all at once. Between sunrise and sunset of the same day, I've endured the worst pain I've ever experienced in my life, and now, in almost the same place on my body, the silkiest pleasure I've ever felt. It doesn't make any sense.

Then I come, jerking my limbs and crying aloud at the irresistible, gushing heat. Melpomene lifts her mouth, my penis droops and chills, and she turns her face away and spits.

'I didn't expect that,' she says, clearing her throat. 'I thought you were too young.'

She flips my tunic back down over my knees, then pushes herself up. She picks the mantle up off the ground, slaps the dirt off it, and shrugs it back on. Then she sits next to me on the bench, puts her arm round my shoulders, and pulls me close, wrapping the mantle round both of us. I'm surrounded by her warmth and overpowered by the smell of her perfume. My limbs are weak, my head is spinning, my ears ring as if I were a coin someone has dropped on the floor. Moving up and down the street on my daily rounds, slipping up and down the hall in the tavern at night, I had thought I understood both worlds better than anybody else, that I saw things that no one else saw, that I knew what no one else knew, that I was above it all, like Sparrow. But I was wrong. Now, trembling in the soft warmth under Melpomene's mantle, I feel as confused and frightened as I did in my earliest memory, when I was a squalling child on the floor of the kitchen, watching giant adults fighting over my head. Starting with Audo roughly thrusting himself inside me and ending with my own involuntary spasm inside Melpomene's mouth, I am learning that the same impulse can result in both pain and pleasure, in humiliation and bliss – often, I will learn soon enough, at the same time.

'Listen to me, Antiochus,' Melpomene says. Her head is only inches above mine, but it feels as if she's speaking from a great height. 'What you felt just now, only a man can feel that.' She squeezes my shoulders. 'I want you to remember that, when you're doing it for a punter. All right?'

I say nothing, just move my head against her shoulder.

'Now I want you to listen carefully as I explain some things to you,' she says. 'Are you listening?'

238

I nod again. She smells different from Euterpe, somehow sweeter and less pleasant at the same time.

'I don't expect you to understand all of this tonight,' she says, 'but from now on, your job is to suck punters off, the way I just sucked you off, and to let them fuck you, the way Audo fucked you this morning.'

I cringe under her arm, and she kisses the top of my head and says, 'I know, but I'll show you ways to make it easier. All right?'

I say nothing, and she takes my face in her hands.

'But you must understand that there are rules,' Melpomene says. 'And the chief rule is that you must never fuck a punter, and you must never let a punter suck you off. Some of them will want you to, but you must learn how to refuse, even if it means taking a beating. Because the greatest shame a man can experience, Antiochus, is to be used like a woman. And if a man is shamed by his friends for being fucked, he will take his shame out on the boy he asked to fuck him. He might even kill you.'

At this, I find my voice at last. 'But they'll be using *me* as a woman,' I say. But I already know what she's going to say.

'Yes,' she says, 'they will.' She leans back and drapes her arm around me. 'You asked me if you were a woman now,' she continues, 'and you're not. But from now on you will be a cinaedus, which means you will be used like a woman. That means you will never be a man like other men.'

I know I ought to cry at this, but I don't think I can anymore. After all the violence and endless work of my life so far, this is no more than I deserve. Why did I ever think my life was my own? That my body belongs to me? My only purpose is to be used by others. It's what Focaria has explained to me, over and over again. It's what Audo teaches me every day with his fists. Has Euterpe really done me any favours by telling me different? Has she been lying to me all along, or is it worse than that? Is it possible she doesn't know her stories are false? At least the others – Focaria,

239

Audo, and now Melpomene – are telling me the truth, even if it isn't as beautiful as Euterpe's lies.

By now Melpomene has pulled out of her mantle the carrot she took from the kitchen. She holds it up in silhouette against the starry sky.

'Let's practise,' she says.

And so for a little while, with the carrot cold and rough in my mouth, she tutors me in fellation, showing me the places along its length where a man will feel pleasure most keenly, teaching me how to keep from biting it, how to breathe through my nose, how not to gag when a punter face-fucks me.

'Which most of them will,' she says, taking the carrot and snapping it in half. 'You're going to have to learn how to protect yourself.' She takes a bite out of one half and hands me the other.

'You didn't really think we were going to take it back, did you?' she says, and as we sit crunching the two halves of the carrot between us, Melpomene tells me her own story. As she talks, she idly twists the rings around her fingers, one at a time. She's a lot like me, she says. She doesn't know who her father was. She thinks she was born in a town called Gades, a long way from Carthago Nova, and she was raised by a wolf who may or may not have been her mother. The wolf brought them both to Carthago when she was younger than me, and, when she was not much older than I am now, the wolf taught her how to live under the arches of the aqueduct and sell herself on the street, just the way she's teaching me now. Then the wolf died, and Melpomene eventually sold herself to Dominus and went to work at the tavern, because no one lasts long under the arches.

'Then I worked my way up to freedom,' she says, 'by hard graft.'

The wolf who may or may not have been her mother taught Melpomene things she's never forgotten, things which have been useful to her, things which will be useful to me, too, if I truly listen to what she says and take them to heart. She tells me that the secret to being a wolf is not just knowing how to move or where to touch a punter, but knowing what he's really after and knowing how to give it to him.

'What a punter says he wants,' she says, 'and what he needs aren't always the same thing.' The wind is colder now, so she pulls me closer and wraps the mantle tighter around us. 'You have to learn how to satisfy both of them.'

Some men will come to you, she says, because they want a boy, but some will come just because you're available, and all they want is a warm, tight place to empty themselves into. They don't care who it is, and they don't care what you think or feel. They just want to relieve themselves inside you and then go away. They're the easiest ones, because they're quick and they're simple. Some of them, though, will think they want to know you, and they're trickier, because they want to believe that you're feeling what they're feeling. And even though that will never happen, you have to act as if you do. They're the ones you have to flatter and tease and reassure, they're the ones you have to pretend with. They're the ones who need you to feel weak with pleasure in order to make themselves feel strong.

'A wolf never comes with a punter, if she can avoid it.' Melpomene is speaking expansively now, as if to the air and not to me. 'Everyone says you can't get pregnant if you don't come, but I don't believe it. I've been pregnant six times, and I haven't come with a punter in years. But you won't have to worry about getting pregnant, of course.' She turns to me on the bench. 'Listen to me now, Antiochus.'

A punter wants to feel like a master, she tells me, especially if he's a slave. Poor men come to us for what rich men can take for free from their slaves, but slaves come to the tavern to use us the way their Dominus uses them. Some of them will want to hurt you, and they're the trickiest ones, because you have to let them do it, but only up to a point. This is the hardest thing to learn.

241

You have to make them think you're in worse pain than you really are, otherwise they'll keep going until they really do hurt you. And you have to learn how to stop them before they hurt you as much as that punter hurt Clio, but you have to learn how to stop them without hurting them in turn, because that can get you killed. These men aren't like the ordinary punters, she says, the ones who just come and go. With these men, it's not just that they don't care what you think, like your ordinary punter. It's that they actually want you to suffer.

'Like Nazarius?' I say. After his kindness to me early today, this feels like a betrayal, but I still remember him with Euterpe.

'Well, Nazarius . . .' She tightens her grip round my shoulder. 'Some of them are worse than Nazarius.'

And here's the thing, she tells me: just like you pretend to feel pleasure for the men who want you to feel pleasure, you have to pretend to feel pain for the men who want you to feel pain. And you have to make them believe it, because the one thing a man can't stand – any of them, it doesn't matter whether he wants to hurt you or please you – the one thing a man can't stand is to be lied to by a woman, even if she's a wolf. Especially if she's a wolf.

'Some of them think they're in on the joke,' she says. 'But they're not, Antiochus. They never, ever are.'

She leans back against the bench, which has grown cold in the dark, and she gazes up at the stars, which are dashed across the sky like white dust. Across the centre of the sky is a river of them that seems to flow and pulse, cutting the night in two.

'The only pleasure a wolf enjoys with a punter,' she says to the blazing sky, 'is knowing the joke.' She folds me in her mantle again, and together we look out across the darkened town.

'I know you love Euterpe,' she says, 'and I'm not going to come between you. But she thinks she's better than the rest of us, because she can read, because she knows things free women know.'

Melpomene smiles to herself. 'But she doesn't know what I know, Antiochus. The others, Thalia, Urania, they do the job all right, but they don't know what I know, either.'

She hugs me tightly under the mantle.

'None of them are going to live to be as old as I will. They're all going to end up like Clio, scarred and diseased, sucking cock under the aqueduct. They're all going to die as wolves. But I'm not. I've already bought my freedom, and I'm not going to die as a whore.'

She kisses the top of my head again.

'And if you listen to me, Antiochus, neither will you.'

And so the world closed in on me, and my horizon contracted once again within the walls of the garden and the tavern. But it didn't happen overnight. I continued to perform my old jobs as if I were watching myself moving through a dream. Maybe Audo would change his mind, I thought. Maybe if I were extra diligent and careful – not dropping anything, not spilling anything, not calling attention to myself – what he did to me upstairs would never happen again. And for several days, it didn't. I still carried food into the tavern, still circled the room collecting cups, still emptied the chamber pots of the other wolves. The men treated me with their usual mixture of indifference and casual abuse. But this lasted only as long as it took for Audo to spread the word about me to the punters. Now when a punter came up to the counter, Audo beckoned him to lean a little closer while he rumbled in his ear and lifted his chin in my direction. Just when I began to think that Audo had forgotten, that my life would go on as before, he began to beckon me, two or three times a night, and I'd cross the room, aware of the gaze of the waiting punter, furtive and avid all at once. I'd lower my eyes, take the man's rough hand, and lead him up the stairs, down the hall, and into Clio's old cell.

Afterward, if she wasn't with a punter herself, Melpomene would appear in the doorway, her gown wrapped loosely around her, smelling of sweat and scent.

'What did he do?' she'd say. 'Be specific.'

The first few times she asked me, I could barely speak. If I remembered what the man had done, it was only because Sparrow had been watching from above, and even then I scarcely had the words to describe it. Still, she coaxed it out of me as we sat together on the cot in the smoky light of the lamp. She'd tell me what I'd done wrong, and how to do it better next time. She told me how to move my hips, how to touch the man, what to say. When to tighten my muscles and bear down and when to let myself go slack. Sometimes, she said, you'll have two punters at once, and one of them only watches. 'It's because the man who's watching wants to fuck the other man, but he's afraid to ask,' Melpomene said. 'So he watches you getting fucked instead.'

She held up the little bottle of oil on the table. 'Whatever happens, never run out of this.' She told me when to look the punter in the eye and when not to. She told me how to lick my lips and look up at him. She told me never to kiss a punter unless he kissed me first.

'It makes them come faster,' she said, 'but you're not always going to be face to face with a punter.' She put her arm around me and made me look at her. 'They're not here for love. They come here so they can do to us what they can't do to the honourable women in the town. That's why the tavern is close to the docks. That's why the bishop doesn't shut us down. We're here to protect their wives and daughters.'

And sons? I almost asked, but I didn't.

'You'll learn.' Melpomene kissed me on the top of my head. 'You're a smart boy.'

* * *

244

Audo worked me both upstairs and down for a few more weeks. I still slept in the kitchen with Focaria, I still rose before cockcrow, I still fetched water in from the tank, still cleaned ash out of the oven, still swept the tavern – but now I did it wearing the bruises I'd earned the night before, still smelling the punters on my skin, still tasting them in my mouth. The day after Audo raped me, I had moved up and down the street thinking that I burned like a brand, that everyone could see what had happened to me. I wasn't entirely wrong – Nazarius had seen it. Now everyone else could see it, too, and the laughter of the men in the tavern followed me into the street. Where I used to move anonymously, just another slave boy on an errand, now the eyes of shopkeepers and slaves and housewives all tracked me. I tried to hide under the basket on my back, but I trailed a cloud of whispers in my wake. I transacted my business in the shops or the stalls in the theatre with averted eyes, to avoid meeting the gaze of a punter who'd had me the night before; whether the punter averted his eyes as well, or gave me a knowing smirk, depended on who he was and who might be watching. The boys at the corner who left me alone because of Audo and my skill with a stone now went back to puckering their lips at me, calling me names, howling like a wolf. The women at the fountain simply stopped speaking when I showed up with my buckets and yoke. After a few days I learned to wait until they were gone and use the fountain when there was no one else there. If Focaria wondered why I carried in the water later than I used to, she didn't say anything.

The only shop I was unafraid to visit anymore was the bakery. At least Renatus's contempt was familiar, and there was something oddly reassuring in the fact that he had known what was going to happen to me before I did. Unlike the other women along the street, Balbina continued to speak to me, though the look she gave me now was even more severe and pitying than ever before.

'It's not too late,' she'd murmur as she took the tavern's money.

But in the end it was the baker and his sister who exiled me permanently upstairs with the wolves.

Renatus and Balbina arrive at the tavern early one afternoon, in the company of the aedile. The magistrate is a different man than the one I saw on the docks a few years before, who was followed by a scribe and preceded by a brawny slave to clear the way. That man was plump and balding, and he wore a toga and a harried look of self-importance. This man, his successor, is thin and grey and reserved, with a wispy beard and hooded eyes. He seems a little lost in his toga, like a boy wrapped in a bed sheet. He's accompanied by only one civic slave, who walks a pace behind and to his master's left, bearing a sheaf of documents in a leather binder, a wax tablet, and a stylus stuck behind his ear. Renatus steps gingerly in their wake on the balls of his feet, as if tiptoeing through shit. Balbina glides behind him, her hands clasped before her, her chin lifted. The aedile and his slave walk straight into the tavern and right up to the counter, where Audo perches heavily on his stool. Renatus makes a wide berth around the tintinnabulum and hesitates in the doorway, coughing discreetly in his fist, while Balbina waits patiently behind him. I watch them all from a corner, where I'm sweeping up the shards of a bowl someone has dropped. Renatus stares straight ahead like a blinkered mule, trying not to see anything in the tavern – not the three early drinkers who have looked up from their wine, not the paintings on the wall, not me lurking in the corner. Balbina's gaze, however, finds me immediately, as if fixing me in place.

Audo places both his hands on the countertop. He lifts his eyebrows at the aedile, glances past him at the baker. 'Your Honour,' he rumbles.

'You're . . .' the aedile begins, and the slave leans forward and whispers in his ear. '. . . Audo. Is that right?'

Audo nods.

'I'm here on behalf of . . .' the aedile continues, in a dry voice. He looks to his right, but no one's there. 'Where is he?' he says, and the slave whispers again in his ear. The aedile turns to see Renatus balanced on the balls of his feet in the doorway, his nose twitching as if at a bad smell.

'What are you doing back there?' says the aedile. Renatus puffs out his narrow chest, tucks his elbows close to his sides, and minces up to the counter, next to the aedile. Balbina steps just inside the door, keeping her unreadable gaze fixed on me. The drinkers look her up and down, then look at Audo as if they expect him to do something. Respectable women never enter the tavern. It makes the punters uncomfortable.

'Right,' the aedile says to Renatus. Then, to Audo, 'You two are familiar with each other?'

Audo grunts. Renatus trembles like a hare – with fear or rage, I can't tell. Probably both.

'The baker here,' the aedile says, 'has registered a complaint. He says you are in violation of your employer's agreement with the city, by allowing one of your girls—'

'Not a girl,' mutters Renatus. '*That* one.' He won't look at me, but he knows where I am.

'Which one?' says the aedile. The slave looks back at Balbina, and she lifts her chin in my direction. The slave glances across the room at me, then whispers in the magistrate's ear. The aedile leans slightly forward to look past Renatus at me in the corner, with my broom and dustpan, one broken bowl sweeping up another. Renatus keeps his eyes fixed on a point just beyond the tip of his nose, but now everyone else in the tavern is looking at me – Balbina, the aedile and his slave, Audo, the wide-eyed early drinkers.

'Ah.' He turns to Audo. 'Renatus is threatening to file a court action against . . .' The slave whispers in his ear again. 'Against Granatus, the owner of this establishment. It's the baker's contention

247

that the owner has agreed not to let his prostitutes go abroad in the street except to the baths and back. He further contends you are in violation of this agreement by sending the, um, boy –' He waves his hand – 'out to do your marketing. Renatus contends that the boy in question is, in fact, a prostitute himself, and subject to the agreement.'

Audo drums his fingers on the countertop, rippling the eagle on the back of his hand. He levels his black gaze at the aedile.

'He's the kitchen boy,' he says.

'That's a lie!' Renatus is practically bouncing up and down.

'Brother,' says Balbina, taking a step further into the tavern.

The aedile touches the baker's wrist. 'I'll do the talking.'

'How do you know he's a wolf?' Audo shifts his gaze to Renatus. 'You never come in here.'

'One of my *slaves*.' Renatus is positively vibrating now. 'He's *soiled* himself with the boy.'

'Did you see it?' Audo says.

'This is outrageous!' Renatus is shouting now. The early drinkers watch slack-jawed in delight. '*Outrageous!*'

The aedile sighs, and Balbina comes all the way into the room and lays her hand on her brother's back. Renatus, red-faced, his veins standing out, checks himself. The baker and his sister are both brave, I'll give them that. It takes some courage to face off with Audo, even in the company of the aedile.

'You need to talk to Granatus, Your Honour,' says Audo. 'The owner.' He's drumming the fingers of both hands now. 'Or his son, Calidus.'

'I have,' says the aedile. 'Calidus tells me that the day-to-day management of this place is your responsibility.'

Audo grunts.

'He also tells me,' says the aedile, 'that he would prefer to avoid the time and expense of a lawsuit.'

Now all ten of Audo's fingers are drumming in unison.

'Which is why I'm here today, informally,' says the aedile, 'to see if we can't settle this to everyone's satisfaction, without going to court.'

'I won't send him to the bakery anymore,' says Audo.

'He needs to be off the street entirely,' says Balbina, from behind her brother.

Renatus makes a sound of disgust in his throat.

'There are *children* on the street,' Balbina says.

The aedile's slave looks at her, but the aedile keeps his eyes on Audo, who ignores her, too, and addresses the aedile.

'He's a child,' says Audo. 'What's the difference?'

'He is not a child!' cries Renatus. Balbina slides her hand up his back and grips his shoulder, as if to keep him from rising into the air.

'Yes, he is,' rumbles Audo. 'Look at him.'

'He's not if he's working as a prostitute,' says the aedile.

'Let's have this slave in here, then,' says Audo. 'The one who *soiled* himself. We'll see if I remember him.'

The aedile lifts an eyebrow at Renatus.

'I sold him,' says the baker. 'I won't have him in my shop any longer.'

'Well, then . . .' Audo sits back and crosses his arms.

'There are others,' says the aedile, 'who say they have had the boy.'

'Bring 'em in,' says Audo. 'It's their word against mine.'

'When you speak to my Dominus . . .' Now the aedile's slave speaks, in a surprisingly loud voice. '. . . you are speaking to the curia. Show some respect.'

Audo sighs and uncrosses his arms. 'Your Honour,' he says.

The aedile, his slave, and Renatus form a tight little triad, the three of them focused on Audo, who glowers back at them. The three early drinkers are sitting with their mouths agape. But Balbina, still gripping her brother's shoulder from behind, is watching me now, her lips pursed and her eyebrows drawn together.

'You have three choices,' the aedile is saying to Audo. 'Take him off the street and keep him upstairs, with the rest of the wolves. Or send him back to the kitchen and never let him work upstairs again . . .'

Renatus starts to protest, but Balbina, still looking at me, tightens her grip on his shoulder. Renatus checks himself, seething.

'Or,' continues the aedile, 'keep doing what you're doing, and Renatus will see you in court.'

The aedile and his slave stand very still. Audo sits on his stool and breathes deeply through his nose. The early drinkers wait breathlessly. Renatus, still red-faced, still vein-popping, trembles where he stands.

'There's a fourth choice.' Balbina releases her brother and steps back. 'I'd like to buy the boy.'

Renatus whirls on his sister, his eyes wide. He's speechless. The aedile and his slave turn more slowly, exchanging a glance. Even Audo looks surprised.

'Sister!' hisses Renatus. 'Be silent!'

'I will not.' Balbina clasps her hands and lifts her chin. 'I will buy the boy.'

'Hm,' says the aedile, and behind him Audo is starting to laugh, a nearly silent rumble deep in his chest.

'Go home!' shouts Renatus, stamping his foot. 'Go home this instant!' He raises his hand to his sister, but Balbina does not flinch.

'Whoever saves one soul,' she says, in a trembling voice, 'saves the whole world.' She dramatically points at me. 'Salvation, brother, means nothing if we cannot save *him*.'

Now every gaze in the room is directed at the boy standing still as a hare in the corner. For an instant, I see my life in the bakery as a slave of Renatus – rising early, eating little, working in silence, pounding dough till my hands ache, burning my fingers on hot loaves – and my heart sinks. Renatus would threaten me and harangue me, Balbina would fill my ears with Christian talk all day, the other slaves would resent and ignore me or worse. I would never see Euterpe again.

But I would not be fucked. I would be beaten and underfed and worked off my feet, I would breathe flour dust until my lungs were ruined, I would spend my life walking endlessly in a circle like the mule round the millstone, I would *never* see Euterpe again. But I would not be fucked. My heart pounds. Nobody's asking me, of course, and it's not up to me, but . . . what kind of choice is this?

'He's not for sale.' Audo is openly laughing now, his shoulders and chest shaking.

'Brother, please!' Balbina pleads with her eyes, but Renatus starts to cough. She touches his arm, but in an instant the coughing has bent him double, as Balbina pounds his back. The aedile and his slave take a step away from him.

'Do you have something to drink?' Balbina says, looking at Audo, still pounding her brother. Audo smiles and considers a joke – do I have something to *drink*? – then reaches under the counter and lifts a cup to one of the spigots over his head, not the expensive wine, but not the cheapest stuff either. He places the cup on the counter. Renatus, meanwhile, grips the edge of the counter with one hand and hangs onto Balbina with the other while he hacks and clears his throat. His back is to me, so I can't see his face, but I can hear him gasp, 'Never.' He looks at his sister, breathing hard. 'Never,' he says again.

Audo sits up straight on his stool, puts both hands on the countertop, and draws a deep breath.

'From now on,' he says, 'Pusus stays off the street.'

Renatus stands slowly erect, his chest heaving. Balbina lets her hand slip away from him. Renatus looks at Audo, who slides the cup closer to him. Then the baker looks at the aedile, who nods toward the cup.

'Brother, please—' Balbina starts to say, but the aedile's slave interrupts her, not unkindly.

'Domina,' he murmurs, 'it's not going to happen.'

Balbina dwindles in front of me, and my fate is decided. She gives me the briefest glance, then looks down at her feet, as if ashamed.

'Let's drink on it,' rumbles Audo.

'Let's all drink on it,' says the aedile, and Audo produces two more cups. He pours one for himself and one for the aedile. Renatus makes no move to take his cup, and Audo pushes it toward him with the tip of his finger.

'It's what you wanted,' says the aedile's slave.

The aedile and Audo take up their cups and salute each other. Still wheezing, his hand shaking, Renatus finally raises the cup and lifts it gingerly to his lips.

'He goes to the baths, though,' says Audo, his cup poised just below his chin. 'With the other wolves.'

The aedile pauses his cup and looks at Renatus, who has already taken a sip. The baker chokes on the wine and waves his finger vehemently in the air. Balbina opens her mouth to speak, but the aedile lays his hand on the baker's shoulder.

'That's fair,' the aedile says, and before Renatus can object, he drinks. Audo drinks, too, and the two men place their cups on the counter at the same time. Renatus, sputtering, puts his cup down, but before he can speak, the aedile has stepped back from the counter.

'Thank you, citizen,' he says to Audo, dipping his head, and he and his slave turn and sail out of the tavern, into the sunlit street, and out of sight. Renatus lifts his finger again, as if he has one more thing to say, but he's still choking a bit on the wine that went down the wrong way. Balbina tugs at his elbow, and Renatus stiffens.

'Brother,' she murmurs, 'it's over. Let's go.'

Audo watches the baker from his stool, and he puts his hands on the counter again. The baker's eyes widen at the flexing hands on the countertop, and he backs away. He stands, breathing heavily, Balbina hovering to the side, not quite touching him. Then he whirls and grabs her arm and marches her out of the tavern, nearly jerking her off her feet.

'God loves you, child!' she calls out as they disappear round the corner. 'I'm sorry!'

The early drinkers exhale and smile at each other over their cups.

Audo sighs heavily. Then he turns to me in the corner, where I'm still as a statue and just as numb. He lifts his chin at the three cups on the countertop.

'Clear these away,' he says.

'I'll have to buy another kitchen boy, Your Honour,' Audo says to Calidus, later that afternoon. They are talking in the garden, which is already cooling in the shadow of the mountain. Audo has temporarily shuttered the tavern so he and Calidus can confer. I am standing to one side, as if on display on the slaver's stage. Melpomene has joined them, and I can't tell if she was invited or came out on her own initiative. She is already made-up and scented for the evening, wearing the gown she works in, and the smell of her perfume nearly overwhelms the ordinary smells of the latrine and the garden and Focaria's kitchen. Focaria herself, wielding her spatula and her tongs, appears in the doorway for a moment before dipping back inside to attend to the food she's grilling.

'Well, that defeats the purpose, doesn't it?' says Calidus. He's pacing up and down.

'Your Honour?' says Audo.

'Of him working upstairs!' Calidus waves in my direction without looking at me. 'What's the point of him bringing in more money if I'm just going to turn around and buy another mouth to feed?'

'Your Honour.'

'We're right back where we started,' says Calidus, restlessly moving. Audo keeps his head lowered, watching from under his eyebrows. Melpomene follows Dominus with her steady gaze, her hands pressed together.

'Your Honour,' she says, 'if I may . . .'

Calidus waves his hand and keeps pacing.

'I'm only a woman,' she says, 'so of course I don't understand anything about money . . .'

Calidus grunts. Audo shoots her a look.

'But little Antiochus here,' she says, gesturing at me, 'offers the punters something that none of the other taverns in town do.' She smiles warmly as Calidus passes her. 'I think we could charge a little more for him.'

Calidus stops. 'Antiochus,' he says. 'Who calls him that? Is that his name?' He turns to me. 'Is that your name, Pusus?'

'It's my nickname for him, Your Honour.' Still smiling, Melpomene lays her hand on Calidus's arm. 'Because he's Syrian.'

'He's Syrian?' He looks at me. 'Are you Syrian?'

Behind him, Melpomene gives me an encouraging nod.

'Yes, Dominus,' I say.

'He's something special,' says Melpomene. 'I think if you added him to the pictures in the main room—'

'More money?' Calidus starts to pace again. 'You want me to pay for a painter, too?'

'Oh, Your Honour,' laughs Melpomene, 'what I don't understand about business, you could fill the harbour with. But I know from experience . . . after your father was kind enough to let me purchase my freedom . . .' She cants her head at him, and Calidus grunts. 'I know from experience that when I spent a little extra – of my own money, of course – on nicer clothes and nicer things for my cell, my traffic increased. I spent a little extra, but I made even more.'

Calidus, pacing, looks at Audo. 'Say something, you brute.'

'Your Honour,' grumbles Audo. 'Maybe she's right.'

'Hm,' says Calidus.

'But if we take him off the street,' adds Audo, 'we still need someone to do the work he's doing now.'

'Didn't Focaria used to do it?' says Calidus. 'Shopping and fetching the water?'

Focaria is peering out the kitchen doorway, looking as though she might attack Calidus with tongs and spatula. But before he can turn round and see her, she slips back into the darkness.

Calidus wheels on Audo. 'What do you do in the morning?'

For the first time in my experience, Audo is flustered.

'I . . . I . . . I . . .' he stammers.

'He escorts us to the baths, Your Honour,' says Melpomene, touching Audo lightly.

'That's right,' grunts Audo. 'The baths.'

'But I could take over that, if you like.' She tilts her head. 'So Audo could do the shopping and so on.'

Behind Calidus's back, Audo looks at Melpomene as if he wants to beat her to death where she stands. He's squeezing both his fists bloodless. She ignores him.

Calidus stops. Audo struggles to control the expression on his face. Melpomene beams at each of us in turn like a watchman's lantern.

Calidus rubs his hands together. 'That's settled then. Focaria and Audo will pick up the boy's work. Right?'

'Your Honour,' says Audo, deep in his throat. His face is coming out in red blotches.

'And you'll take yourself and the wolves to the baths, yes?' says Calidus.

'Your Honour.' Melpomene graciously dips her head. 'And if I may?' she adds. 'I think little Antiochus should come with us.'

'Wait a moment,' says Calidus. 'I thought we were trying to keep him off the street . . .'

'Of course, Your Honour!' Melpomene slips her hand through his arm. 'But it's understood that we —' She gestures grandly at herself – 'that we are allowed to be abroad for an hour or so every morning. By arrangement with your distinguished uncle, the bishop.

I don't see why the boy shouldn't come with us. Under the same dispensation.'

All three turn to look at me. Audo looks as though he wants to beat me to death along with Melpomene, but he says, 'The aedile agreed to it.'

'Taking him with us has the added advantage, Your Honour,' Melpomene continues, low and insinuating, 'of making his availability known to the *better* sort of punter.' Her fingers are stroking the inner arm of the young Dominus. 'Why waste his charms on fishermen and slaves? Especially, Your Honour, if you want to charge more for him . . .'

Calidus is clearly enjoying Melpomene's touch, but he's trying not to show it. 'I don't like the name,' he says.

'Your Honour?' says Melpomene.

'Antiochus is wrong,' he says. 'Antinous is better.'

'Your Honour?'

'I wouldn't expect you to know,' Calidus says. 'Antinous was the lover of the Divine Emperor Hadrian.'

'Of course!' Melpomene laughs with delight. 'What a splendid idea!'

'You see the difference?' Calidus puffs out his chest as Melpomene squeezes his arm with both hands. It's as if she's pumping up a bladder. 'Antiochus was a *king*, but Antinous was the king's *lover*. This way, the punter isn't thinking, I'm having the king, because, seriously, how likely is that? No, he's thinking, I *am* the king.'

Melpomene looks as though she might burst into tears. 'Oh, Your Honour, what a perfectly *splendid* idea! You're *so* clever!' She clings to him like a lover.

Calidus smiles indulgently and disengages himself from her. Audo all but rolls his eyes. The young Dominus looks me up and down.

'He can't look like that, though,' he says.

'No!' gasps Melpomene. 'Of course not!'

'He's too skinny,' says Calidus.

'Of course!' cries Melpomene.

'He needs to be . . .' Calidus spreads his hands, to indicate plumpness. 'Tell your cook to . . .'

'Your Honour,' mutters Audo.

'Oh, and he'll have to dress the part!' Melpomene presses her hand to her chest. 'He can't wear *that* . . .'

Calidus sighs like a beleaguered husband. 'All right. Get him a new tunic.'

'Two,' says Melpomene. 'He'll need a change of clothes while the other's at the laundry.'

'Fine,' says Calidus.

All this time, I stand trembling under their gaze. I feel the way I did when Audo stripped me naked.

'And do something with his hair,' says Calidus. 'And make him up.' He waves his hand at me. 'You know, his eyes, his lips . . .'

'Oh, *yes*!' Melpomene looks at Calidus as if she wants to kiss him. 'Asellina's shop has some lovely paints and ointments . . .'

'Fine. Whatever.' Calidus lifts his hand. 'But you pay for it.'

Melpomene blinks, then beams brightly at the young Dominus. 'Of *course*, Your Honour! I would be honoured . . .'

'Right then.' Calidus claps his hands together. He takes a step toward me and looks me slowly up and down. Behind him, Melpomene closes her eyes and sighs silently, then opens them again, appraising me. Audo, glowering, shifts his weight. From the corner of my eye, I can even see Focaria peering at me round the side of the kitchen doorway.

'Peace of God,' says Calidus, and then he's gone, through the garden door and away. Audo hovers for a moment over Melpomene, squeezing his fists, but she gives him a hard stare, as if to say, 'You wouldn't dare . . .' And he wouldn't, apparently. He turns away grumbling and disappears into the tavern. Focaria recedes into the smoky shadows of the kitchen. Melpomene approaches me slowly, looking grandly down her nose at me. I lower my eyes to the toes of her slippers.

'You're a lucky boy.' She grasps my chin and tilts my face up to hers. 'I hope you appreciate that.' She speaks softly to me, but I can hear the iron underneath it. 'You're going to sleep in a bed from now on. You're going to have your own room. You're going have a nice, soft tunic. You're going to come to the baths with us every day.'

My heart is beating fast. From now on, I'm going to be used by punters every night, but I won't have to work during the day. I won't have to sleep on the kitchen floor. I'm going to eat better, I'm going to sleep later, I'm going to be closer to Euterpe. I'm confused and afraid and hopeful all at once, but one thing I know for certain: I belong to Melpomene now.

I say nothing. She releases my chin and strokes the side of my face.

'You're going to be beautiful,' she whispers.

The following morning, Melpomene comes into my cell with two new tunics. She pulls off my old coarse tunic and slips one of the new ones over my head. It's bright red linen, and it's so light and smooth I scarcely know it's on at first. Unlike my old one, this one has no sleeves, the better to show off my arms. Melpomene kneels and fusses with it, nipping in the waist with a little belt, puffing up the chest a bit, tugging the hem down. Then she sits me on the bed and straps a new pair of shoes on my feet. Up until now, I've only worn second-hand shoes, purchased from a ragpicker's stall in the theatre, but this pair is new and finely tooled, with straps that twist up my ankles. Melpomene stands me up, turns me round, and leads me across the hall into the empty cell, and she covers a bruise around my throat from the night before with a smear of make-up that doesn't quite match my skin. Then we go down into the garden, where the other wolves are already waiting in their mantles. This will be my first Parade of the Wolves.

'Mouse!' says Thalia. 'Look at you!' Euterpe glares at her, and Thalia falls silent.

Melpomene lines us up and ushers us out of the garden, bringing up the rear and pulling the door shut behind her. I look back and hear Focaria bolt it after us, and I know my old life is now well and truly locked away from me. We five walk single file up the middle of the street, along the wide ridge between the cart ruts. On my first moment in public as a wolf, I imagine myself from above, the way Sparrow might see me, the brightest marcher in the parade. Ahead of me Thalia and Urania walk with their hoods up, while behind me Euterpe sinks deep into her mantle. Only Melpomene leaves her hood dangling down her back, leading with her hips, lowering her chin, pursing her mouth, casting provocative glances from side to side. In my new shoes, I can scarcely feel the pavement under my feet; it's as if I'm floating. My new tunic is loose in the chest, but clingy below the waist, and it swings a bit as I walk. Every eye on the street is drawn to me. The pressure of their collective gaze is like heat on my skin.

Traffic parts for us. The street doesn't fall silent, but conversations stutter as we pass. Priscianus lets his hooded eyes flicker from his customer to watch us pass. Nazarius, laughing with a housewife, pauses mid-joke to let his eyes glide up and down Melpomene, then broadens his smile and resumes his story. Brutus is loading boxes into his cart in front of a shop, and without breaking rhythm, his eyes shift from me to Euterpe. The butcher watches from his cloud of flies, the barber halts his razor under his customer's chin, the cobbler pauses mid-stitch, glances to make sure his wife isn't watching, then slowly swivels his head to follow us until we're out of sight.

Women, on the other hand, scowl at us or avert their eyes. Perpetua and Felicitas, the carpenter's daughters, one of whom is married and pregnant now, whisper with their heads together, tracking us in tandem. Afra, with her silent male slave in tow, marches past us with her chin lifted as if we don't exist. Lucilia and the girl who follows her everywhere scowl as we pass. Balbina,

259

her hands and hair and apron dusted with flour, watches us from the open archway of the bakery with the mule circling the millstone behind her. For a moment she looks as though she might say something to me, but then she turns away.

Only children watch us without embarrassment, unless their mothers hustle them inside. The boys drowsing under the schoolmaster's portico sit up straighter as we pass, nudging each other and pointing. The schoolmaster whacks the closest boy with his stick, and the others lower their heads and stifle their laughter. At the crossroads, the boys on the corner erupt in catcalls and jokes. One of them launches off the bench and falls in alongside, mimicking Melpomene's louche walk to the hilarity of his mates. Then he jogs past her and minces alongside me. I fix my eyes straight ahead, at the back of Urania's mantle.

'Hey, cocksucker,' the boy says.

My throat is so dry I couldn't talk even if I wanted to. The boy walks backwards next to me, puckering his lips. His mates hoot at him.

'I want to *kiss* you,' he says. 'You're so *pretty*.'

'Not as pretty as you.' Euterpe throws back her hood and steps between the boy and me, taking my shoulder. The boy dances off to the hooting of the others. Ahead of me, Thalia and Urania have turned left into a narrow lane, and Euterpe directs me into the shadows after them. I glance back to see Melpomene slipping her little knife back inside her mantle.

The sun doesn't shine into the crosstown lane that leads to the baths, and the sky is a slot of blue overhead. The lane isn't wide enough for a cart, and there are no shops, just the back ends of houses with high, barred windows and stout back doors, securely bolted. Weeds sprout between the paving stones, and the lane is dotted along its entire length with both fresh and dried dog turds. I step carefully, glad of my new shoes. Our footsteps reverberate off the walls, which are scrawled with graffiti I can't read as well as the usual crude drawings of giant phalluses and cavernous vaginas. Halfway along we pass a lone slave nodding in a doorway, stealing time from his Dominus. He lifts his hand at Thalia, then Urania, who both ignore him. He lets his eyes glide over me, then holds up a coin as Euterpe passes. She ignores him, too. Melpomene wags her finger as she brings up the rear.

'You know where to find us, lover,' she says.

At last the narrow lane empties into a wider street lined with busy shops and cook stalls. Beyond the carts and people crossing back and forth, the humpback dome of the baths rises against the rocky hill along the north side of the city. Thin columns of grey smoke from the boilers wisp away over the roof, overlaying the smell of the street – food, shit, people – with the rich aroma of burning wood. Like everything else in Carthago Nova, the baths have seen better days. The blue paint on the dome is stained and cracked, and patches of it have flaked away, revealing the dingy plaster underneath. The doorkeeper leans in the entrance, idly picking his teeth with his thumbnail. Up the street to the right, I can see a broad space open to the sky above. This is as close as I will ever get to the forum of Carthago Nova, where the curia meets and the provincial governor has his suite of offices. I glimpse brightly painted pillars and tall statues in the shadow of the colonnade.

Melpomene comes up from behind, steps into the traffic, and raises her hands to make way. A carter yanks his mule to a halt, and Melpomene waves us past. Men stop in their tracks and appraise us. Women pull up suddenly and shorten their gazes, or swerve around us without a word. Thalia skips across as if from stepping-stone to stepping-stone. Urania crosses with long strides, her chin lifted as if to keep her head above water. Euterpe follows, hood lowered, eyes on the pavement. Melpomene clutches my shoulder and drags me across in my vivid red tunic. In the middle of the street, she pulls me up short. I hear a voice I recognize.

'. . . anyway, that's what he said to me,' it says, and I look up to see Calidus in a bright white toga, leading a gaggle of younger men in tunics who eagerly hang on his every word.

'And what did you tell him?' says one of the young men, avidly.

'Not if I get in first,' says Calidus slyly, and the young men burst out laughing. The young Dominus's eyes glide over Melpomene and me as if we aren't even there. The gaggle follows him toward the forum, and Melpomene pinches the shoulder of my tunic and tugs me across the street and into the baths. The doorkeeper pauses from picking his teeth long enough to take a few coins from her and drop them through the slot into the cashbox. I follow Melpomene down a wide corridor into a dim, high-ceilinged changing room lined with niches for customers' clothes. A bony slave is slapping a mop between the wooden benches, and he pauses when Melpomene and I come in. His tunic is too big for him and belted tightly in the middle. A ring of keys jangles from the belt.

'Who's this?' the slave says, leaning on his mop.

'Antinous,' says Melpomene. 'He's new.'

'No, he's not,' says the slave. 'I've seen him on the street.'

'Well, he's Antinous now,' says Melpomene. 'Antinous, say hello to Simplex.'

But I'm staring at the floor, at the first mosaic I've ever seen, a dense pattern of black and white with deltas at the doorways where foot traffic has worn the tiles down to the concrete. The images are dulled by years of feet and dirt, but I can make out fish and octopuses and, at the centre of it, a huge figure with the head and shoulders of a man, the body of horse, and the tail of a fish.

'Is that real?' I say, and Simplex laughs.

'You bet, sonny,' he says in his rasping voice. 'There's one just like him in the pool.' He winks and laughs again, and Melpomene propels me through a low arch and into the next room, where a pool of cool water lies under a dripping dome. The water is perfectly still, but I move to the other side of Melpomene, in case Simplex is telling the truth about the monster in the mosaic.

'He's teasing you,' she says, hauling me through another arch. 'There's nothing in the water.'

We arrive in the caldarium, a hot, humid, and cavernous space lit by a shaft of sunlight that falls through a hole in the vault overhead and slants through the steam rising off the water below. Thalia has already dropped her mantle, kicked off her shoes, and stripped off her gown, and her sigh echoes round the vault as she eases herself into the water, sending ripples across the pool. Urania follows a moment later, sinking up to her chin in the water. Around the pool is a wide margin of red and yellow marble, cracked in places, slippery everywhere, and warm underfoot, even through my new shoes. Another slave is sweeping round the pool with a broom.

'Gracilis!' Melpomene waggles her fingers at him. 'This is Antinous. He'll be joining us from now on.'

Gracilis is fatter than Simplex, and his tunic bulges round his middle, making me wonder if the two slaves have put on each other's clothes in the dark by mistake. He stares at Thalia and Urania in the pool as he sweeps, and barely glances at me. Melpomene takes off her mantle and her gown, folds them, and leaves them carefully on a bench along the wall. She ties her hair up in a knot and descends grandly into the water.

'Little One.' Euterpe touches me from behind and leads me to a bench.

Meanwhile, Simplex has come in from the other room, and he and Gracilis aren't even pretending to work. They just stand and watch the wolves in the water.

Euterpe sits me on the bench and kneels to take off my shoes.

'Where's everybody else?' My voice ricochets round the room, so I whisper, 'Why are we the only ones here?'

'That's the arrangement.' Euterpe sits next to me to take off her own shoes. 'The aedile lets us come first thing in the morning, before

263

the baths are open to the public.' She stands and shrugs off her mantle, draping it over the bench. 'Women aren't allowed to bathe at the same time as men anymore, and wolves aren't allowed to bathe with decent women. So . . .' She strips off her gown and lays it on top of the mantle. 'Here we are.' She stands me up and lifts off my tunic, laying it next to her clothes, then she takes my hand and leads me to the pool. 'Come on, Little One. You'll like this.'

The floor is almost too hot under my bare feet, but even so, at the edge of the pool, I hesitate. I have never been immersed in water before, not once in my entire life. Along the docks, I have seen boys leaping from masts into the harbour, where they laugh and splash and push each other's heads under the water. Once one of them hit his head on the way down and drowned. A chain of men handed his body, slack-mouthed and limp, up onto the quay. I watched from the edge of the crowd as his father clutched him from behind and squeezed the water from his lungs, then pushed and pushed and pushed on his chest until Rufus, the chief fisherman, pulled him away.

'It's not very deep,' Euterpe says, as if she knows what I'm thinking, 'and the water is very warm.' She's standing in it up to her thighs, steam curling round her hips. She takes my hand and guides me in, and a moment later we're sitting together on a wide step under the water, up to our chins.

All these years later, I still remember that first flush of enervating, limb-loosening heat as I sank into the caldarium in Carthago Nova. It was the nicest feeling I'd ever experienced, and, though I didn't know it yet, it was probably the nicest feeling I ever would experience. All the baths in Britannia, where I live now, are dried-up and overgrown, but I can still conjure in my old flesh the sensation of half-sitting, half-floating in the water, hand-in-hand with Euterpe, the water sloshing over my lower lip and up my nose, the sweat trickling through my hair and down the sides of my face, the little tendrils of steam rising right before my eyes, the heat soaking all the way into my bones. I live in a library now, surrounded by the greatest works of literature in the world, but I'm here to tell you, reader, literature is not the foundation of civilization. The foundation of civilization is hot water. Civilization is plumbing.

Along the rim of the pool, Urania sits with just her nose above water, her eyes closed, her hair plastered to her head. Thalia ducks her head, then flings it back in a shower of droplets, pushing her fingers through her hair and blinking the water out of her eyes. Melpomene briskly rubs herself down with a sponge, reddening her skin. The splashing of the wolves echoes round the vault overhead, and Euterpe lifts her dripping hand to direct my gaze upward. Through the shaft of light falling through the steam, I can make out dim paintings on the vaulted ceiling. Between the cracks and patches in the plaster, I see naked men and women, as well as beasts and monsters, all of them huge. One is a man holding a bloody sword in one hand and the severed head of a woman in the other. The woman's eyes are closed and her mouth is slack, and her hair seems to be made of snakes.

'That's Perseus and Medusa,' murmurs Euterpe.

'Which one is the man?'

'Perseus. That's Medusa's head, with the snaky hair. She was one of the old gods.'

'Is that why he cut her head off? Was he a Christian?'

'No,' says Euterpe. 'He was one of the old gods himself. Well, half a god.'

'Why are they still up there?' I'm thinking of the old god Asclepius, smashed and defaced in his temple on the hill behind the theatre, his pedestal painted over in red. 'Why don't the Christians cover him up?'

Euterpe sighs, partly in comic annoyance, partly out of pleasure at the warmth of the water.

'Christians don't come to the baths anymore. They're not supposed to, anyway. By order of the bishop.'

'Why not?'

'They think it's sinful to be naked, especially in front of other people.'

'Thalia's a Christian,' I say, keeping my voice low. 'She's naked in front of other people all the time.'

'Well, according to the emperor, we're all Christians now, so . . .' Euterpe cups a handful of water and slowly drizzles it over my head, making me sputter. She laughs.

A sharp rapping makes us all look up. Simplex is squatting not far from Thalia, tapping the edge of a coin against the lip of the pool. When Thalia turns to him, he holds up the coin and lifts his eyebrows.

'Hey, Cleopatra,' he says. 'What will this get me?'

She reaches up to take the coin, rubs the water out of her eyes, and peers at it. Then she pushes herself up out of the pool and shakes herself like a dog, flinging droplets in all directions. She walks round the rim of the pool and disappears into an alcove. Simplex follows her, his keys tinkling at his belt.

'Why does he call her that?' I whisper.

'Because she's Egyptian.' Euterpe tilts her head back into the water. 'Cleopatra was the queen of the Egyptians.' She blows a sigh at the ceiling. 'It's their little joke. He says it to her every time.'

Now Gracilis, his broom propped against the wall, is fumbling at coins in his palm, his lips moving as he tallies them up, and he squats down heavily next to Urania. But before he can say a word, Urania lifts herself just far enough out of the water to shake her head. Then she sinks into the water again, up to her nose.

'How about him?' Gracilis gestures at me. 'He hasn't been here before.'

'No.' Euterpe sits bolt upright in the water. 'You can have me if you want.'

'Maybe I want him.' Gracilis pushes himself up with a grunt and lumbers toward us round the rim of the pool. 'I've never had a boy before.'

266

'Well, you're not going to have this one.' Euterpe shifts on the step, sloshing water over the edge of the pool, putting herself between me and the slave. 'That's not what he's here for.'

Gracilis turns to Melpomene, who has paused in her scrubbing to watch.

'Seriously?' says Gracilis.

'Well actually, Antinous . . .' Melpomene beams at me across the pool. 'You can if want to.'

'No.' Euterpe stands up, water cascading off her. 'Not today, Mel. It's his first time.'

I sit very quietly. The water slowly stills as the silence grows between the slave and the two wolves. For a moment, the only sound is the echoing drip of condensation from the ceiling. Then Gracilis sighs and turns away.

'My money's as good as anybody's.' He pads round the rim of the pool and disappears into the alcove where Thalia and Simplex went. Euterpe lowers herself onto the step next to me, but she's not relaxed any longer.

Melpomene wades across the pool and squats down near us. She's careful to keep her hair dry, but the water laps at her collarbone.

'I want to explain something to you, Antinous,' she says in a very level voice. 'Not so long ago, wolves used to work at the baths. Not in my lifetime, but my mother did, back in Gades.' She glances at Euterpe, who frowns but says nothing.

'It's against the law now,' Melpomene says, 'but when we're here, before they're open to the public, nobody's keeping track. The slaves here –' She lifts her chin toward the alcove – 'they make a little extra money on the side, the way we all do. It's expected. And they're happy to spend it on us.'

She edges a bit closer to me, and the little tide she generates washes over my shoulders. Euterpe stares straight ahead.

'Anything you make here, Antinous,' Melpomene says, 'you get to keep. Especially since Audo isn't coming with us anymore.

All you have to do is what you do at the tavern, every night. And you get to keep it all.'

Beside me, Euterpe has lifted her face to the ceiling again. She says nothing. We both sit very still in the water.

'You don't have to do anything if you don't want to,' says Melpomene, her eyes bright, 'but if you *do*, it's pure profit.'

Just then Simplex comes out of the alcove, whistling tunelessly, and he picks up his mop and saunters round the pool and through the arch where he came in. Melpomene kicks away from us, floating on her back in the water, her chin pointed at the fading gods above.

On the way back to the tavern, Melpomene walks in front, with Thalia and Urania behind her. I walk behind them, and Euterpe brings up the rear. In the narrow, sunless lane, the malingering slave is nowhere to be seen. I look back at Euterpe. She silently picks her way through the weeds and the dog turds, her lips pursed, her brows knitted. I've seen this look on her face when she's arguing with Focaria, or when she's facing off with Melpomene. I glance ahead at the others, then I step in front of Euterpe. She stops short, and her blank gaze comes to rest on me.

'Is Audo ever going to let me go out on the street again?' I say. 'By myself?'

Euterpe stares at me for a moment, then says, 'No. Not anymore.'

'Are they always going to look at me like that?'

She knows who I mean: the boys on the corner, the women shooing their children indoors, the men looking me up and down.

'They'll get used to you.' She starts to walk around me.

I clutch her mantle. 'Is it too late to run?' I whisper.

Euterpe stops short again. Glancing ahead at the others, she tugs me into someone's back entrance, a heavy, battered door with no keyhole on this side, and she crouches down before me, her hands gripping my upper arms. Gazing into my eyes, she opens her mouth to speak and then doesn't. She opens her mouth again, and still the words won't come. She looks like she's about to cry. In a moment, I'll be crying, too.

'Is it?' I'm barely breathing. 'Too late?'

Euterpe squeezes her eyes shut and tightens her fingers on my arms. Then she opens her eyes and tries to smile.

'Did I ever tell you,' she whispers, 'the story of the jackdaw and the string?'

I shake my head and swallow my tears.

'A man catches a jackdaw,' she says, her voice low and hoarse, 'and he attaches a little string to its leg, so that it can't escape. But the jackdaw hates being trapped, so one day, when the man loosens the string from the perch just for a moment, the jackdaw takes his chance and flies away.'

I think of all the enslaved birds I've seen, in the theatre, in the street – the songbirds in cages, the parrots chained to their perches – and I imagine them erupting all at once into the air, in a thumping fury of wings.

'But when the jackdaw has nearly returned to his nest,' Euterpe whispers, 'he pauses to rest in a tree, and the string gets caught on a branch. Try as he might, he can't loosen it.' She glances up the street. Thalia and Urania are waiting at the end of the lane, and Melpomene is walking back toward us, looking stern.

'What happens to him?' I whisper.

'He starves to death.' Her eyes are bright and glistening. 'All because he couldn't get used to being a slave.'

The flurrying wings in my imagination evaporate in a mist that clouds my vision. Euterpe releases my shoulders and cups my face and wipes my tears with her thumbs.

'I wish it wasn't true, Little One,' she whispers. 'But it is.'

'Is there a problem?' Melpomene is standing in the middle of the lane in her pose – back erect, palms pressed together, eyebrows lifted.

Euterpe stands, but keeps her hand lightly on my shoulder.

'I was just telling him,' she says, her voice still trembling, 'that you're right.' She draws a deep breath. 'He ought to start making his own money at the bath. If he wants to.'

Melpomene looks at me.

'Is that what you were talking about, Antinous?'

I swallow. I nod.

'Well.' Melpomene narrows her eyes at us. 'Don't fall behind. You can talk when we get home.' She steps aside and waits for us to pass ahead of her, and Euterpe and I fall into single file, picking our way up the street.

Now I was well and truly a wolf. I spent most of my time in my cell, which used to be Clio's, either alone or with a punter. Poor little Pusus, poor little Mouse, poor little Antinous, trapped like a caged bird, the sole inhabitant of a room in a house on a street in a town by the sea at the centre of the world. I had my new red tunic and my new pair of shoes. My spare tunic and my old one hung on pegs by the door. I had Clio's old bowl and spoon, I had her wine cup, her lamp, her jar of oil. I had her table, her stool, her pitcher, her washbasin, her chamber pot. None of it had actually been hers, of course, just as none of it was mine now. I had a little cache of coins wrapped in a cloth and hidden in a hole in the mattress – gratuities I earned from punters – but none of that was mine, either. Dominus or Audo could take it away from me at any time. Everything I had was theirs and nothing in the room was mine, especially not me. The room did not belong to me. I belonged to the room.

I had Clio's old bed, but the very first night I spent alone in the cell, I learned I could not sleep on it. No matter how exhausted I was, no matter how bruised and sore and sticky and half drunk I was at end of my working night, when I collapsed on the mattress and closed my eyes, I started to shake and sweat. No matter how much wine I'd swallowed throughout the evening, I could still taste the punters in my mouth. I could tell you where every flavour of a man's body landed on my tongue, the taste of sweat, the taste of cum, the taste of piss, the taste of shit, the taste of blood, the taste of tears. I could not breathe. It was as if a punter was still smothering me or throttling me or stopping-up my throat. So each night, after the last punter left, I slid off the stained sheet and crawled under the bed to curl up on the floor. It was the way I used to sleep in the kitchen. On the floor I felt comfortable. On the floor I felt safe.

My fellow wolves, meanwhile, went from being my aunties to being my sisters. I already knew what they sounded like when they were working, but now I knew what they sounded like when they weren't. Late at night, after the punters were gone and the lamps were extinguished, I heard them shifting on their mattresses. I heard them coughing and sighing and sneezing and passing wind, their exhalations contributing to the fug of smoke and sweat that permeated the hall. Sometimes Thalia cried at night, and I heard Urania's tread on the floorboards and the creak of Thalia's bed as Urania got in with her. Sometimes Urania cursed in her dreams, and I heard Thalia go to her, singing softly to her friend until Urania went back to sleep or Melpomene called out to them to knock it off.

In the afternoon, before the punters came upstairs, I sat on the bed of the empty cell across from mine as Euterpe, Urania, and Thalia did each other's hair and make-up, preparing their masks for the evening. Melpomene did her own, with her own tools in her cell, and in Calliope's old cell, the others began to teach me how to put on my own mask. Urania showed me how to wash my hair with vinegar, to make it shine. Thalia, whose skin was nearly the same colour as mine, showed me how to make my cheeks ruddy with paint, how to make my lips bright red, how to tousle my hair just so. Even Euterpe showed me how to make my eyes stand out by lining them with kohl.

271

'The punters like it,' she said. 'I don't know why.'

Now that I saw it every day, the face in the mirror was no longer a novelty to me, but he was still a stranger. Without the paints and creams, he was still a boy whose thoughts I couldn't read, and who couldn't read mine. But when he was made up for the evening, all I saw in the mirror was the mask, and the boy and I receded even further from each other. One night, when we were alone in the cell, Euterpe wrapped her arms around me from behind and pressed her face next to mine in the mirror. Two masks, looking back at each other.

'That's not me,' she whispered. 'And that's not you.'

Our eyes, rimmed with kohl, met in the mirror.

'Who are we, then?'

'We are sparks of light,' she said. 'Trapped in bodies.' She squeezed me and pressed our greasy cheeks together. 'It's the spark that matters.'

I looked away from her, into my own kohl-rimmed eyes. I didn't see any spark there.

As for Melpomene, she taught me techniques to make the work quicker and easier. She showed me how to oil the inside of my thighs so that a man might think he was inside me when he wasn't. She told me how to stick my middle finger up his ass and tickle the little bump inside him to make him come faster. She warned me about certain regular punters – this one's a biter, this one laughs when he comes, this one cries afterwards, this one will pull your hair and try to choke you.

'What do I do?' I said.

'Thrash about like you're dying,' she said, 'even if you aren't. The more he thinks he's hurting you, the quicker he'll finish.'

She also taught me how to defend myself, if it came to that. 'Call for Audo, if you can,' she said, but since a punter could still hurt me in the time it took Audo to hoist himself up the stairs, she showed me how to close my fist around his balls, how to put my thumb in his eye, how to curl up with my arms over my head to protect my face.

As for Audo, he seemed older now, and slower. During the day he did the jobs I used to do, and at night he was also doing my old job, wheezing up and down the stairs, bringing us food and water and wine and carrying away our chamber pots. When he was at the counter below my room, I could hear him snarling and snapping at the punters. Late at night, after we closed, I could hear the alarming stop and start of his snoring from the little cell where he slept under the stairs, and sometimes I heard him shouting and screaming in his dreams, fighting some long ago skirmish along the German frontier. Either way, his sleep was fitful, and on those rare occasions during the day when we came face to face, he turned a blotchy red – from anger, I suppose, at having to do all my work. If he didn't hit me as much as he used to, it was only because he rarely saw me. Yet whenever we came face to face, my breath came short and my heart pounded, as I thought of what he had done to me and what he could still do to me again at any moment, without warning.

Focaria was under orders from Calidus to give me more food, to make me less scrawny, but she gave me bruised fruit, the grittiest sausage, the oldest, driest bread. She also gave me the sharp edge of her tongue, laughing at my make-up and red tunic, asking me if I missed my old friends on the street, reminding me nearly every time she saw me, at great length and in copious detail, that she was doing my jobs now as well as her own.

'That's a lot of food,' she'd say, slamming a plate of scraps onto the kitchen table in front of me, 'for someone who works lying down.'

Even so, my limbs grew rounder, my ribs receded into my flesh, and, in the mirror, the face behind the mask began to fill out. I became smoother and shinier, like a cheap new pot rendered glossy by the oils of many hands. I think that made Focaria even angrier, and it didn't help that we seemed to be in competition for the attentions of Euterpe. Now that I wasn't sleeping in the kitchen anymore, and Audo's slumber was guaranteed by his wall-shuddering snores, Euterpe crept downstairs some nights to sleep in the kitchen with Focaria, and some nights Focaria crept upstairs to sleep with her. I could hear them whispering or moving together in the next room. At cockcrow, I heard the rasp of Euterpe's curtain being pulled aside, then Focaria tiptoeing along the hall and down the creaking stairs.

But some nights, Focaria came upstairs and lifted aside Euterpe's curtain to find me huddled in Euterpe's bed. This had started when Euterpe had come looking for me in my cell one morning, not long after I started working upstairs. She stopped short in my doorway, puzzled because I wasn't on the mattress, and she was about to turn away and look for me downstairs when she heard me stir. She sank to her knees and peered under the bed, and we watched each other for a moment without speaking.

'What are you doing down there?' she said.

'Sleeping.'

'Why not use the bed?'

'No one can find me down here,' I said.

Euterpe beckoned me to come out. 'Come lie with me for a little while.'

And so Euterpe began to bring me into her bed. Sometimes she waited until morning, after Focaria had gone downstairs, but sometimes she sent Focaria away and let me spend all night with her. Waking together in the morning, we stared at the ceiling as the other wolves stirred in their cells. These first mornings of my new life were both the closest I had ever been to Euterpe and the most remote. The times when she'd held me in the garden, before I moved upstairs, had lasted only a few moments each day, but we'd had a lot to talk about. Now that we lay like mother and son in the same bed, neither of us spoke at first, because what was there to say? Instead we simply nestled into each other, feeling each other's stomachs rumble, breathing in each other's scent, listening to each other's sighs.

One morning, lying with her arm around me, facing the wall, I attempt to restore what we used to have in the garden. I touch a graffito next to her bed and ask her, 'What's that say?'

Euterpe lifts her head to see what I'm touching. 'I fucked, I came, I left.'

'And that?' I say, touching another.

'Melpomene fucks the best,' she says.

I twist my head to look at her. 'Really?'

Euterpe's eyes are sad, but she smiles. 'There's no accounting for taste,' she says.

My eyes glide over the crude stick figures scratched into the wall, the rudimentary letters. I touch another word. 'And that?'

'Festus,' she sighs. 'It's just his name, Little One.' She lifts her arm from around me and rolls onto her back.

'Why do they do it?' I roll over to face her, my head next to hers on the thin pillow.

'Why do they do what?' She doesn't look at me, but only stares at the ceiling.

'Why do they write on the wall?'

Euterpe sighs, then says, 'It's a way of saying, "I was here. Don't forget me."'

I stare at her cheek, just beyond my nose. Her skin is still oily with last night's make-up.

'The rich put their names on everything,' she says. 'Why shouldn't punters do the same?'

I want her to look at me, to smile and hold me like she used to in the garden, but she just stares at something on the ceiling, something that I can't see. I'm wondering if I've lost her for ever, and as if she knows what I'm thinking, she rolls suddenly onto her side to face me, making the narrow bed shake. She presses her hand to my chest.

'Little One,' she says, 'did I ever tell you about the philosopher Seneca?'

'No.' The warmth of her hand spreads through my chest and down my limbs.

'My father told me about him,' she says, her sour breath warm on my face. 'Seneca led a turbulent life, with many problems and difficulties. But he believed that no matter how difficult or painful his life was, true happiness came from being virtuous. He believed a virtuous man could be happy even if he was being . . . even if things weren't going his way. Even if he was a slave.'

'Was Seneca a slave?'

'No.'

'Was he an emperor?' Some of the famous Romans she's told me about were emperors.

'No,' she says, 'but he worked for one.'

Then what's he to do with me? I wonder, but I don't say it out loud. I'm just happy that she's touching me, and teaching me, one more time.

'Seneca said,' Euterpe begins again, 'that the greatest empire is to be emperor over yourself.' She narrows her eyes at me. 'He said you could be happy and free, even if you're a slave, as long as you're virtuous.'

'Even if I'm tied to my perch?'

Euterpe smiles. 'Yes, you little jackdaw, even if you're tied to your perch.'

'What does "virtuous" mean?'

Euterpe thinks for a moment.

'It's a way of . . .' she begins. 'It's a way of being a man. It means . . . understanding how the world works, and accepting it, not trying to fight it. Virtue is . . . true knowledge. It's what the jackdaw realized, too late.' She looks at me. 'Do you understand?'

I don't say anything. I try to think if any of the men I know are virtuous. It doesn't seem likely. Most of them know the world better than I do, but they seem to be fighting it, and each other, all the time. Certainly none of them seem happy. Audo's always in a rage. Calidus is either angry or petulant. Quartus torments himself over Thalia. Nazarius swings between bonhomie in his shop and fury in a wolf's cell. Renatus winces through life as if he's tiptoeing through shit. Festus, whoever he is, could die tomorrow, and the only thing he'll leave behind is his name, scratched into a wall. The nameless men who use me all seem spent afterwards, or relieved, or bored, but never happy. Most of them leave my cell as angry or as sad as when they came in.

Before I became a wolf, I foolishly thought I was learning how the world works, that I was learning to make my way in it as I moved up and down the street, seeing, every day, people I knew, and who knew me. Not friends, exactly, but people who might share a joke or a bit of gossip with the little slave boy from the tavern. But then that world disappeared. Well, that's not true – all the people I used to know were still where they'd always been, on the street, without me. I could still hear them from my window: the women laughing at the fountain, the men singing in Nazarius's shop, the town crier braying about runaways. That world was still there, but I was plucked from it and placed in this room like a bird in a cage. A spark embedded in a body meant for the use of others, shining for no one in the dark. So how can I be virtuous in here, especially if all I ever see are men with no virtue at all?

'Melpomene . . .' I say, and just her name makes Euterpe tense up. 'Melpomene says I'm never going to be a man. Not like other men.'

'That may be true.' She sighs. 'None of us have any control over our lives. But that doesn't mean you can't find . . . some sort of happiness.'

'Are you happy?'

It's a cruel thing to say, and I regret it instantly. But to my surprise, she smiles.

'Sometimes,' she says.

'When?'

'When I'm with you.' She slides her hand up my chest to caress my cheek. She kisses me.

'Or when you're with Focaria,' I say.

She laughs. 'Sometimes.'

'But never with a punter.'

'No,' she says. 'Never with a punter.' She presses her forehead to mine and closes her eyes. 'But when I'm with a punter, I'm not really there.'

'Me neither,' I say.

She opens her eyes. 'What do you mean?'

We breathe in each other's sour morning breath, smelling of last night's wine.

'I go away,' I whisper.

'Where do you go?'

Even with Euterpe, even with the woman I love more than anyone else in the world, I'm afraid to say. There's no room in Sparrow for anyone else but me.

'Just somewhere else,' I whisper. 'Till it's over.'

Euterpe pulls me close. 'My child,' she breathes, 'my child, my child, my child.' She loosens her embrace to look at me. The space between us is humid with our breath and her tears. 'I'd take you away if I could.'

'Why don't you?'

She inhales sharply, and then the curtain rasps open, startling us both. Melpomene poses in the doorway, watching us without speaking as we slowly pull apart and look up at her from the bed.

'Time for the baths.' She holds out her hand. 'Come, Antinous.'

I rise from the bed, leaving Euterpe behind me, staring at the ceiling. Melpomene ushers me into my own cell. I sit on the bed while she kneels before me and ties on my shoes.

'What were you two talking about?' she says.

I say nothing, and she places her hands on my knees. 'What were you talking about?'

'Birds,' I say.

She raises her eyebrows and waits for me to say something more, but I just look down at the bed.

'Are you two going to run away?' she says.

What did she hear? I can feel Sparrow fluttering at my shoulder, ready to take flight. I shake my head.

'Because that would be stupid,' she says. 'You'd be caught, and your life would be much, much worse. You might even be killed.'

I say nothing. Sparrow hovers just over our heads, watching the woman and the boy below. Melpomene pushes herself up and sits next to me on the bed. She puts her arm around me.

'I know what it's like to be scared in the night,' she says, stroking my hair. 'If you're lonely, you can come sleep with me.'

I still say nothing, so Melpomene takes my chin and makes me look at her.

'If you're confused,' she says, 'you can always talk to me. Euterpe's not the only one who knows things.'

Euterpe is just beyond the wall, and I know she can hear us. Melpomene knows it, too. I try not to look at her, but she fills my sight, staring deep into my eyes. My heart is beating, my mouth is dry. Sparrow is ready to take flight.

'We'll be late.' It's Euterpe, standing in my doorway.

Melpomene hangs on to me a moment longer, then she looks away and releases me. She rises and brushes past Euterpe.

'Let's go, then,' she says.

Those were my days. What about my nights?

A man enters. Sometimes he tells me what he wants, sometimes he just begins. At that moment, I leave. As man and wolf grapple on the bed or on the floor, Sparrow lifts his wings and takes flight. Sometimes he only flies as far as the window, where he folds his wings and watches what's happening below, turning his head from side to side, first one eye and then the other. But more often he leaves the room entirely and soars above the garden, where he can see Focaria below, doing Mouse's old jobs – carrying water, weeding the garden, emptying ash into the latrine. Her hair is thinning on top, her shoulders are stooped under the weight of her iron collar. She looks older from above.

Sparrow keeps going, sailing above the street, where he sees the women at the fountain, who never talk about him anymore. He sees Audo, fat and angry and out of shape, stumping along the street with an old leather satchel, doing the shopping. He sees through the skylight of the fuller's shop, looking down at his own reflection in the trembling water of the rinsing pool. He sees the perfect circle the mule makes round the baker's millstone. He sails higher and sees the line of slaves on auction on the stage of the old theatre, he sees the ragged fringe of Opitria's awning, he sees the cracked roof of the temple on the hillside. He sees the dank lane where the sun never shines, he passes through the smoke rising from the baths, he sees the crowds of men in the forum like particles suspended in water, swirling and congealing and swirling again. Higher still, and he sees threads of slaves like ants, carrying bales like breadcrumbs along the quay. He sees a galley stroking its oars like a water bug walking across the glittering surface of the harbour. Spiralling higher and higher and higher, he sees the brackish lagoon like grey silk, he sees the folded hills studded with the red roofs of villas. He sees the blue, blue sea that stretches to the horizon, he sees long lines of ships at sail, on their way to Africa, to Italia, to Egypt, to Syria, to Greece, to Asia.

Then he's soaring among the stars. He sails toward them, but they never get any closer. He banks toward the moon, but it never gets any closer, either. There's no wind up here and no warmth, only the beating of his wings and the frantic fluttering of his heart. He's gasping for breath now, but he keeps trying, because if he climbs just a little higher, he can escape, he can sail away and never come back. He can be Sparrow for ever. But of course, he's forgotten about the string, the one they tied around his leg. He's pulled it as taut as he can, higher and higher, further and further away from the city below, but he can never pull it far enough. He can never pull it until it breaks.

Then Sparrow can't rise any more. The string pulls tight, his wings flail and lose their lift, and he plummets, spiralling back down the way he came, past the moon, through the stars. The hills spin around him, the harbour flashes, the roofs and streets tilt and heave. Something's reeling him in, and he's falling, falling, falling, past the hillside, past the theatre, past the baker, past the fuller, past Audo, past the fountain, past Focaria stooped in the garden, past the bars of his window, and straight back into the bruised and tender flesh of the boy, alone on the bed.

The Stoics say that the world goes on for ever, but also that it is regularly destroyed by fire and then remade. When my own world burned down, the first sparks of the fire came from Audo. I won't ask you to feel sorry for him – I never did – but in the time after I began working in the tavern but before I became a wolf, he had gotten used to sitting behind the counter downstairs, drinking wine and nibbling food all night, getting drunker and fatter while I did most of the work. Then I started to do his work upstairs as well, and he only lifted himself from his stool and struggled up the steps if there was trouble. Now, between the two of them, he and Focaria were doing all the work I used to do, and sometimes as I lay in bed in the morning, I could hear them bickering in the garden below my window like an old married couple.

'The fish you brought me yesterday were unusable,' Focaria says.

'They were cheap,' grumbles Audo.

'Of course they were,' she says. 'How long did they lie in the bottom of Rufus's boat before he dredged them up and sold them to you?'

'Rufus knows not to cheat me.'

'Rufus sees you coming, every fucking day. You think because he tells you jokes every night he won't cheat you like he cheats everyone else?'

And so on. The remarkable thing about these exchanges was how rarely they ended in Audo hitting Focaria. Something had diminished in him, and we all could see it. He wasn't just getting older and fatter – he had begun to limp. We often passed him on the street on our way to baths, as he stumped along on his way back from the shops, favouring his right leg and swinging his left one like a dead weight. He heeled over like a ship in a crosswind, the bulging leather satchel full of bread or laundry hanging at his side like ballast. Even over the racket of the street, we could hear him wheezing from a block away. Focaria began to do all the shopping in the old theatre, which required climbing steps. They negotiated this arrangement every morning.

'I can climb the fucking steps,' shouts Audo, 'if you'll just tell me what you fucking need.'

'I'll do it myself, Audo,' Focaria shouts back. 'Just get the bread.'

It was as ritualized as a pantomime, and it always had the same result – Audo avoided the steps, and Focaria spent a few minutes every day with Opitria, coming home with another useless prediction or a curse on a slip of papyrus. ('Don't ever tell her,' Euterpe whispered to me one morning, when we were sharing her bed, 'but the words Opitria writes on those slips are just gibberish.') Now and then Audo still swung his fist at Focaria, for old time's sake, just to remind her that he could. But he didn't connect as often as he used to, and I could hear him breathing hard afterwards. He also breathed harder climbing the steps to the second floor, and even over the uproar of the tavern and the noisy exertions of the punters, I heard his heavy, uneven tread all the way up the creaking steps, his rasping breath in the hall, his grunt as he bent to set the pitcher outside my cell, then another grunt as he stood and tugged the curtain.

'Water,' he rasped, and then limped off, wheezing all the way back down again.

Even when he made it upstairs for sex in the morning, he never got on top anymore. Instead one of the wolves straddled or fellated him, while he lay on his back and stared at the ceiling like a weary old dog until it was over. Sometimes it took two of us, one hauling at each hand, to help him up off the cot afterwards.

One night, there's trouble upstairs, and Audo only shows up when it's nearly over. I am between punters when it happens, my curtain drawn as I wash the smell of the last one off me with a wet cloth and chew a couple of mint leaves to freshen my breath. Someone across the hall starts shouting, and I hold still over my washbasin. It's Urania.

'My name?' she's shouting. 'You want to know my *name*?'

I peek through my curtain. In the smoky light of the lamps, I see Thalia peering out of her cell and Euterpe sticking her head out from behind her curtain. Melpomene comes right out into the hall, wrapping her gown around her. She's holding her little knife.

Suddenly a man erupts backwards through Urania's curtain, naked and crouching, clutching his wadded-up tunic over his crotch. Urania rips the curtain aside and stands naked in a bony fury in her doorway.

'I'm your *daughter*, you fuck!' she shouts, eyes blazing. 'I'm Izar, the girl you sold like a sow! Don't you fucking recognize me?'

The red-faced man backs toward the stairs, bent nearly double. His eyes are frantic, looking everywhere but at Urania. Thalia's mouth is hanging open, and even Melpomene retreats a step. Euterpe sees me watching and gestures for me to go back into my cell. But I keep watching. The man backs into the stairwell like a rat, but Urania stalks after him.

'You know how I know it's you?' she shouts down the stairs. 'You still smell like pig shit!'

283

None of us move or say anything. Even the tavern below has fallen silent. We hear the man stumbling halfway down the stairs, then a series of brutal thumps as he falls the rest of the way.

'Tell mother I said hello!' Urania shouts after him. Then she turns back into the hall and just stands there, shaking with rage, her chest heaving. None of the rest of us move or say anything, not even Melpomene. We all listen to Audo wheezing up the stairs, step by leaden step, until he appears at the top, made nearly as red-faced by the climb as Urania's father. Urania wheels, spreads her arms, and pushes her face at him.

'What?' she shouts.

For the first time in my experience, Audo, sweating and breathing hard, does nothing, says nothing, hits no one. He only turns and stumps slowly back down the steps, wheezing all the way. Urania disappears into her cell and yanks her curtain shut.

That was the last time Audo ever came upstairs.

A few days later, I'm having my breakfast in the kitchen. Focaria glowers at me, still angry at the extra work my elevation to a wolf has caused her. Lately I have tried to avoid her, ducking into my cell and under my bed if I hear her coming up the stairs, or slipping into Euterpe's bed in the morning only after Focaria has gone back to the kitchen. But once a day we come face to face while she feeds me half a loaf of bread and a wedge of cheese, and now that I know I won't be working for her anymore, I've started to talk back to her a little bit.

'You're getting fat,' she says.

'I'm supposed to,' I say, my mouth full.

'You're luckier than I thought you were,' she says.

I must have made a look, because she continues: 'You have a bed to sleep in. You get as much to eat as you want. You work lying down.'

'You get a bed to sleep in, too.' I tear off another mouthful of bread. 'And I hear you working on your back.' I pucker my lips at her. 'You and Euterpe.'

She slaps me, knocking the bread out of my mouth.

'Everybody knows!' I cry. My cheek burns.

'Yes, and everybody knows *not to talk about it*.'

For the first time in my life, I have the urge to hit her back. Focaria pushes her face close to me. I cringe, but I don't back up.

'I fed you when you first came here,' she says. 'I wiped your ass. I kept you alive.'

'I know.'

'Nobody cared if you lived or died,' she says. 'Not even me. Especially not me.'

'I know.'

She stands up straight. 'You think that little red tunic makes you special now? It doesn't. You look like a cunt.'

'I know.'

Outside, someone is hammering on the garden door.

'You're just another hole for punters to stick it into.'

'I *know*.' I'm starting to cry.

She tears off another piece of bread and tosses it at me. 'Here,' she says. 'Get fat.'

The bread bounces off my chest. I'm afraid she'll hit me again if I pick it up.

'Let me in,' rasps Audo from beyond the door. His pounding slows.

'For fuck's sake.' Focaria pushes past me and out the kitchen door. I snatch the bread off the floor and wipe my tears as she strides through the garden.

'Calm the fuck down,' she calls out. 'I'm coming.'

'Open . . . up . . .' wheezes Audo.

Focaria raises herself on the balls of her feet, and as soon as she hauls the bolt back, the door pushes violently open, knocking her onto her backside. Audo stumbles through, breathing hard. He pulls himself along the wall with one hand while his other hand dangles at his side. As Focaria scrambles to her feet, he drags his leather satchel over his head and drops it, spilling fresh bread into the dirt. Then his knees buckle and he topples sideways onto the ground. Focaria starts picking up the loaves, slapping the dirt off them, and pushing them back into the satchel. But Audo doesn't get up. He lies on his side, panting. He pushes himself up on one elbow, then collapses into the dirt again. Focaria sees me in the kitchen doorway, my mouth hanging open, half full of bread.

'Pusus,' she says. 'Come here.'

I drop my bread and run across the garden. She shoves the satchel at me and says, 'Put this in the kitchen.' I run inside, dump it on the table, then run back out again. Focaria is trying to roll Audo onto his back, but he's a dead weight, sweating and pale and panting like a dog.

'Help me,' she says, and together we drag Audo's legs around, roll him onto his back, and lift the back of his head against the wall. His eyes show a lot of white. He's trying to say something, but all he can do is choke and gasp. Focaria stands and pushes the door shut. I back away from Audo.

'Get Mel,' Focaria says. I stand gawping, and she shoves me. 'Now! Get Mel!'

I run through the empty tavern and up the stairs. I yank Melpomene's curtain aside and startle her at her make-up table, peering at herself in her mirror. She thrusts the mirror behind her back, as if afraid I'll see what's in it.

'Audo.' I'm breathless. 'In the garden.'

She stares at me for an instant, then tosses the mirror on the bed and brushes past me. The other wolves come out of their cells as her feet pound down the stairs.

'What is it?' Euterpe says, shrugging on her mantle.

'It's Audo,' I say. 'He's sick.'

Euterpe pushes me past me and down the stairs. I follow, with Thalia and Urania right behind me.

In the garden, Melpomene is bending over Audo without touching him. The garden door is closed now, and Focaria stands with her back to it, pressing her palms against it as if to keep someone from coming in. Audo's mouth is opening and closing like a fish drowning in air, and there's a foam of spittle in the corners of his lips. He's clutching his chest with one hand, clawing the ground with the other. His legs slowly pump as if he's walking in place, his heels gouging the dirt. His eyes roll from side to side, as if looking for something or someone.

'He needs a physician.' Euterpe bends and puts her hand on his forehead. He looks at her like a terrified dog. His lips move but only a liquid gurgling comes out. Euterpe looks up at Focaria. 'You must know where there's a physician.'

Focaria says nothing. She and Melpomene exchange a look.

'Punch him in the chest,' Urania says, from behind me. Everyone looks at her, and she says, 'I saw my father do it to a pig once. I did it myself once with a punter. It gets the heart going.'

'For God's sake.' Euterpe shrugs her mantle off into the dirt. 'Help me lie him flat.'

Melpomene throws her arm across Euterpe's chest.

'Not so fast,' she says.

'If we don't do something,' Euterpe says, 'he's going to die.'

She tries to push past, but Melpomene holds steady.

'Stop and think about it,' she says, but Euterpe wrenches free.

'Little One!' she says to me. 'Run to Nazarius as fast you can and ask him where there's a physician.'

It seems as if the light in the garden is brighter. The blue of the sky is deeper, the red of my tunic more vivid, Melpomene's hair more unnaturally golden than usual. At the same time, I can smell every individual herb in the garden – thyme and oregano and rosemary – as well as the rich reek of the latrine. Before me Melpomene and Euterpe are squaring off like wrestlers, while Urania looks on with no expression, her gown hanging from her shoulders

287

like a shroud. Thalia peers out of the tavern arch, wringing her hands, ready to flee.

'Little One!' cries Euterpe. 'Do as I say!'

Startled, I dash across the garden. Melpomene reaches for me, but I slip around her. Before I can get to the door, Focaria reaches up and bolts it. Then she presses her hands against the door behind her again, staring me down.

Audo cries out wordlessly, and everyone turns to him. His mouth is foaming and contorted, his eyes are squeezed shut. He clutches his chest and kicks the dirt. From where I'm standing I can see every pore in his face. Euterpe yanks on my arm and swings me toward the arch. 'Go out the other way!' But Melpomene grabs me by the shoulders and shakes me.

'Stay where you are,' she says. Now Euterpe makes a dash for the arch, but Melpomene and Focaria grab her by the arms, holding her back.

'We're killing him!' she cries.

'We're not killing anybody.' Melpomene's voice is as hard as iron.

'The gods are taking him.' Focaria's voice is hoarse, her eyes wild. 'Finally.'

Euterpe wrenches free, but instead of going to Audo or through the arch, she backs away, breathing hard. Melpomene lifts her hands to Euterpe as if calming a terrified beast.

'Think about what this means,' she says in a low voice. She turns to me.

'Think about what he did to you,' she says, and for an instant, I am Sparrow, hovering over my own shoulder.

'It was *your idea*,' shouts Euterpe, but Melpomene ignores her and turns to Urania.

'Why should you care if he dies?' she says.

Urania says nothing.

Melpomene turns to Thalia. 'You were with Clio after she was cut. Do you think he cared if she lived or died?'

Thalia cringes in the archway. Tears are streaming down her face.

Melpomene says, 'Why should any of us care if he lives or dies?'

'Dominus,' says Euterpe. 'Calidus might replace him with someone worse.'

'That's true,' says Urania. She's staring expressionlessly at Audo, writhing in the dirt. She lifts her gaze to Melpomene. 'We're used to him.'

'True,' says Melpomene. 'But what if Dominus doesn't replace him?'

Audo has stopped moving his legs and working the dirt with his fingers, but he's still panting.

'What are you talking about?' says Euterpe.

'Listen to me.' Melpomene turns slowly, regarding each of us in turn. 'I'm a freedwoman now, and I've been doing this for longer than any of you. I know this city. I know the punters. I know every detail of running this place. I'm practically running it now. If I go to Dominus tonight, before anyone hears about this, I think I can persuade him to let me take over.'

'You're not serious,' says Euterpe.

'We'll all be better off,' says Melpomene, 'if I'm in charge.'

Euterpe goggles at her. 'Are you going to *free* us?'

'You know I can't do that,' says Melpomene. 'You don't belong to me. But . . .' She looks at each of us in turn again. 'I used to be one of you. Think about that. Who would you rather have in charge? Someone who knows what your life is like?' Her gaze lands on Audo. 'Or him?'

Audo is flat in the dirt, sweating and pale and blinking sightlessly at the sky. Only his belly is moving, his breath shallow and uneven. Euterpe looks over at Urania, who is looking back at Thalia, who is crying with her hands over her mouth. No one looks at me except Sparrow, from above.

'What are we waiting for?' Focaria drops to her knees next to Audo. With one hand she pinches his nostrils shut and with her other, she snatches up Euterpe's discarded mantle and stuffs a corner of it deep into his mouth. Audo gags and clutches weakly at Focaria's wrists, but she doesn't let go. Without a word, Urania drops to her knees on the other side of him and pries his hands away, pinning his fat wrists to the ground. Melpomene turns to block Euterpe, but Euterpe doesn't move. She only stands and watches, her chest rising and falling. Thalia is on her knees in the archway, her hands folded under her chin, and she's murmuring, 'Our Father, who is in the heavens, let your name be held holy . . .'

I am stock still and trembling all at once. Is this the worst thing that could happen, or the best? Audo will never hit me again – he'll never hit anyone again – but will Melpomene be worse? Silently I start to count to one hundred, the way I was supposed to that day in the temple of Asclepius. But before I even get to twenty, it's over. First Audo's arms go limp, then his belly stops rising. His choking stops, and sounds from the street – a creaking cart, a dog barking, someone laughing at the fountain – once again flow over the wall.

'. . . but rescue us from the evil one,' whispers Thalia. 'Amen.'

Urania tentatively lifts her hands from Audo's wrists. Then she picks up one of his hands and drops it into the dirt. It lies there, the eagle over his knuckles as still as Audo himself. Urania gently pries Focaria's fingers from his nose and mouth, then she drags the mantle out of his throat and pushes it away. Focaria settles back on her haunches, looking pale and exhausted.

'So,' she pants, 'who's a cunt-licker now?'

No one else says anything. None of us look at each other, except for Euterpe, who looks around at all of us. 'Now what?' she says.

'Listen carefully,' says Melpomene.

Audo lies naked on his stomach on Melpomene's bed, his flesh sagging over the sides. His face is slack against the pillow, his dead eyes stare into the room, one pale, mottled leg droops off the bed to the floor. It took all six of us to haul him up the stairs, hoist him onto the bed, and strip off his tunic and his shoes. While Melpomene arranges the scene in her cell, she sends me back down into the garden to scuff away the tracks where we dragged him away. Then she insists that we make our daily trip to the baths. For a moment, on the way, Sparrow hovers over the Parade of the Wolves, watching the four silent women and the stunned boy in the red tunic, all of them gilded with the gazes of women and shopkeepers and children, who can surely see what we have done. At the baths, Thalia declines to disappear into the alcove with either of the slaves in the caldarium. Instead she sinks into the pool with her head on Urania's shoulder, neither of them moving, neither of them speaking. Melpomene takes it upon herself to entertain both Simplex and Gracilis, one after another, her enthusiasm reverberating out of the alcove. Then she bathes, vigorously scrubbing herself with a sponge as if nothing has happened.

Euterpe and I sit shoulder to shoulder and hold hands under the water.

'Are we free now?' I speak as quietly as I can, but the vault amplifies my whisper. Euterpe squeezes my hand and murmurs, 'No.'

When we return to the tavern, Focaria bursts out of the kitchen, where she has been cooling her heels all morning.

'What if Calidus comes?' she cries, practically flying at Melpomene. Her hair is pulled back tight, but stray strands fly round her face. Her eyes are wide with panic.

'He never comes on Monday.' Melpomene coolly shuts and bolts the door. Thalia and Urania huddle together near the archway, away from the spot where Audo died. Euterpe steadies herself with her hands on my shoulders.

'What if he hears we're closed for the day?' insists Focaria. 'He'll come to see what's wrong.'

'If that happens,' says Melpomene, 'let me do the talking. That's why we put Audo in my cell.'

She tries to move around the cook, but Focaria plants herself in Melpomene's way.

'Why not tell him now?' Focaria demands. 'Send Pusus to fetch him.'

Euterpe tightens her hands on my shoulders.

'I need to talk to both father and son, not just Calidus.' Melpomene speaks slowly, as if to a child. 'Granatus won't come here, so I have to go to him, and I can't be seen at his house until after dark.'

'What if he won't let you in?' Focaria says. 'They're all going to think we killed him.'

'We did,' murmurs Euterpe.

'They're going to crucify us!' cries Focaria.

Melpomene straightens her back. 'What do you suggest?'

'We run!' cries Focaria. 'We set fire to the tavern, and we all run, in different directions. They'll think the fire killed him, and they won't even notice we're gone until it's too late.' She looks wildly at each of us. 'It's our only chance!'

Focaria's chest is heaving, her eyes are wild. Melpomene steps up to her, hooks her fingers through the collar round her neck, and swings her forcefully against the wall, knocking the breath out of her. Urania and Thalia leap back, clutching each other. Euterpe folds me in her mantle.

'How far do you think you'll get with *this*.' Melpomene tightens her grip on the collar and bangs Focaria's head against the wall. 'If you run, it's as good as a confession. They will catch you and crucify you for sure, and probably the rest of us as well.'

Focaria trembles against the wall.

'This is going to work,' says Melpomene, 'if you just do what I say.'

Focaria grabs Melpomene's wrist. 'What's in it for me?' she says. 'Are you going to set me free?'

'No,' says Melpomene. 'I don't own you.' She loosens her grip on Focaria's collar without letting go. 'But if I'm in charge, I can persuade Calidus to take this off.'

Focaria loosens her hold on Melpomene's wrist. She says nothing.

'Would anyone else do that for you?' Melpomene says.

Focaria lets go of her wrist. Melpomene releases the collar and steps back. Urania and Thalia, still clutching each other, crouch against the wall. I huddle inside Euterpe's mantle, her hands still on my shoulders. I can hear her breathing over my head. Melpomene turns to her.

'Euterpe,' she says, 'can you write?'

We usually open the hour after noon, but today Melpomene keeps the shutters latched. Euterpe writes a note in charcoal on a piece of wood, and Melpomene props it against the wall outside. 'Closed,' it says, in both Latin and Greek. 'Food poisoning.'

'Of course,' says Focaria. 'Blame the cook.'

All afternoon, Melpomene sits in the hot, dim main room, and when punters who can't read the sign rattle the shutters, she shouts, 'We've all got the shits. Come back tomorrow.' Sometimes she retches noisily for effect. If a punter shouts, 'Can't I at least have a drink?' she calls out, 'Audo's sick, too,' and the punter goes away, cursing or grumbling.

Audo lies upstairs by himself. Thalia is afraid to be up there with him, so she spends all afternoon in the garden, sitting against the water tank with her knees drawn up to her chest, fingering her chi-rho medallion and praying silently to herself. Urania keeps her company, sometimes sitting with her arm around her friend, sometimes walking up and down the garden with her head down. Euterpe hides in the kitchen with Focaria, sitting in the corner where I used to sleep, wrapped in her mantle. I can hear them talking in low voices, but when I come in, they stop. Euterpe pulls me down next to her, and we sit without talking while Focaria makes us all something to eat. Usually all we get is bread and cheese and chick-peas, but today she fries us the sausages she was going to serve the punters tonight.

'Do you really think she'll do it?' she says at last, turning away from the stove.

'Do what?' Euterpe has her eyes closed and her head tipped back against the wall. The kitchen is full of the smell of hot grease.

'Take this collar off me,' says Focaria.

'Maybe she will, maybe she won't,' says Euterpe. 'Either way, she's in charge now.'

'Is she?' says Focaria.

'Yes.' Euterpe opens her eyes. 'You made sure of that.'

Focaria says nothing. She stabs with her spatula at the sausages sizzling in the pan. When they're ready, she sends me out with a plate for Thalia and Urania. Thalia turns away, but Urania gulps down all the sausages and licks the plate afterwards. Focaria sends me into the main room with another plate for Melpomene, who sets it on a table and sits me down on a stool beside her.

'You can't ever tell anyone what happened here this morning,' she whispers. 'You understand that, right?'

I nod.

'If they find out,' she says, 'they'd crucify us all.'

I nod again. Once, just for fun, Focaria explained crucifixion to me in gruesome detail.

'Good,' says Melpomene. 'You're a smart boy.' She cuts a sausage in two with her little knife and pushes half of it to me. I pick it up and sniff at it. I've never had so much meat at once, only a few stolen mouthfuls now and then. I take a bite, and the flavour of fat coats my tongue. I make a face. It's almost too much. Melpomene goes to the counter and returns with two cups of unwatered wine.

'It's better with wine,' she says. 'Drink.' She cuts a slice of sausage for herself and lifts it on the tip of her knife.

'You're going to come with me tonight, Antinous,' she says. 'If I show up at Dominus's house by myself, the doorkeeper won't let me in. So I need you to go inside with a message for Granatus and make sure he'll see me.'

'How do I do that?'

'I'll tell you what to say,' she says.

I force another bite of sausage down. 'What will I say?'

'I don't know yet.' Melpomene regards the piece of sausage on the point of her knife. 'Eat up and let me think.'

After sunset, Melpomene installs Urania in the main room to turn the punters away. Thalia still won't go upstairs, so she sits near Urania with her medallion and a pitcher of wine, quietly getting drunk. Focaria and Euterpe disappear into the kitchen. Melpomene takes me upstairs, where Audo's collapsed backside seems to glow in the dusk of her cell. She sees me staring at him, so she yanks the curtain shut and sends me into my cell to put on my old tunic, which is a little tighter than it used to be. She scrubs any trace of make-up off her face and off mine, and she washes the scented oil out of my hair. Then she puts on her mantle, and we go downstairs and out through the garden door. We leave it unbolted behind us.

Melpomene takes my hand as we walk up the middle of the street toward the centre of town. The shops and workshops and houses along the way are all shut up for the night. Lamplight flickers through chinks in their shutters and trembles from barred windows, and the stars are coming out in the slot of sky overhead. No one else is abroad. Our footsteps are the only sound. I stumble along beside her in the dark, negotiating the wagon ruts. When I look up at her, she's staring straight ahead and moving her lips, silently rehearsing what she's planning to say. We walk further up the street than I've ever been before, and when we turn left into a darker street, Melpomene clutches my hand even tighter and openly displays her knife, even though we can't see anyone else.

We turn right again and walk to the middle of the block, where Melpomene pulls me to a stop before the broad front of a tall house with shuttered shops on either side. At the centre of the facade is a massive door flanked by squat pillars and lit by a pair of cressets full of burning, softly crackling pitch. The door and the walls to either side are painted in a complicated pattern that might be red and green, though it's hard to tell in the smoky light. There are stone benches on either side of the door, and up above, three windows in the second storey, each covered with a metal grille. One is full of lamplight, the other two are dark.

'I think this is it,' murmurs Melpomene.

'Don't you know?' I whisper.

'I was only here once before.' She takes a deep breath. 'Yes, this is it.' She stoops over me. 'Do you remember what to say?'

I look at the massive front of the house. Apart from the baths, it's the biggest building I've ever seen.

'Why can't *you* knock?' I say.

'The doorkeeper is a punter,' she says. 'He knows me. He won't let me in.'

'What if he knows me?'

'He won't.'

'But what if he does?'

'Then we go back to the tavern and hope for the best. Is that what you want to happen?'

I think of crucifixion, and I shake my head.

She squats before me. 'This is a game, Antinous. All you need to do is pretend, just like you do with the punters. You can do that, can't you?'

I nod.

'All right, then.' Melpomene pushes me toward the door, and a black dog I hadn't seen before – teeth bared, leash yanked to its limit – seems to lunge at me from the doorstep. I gasp and leap back, and Melpomene grabs me from behind and claps her palm over my mouth.

'It's just a picture.' Her breath is hot in my ear. 'See?'

My heart pounding, I look again. It's a mosaic, a pattern of black and white stones that seem to move in the reddish flicker from the cressets. There are some words across the bottom that I can't read.

'Come.' She guides me up to the door. Picture or not, I'm careful not to step on the dog. Melpomene takes a deep breath, then grips the knocker and raps it sharply. We hear someone clearing his throat on the other side, and she slips behind one of the pillars. I hear a bolt sliding back, then the door swings open, and the silhouette of a man blocks the light from within. I draw a deep breath and step closer, as Melpomene instructed me to.

'I beg pardon, Your Honour,' I say, 'but I have an important message for your Dominus.'

I can't make out the doorkeeper's face against the light, so I can't tell if I recognize him or not. He's wearing a simple tunic, though, so I can see he's a slave.

'Who are you?' He has an accent. 'What's your business?'

'I come from Helicon.'

'Helicon!' The doorkeeper glances back into the house and pushes the door partway shut. 'What are you doing here?' he hisses.

'I have a very important message for Dominus.'

'Keep your voice down,' he says. 'Tell me what it is, and I'll pass it along.'

'This is for his ears only.' Don't back up, Melpomene told me. Don't let him shut the door. 'It's very important.'

'Go back to Helicon,' says the man. 'I'll tell him you were here, and he'll come along when he can.'

He starts to close the door, but to his surprise, and to mine, I put my hand on it and push back. I lower my voice, the way Melpomene lowered hers when she was threatening Focaria earlier today.

'He needs to hear this news tonight,' I say. 'He'll be very upset if he doesn't hear it immediately.'

Is this Sparrow speaking, I wonder? Or does Sparrow only come out when I'm frightened? I let my eyes flicker past the doorkeeper into the house, wondering if there's a real dog in there. I'm aware of Melpomene listening from behind the pillar.

The doorkeeper glares down at me, then plucks me by the tunic into the house, shuts the door, and backs me up against it. He has unruly hair and a beard. I can smell wine on his breath.

'If you're lying to me, pusus,' he says in a low voice, 'I'm going to beat you senseless.'

I meet his gaze and start counting silently to myself, but before I get to five, he lets go of me.

'Wait here.' He walks away up the short hall and into the bright room beyond. As I watch him go, the real dog I was fearing appears, rising from just around the corner. But unlike the fierce beast on the doorstep, this is an old mutt with a grey muzzle, prominent ribs, and shaky legs. It doesn't even look at me as it follows the doorkeeper into the house, its nails clicking against the tiles.

As soon as I can't see the doorkeeper or the dog anymore, I open the door. Melpomene slips in and squeezes my shoulder.

'Nicely done, Antinous!' she whispers.

'There's a dog,' I whisper back, but Melpomene pushes me further up the hall, into the light.

I've never seen an atrium, and at first sight, I want to turn around, bang through the door, and run all the way back to the tavern. You could fit our whole garden and kitchen into this room. It's wide and tall and square and clean, with a skylight full of stars above, and at the centre of it, a statue of a naked boy pouring an endless stream from a pot on his shoulder into a trembling pool of water. The room is full of golden light from brass lamps suspended from tall brass stands, one in each corner, and there are low wooden doors along the walls, surrounded by the most beautiful paintings

I've ever seen, colourful pictures of men fighting other men, men fighting beasts, men wooing women. Even the floor is beautiful, an intricate pattern of red and green. Everything gleams in the lamplight – the floor, the polished wooden doors, the lampstands themselves. In a corner across from us a small stone altar is lit by three candles, and above it is a painting of a bearded man with his hair parted in the middle. It's the new god, the Christ. He raises one hand in a two-fingered gesture, and his grave eyes stare right at me from across the room. I step back, and Melpomene catches me by the shoulders.

'Remember, Antinous,' she whispers, 'we pay for all of this.'

On the far side of the atrium beyond the pool is a smaller room with a table and some chairs, lit by a single lampstand. Beyond that, through a wide archway, lamps twinkle in a dark garden, and shadowy figures move among the trees. We can hear talk and laughter. Then two figures step out of the dark and into the light of the office. Melpomene's hands slip from my shoulders. I turn to see her disappear into a low doorway just off the hallway behind me, but before I can follow her, someone says, 'Who are you?'

A young man only a couple of years older than me is standing by the table in the other room. The table is heaped with scrolls, and he's holding one of them in one hand, his other hand cocked on his hip. The office is a step up from the atrium, so he looks taller than he really is. A slave boy my age glares at me from behind him.

'Are you new?' The young man steps down into the atrium and comes around the pool. The slave follows, still glaring at me.

I don't know what to do. This isn't Calidus, and it obviously isn't Granatus. Melpomene didn't prepare me for this.

The young man stops a few paces from me, balancing the scroll on his hip. He has rings on his fingers and a gold locket on a leather thong around his neck. His tunic is expensive, and I can smell the scented oil in his hair. For a moment, I wonder if he might be a wolf, like me, but why would a wolf have a slave? The young man looks me up and down. Once, a look like that would have frightened me, but now I'm used to it. It's the same look I get from punters every night of my life.

'Do . . . you . . . under . . . stand . . . me?' the young man says. From behind him, the slave boy, who has pale skin and almost colourless hair, speaks sharply in a language I don't understand.

'I don't know what you're saying.' It just slips out of me, and the young man slowly starts to smile.

'You're the boy from Helicon.' He narrows his eyes at me. 'Did my brother send for you?'

'Marius!'

Calidus is striding quickly round the pool, followed by the anxious doorkeeper. The dog is not with them. 'Father wants the scroll,' he says. 'Now.'

Marius waves his hand at me. 'Is *this* Antinous?'

Calidus is taller than his younger brother, and he looms over him. 'What did I just say?' The doorkeeper hovers a few paces back, glaring at me.

Marius sighs. 'Fine.' As he turns, the slave boy behind him doesn't get out of his master's way quick enough, so Marius shoves him. 'Idiot.' The slave gives me one more evil glance, then trots after Marius back through the office and into the garden. As soon as they're out of earshot, Calidus shoves me roughly back into the front hallway.

'The *fuck* are you doing here?' Then, over his shoulder, to the doorkeeper, 'What the fuck were you thinking?'

'He said he had a message, Dominus.' The doorkeeper cringes. 'He said it was for the ears of Dominus only. He said—'

Without looking at the man, Calidus raises his finger to silence him. He pushes his face close to mine. 'You don't *ever* come here.' I can smell the wine on his breath. 'Tomorrow I'm going to have Audo beat you bloody, if I don't do it myself.'

300

'Audo's dead.' Again, it just pops out of me. Whatever Melpomene prepared for me to say is pointless now.

Calidus stands bolt upright. He looks at the doorkeeper. 'Did you know this?'

'Dominus, I . . .' The doorkeeper spreads his hands.

Calidus turns back to me. 'How did he die?'

'He, um . . . he . . .' I don't know what to say.

'I killed him, Your Honour.'

We all turn to see Melpomene standing in the hall, back erect, palms pressed together.

'Dominus, I swear I didn't let her in.' The doorkeeper's eyes are wide. 'This boy must have . . .'

'I killed him in the act of love, Your Honour.' Melpomene steps forward into the light. Her lower lip trembles, as if she might cry. 'At the peak of his ecstasy, Audo's noble heart just . . . gave out.' She lowers her eyes. 'I humbly beg your pardon, Your Honour. I wish it weren't so.' She looks up at him again. 'But it is.'

'Oh, fuck,' Calidus groans. 'Where is he now?'

'In my bed, Your Honour. Where I left him.'

'Fuck!' shouts Calidus. He spins on the ball of his foot, running his hands back over his hair. He looks at Melpomene. 'Nice work, bitch. You picked a great fucking night to kill my pimp.'

'Your Honour, I . . .'

He walks straight up to her. 'My uncle's here tonight.'

'Your Honour?'

'My *uncle*!' says Calidus. 'The *bishop*.'

'Your Honour, if I may,' says Melpomene, lowering her voice as well. 'I'll be brief . . .'

'Calidus!'

Now an older man is coming into the atrium. He's heavier and balder than Calidus, but they have the same features. This must be his father, Granatus, our other Dominus.

301

'Your brother tells me we have a special visitor.' He stares at me as he comes round the pool.

'I'm taking care of it, Father.' Calidus moves into the older man's path.

Granatus raises his hand, the way Calidus lifted his finger to the doorkeeper, and Calidus lowers his head and steps aside. Granatus's gaze turns to the wolf.

'Melpomene, isn't it?' he says.

'Your Honour.' She dips her head.

'Who's this?' Granatus lifts his chin at me.

'Nobody,' says Calidus. 'The kitchen boy.'

'This is Antinous,' says Melpomene. She nudges me.

'Your Honour.' I make a stiff little bow.

'You say "Dominus",' Melpomene corrects me.

'Dominus,' I say, and retreat behind Melpomene.

'It's been a long time,' Granatus says to Melpomene. 'Why are you here?'

Melpomene glances at Calidus, who widens his eyes and throws up his hands. She fixes her gaze on Granatus and says, 'Audo has died, Your Honour, in the throes of—'

Granatus lifts his hand. 'I don't need to know. As long as he wasn't murdered.'

Behind Melpomene I draw my breath in sharply, but no one notices.

'Oh, no, Your Honour!' cries Melpomene. 'It was his noble heart . . .'

'Well, noble.' Granatus purses his lips and glances at Calidus. 'Who's minding the tavern?'

'We shuttered it for the evening, Your Honour.' Melpomene steps forward. 'Or rather . . . I did, Your Honour.'

'Oh, *fuck*,' breathes Calidus.

'Out of respect,' Melpomene continues, licking her lips. 'It wasn't safe, Your Honour, to keep it open, without . . .' She takes another

302

step forward. 'Your Honour, if I might be so presumptuous . . . you're going to need to replace Audo . . .'

Calidus's mouth drops open.

'You need someone with experience . . .' Melpomene's voice is pulled tight like a cord. I've never seen her this nervous before. 'Someone who knows the profession . . .'

'No, no, no, no, no,' breathes Calidus. He turns to Granatus. 'I can find someone,' he says, but his father silences him again.

'Running a business,' Granatus says to Melpomene, 'it isn't the same as—'

'If you'll pardon me, Your Honour, but it is!' She steps closer. 'I know you'll have no reason to remember, but I made my living on the streets before I sold myself to you. Then I worked my way back to freedom, which you were so gracious as to—'

Granatus waves his hand.

'I know how to make money for you.' The words rush out of her. 'I've been doing it for years. I know all the secrets and tricks that wolves might use to cheat you, and I know how to keep them in line. And I've thought of some new ways to make money for you . . .' She glances back at me. 'I have some ideas . . .'

'Father, please,' says Calidus, 'let me handle this.'

Granatus lifts his hand and Melpomene and Calidus stop talking.

'Antinous,' he says. 'Step into the light where I can see you.'

Melpomene ushers me into the atrium. I stand at the centre of the four adults – Melpomene, Calidus, Granatus, the doorkeeper, all of them looking down at me.

'Father.' Calidus sidles up to him. 'He wasn't my idea. Melpomene—'

'Shut up.' Granatus isn't looking at me like a punter, but like a man buying a horse. 'How old are you?'

My mouth hangs open, but nothing comes out. By this point, Melpomene assured me, she was going to be doing all the talking. I have no idea how old I am, and Sparrow has abandoned me. I'm forced to endure this moment in my own flesh.

303

'What's keeping you, brother?'

Another man is coming into the atrium. He's of an age with Granatus, and maybe even older. He has the same bald dome and fringe of hair, but his lips and the line of his jaw are buried in a full beard, black with streaks of grey in it. He's less robust than Granatus, wearing a long-sleeved black robe belted around his narrow waist. No one speaks as he comes round the pool. Calidus and the doorkeeper exchange a look. Granatus straightens his back and lifts his jaw. Melpomene stares wide-eyed at the man and squeezes her hands so tightly her knuckles are white. The man looks at each of the adults in turn.

'Go back into the garden, brother,' says Granatus. 'Just a little business emergency.'

'Who's this?' says the bishop of Carthago Nova, as his gaze alights on me.

Everyone speaks at once.

'The kitchen boy,' says Calidus.

'I don't know,' says the doorkeeper.

'Antinous,' says Granatus.

'A wolf,' says Melpomene, and everyone else falls silent. 'Like me.'

The bishop shifts his gaze to her, and Melpomene holds it. She is taking deep, steady breaths.

The bishop levels his gaze at me. 'Who do *you* say you are?'

I look up at Melpomene.

'Don't look at her,' the bishop says. 'I'm asking you.'

'Your Honour . . .' I say.

'Your Grace,' says Granatus. He's getting red in the face. 'You address the bishop as Your Grace.'

'Your Grace,' I say. 'I am a wolf.'

'And why are you here?' says the bishop.

'Your Grace.' Melpomene suddenly drops to her knees. She tugs me down next to her. She bows her head, so I bow mine.

'Your Grace,' she says, 'I know I'm a vile, dirty, sinful woman, and I know I'm not fit to touch the soles of your shoes.'

'We are all sinners,' the bishop says.

'Your Grace,' she says.

'But the question is,' the bishop says, 'are you prepared to renounce the sinful life of the flesh and live in the light of your saviour?'

Melpomene lifts her head, so I lift mine, too. Calidus has gone white. He looks as if he might pass out. Granatus grinds his teeth as he calculates the loss in income if he loses another couple of wolves on the same day he's losing his pimp.

'Brother,' he says tensely, 'we have an agreement . . .'

'I know,' says the bishop. His lips are obscured by his beard. It's hard to read his expression.

'It's *expensive* being a member of the curia,' Granatus says. 'I only did it for you . . .'

The bishop lifts his hand. 'I know I'm not supposed to enquire where the money comes from.' He gestures at Melpomene. 'But here is this woman, right in front of me, on her knees.'

'She's on her knees every fucking day,' mutters Calidus, and Granatus slaps him. In the silence afterwards, all we hear is the trickle from the fountain.

'It's true, Your Grace,' says Melpomene. 'I only know one way to make a living, the worst way a woman can. I've swallowed so much filth, I'm rotten with it. There is no help for me, not even from God.' She lifts her eyes to meet the gaze of the bishop. 'But I serve a purpose.'

Granatus starts to say something, but the bishop lifts his hand. 'Let her speak.'

'I am a guard,' Melpomene says, fixing him with her gaze. 'I stand between rough men full of lust and sin and the honourable women of Carthago Nova. I let those men do what they want with me, because if they don't do it with me, then they will do it to your wives and daughters.'

305

She pauses, but she's not as nervous anymore. Her voice is steadier. Her breathing is slow. She and the bishop gaze at each other. The bishop slowly strokes his moustache and beard.

'You're not wrong.' He breaks his gaze with her to look at the others. 'She's not wrong.'

'Brother?' says Granatus. His face isn't as red now.

'A reverend correspondent of mine has said much the same thing to me,' says the bishop, 'in a recent letter.'

'Brother?'

'The bishop of Hippo?' He pauses for effect, but no one says anything. He sighs. 'Women like this are evil, but necessary, my correspondent says, like the public executioner.' He looks down at Melpomene. 'Or a sewer.'

'Your Grace.' Melpomene dips her head.

'So why *are* you here?' says the bishop.

She looks up at him again.

'Our pimp has died,' she says. 'He was with me when it happened. You might even say I killed him. So I'm here to offer myself as a sacrifice. I'm offering to take his place and run the tavern in his stead. To keep the women of this city safe.' She pauses. 'To be your sewer.'

The bishop sighs. 'Rise,' he says, and Melpomene rises to her feet, tugging me up beside her. The bishop turns to his brother.

'Will my church be finished without the income from . . . this establishment?'

'Yes,' says Granatus, 'but not as quickly.'

'Ah.' The bishop sighs again. 'This is not how the world should work, but it's how the world is, at least until the Day of Judgement. I'm sure the bishop of Hippo would agree.'

'So you're saying . . . ?' says Granatus.

'I'm saying,' says the bishop, 'that if this woman is willing to take on the burden of running this place, and if she's willing to suffer the consequences to her immortal soul, I don't see why

306

you shouldn't let her do it. Unless you plan to get out of the business altogether.'

Granatus clenches his teeth and says nothing.

'It's settled, then,' says the bishop.

'What about him?' says Calidus. Everyone turns to the young Dominus. His cheek is still red where his father slapped him. They all follow his gaze and look at me. I can hardly stand it, and I lift my eyes to the skylight above the pool, where the stars I can never reach stare brightly back at me.

'Well.' The bishop is already turning away. 'One does not gaze too deeply into a sewer.'

On the way back to the tavern, Melpomene holds her knife in one hand and my hand in the other. Even in the starlight, I can see she's smiling to herself. At first I think it's because of what she and the doorkeeper said to each other as he ejected us into the street – 'You're a lucky bitch,' he said, and she sang out, 'See you soon!' But then she starts to laugh, quietly at first, and as we come into our own street, treading carefully in the dark between the wagon ruts, her shoulders start to shake and her mirth echoes off the walls around us. She stops and throws her head back, looking up at the river of stars above, laughing out loud.

'What's so funny?' I say.

'That old man,' she says.

'Which old man?'

'The bishop,' she says. 'I like him.'

'But he hates us,' I say.

Melpomene takes my hand and leads me again down the street.

'No, he doesn't,' she says. 'He's as much of a whore as I am.'

'I don't understand,' I say.

'Yes, you do. You just don't know it yet.' She stops again and looks down at me. Her eyes are as bright as the stars. 'The whole world is a whorehouse, Antinous. Everyone's a whore. You are, I am, Euterpe is. The punters who use us are whores. Their wives and daughters are whores. All those men in their fancy house back there?' She tips her head back up the street. 'They're the biggest whores of all. The only reason that men like that hate wolves like us is because we're the only ones who are willing to say it out loud.'

She drags me along again, past Nazarius's shuttered shop, past the trickling fountain, along the wall of the tavern garden. She pauses with her hand on the door.

'I know you don't believe it when I say it, but you're a lucky boy.' She pushes the door open. 'You got to look behind the mask tonight and see how the world really works.'

She pushes me ahead of her into the shadowy garden.

'Buck up, Antinous,' Melpomene says. 'We have a lot of work to do.'

III

I am old now, and I live in a library. Most of my time I spend at this desk, in this chair, pushing this pen across this papyrus, using the last store of ink, so far as I know, in Britannia. When I'm not doing that, I'm reading one of the mouldering old books that crowd the walls around me. My reading is not disciplined or purposeful. I'm just passing the time. 'The reading of many books is a distraction,' says Seneca. 'If you're reading everything, you're reading nothing.' But for all his fine sentiments, Seneca was the willing tool of a monstrous emperor, so why should I follow that old hypocrite's advice on anything, when he never followed it himself? So I pick a book at random and read until I get bored. At my age, one book is as good as another. Maybe Seneca was right about that.

Don't worry, reader, I won't bore you with my indiscriminate erudition. If you're reading this – and you're probably not – you no doubt have a library of your own to bore yourself with. If your library is like mine, half the books are summaries of long-dead authors, and some are even summaries of summaries, written in the floridly allusive and overwrought style of the age. You don't need to read the original, the argument goes, when someone more intelligent and more learned has already done it for you. Maybe, maybe not, but either way, these latter-day histories tend to be unreadable and unfinishable. For all I know, so is mine. I apologize if my own style is overwrought. I, too, am a product of the age. Nobody's perfect.

Perhaps the most honest thing I've ever written is a simple list of all the words that name what the tavern turned me into. Over the years I've come across these words in the works of angry writers like Juvenal, sneering ones like Petronius, and lubricious ones like Martial, and one by one I've recorded them in my best script on a piece of parchment. Then I nailed the parchment to the wall of the library, just inside the door, where the sun would never shine and fade my careful lettering. It hangs there still, long since curled into a tight scroll by the damp – it rains all the time in Britannia – but the words are still nearly as bright as when I first wrote them down:

cinaedus
cinaedius
cinaedicus
cinaedulus
puellus
puer delicatus
agaga
cillo
concubinus
catamitus

There were others, but I ran out of parchment. There were also the proper names that others have bestowed on me – Mouse, Little One, Antiochus, Antinous, and that's just during my life in the tavern – but I've never kept a list of those. This is one of the techniques of empire, to possess things by naming them. It's not the principal technique, of course – that would be the expenditure of actual violence. But once the violence has been expended and empire has taken some person, place, or thing as its own, it gives that person, place, or thing a new name and erases the old one. This new name also erases the history of that person, place, or thing, as if everything that came before never happened. That's another of the conqueror's techniques: the pretence that empire is eternal, that it will not only last for ever, but has always existed. I don't know if the latter is the case; how can I know the truth about the past? I don't even know my own. But I can say with some confidence that empires don't last for ever – or at least not the empire I once belonged to. I'm living proof of that, as I sit alone in this crumbling library, the last of my kind, choosing my own name at the end, free by default, writing empire's epitaph.

Jacob is the name I am calling myself at the end, and it is the last name I will ever have. I chose it myself – or someone chose it for me, I don't remember – because I might be a Jew, and Jacob was the father of the Jews. But of course I've never wrestled with an angel, I've never fathered twelve sons, I've never led anyone into Egypt. I may even be an Egyptian myself, and I might not be a Jew at all. In the words of Varro, I used to be a tool who speaks. Now I am a tool which no longer serves any useful purpose, but which somehow still has the power of speech. Unlike other men – insofar as you can think of me as a man at all – I've never been bound by history or family honour. I have no history, I do not know my family, and God knows I am not honourable. I've never felt the weight that free men carried, of a thousand years of empire, of all those slaves and conquered peoples, of all those slaughtered men, women, and children. If I had been a free Roman, I'd have had to carry empire's weight my whole life, every day, all day long, with no rest and no relief. Instead, I have the freedom of the unremarkable, the powerless, and the insignificant. A broken tool myself, I live in a house full of unread books and broken tools, the irreparable detritus of a dead empire. I am the last Roman, the emperor of junk.

The morning after Audo's death, I woke up in the kitchen, nestled between Focaria and Euterpe in the corner by the oven. The night before, Melpomene and I had found Urania and Thalia huddled together by the water tank – Urania with her head tilted on Thalia's shoulder, fast asleep, Thalia fingering her medallion and keeping watch on the window to Melpomene's cell, where Audo lay. Melpomene said nothing, but disappeared into the arch. I crept into the kitchen and insinuated myself between Focaria and Euterpe. Focaria mumbled something and turned away, but Euterpe gathered me in next to her.

The next morning I'm awakened by Focaria pushing herself to her feet. Then I hear someone pounding on the garden door, and I watch Focaria stumble out of the kitchen, muttering. Euterpe is still asleep, so I creep to the door and peer out. On tiptoe Focaria pulls back the bolt, and Calidus and five more men come in after him – four labourers and a young Christian priest in a long, belted black robe. They leave the door open behind them, and in the street I see the back end of Brutus's cart, and beyond it, Brutus himself, in his ragged straw hat.

'Melpomene,' Calidus says, and Focaria yawns and looks around the garden. Thalia and Urania are stirring by the water tank.

'Upstairs,' says Focaria.

'Wait here,' Calidus says to the men, and he steps through the arch.

Focaria brushes by me into the kitchen without saying anything. I recognize the four labourers from a private dinner as members of the funeral workers collegium. They're all regular punters as well, and one of them has had me several times. As the other three eye Thalia and Urania by the water tank, he sees me in the kitchen doorway and smirks. The young priest stands apart, shoving his hands up the sleeves of his black robe and staring at the ground. He has a boyish beard, mere wisps along his upper lip and jaw.

Euterpe comes into the doorway and puts her arm around me. 'They're funeral workers,' I say.

'I know.' She touches the back of my head. 'What happened last night?' she says.

'We saw Calidus and his father,' I say. 'And the bishop.'

Euterpe frowns. 'The bishop saw you?'

Before I can answer, Melpomene marches out of the arch, with the wolves' mantles heaped over her arm.

'Everyone up!' she says. 'We're going to be Audo's mourners.'

'What?' Euterpe says. 'Why?'

'Calidus won't pay for mourners, so it's up to us,' says Melpomene briskly. 'Let's go, ladies. Everyone needs to wash up.' Then, to the men, 'Calidus needs you all upstairs.' As the four workers shuffle through the arch, she adds, 'You too, Father.' The priest nods without meeting her eye and follows the other men into the tavern.

As we take turns washing our faces and limbs over a bucket, we hear the voices of the men through the window of Melpomene's cell. Audo has been lying upstairs for nearly a day, and as I scrub under my arms, I hear a series of sharp cracks as they straighten his stiffened limbs. We all look up at the sound, Focaria especially. Now she's wide awake, handing round bread and cheese for our breakfast, and she looks as though at any moment she might drop the bowl and bolt through the open garden door. Melpomene puts her hand on Focaria's shoulder and whispers something in her ear, and Focaria disappears into the kitchen. Euterpe watches her go, but says nothing.

It takes all four of the funeral workers to carry Audo down. We hear them bumping down the stairs as Calidus uselessly directs them. 'To the left . . . I said left . . . no, *my* left . . .'

'Your Honour,' one of them says finally, grunting under the weight of Audo, 'we've done this before.'

They bring the body through the tavern and into the garden. It's already wrapped in a winding sheet, a long bundle that bulges in the middle and narrows at the ends. None of us say anything, but we all stop what we're doing and stare. The grunting men stutter-step Audo out the open door, with Calidus hovering behind them. Urania puts her arm around Thalia, and Euterpe does the same for me. The priest approaches us, averting his gaze.

315

'It's customary to, um, sing something, um, as you follow the, um, body,' he says. 'Or wail, or . . .' He makes a nervous gesture.

'We understand, Father,' says Melpomene. 'We will do whatever is appropriate.'

The priest nods and hurries out to the street. Melpomene announces, 'Put on your mantles.' Then, to me, 'You're fine, Antinous.' I'm still wearing my old tunic from the night before.

As the women slip into their mantles, I watch through the door as the men manoeuvre Audo into the cart. The cart's wheels creak a half turn, and up ahead Brutus shouts, 'Whoa whoa whoa,' as the mule at the front of the cart starts to walk forward. Focaria comes out of the kitchen with Audo's leather satchel, stuffed with bread and cheese and a wineskin. She hangs it round my neck and says, 'For the funeral meal, afterward.' Then she turns me round and makes me look at her.

'What did he say last night?' she whispers.

'Who?'

'Him.' She lifts her chin toward the street. 'The young Dominus.'

'About what?'

'How Audo died.'

'Mel told him Audo died in her bed. While they were fucking.'

She glances at the doorway. Calidus is already in the street, out of sight. 'And he believed that?' she says.

'I guess so.'

'What do you mean, *I guess so?*'

'He didn't ask her about it.'

She digs her fingers into my shoulders. 'Don't lie to me.'

'Focaria,' I say, 'Dominus doesn't care how Audo died. Nobody does.'

Focaria releases me. Euterpe murmurs something to her, but Focaria shrugs her off and disappears into the kitchen. Euterpe holds her hand out to me and I take it.

'Isn't she coming?' I say.

316

'I guess not.'

'Will she be here when we get back?'

Euterpe stares after her and says, 'I don't know.'

In the street, Melpomene confers again with the priest while Calidus distributes coins to the funeral workers. Brutus is already up front with his back to us and his fingers hooked through the bridle of his mule, Potiscus. Audo's swaddled feet poke out over the back end of the cart. Also in the cart are a pickaxe and several spades, and Euterpe takes the satchel of food off me and lifts it into the cart as well. Then we join Thalia and Urania, turning our backs on the small crowd that has gathered at the fountain across the street, watching and whispering. Melpomene bustles up to us, but before she can speak, Euterpe says, 'You don't really expect us to wail, do you?'

Melpomene doesn't want to lose her temper in front of the watching crowd, so she looks away from Euterpe to Thalia.

'You know some prayers, don't you?'

Thalia shrinks into her mantle and nods. She's clutching her chi-rho medallion. She glances past Melpomene at the crowd and says, in a small voice, 'I know some songs, too.'

'Funeral songs?' says Melpomene.

Thalia shrugs. 'Songs about death.'

'In Latin?'

Thalia shakes her head.

'They'll have to do.'

'All right, then.' Calidus interrupts us in a low voice. The priest moves up to the front of the cart next to Brutus. The funeral workers climb into the cart. Two of them stand up near the front, bracing themselves against the sides, while the other two sit on either side of Audo's feet with their legs hanging off the back.

'This isn't a holiday,' Calidus says. 'I need you all back here by this afternoon. I can't lose another day of business.'

'Your Honour,' says Melpomene. 'We'll do what's proper and come right back.'

317

'Right.' With no ceremony, Calidus turns and pushes through the crowd round the fountain, disappearing up the street. At the same time, Focaria slams the garden door behind us and slides the bolt, locking Audo out one last time.

Melpomene lifts her voice. 'We're ready, Father.'

Without looking back, the priest starts to pace slowly up the street toward the harbour. Brutus clicks his tongue and tugs on the mule's bridle, and the cart crunches forward. Melpomene ushers the wolves after it, first Thalia and Urania, then Euterpe and me. She brings up the rear. On the back of my neck I feel the gaze of the crowd behind us.

'Sing something, Thalia,' Euterpe says in a low voice.

Uncertainly at first, in a high, thin voice, Thalia begins to sing one of her sad Egyptian songs.

The little procession rounds the corner of the tavern past the dangling tintinnabulum, and we walk up the lane that runs behind the warehouses along the waterfront. The street is still full of cool shadow, but above the warehouses, the mountain across the harbour looms brightly, every bush and rock picked out in the morning light, the sky above it a brilliant, spotless blue. We pass a few shopfronts, all shuttered this early in the morning. There's no one else about, and the narrow street echoes with the clop of the mule's hooves and the rumble of the cart. Their legs swinging, the men in the back of the cart stare blankly back at us. Thalia's voice, high and pure, trembles in the air, seeming to come from everywhere and nowhere all at once. Her voice begins to falter, and Melpomene says, 'Keep singing.'

We pace steadily along the empty street until we come to the north-west corner of the city, where the aqueduct slopes down from the mountain. Here we pass through one of the old city gates, through the muttering chorus of cripples and beggars who huddle there. Then we pass under the dripping aqueduct, where the free-lance wolves under the tall archways stir in the shadows. It's even earlier for them than it is for us, and most of them are still sleeping, huddled together like dogs. At the sound of the cart and of Thalia's tremulous song, their gaunt faces lift toward us out of the shadows. One of the pale faces has a seam across it which might be a scar, but the face is much thinner than I remember Clio's being. We pass beyond the aqueduct. No one says a word.

We come to the bridge across the passage that runs from the brackish lagoon to the harbour, and over the low parapet I glimpse the cloudy, motionless stream, I smell the sour water and dried mud below. Out in the open air, Thalia's singing sounds even thinner than it did in the town, and once we reach the hump of the bridge, Melpomene says, 'That's enough, Thalia. You can stop now.'

At the crossroads on the far side, we turn right and walk along the side of the lagoon, where slow ripples of murky water lap among the reeds along the shore. This is the first time I have ever left the city, and now I'm even farther from the tavern than I was last night. To my left the mountain looms against the brilliant sky, with spiky green bushes and tufts of bleached grass among the rocks. A few huts cling to the steep slope, and in a stand of stunted trees higher up, I glimpse the creamy walls and red tiles of a villa. To the right, across the flat surface of the lake, I see the silhouettes of a boat and two stick figures casting a net over the glittering water.

'Eyes front, Antinous,' says Melpomene.

The cart creaks along ahead of us, the priest walking in front with his hands in his sleeves. All I can see of Brutus are his broad shoulders and the top of his hat. It's as if he doesn't know us. One of the men sitting on the back of the cart is napping, his head bobbing over his chest. The other one, the man who's had me, continues to stare back at me. We pass between small monuments on either side of the road, some of them like little houses with pillared doorways and steep roofs. They all have writing etched into them, and some have faces carved into their sides, their eyes and mouths closed, their features blunted by exposure to the sun and the rain. A few of the monuments are brightly painted, but on most of them the colours have faded or flaked away, leaving only the pale, weathered stone. Almost all of them are stained with graffiti, slogans I can't read as well as the usual obscene drawings.

'Are these houses?' I whisper. 'Do people live here?'

'They're tombs, Little One,' Euterpe says. 'Only the dead live here.'

We start to walk alongside a wall of rough bricks between the road and the lagoon. The wall only comes up to my shoulder, and over it I see a long enclosure of low mounds, about knee-high to a man. Some of them are square, some rectangular, some semi-circular, and they crowd the ground all the way from the wall down to the water. Some of the mounds have flat, mortared tops, while others are just rounded heaps of stones tufted with dry grass. Up ahead, the priest turns off the road and through an opening in the wall, and the creaking cart turns to follow the priest, jouncing over the ruts in the lane. Inside the wall, the funeral workers jump off the back of the cart while it's still moving and pluck out the pickaxe and the spades. Brutus turns the cart slowly around and tethers the mule to a wooden post, and for the first time, he and Euterpe exchange a glance. Melpomene approaches the priest, and while they murmur together, the four men with the tools filter through the mounds and find a spot down by the water. The one with the pickaxe spits on his hands, rubs them together, and begins to strike at the rocky soil.

'What do we do now?' I whisper.

'I don't know.' Euterpe is still watching Brutus, but he has turned away, gazing back down the road toward the city.

'Ladies.' Melpomene addresses us all. 'We have to wait while they dig the grave. Let's all have a sip of wine and make ourselves comfortable.' She pulls the wineskin out of Audo's satchel, jerks out the stopper, and passes it around. After we each take a mouthful, she offers it to the priest, who shakes his head and walks away between the mounds. She offers it to Brutus, who takes a pull and hands it back to her with a nod. Thalia and Urania, hand in hand, start to wend their way through the mounds, in a different direction from the priest.

'Don't leave the cemetery,' Melpomene calls after them. With one more glance at Brutus, Euterpe takes my hand and leads me away from the others, down toward the waterside.

'What's a cemetery?' I say.

'It's a place where they bury the dead,' says Euterpe. 'All these mounds have bones under them.'

'Bones?'

'When you die,' she says, 'your flesh rots away and only the bones are left. Here.' She stops us by one of the mounds close to the water. In front of it a stone marker nearly as tall as I am displays a crude carving of a man in a toga, his hand raised in the same two-fingered gesture as the painting of the grave-eyed Christ I saw in the atrium the night before. The figure's limbs and the folds of his toga are still fairly sharp, but his face has vanished.

'What happened to his face?' I say.

Euterpe brushes the figure's head with her fingers. 'His family probably rubbed it away.'

She leads me down to the side of the lake, where the flat water smells faintly of decay. The sun is getting higher and hotter, and Euterpe glances back at Melpomene before shrugging off her mantle and sitting on top of one of the mortared mounds, crossing her legs under her gown. She shields her eyes against the glare off the lagoon. I scuff along the shore, dipping my toe into the water.

'Take your shoes off if you're going to do that,' she says, and I take them off. I wade into the warm water up to my calves, sending ripples across the flat, featureless surface of the lagoon. Not far off along the shore, all four of the funeral workers are hacking a hole into the earth, making a heap of stones and dirt. Close to the road, Brutus sits next to Audo's body in the cart, taking a nap, his legs stretched out, his arms crossed, his head down, his hat tipped over his face. Across the lagoon, the two men in the boat are still casting their net over the water. Beyond them Carthago Nova shines under the morning sun, its pale wall overtopped by a jumble of red roofs, the upper rows of the theatre, and the hill of Asclepius, where the little temple shines against the blue. The city looks small, surrounded all around by mountains. The closer peaks are reddish under the bright sunlight, but the ones in the distance are only hazy blue silhouettes. Overhead, the featureless bowl of the sky is wider than I've ever seen it before. Beneath it I feel both free and insignificant at the same time, as if I could disappear into the blue and no one would notice.

'What did Mel say to Dominus last night?' Euterpe is leaning back on her arms, with her face lifted to the sun.

I check to see where Melpomene is. She's hovering over the men digging the grave and offering suggestions. Beyond her, the priest stands on the shore, staring across the lagoon and self-consciously stroking his nearly non-existent beard. Thalia and Urania are nowhere to be seen.

'The same thing she said to us.' I wade through the water, working the gritty ooze of the lakebed between my toes. 'She's the best person to run the tavern.'

'What did Granatus say? What did Calidus say?'

'They didn't think so, especially not Calidus.' I look at her. 'It was the bishop who thought it was a good idea.'

Euterpe sits up straight and looks at me, shading her eyes. 'The bishop?'

'Yes.' I kick some of the muck into the air and it plops in the water. 'He said she might as well.'

'Did he really?'

'He said she was going to hell anyway, so she might as well protect the city. Or something.' I splash about a bit more vigorously in the water.

'Little One, stop that.'

I look at her.

'Out of respect,' she says. 'For where we are.'

Along the shore, Melpomene is standing closer to the grave and pointing this way and that. Two of the men look at each other behind her back. One of them makes a rude gesture.

'Melpomene said the bishop was a whore,' I say. 'Just like us.'

'She said that to *him*?'

'No. To me, on the way home.'

Euterpe snorts. 'Well, she ought to know.'

'She said everybody in the world is a whore.'

Euterpe looks away across the lagoon. For a moment, the only sound is the uneven chunk and scrape of spades and pickaxe. Then she says, 'Did the bishop speak to you?'

'Not really.'

'What did he say?'

That I'm a sewer, I remember. *That I'm shit.* 'Nothing,' I say, and kick the water again. Before Euterpe can scold me, we hear raised voices near the grave. The digging has stopped.

'If you want it deeper,' one of the men is saying, 'we'll need more money.'

'The first time it rains,' Melpomene says, 'the lake is going to wash over it.'

'The lake's going to get into it anyway,' says another one of the men. 'Sooner or later.'

'That's not what we paid for,' protests Melpomene.

'This is exactly what you paid for,' says the first man. 'If your Dominus wanted it deeper and higher up, he needed to pay us for that.'

'He's not my Dominus,' says Melpomene. 'I am a freedwoman.'

The man in the grave leans on his spade and spits. Then he lifts his face to Melpomene and says something that I can't hear. He looks toward Euterpe and me, and then he looks in the other direction, toward the unseen Thalia and Urania. Melpomene says something back to him, casting a significant look further down the shore to the priest, who is idly poking the dirt with the toe of his shoe. The man shrugs and climbs out of the grave, then he reaches down and hauls out each of his mates. While Melpomene stares fixedly out across the lagoon, the men, laughing among themselves, let their spades drop against a nearby mound. One of them shoulders the pickaxe, and they filter back up through the mounds to the cart. Melpomene claps her hands.

'Ladies!' she says. 'Gather round.'

Up near the road, Brutus stirs from his nap, pushes himself out of the cart, and steps aside. The worker carrying the pickaxe tosses it into the cart, then all four men drag Audo off the back of it and start to lug him through the mounds, grunting and gasping as they turn him this way and that. Thalia and Urania stand up from behind a mound and start to work their way along the shore, followed by the priest. Euterpe hands me my shoes, and she shrugs on her mantle while I strap them on. Then we walk up the shore to the grave. It's rough and oblong and about thigh deep to a man, surrounded by a rim of displaced earth and stones. The wolves all line up on the lagoon side of it, and the priest stands at one end. The workers arrive, panting and sweating under the stiff weight of Audo, and they manoeuvre him alongside the grave. One of them says, 'On three,' and they start to swing him between them.

'One . . . two . . . *three* . . .'

Audo thumps into the grave, raising a cloud of dust. The workers step back, and everyone lowers their heads. The priest clears his throat as the dust settles.

'Did any of you know his full name?' he says, still not looking at any of the wolves.

The five of us look at each other, and Melpomene says, 'He was a German, I think. A soldier. Audo is the only name we know.'

The priest clears his throat and begins to pray. 'Dominus is my light and rescue, whom should I fear? Dominus is my life's stronghold. Of whom should I be afraid?'

Euterpe takes my hand on one side and Urania's hand on the other. Urania takes Thalia's hand, and she takes Melpomene's, and the five of us stand linked in a chain, heads down. The sun beats on the back of my neck. There is no wind. The only sounds are a bird chirping somewhere and the low droning of the priest. I sneak a glance at the cart, where Brutus is napping again, lying full length in the back of the cart where Audo's body had been, his hat over his face.

'Though a camp is marshalled against me, my heart shall not fear,' the priest is saying. 'Though battle is roused against me, nonetheless do I trust.'

Perhaps the priest picked this prayer because Audo was a soldier, but it doesn't seem right to me. Everyone was afraid of Audo, but he was afraid of Dominus. Not the Dominus in the prayer – well, maybe the Dominus in the prayer, too, but certainly Audo was afraid of Calidus and his father.

'One thing do I ask of Dominus, it is this I seek,' the priest is saying, 'that I dwell in the house of Dominus all the days of my life, to behold the sweetness of Dominus and to gaze on his palace.'

Did Audo ever enter the atrium of Dominus and stand there nervous and unwanted, like I did? I look up at Euterpe to see if she's wondering any of this too, but her eyes are closed. Across the grave, the funeral worker who has fucked me is peering at me from under his lowered brow. When he sees me looking back, he winks. I look down again into the grave, at the long, wrapped bulk of Audo lying stiff among the stones and dirt. As the priest drones on, I wonder what would happen if that bulk below me moved, if it sat up and clawed off the winding sheet, moaning and angry, and then reached up and dragged the five of us – his murderers – one by one into the grave with him? I shuffle my feet and glance

325

along the shore, wondering how far I would have to run to escape him. Euterpe tightens her grip on my hand.

Everyone's getting restless now. The four funeral workers look off to the side, or up at the sky. I feel the restlessness of the wolves, too, like a little wave that travels down the chain of our linked hands, all of us wondering, are we really done with Audo? Will he truly never hurt us again? Even the priest is speaking faster now, as if he too would rather be someplace else.

'If I but trust to see the goodness of Dominus in the land of the living,' he mutters quickly. 'Hope for Dominus! Let your heart be firm and bold and hope for Dominus. Amen.'

Even before he says, 'Amen', the funeral workers are stooping to retrieve their spades. As we five wolves release each other's hands and step away from the grave, the men start pitching dirt back into the hole, where it thumps and rattles and hisses against Audo. The priest walks away, and the wolves all troop after him. Euterpe pulls me along after her, but I glance back one more time at the white form of Audo, dirt and pebbles slithering off him. I wonder if there's enough earth in the world to cover him up.

'We've brought some food, Father, for a little meal in Audo's honour,' Melpomene is saying. 'Would you care to join us?'

'Thank you, no,' says the priest, still not looking at us, his hands thrust back up his sleeves. 'I have to, um, I need to, um, I have to get back . . .'

'Of course, Father,' says Melpomene. 'We understand.' As the priest hurries back through the mounds toward the road, Melpomene says to me, 'Antinous, go fetch the satchel out of the cart. Quickly.'

I run up to the road, making a wide berth of the priest. At the cart I try to lift the satchel full of food without waking Brutus, but he raises his hat and lifts his head.

'Is it over?' he says.

'We're sharing some food,' I say, clutching the satchel to my chest, 'if you want to . . .'

But Brutus only grunts and levers himself up and out of the cart. As I turn to go back, the priest and I come face to face. He blushes bright red, and we do a little dance, each of us looking past the other. Finally he steps around me and into the road, and I run back to where the wolves are gathering around one of the flat-topped mounds covered with mortar. Melpomene tosses away a desiccated bunch of flowers, then the wolves all crawl up on top of it, arranging themselves cross-legged under their mantles. I clamber on top of it, too.

'Is Brutus coming?' Euterpe murmurs.

'No,' I say.

We sit in a circle, and I drop the satchel in the middle. I wonder if the bones below can hear us moving about. As I'm settling on my knees, Melpomene looks past me, and we all turn to see one of the funeral workers coming toward us. Behind him, his mates are already finishing up with the grave, stomping on the dirt and tamping it flat with their spades. The man approaches the mound where we're all sitting. He rattles a fistful of coins.

'How about it?' He glances back at the men stamping on Audo's grave. 'We can pay.'

Melpomene fixes him with a look, but it's Euterpe who says, 'It's a funeral.'

'The priest is gone,' the man says, and it's true. Up the road, the priest is already halfway back to the bridge, walking quickly with his head down, and Brutus is untethering his mule from the post.

Euterpe looks to Melpomene for support, but it's clear Melpomene is thinking about it. Thalia and Urania watch the other two women.

'Not here, Mel,' Euterpe says. 'Not now.'

Melpomene narrows her eyes at the man, perhaps remembering her argument with him over the grave. 'No,' she says at last. 'Not today.'

The man shrugs and turns away. 'No,' he shouts back to his mates leaning on their spades. Two of them jerk their spades out of the ground, but one of them, the man who's had me before, continues to stare in our direction until one of the others hauls him away. A few moments later, they are tossing their clanging spades into the cart and clambering in after them. Without looking back, without a word, Brutus leads the mule and the creaking cart into the road.

Melpomene, meanwhile, is already hauling food out of the satchel. She passes the wineskin to Thalia, who gulps from it and passes it on. Melpomene cuts wedges of cheese with her knife, then breaks the loaf of bread into equal sections. She hands the bread and cheese around.

'This is my body,' Euterpe mutters. 'Think of me when you eat this bread.'

Thalia looks hurt. 'That's blasphemy. You shouldn't say that.'

'Why not?' says Euterpe. 'Audo died for our sins.'

'That's not funny,' says Thalia.

'I don't get it,' says Melpomene.

'Never mind.' Euterpe breaks off a piece of bread and puts it in her mouth.

The wineskin circles again. Urania hands it to me and wipes her mouth with the back of her hand. 'What happens now?'

'I'd like to know that, too,' Euterpe says. 'What did you say to Dominus last night?'

'What I needed to,' says Melpomene. 'Things are going to get better.'

'So, you're going to free us?'

'I keep telling you,' Melpomene says, 'you're not mine to free. But if we all work a little harder and a little smarter, each of you can save enough to do what I did, and buy your freedom.'

'If we live that long,' says Euterpe.

'Who's going to protect us?' Thalia is only picking at her food. She huddles in her mantle, fingering her medallion.

'Audo let things get out of hand too often,' Melpomene says. 'The trick is to make sure the punters are having a good time before they even come upstairs.'

'Who's going to do that?' says Euterpe. 'Are you going to watch the counter *and* work upstairs?'

'Well.' Melpomene smiles. 'I was thinking of having Focaria mind the counter.'

We all look up from our food.

'Focaria?' says Euterpe. 'Who's going to cook?'

'I'm thinking of buying a new cook,' says Melpomene.

'Will Calidus pay for that?' says Urania.

'He won't have to,' says Melpomene. 'I'll buy one with my own money.'

The rest of us glance round the circle at each other.

'I think Focaria's talents are better suited to working in the main room,' Melpomene says. 'She's never been much of a cook, but I think she can keep the punters in line.'

'Will they take her seriously?' Urania touches her own throat to indicate Focaria's collar. 'What about . . . ?'

'I'm going to have that removed,' Melpomene says.

Euterpe snorts.

'Look,' says Melpomene, 'as long as she keeps her mouth shut about what happened to Audo, and as long she doesn't run, there's no reason to keep it on. Dominus doesn't care if she wears the collar. Only Audo did. She has no reason to run now.' She looks meaningfully at Euterpe. 'She has every reason to stay.'

Euterpe says nothing.

'If I buy another cook,' says Melpomene, 'Focaria has no reason to sleep in the kitchen anymore, either. She can sleep where she likes.'

She watches Euterpe for a reaction – for gratitude, perhaps – but Euterpe looks away. Melpomene breaks off a piece of bread and regards it in the sunlight.

'Or I can have Dominus sell her,' she says. 'I can have him sell all of you, come to that. Start with a clean slate – a new Focaria and a new Audo and new wolves. Is that what you want?'

Thalia and Urania look down at their food, but Euterpe stares at Melpomene without speaking. Melpomene puts the bread in her mouth and chews slowly, staring steadily back at Euterpe.

'It doesn't have to be this way,' Melpomene says. 'I'm not your enemy.'

'You're not our friend, either,' says Euterpe.

'No, I'm not,' says Melpomene. 'But it's the world you're angry at, Euterpe, not me. And I didn't make the world. I've just learned how to live in it.'

Euterpe looks away across the lagoon. The sun beats down on our heads. Somewhere the bird is still chirping. No one speaks. Finally Euterpe looks back at Melpomene.

'You're not really going to sell us,' she says quietly. 'Are you?'

'That's not what I want,' Melpomene says. 'But don't ever forget – I don't need anyone's permission to do what I'm going to do.' She pauses. 'Well, I need the permission of Calidus and his father, but as long we make them money, without any more interruptions, I don't see any reason why I can't make your lives better. Happy slaves are profitable slaves.'

'But still slaves,' says Euterpe.

'Again, Euterpe,' says Melpomene, 'I didn't make the world.'

On the way back to the city, Melpomene slings the empty satchel over her shoulder and walks ahead of us up the road. Thalia and Urania walk arm in arm after her, whispering together. Euterpe and I bring up the rear, walking hand in hand.

'Is it really going to be better?' I say.

'Probably not,' says Euterpe. 'But if we're lucky, it won't get any worse.'

'If Mel takes her collar off, will Focaria stay?'

Euterpe is silent for a moment. 'I don't know.'

'You want her to, don't you?'

'I want . . .' She pauses. 'I want what she wants.' She looks down at me. 'That's what love is.'

'What if she wants to run?'

'Then I hope God smiles on her.'

We walk along the road in the sunlight, between the little houses of the dead. Off to our left, across the lagoon, the men in the boat are rowing back toward the city.

'Melpomene is wrong, Little One,' Euterpe says. 'Not everyone in the world is a whore.'

'We are,' I say.

'No.' Euterpe kneels in the lane before me. 'We're not. A whore sells herself, willingly. Melpomene is a whore, and for some reason, it's the nature of whores to think that everyone else is just like them. But you and me and Thalia and Urania, we're not whores. We're slaves. We have no choice. We can't sell what we don't own.'

'We do the same things Melpomene does,' I say.

'I know.' She kisses me. 'But it's not our choice. It's not our fault.'

'Everyone else thinks it is. The bishop called me a sewer.'

Euterpe closes her eyes, as if in pain. Then she opens them again. 'Listen to me,' she says. 'A wiser man than the bishop once said, there is neither Jew nor Greek, nor slave nor free, nor man nor woman. We're all the same in the eyes of God.'

'Even Audo?'

'Well.' Euterpe almost smiles. 'Maybe not Audo.'

'Who said that? Seneca?'

'No,' Euterpe says. 'A man named Paul.'

'Is he right?'

We hear a shout, and we turn to look. Melpomene is hailing us from the crossroads. Thalia and Urania are already halfway across the bridge.

'It's nearly noon!' Melpomene shouts.

Euterpe waves at her, then she stands and takes my hand again. We start toward the bridge.

'What Paul said,' I say. 'Is it true?'

'I hope so,' Euterpe says.

Now that Audo is dead, it's as if a lid has been taken off the tavern. The night after his burial, the main room is in uproar all night long. Word has spread of Audo's demise, and all our regulars are here, singing and laughing, toasting Audo at the top of their lungs, making obscene jokes at his expense.

'Eating, drinking, you name it, he never knew when to stop,' shouts Rufus the fishing captain. 'It don't surprise me he went one fuck too far.'

'There are worse ways to go,' shouts Nazarius the fuller, 'than dying in the saddle!'

The punters who come upstairs are drunker than usual, which makes them either much easier or much harder to handle. Quartus is even weepier tonight, and he gives Thalia a long, heartfelt speech which we can all hear in our cells, even over the riot downstairs, thanking the gods that it wasn't his own true love upon whom Audo collapsed in his final passion. When it begins to sound as if he won't stop talking, Thalia, for the first time ever, finally asks him to leave, rather testily pointing out that other punters are waiting. Late in the evening, Musa lurches into my cell, his face sweaty from the climb up the stairs, his eyes swimming in wine. He's never had me before, and as he stands in the doorway wobbling like a round-bottomed pot, I can't tell if he's walked into the wrong cell or if he's decided to try something new on this special occasion. His smell of garlic is even more overpowering than usual, and when he lurches toward me, I scamper off the mattress, terrified of being smothered. Whatever his intention, he passes out full length on my bed, so I draw the curtain and sit against the wall across from him, my knees drawn up to my chin, listening to the riot below while Musa drools on my pillow.

Melpomene is busier than ever, as punters line up for the extra thrill of risking the fuck that killed Audo. In between punters, she charges up and down the stairs in her dishevelled gown to supervise Focaria, who has been installed behind the counter against her will.

'I have to cook *and* wait on them?' she complained when Melpomene explained her new duties to her that afternoon. 'Do you want me to fuck them all while I'm at it?'

Focaria starts the evening angry, barking at the men to wait their turn, but as the night goes on and she helps herself to wine, she begins to give as good as she gets, to the great delight of the punters. Sitting on the floor of my cell while Musa snores on my bed, I hear the same jokes about Audo rising through the floorboards, over and over again – *fucked to death, died in the saddle, worse ways to go* – but it's Focaria who finally gets the biggest laugh of the night.

'You know what they say,' she shouts. 'A cunt's like a whirlpool. Once a man goes in, he never comes out again.'

The roar of laughter shakes the floor beneath my backside. On the bed, Musa stirs, breaks wind at both ends – yes, reader, it smelled of garlic – and passes out again.

'How many poor bastards have *you* swallowed?' Rufus shouts.

'Well, don't tell anybody,' Focaria shouts back, 'but I killed the son of a bitch.'

There's another eruption of laughter, and Melpomene pushes herself out from under her grunting punter to race down the stairs, where she sends Focaria back into the kitchen to fetch more food. Then she steps behind the counter and begins bantering with the punters herself.

'Don't believe it, lads, no one's been inside Focaria in years,' she shouts. '*I'm* the one who killed Audo.'

Over the uproar, I hear Nazarius shout, one more time, 'Well, if you gotta go . . .'

'That's our new motto here at Helicon!' Melpomene cries. 'Die happy, or your money back!'

At last I fall asleep, curled up on the floor. Sometime deep in the night, I wake briefly to see Musa's man, Deodatus, stooping over my bed, feeling the pulse of his master at his throat. My lamp is still burning, but downstairs, the tavern is quiet. I sit up, and Deodatus plucks a couple of coins out of Musa's purse, holds them up so I can see them, and lays them on my table, without saying a word. Then he doubles his master over his shoulder like a sack of grain and lumbers with him down the creaking stairs. For a moment I think, if Audo's truly gone, maybe it's safe to sleep on the mattress. But it still smells of Musa, so I blow out the lamp, crawl under the bed, and go back to sleep.

When I wake at dawn, I find the coins still on my table. Kneeling beside my bed, I pull my little cloth pouch out of a slit in my mattress and add the coins to my stash of tip money. In the hall, I lift Euterpe's curtain. She's sitting on the floor with her back against her bed. Behind her Focaria is face down on the mattress, just like Musa. Her wild red hair is spread over her eyes, and she's breathing open-mouthed like a beached fish. Euterpe says, 'You're going to have to get your own breakfast, Little One.'

Melpomene comes out of her cell, her gown hanging off her like a shroud. She looks older than I've ever seen her. Under last night's make-up, her eyes are gaunt and her skin is creased and sallow. She sees me, and she pulls Euterpe's curtain back. Euterpe looks up.

'So,' she says, 'are things better yet?'

Melpomene says nothing, but turns to lift the curtains of Thalia and Urania's cells. Then she returns to Euterpe, who glances over her shoulder at Focaria, lying insensible on the bed.

'Are you going to sell her?' Euterpe says.

'No,' Melpomene says. 'The punters loved her last night. But she and I are going to have a serious talk this morning. Can you take everyone to the baths today?'

'Me?' says Euterpe.

'Yes, you,' says Melpomene. 'Can I trust you?'

After a moment, Euterpe nods. Melpomene lays her hand on my shoulder.

'Not you, though,' she says. 'I need you.'

Melpomene sends me downstairs, and one last time, wearing my old tunic, I perform my old jobs, at least the ones that don't require me to go into the street. I tidy up the chaos in the main room – the overturned stools, the broken cups, the pools of piss and vomit in the corners. I bring in firewood, I clean out the ovens and start new fires. I scrub pots and pans, I sweep the kitchen, I feed the chickens. The other wolves, groggy and sore, help me out by emptying their own chamber pots and pulling their own sheets off the beds. Meanwhile, Melpomene gives Focaria a stern talking to in Euterpe's cell. In the garden, we can't hear what Melpomene's saying, but we can hear the steady, insistent rise and fall of her voice. To our surprise, we hear no response from Focaria, not a word. It's the first time in my experience that Focaria has nothing to say. When at last she comes downstairs, pale and hungover, her hair in a tangle, she makes a beeline for the kitchen. A moment later she comes out with her hair pulled back in a bun and the wicker basket over one shoulder. A moment after that, she's left the garden for the street, without saying a word to anyone.

'What's with her?' Urania asks Euterpe.

'I don't know,' says Euterpe, gazing at the door where Focaria has just left.

By time Focaria returns with a basket of fish, it's time for the Parade of the Wolves, and Euterpe, Thalia, and Urania put on their mantles and head for the baths. Melpomene tells me to stay behind and takes me into the kitchen. The fish are spilled across the tabletop, but Focaria is squatting in front of the glowing oven. There is a little heap of folded strips of papyrus on the floor next

335

to her, and she's feeding them one at a time into the fire. She stops when she senses us standing behind her.

'What are you burning?' says Melpomene.

I know, but I don't say. They're the curses Focaria bought from Opitria the fortune teller over the past few years. Until now they've been stashed in cracks and crevices all over the kitchen. I used to see them wedged between bricks and wondered what they said, until Euterpe told me they said nothing, just Opitria's gibberish.

'Nothing.' Focaria scoops up the last handful of strips and flings them into oven, where they begin to crisp and curl and burn. Then she pushes herself up and turns to us, her face a rigid mask.

'Antinous,' Melpomene says, 'can you clean the fish? Do you know how to get a stew started?'

I nod. I've watched Focaria do it often enough, I reckon I can fake it. Melpomene shrugs on her mantle, hooks Focaria by the arm, and tugs her into the garden. 'Leave the door unbolted,' Melpomene calls back to me as she pushes Focaria ahead of her into the street.

I start gutting the fish on the kitchen table, mostly making a mess of it. Then I shovel the bloody mess I've made into a pot of water on the stove and start chopping up vegetables. The wolves are the first to return, and Euterpe comes into the kitchen.

'Where is she?' She hunches in the doorway, still wearing her mantle. I'm at the stove, where I'm stirring the big pot of stew, hoping I've got it right. I threw in everything I remember Focaria putting in, but it doesn't smell the same.

'They went out,' I say. 'They haven't come back yet.'

'Did Mel say where she was taking her?'

'No.' We look at each other as the stew bubbles and fills the kitchen with steam. Neither of us wants to say out loud what we're thinking. Melpomene said she wasn't going to sell Focaria, but where else would she have taken her? But before either of us can break the silence, we hear the garden door open. Euterpe hurries out, and I hurry after her.

Melpomene is bolting the door. Focaria stands in the garden looking dazed. Her old iron collar is no longer around her neck, but dangling from her hand, though I can still see the calluses it has left on her shoulders and her clavicles. Standing off to one side, holding a little bundle of belongings, is an older, bearded man with dark skin and wiry grey hair. He's wearing a shapeless old tunic that hangs to his bony knees, and he's looking around the garden with watchful eyes. Euterpe and I stop in our tracks.

'This is Digitus, the new cook.' Melpomene shrugs off her mantle and drapes it over her arm. 'Show them your hand,' she says to the man.

He raises his left hand. It's missing the last two fingers. 'Digitus, get it?' he says in a heavy accent. 'My master make joke.' He smiles, and it turns out he's missing teeth as well.

'Euterpe. Antinous.' Melpomene points us out. 'They're wolves, they work upstairs. You'll meet Thalia and Urania later.' She points across the garden. 'Kitchen's in there.'

'Domina.' Digitus offers Euterpe and me his broken smile, then limps into the kitchen.

Melpomene turns to Focaria and takes the iron collar from her. It's no longer a perfect circle – there's a gap in it now where the bolt that held it together has been cut. She lifts it up in front of Focaria.

'I can always put this back,' Melpomene says. 'Do we understand each other?'

Focaria nods. Melpomene hands her the collar and turns her toward the kitchen. 'You're still in charge of all the cooking and shopping,' she says, 'but he'll do most of the work, under your direction. Starting today, you're the new Audo, and you'll work behind the counter whenever we're open. Remember what we talked about. No drinking till we close. Got that?'

Focaria nods again.

'Ladies, let's go,' Melpomene says briskly to Euterpe and me. 'We're open for business.'

Melpomene disappears through the arch, but Euterpe doesn't follow. Instead, she wraps Focaria in a tight embrace. The two women bury their faces in each other's necks, and behind Euterpe's back, Focaria's old collar dangles from her hand. Meanwhile I hear Digitus in the kitchen, theatrically gagging – 'Who made shitty stew?' – and I duck through the archway after Melpomene.

Over the following weeks, the tavern settles into a new routine, which is essentially the old routine, without Audo. In that respect, Melpomene is true to her word – life at the tavern does get better, if only because we no longer live under the eternal overcast of Audo's rage and the constant threat of his fists and feet. Melpomene's right about Focaria as well – now that she's literally off her leash, she turns out to be a livelier presence in the tavern than Audo ever was. She jokes and banters with the punters, she comes out from behind the counter herself to dispense wine from a pitcher, she swats away wandering hands with surprising good humour.

'Hands off,' she says. 'I've done my time in hell.'

To my astonishment, and Euterpe's, Focaria even leads the punters in song once in a while. She has a surprisingly robust singing voice, and through the floorboards I can easily hear her over the roar of the men joining in. Unlike them, she can carry a tune, and she knows all the words. She often sings the verses on her own –

> I don't know where I'm going
> I don't know where I've been
> But when I get between her legs
> I come right quick, and then
> I come right quick again!

338

Then she leads the punters in the chorus —

> Oh, oh, oh, oh
> My girl is simply the best
> On her back or on her knees
> She's always and ever eager to please
> When I'm deep in her cuckoo's nest!
> When I'm deep in her cuckoo's nest!

'Did you know she could sing?' Euterpe asks me one morning.

'She sang a bit in the kitchen,' I say, 'but always under her breath.'

'How does she know the words?'

'The same way I do,' I say. 'Punters only know six songs, and they all sing them all the time.'

Melpomene is right about something else as well — the punters are coming upstairs in a better mood than they did when Audo was running the tavern. Some of them come up laughing or still singing one of Focaria's songs, and it's a relief to have my curtain pulled shut by a man who is already smiling. Even when a fight breaks out down below, Focaria handles it with authority and dispatch, bellowing above everybody else, putting herself quickly between the combatants, puncturing their bluster with a well-deployed insult.

'If you boys want to fuck each other,' she says, 'take it upstairs.'

The punters love this, of course, and the tide of laughter is usually enough to dissolve whatever anger provoked the fight in the first place. On those rare occasions when the violence isn't deflated by one of Focaria's wisecracks, the other punters step in and eject the combatants into the street. This would never have happened under Audo — I've been in the tavern many times when the crowd reflexively retreated to the walls while Audo hammered some poor miscreant to the floor and then flung him into the street. Now they gather round Focaria, backing her up and even protecting her, if necessary.

'Stay the fuck out of my way,' she says when they do. 'I could've handled it.'

Meanwhile, Digitus, the new cook, has taken on my old night-time duties, carrying water, wine, and food up to the wolves, and carrying away our chamber pots. Thalia is the first to call him Diggy, and soon we all do. He also takes on Audo's old job of protecting us when necessary. He's old and bony, but he's remarkably deft with his cosh, a little leather tube filled with lead pellets that he carries in his tunic. Unlike Audo, he can't overpower a troublesome punter, but he can step in quickly and stun him with a sharp tap to the base of his skull. To begin with, though, he's also much too interested in what happens in the cells. I look up from under a punter one night to see Diggy's bright eyes peering through the gap in my curtain. That same night, I come out of my cell to find him outside Thalia's curtain, watching her with a punter through the gap and pleasuring himself with his hand. He sees me, but keeps going. When Melpomene finally catches him at it, she dresses him down in the hallway where we all can hear.

'Do you like it here?' she demands.

'Yes, Domina,' he says mournfully, in his heavy accent.

'Then wank in the kitchen,' she says. 'Punters don't pay for you to watch them.'

'Apology, Domina,' he says.

'If you want sex, you pay for it, just like everyone else.'

'Yes, Domina.'

'I catch you watching again, I'll sell you.'

'Please don't, Domina.'

She slaps the back of his head, then hands him her chamber pot. 'Do your job, and we don't have a problem.'

'Domina,' he says, and scurries down the stairs.

340

'If you see him doing that again, ladies,' she announces from the hallway, 'let me know.' Then she swishes through her curtain and back to her punter.

Even late in the evening, after the last punter staggers away and Focaria latches the shutters, the tavern feels different. We used to hear Audo lumbering about below, breathing heavily and muttering drunkenly to himself as he collected empty cups and moved tables and stools about. Most nights we heard him snoring, and sometimes shouting in his dreams, from the little room where he slept under the stairs. Now that he's gone, the silence from the main room is eerie, and for the first few nights, I can't sleep. I strip off my red tunic and lie naked in the heat under my bed, aching and sticky and bruised from my labours. In the ticking silence of the night, I can't help thinking of Audo wrapped in his sheet under a heap of earth and stones beyond the city wall, the brackish water of the lagoon seeping into his flesh and dissolving him down to his bones. If I hear a step in the street or the scrabbling of a rat in the walls or even one of the wolves shifting on her mattress, I start awake, my heart pounding, my eyes wide to the blackness of my cell, certain that the next sound I hear will be Audo's rotten corpse stumping up the stairs, or his skeleton rattling in the hallway, come to exact revenge for his murder. I wonder if the other wolves are awake, too, thinking the same thing. I want to seek comfort in Euterpe's bed, but now that Focaria has been liberated from the kitchen, she often sleeps with Euterpe, or at least spends some time with her before going downstairs to sleep in Audo's old room. It makes me feel even lonelier at first, because it feels as if Euterpe is choosing her over me. But I still crawl into bed with her in the morning, and in time I come to find it comforting at night to fall asleep to the murmur of their conversation or the creak of the cot as they make love.

The only one more restless than me, it seems, is Melpomene. I hear her rise in the middle of the night when the street is silent and she thinks the rest of us are asleep. She tiptoes down the stairs into the tavern, and, with my ear to the floor under my bed, I can hear the trickle of wine being poured, then the scrape of a stool, then the lightest tap of a cup being set on a tabletop, as our new pimp sits in the dark and thinks about what she wants to do next.

The changes Melpomene wanted to make didn't happen quickly, at least not at first. She wanted to replaster the cells upstairs, she wanted to buy new beds and mattresses, she wanted to kit all the cells out with cheap draperies like hers. She wanted to buy new gowns and mantles for the wolves, she wanted to replace the chipped old crockery in the main room with plates and cups of tin, she wanted to serve a wider variety of foods. It had been a long time since anyone had rented the private dining room, and she wanted to revive that as well, with a new table and new benches. She wanted to hire someone to repaint the menu in the main room from scratch, so that the pictures looked more like the five of us. She wanted to add Antinous to the menu, a picture of a young, willing, and limber boy who looked vaguely like me, submitting to a faceless punter.

But she was either going to have to persuade Calidus to pay for all these improvements, or pay for them herself. Once or twice a week, when he came to collect the profits, they engaged in spirited discussions in the garden or the tavern, while the rest of us got ready to go to the baths. It was an uphill fight for Melpomene, but she was not without her resources.

'Nobody even looks at the pictures,' I hear Calidus say one morning, as I lie under my bed with my hands behind my head. 'Why not just paint them over?'

'I'm sure you're right, Your Honour.' Melpomene's voice comes up through the floorboards. 'But a lot of our punters are men off ships in the harbour, men who've never been here before . . .'

'Yes, but they've all been in taverns,' Calidus insists. 'There isn't a sailor in the world who expects to get upstairs what he sees on the wall.'

'Of course not, Your Honour,' she says, and then lowers her voice. As the other wolves stir in their cells, I hold my breath, straining to hear. I roll onto my side and press my ear to the floorboards. I can just make out her voice, silky and insinuating.

'They pay more for me than they do for the other girls,' she's saying. 'Not because I'm so much better, but because I offer a man more when he comes into my cell. It's not just a bare room with a tired girl on an old mattress who's already had five or six men before him. He gets soft light and incense and something to look at besides crumbling plaster.'

Calidus says something I can't hear, and Melpomene continues, insistently, 'Because, Your Honour, you will make *more money*.' He says something else, and she says, 'I know I don't have to explain business to you, Your Honour. But surely you understand that the way to make money is to spend money.'

'All right,' he says. 'Say I pay to paint the place. Say I buy you new mattresses and . . . whatever. How does that make me more money?'

'Because we will attract more punters,' Melpomene says. 'We'll be the most popular fuck in the city.'

'If my uncle has his way, pretty soon we'll be the only fuck in the city.'

'All the more reason to make it special!'

'Next you're going to tell me I'll have to buy more wolves.'

'No, Your Honour!' Melpomene says. 'We will charge more, and we'll work faster!' Before Calidus can object, she rushes on. 'Every girl here has been a wolf for years already. They're experienced. They're skilled. They all know what to do.'

'Antinous . . .' Calidus says.

'Antinous is learning fast,' Mel says. 'He's one of our best earners.'

'You're talking about a lot of money.'

'We don't have to do it all at once,' Melpomene says. 'We can do it in stages. We redo one cell a week, and while it's being done, we rotate the girl into the empty cell at the end of the hall. The work can get done in the morning. We never close, not a single day.'

'So I'm paying a plasterer for five separate days . . .'

'I can negotiate a rate. Half the plasterers in town are regular punters.'

'How do I know . . .' Calidus says, and lowers his voice so I can't hear the rest.

'Tell me,' Melpomene says, in her deepest, breathiest voice, 'how have we been doing since Audo died?'

There's a pause before Calidus says, 'Better.'

'And why do think that is?' she says slyly. I can't see her, but I know she's close to him, touching him.

Calidus laughs. 'Audo never gave me this much trouble.'

'Your Honour,' Melpomene says, 'did Audo ever get you off the way I do?'

They fall silent and then, after a moment, I hear through the floorboards a soft grunt from the young Dominus. As quietly as I can, I push myself out from under my bed and sit cross-legged on the floor. Euterpe is watching me from my doorway.

'What are they talking about?' she says.

'She wants us to work harder,' I say.

Euterpe starts to reply, but she's interrupted by a long groan from below. We wait until he finishes, then we hear Calidus sigh heavily and say, 'I'll pay for a new wall menu. If you get results from that, we'll see about plastering the cells and . . . the rest of it. But not all at once.'

'You know best, Your Honour,' says Melpomene. 'I'm only trying to serve you as best I can.'

'Remember that,' he says.

'Always, Your Honour.'

344

Euterpe and I hear a shutter open and close as Calidus leaves, then we hear Melpomene sighing as she comes up the stairs. Euterpe turns to look down the hall.

'Euterpe,' I hear Melpomene say briskly. 'I need you to take everyone to the baths today. I have things to do this morning.'

'Yes, Domina,' Euterpe says. 'Whatever you say.'

Over the next few days, an artist and his slave repaint the menu in the main room of the tavern. They work only in the mornings, when we're closed, and since they need the shutters open to see what they're doing, Melpomene posts me on the bench outside, under the tintinnabulum, to turn away any stray punters who might think we've opened early. It's the easiest job I've ever had in my life so far. Wearing my old tunic, I sit in the cool shadow of the tavern with my back against the wall and my legs stretched out in front of me, listening to the racket from the harbour and the bustle of the street around the corner. I watch the little tangle of winged penises twist in the breeze above me, and I tell the odd passer-by, 'We're actually closed. We're just having some work done.'

The painter is a solemn, jowly man named Astius, and his slave is a boy named Petrus, a couple of years older than me. When I'm not staring at the sky or napping on the bench, I turn around to watch them through the doorway. On the first day, Astius and the boy cover the old menu with a thick coat of whitewash. On the second day, Astius sketches out each frame of the new menu in light strokes of charcoal, then Petrus fills in the background while Astius moves on to the next frame. They work in slow rotation, standing on the bench against the wall to do the top row, then standing on the floor to do the bottom row. When the first frame is dry, Astius starts to fill in the details, doing close work with his little brushes while Petrus hands him pots of paint, usually without a word passing between them. On the third day, Astius sketches each of the wolves in charcoal on a piece of wood. Melpomene hovers over his shoulder during these sessions and makes suggestions. Astius refrains from answering, but with each interruption from Melpomene, he draws a deep breath, rubs out the offending portion, and does it over.

'Do you want faces?' he asks her in a gravelly voice.

'Are faces more?'

'Yes,' he says.

Melpomene chews her lip and says all right, but only the wolves. We should only see the punters from behind.

During my session, Astius has me stand on a stool, and he looks me up and down, but not like a punter does. It's a strange feeling – he's looking at me more intently than any man has ever looked at me before, but there's not a flicker of interest in him.

'Lift your head, Antinous.' Melpomene taps the underside of her own chin with two fingers. Then, to Astius, 'I'm concerned about skin tone.'

'It's just a sketch,' Astius murmurs, his hand moving quickly and decisively.

'I know,' says Melpomene, 'but when you get to the actual pictures, I want Euterpe to look dark, but not too dark, and I want Antinous and Thalia to look about the same, almost as if they're brother and sister. And I'd like you to highlight the contrast between Urania's skin and her hair. I want to be the palest one, but not too pale. Not . . . ghostly.'

Astius says nothing, but just frowns at his sketch of me.

'I want the pictures to look like us, only more. . . .' Melpomene circles her hands in the air.

'They will,' says Astius.

By the third day, I catch Petrus looking at me. His glances show a little more interest than his master's professional gaze, but when he sees me looking back, he immediately looks away. By the fourth day, while Astius is making his finishing touches, Petrus meets my gaze and holds it, and later that morning, when they're almost done, I look up from a nap on the bench outside to see him standing beside me. He's taller than me, and his hair has been shaved down to stubble, emphasizing the shape of his skull. The first wispy hairs of a beard are coming in along his jaw and above his upper lip, and he wears splashes of paint on his tunic, his face, and his hands. He has the bluest eyes I've ever seen, even bluer than Focaria's. I sit up on the bench and glance back into the tavern.

'Where's your Dominus?' I say.

'Latrine,' says Petrus.

I look past him at the paintings, which are almost finished. Astius is a better artist than the man who painted our original menu. I was no expert at that stage of my life, of course, but even then I could tell that the figures were more lifelike, the poses more energetic. In each one, the punter has his back to the viewer, while the wolf is looking up at him or down at him or over her shoulder at him, her face clearly visible, her eyes moist with desire. Since there are six frames and only five wolves, the middle picture in the lower row is of a goddess reclining naked on a giant clamshell. In my picture, on the lower right, Melpomene wanted to show me sucking a punter's cock, but the painter told her the bishop wouldn't allow it. 'The aedile will shut you down if you show the boy doing that,' he said, 'and he'll prosecute me for painting it.' So Melpomene has settled for me on my knees, eyes shining, smiling up at the faceless punter.

'Are you really a wolf?' Petrus says.

'Yes,' I say.

'What's that like?'

'Don't you know?' I let my eyes flicker across the room, to indicate his Dominus.

'He doesn't use me like that,' Petrus says. 'He has a girl at home he prefers to me.'

'So you've never . . . ?'

'I have,' Petrus says, defensively. 'With the girl. Sometimes. When he's not around.'

'Oh,' I say. 'I've never done it with a girl.'

'Really? Not even with . . . ?' He gestures over his shoulder at the menu.

'Well, once,' I say. 'With Melpomene. But that was . . .'

'Which one is Melpomene?'

I point at the menu. 'Top left.'

Petrus widens his eyes. 'She's the old one.'

'She was just showing me how to do it.'

'Do you get to keep any of the money?'

I look back into the tavern. We're all alone.

'Sometimes punters give us a little extra,' I say. 'If they like us.'

'But you've only ever done it with men.' He lets his eyes flicker over the tintinnabulum hanging from the eaves. I look up at it, too. I've seen many more penises than that by now, and not a single one with legs or a tail or a pair of wings.

'Mostly,' I say, 'they do it to me.'

Petrus chews the inside of his lip. I can see a scar on his scalp, a thin white line through the stubble.

'What does the writing say?' I ask him. 'Under my picture?'

He looks back at the menu.

'"Antinous fellator",' he says. 'Do you get to keep the money?'

'You mean the tips?'

He nods.

'Yes.'

'What do you do with it?'

'I'm saving it,' I say, 'to buy my freedom.'

'Huh.' He thinks about this. 'You never think about spending it on one of the other wolves?'

I laugh.

'What's so funny?' He looks annoyed.

'Nothing,' I say.

Petrus stiffens his back and lifts his chin. 'Astius tells me I can't be free till I'm thirty. He says it's the law.'

'I've heard that, too.'

'How old are you?'

'I don't know,' I say. 'Ten, maybe.'

'You have a long way to go.'

'Yes.'

'Bet you'll have a lot of money by then.'

'If I live that long,' I say.

'Petrus!' It's Astius, coming back from the latrine. He snaps his fingers, and without even a look, Petrus turns away and goes back to work.

Early that afternoon, just before we open, Melpomene gathers us all in the main room and pours us each a cup of wine. Except for Focaria and Digitus, each of us is dressed for the evening, the wolves in their gowns and me in my red tunic, all of us freshly made-up and scented. It's like being behind the scenes at a theatre just before the actors go on stage. The room still smells of Astius's paints. Behind the counter, Melpomene raises her cup.

'To Audo,' she says. 'May the earth rest lightly upon him.'

'Not too lightly,' Urania says under her breath, but we all drink anyway.

'So, what do you think?' Melpomene gestures with her cup to the new menu. 'Don't we look gorgeous?'

'It's pretty,' says Thalia.

'What are they doing in that one?' Focaria says, pointing to the picture on the upper right.

'I'm sure someone can explain it to you,' Melpomene says, laughing.

'Mine doesn't look like me,' says Urania.

Melpomene ignores her. Instead she lifts her chin to Digitus, who sits apart from us in the corner, openly ogling the wolves in

349

their gowns. 'What do you think, Diggy? Do the pictures make you hard?'

'Yes, Domina,' he says mournfully, clutching his cup with his three fingers.

'Everything makes him hard,' mutters Urania.

'Antinous,' says Melpomene, 'what do you think?'

I look at the doe-eyed boy in the picture. I promise you, reader, I never looked at anyone like that in my life.

'It looks like me,' I say. 'I guess.'

'How does this make our lives better, Mel?' Euterpe says. 'What good do those pictures do us?'

I watch Melpomene decide not to get angry.

'Because we're all going to make more money,' she says. 'The better the place looks, the more punters we bring in. The more punters we bring in, the more money we make for the owner. The more money we make for the owner, the more he'll be willing to make our rooms nicer.' She takes a sip of her wine. 'Not to mention the extra money we'll each make.'

'More punters,' says Euterpe. 'So are we going to work later every night? Or faster? Or both?'

Melpomene still won't take the bait. 'Punters are easy to please. The faster you get one off, the quicker it's over.'

'And the faster we go to the next one,' says Euterpe.

'We all know how much you enjoy talking to the punters,' Melpomene says. 'If all Brutus wants is conversation, he can get married.'

Euterpe bristles at this, but says nothing. The others sneak glances at her.

'Listen, all of you.' Melpomene leans on the counter. 'How do you think I earned my freedom? By raging at what I couldn't change? Or by working smart and watching for my opportunity?'

The others wait for Euterpe to say something, but she's still silent. Finally Urania speaks up.

'How many more?' she says. 'Each night, how many more?'

'I've been keeping track for a long time,' Melpomene says, 'even before Audo died. Each of us is doing between six and eight punters a night. I want to get that up to between eight and twelve.'

'That could be twice as many,' says Thalia, as mournfully as Digitus.

'Possibly,' says Melpomene. 'Some nights it'll be less.'

'And some nights it'll be more,' says Urania.

'Well,' says Euterpe at last. The others stop talking and look at her. 'As long we get a nice painting out of it . . .'

Under her breath, Focaria mutters, 'Be quiet.'

'. . . and who knows,' Euterpe persists, 'maybe a new gown and a better mattress and if we're really lucky, a chamber pot with a lid on it. Then, yes, sure, it's all wonderful. We're happy to work twice as hard.'

'Do you want to take your chances with a new Dominus?' Melpomene says. 'It's easily done.'

'I don't think that's what she's saying,' says Thalia. 'You're one of us. You know what it's like—'

Melpomene cuts her off. 'I *do* know what it's like. I *was* one of you, but I'm not anymore. Before any of you came to Helicon, I earned my freedom the hard way. Only Clio was here when I was still a slave, and look what happened to her.'

'What happened to Clio wasn't her fault,' Euterpe says.

Under the table, Focaria squeezes her lover's hand. '*Please*,' she whispers. '*Just shut up.*'

'Maybe it was and maybe it wasn't,' says Melpomene. 'I used to be where you are now, true. But through hard work and a little luck, I pulled myself up.' She pauses. 'How old are you now, Euterpe? Twenty, twenty-one?'

Euterpe says nothing. Under the table she lets Focaria squeeze her hand, but she doesn't squeeze back.

'Well sister, I was sucking cock before you were born,' says Melpomene. 'I've swallowed an ocean of cum over the past twenty-five years. But because I didn't *whine* about it and wish for a life I will never have . . .' She stands up straight and spreads her hands. 'Here I am, now. In charge. Running the place.'

We're all looking at her now. It's not possible to look away. Even Digitus is trying to make himself as small as possible.

'I said it was going to get better,' Melpomene says. 'I never said it was going to get easier. I'm a freedwoman now, because for years – *years*, ladies – I took care of myself at the same time as I did what I was told. If you do as I say, and follow my example, I can help you stay alive until you have a chance to do what I did.'

She comes around from behind the counter and stands over us. Behind us, Digitus shrinks into his corner.

'Or,' she says, 'you can take your chances with a new Dominus. Or you can get some lonely punter to buy you. Or you can go live under the arches with Clio and suck the cocks of cripples and lepers. Or you can just die. Those are your choices.' She looks at each of us in turn, holding our gazes whether we want her to or not. 'I'm saying this to all of you, not just Euterpe. I may not be your friend, but I am the best thing that ever happened to you.'

'Thank you.' It's Focaria, speaking under her breath. She looks up at Melpomene. She swallows and says, 'Thank you,' a little louder.

After a moment, Thalia says, 'Thank you.'

'Yes,' says Urania. 'Thank you.'

'Gratitude, Domina,' says Digitus from his corner.

I hear a ringing in the air, as if someone has boxed my ears, and then I hear myself say, 'Thank you.'

Under the table, Euterpe lets go of Focaria's hand. She says nothing.

*　*　*

Do you see how it works, reader? A slave learns to look at herself and see only what the master sees. She learns to be grateful when her master lets her eat, when he lets her sleep, when he lets her live. Any day she wakes up to another dawn is a good day, any night she doesn't get hurt is a good night. Any food she eats is a gift that she doesn't deserve and shouldn't expect to get. An hour's rest – an hour when she isn't being pawed or fucked or beaten – is an hour in paradise. An hour to herself is almost unthinkable. A slave helps to forge his own chains. A slave narrows his own horizons. A slave digs his own pit and stands in it, peering over the edge at everyone else's feet and counting himself lucky whenever they don't step on him.

That's what Aristotle thought, anyway. I haven't read him in years, but as I recall, the argument goes something like this: there are superior people and there are inferior people, and the inferior people are actually better off if they serve as the tools of the superior people, because that's all they're good for. A slave is to the master as the body is to the soul, or as the animal to the human being, or the tool to the craftsman, or the child to the father, or the woman to the man. Or something like that. A man who is by nature another's possession is, by nature, a slave. Natural slaves have no interests of their own, and they benefit only from being part of the larger whole, like a hand benefits from being part of the body. A hand doesn't play the harp by itself, it needs the musician's superior mind to guide it. And how can you tell the inferior people from the superior people? It's simple: the superior people are the ones who are masters, and the inferior people are the ones who are slaves. If that's not perfectly reasoned, I don't know what is. QED.

Seneca, that old whore, was more subtle than Aristotle. He said that a free man and a freedman and a slave all live under the same sky and walk the same streets and breathe the same air. He said that the soul of a god could descend with equal ease into a senator or into a slave, and that someone with a great soul could leap straight from the gutter to heaven. He said that all bad men are slaves, whatever their station in life, and that only the wise man is free, no matter how lowborn he is. But then he said that the vast majority of men are bad and only a very few are wise, and so, worse luck, we're all slaves really, when you think about it. You might be a slave in real life, Seneca says, you might spend your days at the beck and call of your master, leaping to service his every need and anticipate his every whim, but the hardship of your life doesn't matter as long as you're the emperor of your own soul. And you might be a master whose every need is catered to by other people, you might rely on them to feed you and bathe you and keep you warm, but if you are ruled by your desires and do not discipline your soul, then you are a slave.

'And so,' Seneca explains to his weary body slave, who sits against the wall just outside the circle of lamplight on the philosopher's desk, 'you're potentially the master, and it's possible I'm really the slave.' The slave who might be a master blinks in the shadows, fighting to stay awake. 'Now fetch me another pen,' says Seneca, 'this one has gone dull.'

I don't know which one of these philosophers is right. They're both long dead, so perhaps they know now. As I keep telling you, reader, I'm no philosopher myself, but I do know that philosophers love paradoxes and tautologies. Perhaps what Aristotle and Seneca were saying boils down to the same infinite regress, a pair of facing mirrors in which my own image recedes into the distance, until I dissolve in the darkness: I do what I'm told because I'm a slave, and I'm a slave because I do what I'm told.

And so we worked faster. No more poetry readings from Quartus, no more pillow talk with Brutus, no more patiently waiting for the Garlic Farter to huff and puff himself to climax. They fucked, they came, they left.

Now that Melpomene had planted the idea in my head, I began to keep track of the number of punters who entered my cell each evening. This was a bad idea, because it only made the work harder. It discouraged me to realize, late in the evening, that I had serviced only half the punters Melpomene expected me to, and that I had that many again to do before I could curl up under my bed and fall into an exhausted sleep. This made me even more tired and listless as the night went on, which required me to work that much harder to show enthusiasm, which in turn made me feel even more tired and listless. I saw the same fatigue in the faces of the other wolves each morning, even Melpomene. She tried to hide it by wearing her make-up all the time now, but you could see how tired she was underneath the paint. The others didn't even try to hide it. It was as if we were spiralling into a whirlpool, knowing that no matter how hard we struggled, we were all going to drown.

Meanwhile, in the room below, Focaria led a nightly party — singing songs, trading jokes, breaking up fights without dispensing any blows or spilling anyone's blood. Her prickly bonhomie became one of the tavern's chief attractions, drawing a larger and more boisterous crowd than we'd ever had before. Punters began to line up for the wolves, waiting on the bench under the bright new menu, and Digitus became the unofficial doorkeeper, taking note of each man's preference and letting him know when his wolf was available. From my cell upstairs, I could hear his croaking voice joining in on the singing sometimes as well.

In the mornings, we rose later than we used to, bruised and sore and hungover. Melpomene rarely came to the baths with us now, staying behind instead to meet with Calidus or oversee improvements that she hoped Calidus would pay for. Using her own money, she came back one day with an armload of erotic lamps from one of the stalls in the theatre, each one showing some obscene image like the pictures on our wall.

'I got them for a song,' she said happily. 'The man said no one would buy them anymore.'

She finally persuaded Calidus to hire a plasterer, and over the course of a couple of weeks, each of us moved temporarily into the empty cell across from mine while the artisan and his slave replastered our walls. To the annoyance of Calidus, this took longer than expected, because the new plaster in each dank, sunless cell didn't dry as quickly as the plasterer promised. The overwhelming smell of fresh plaster also had the effect of discouraging the punters, which made our lives briefly easier. But we were soon each back in our cells, which were now little white boxes, temporarily clean and bright, with no stains, no cracks, and no graffiti. That didn't last long, of course, and I'll confess I was the first to deface my own wall. In the morning before the other wolves stirred, unable to sleep, I used a stone to scratch a sparrow on the wall under my bed. I'm no artist, but I sketched him in flight, his wings curved out from the crude oval of his body, his little beak pointed at the sky, his legs hanging down below, unchained and free.

Our chief moment of respite was at the baths, and now that Melpomene rarely joined us, Urania and Thalia began to decline the money of Gracilis and Simplex, refusing to sneak off for a quick one in an alcove. They preferred instead to soak their bruises and sore muscles in the caldarium, sitting with their eyes closed and their heads tipped together. Now that Diggy was doing most of the shopping in the morning, Focaria sometimes joined us. I had never seen her naked before, and at the baths, she turned shy, retreating even from Euterpe to the farthest point around the rim of the pool and stripping off her dress with her back to us. In the moment before she sank into the water, I could see the ropy muscles around her arms, the loose flesh around her middle. Unlike the rest of us, she didn't use the baths to catch up on her sleep, but sat up to her chin in the water with her hair tied up, gazing wide-eyed at the patched and mildewed gods overhead. Sometimes, without warning, a chunk of plaster fell from the ceiling into the water, and she started and hunched her shoulders against the little circular wave that spread across the pool. The rest of us barely moved. We were used to it.

'Why doesn't she sit with us?' I whisper to Euterpe one morning.

I knew that Focaria still spent most nights in Euterpe's bed. They often fell quickly into an exhausted sleep, without talking or making love. When they did talk, their voices often descended into a hissing argument, which usually ended with Focaria stumping down the stairs in the dead of night to sleep in Audo's old room.

'She's a Briton,' Euterpe whispers back. She watches Focaria across the pool, something remote in her gaze. 'She wasn't raised as a slave like we were. She isn't used to taking her clothes off in front of other people.'

'Don't Britons fuck?'

'I think they leave their clothes on,' says Euterpe. 'It's too cold in Britannia to take them off.'

'Do you still love her?' I whisper.

Euterpe tips her head back and lets the water lap the underside of her chin. 'Yes,' she says, though she doesn't sound happy about it. 'Do you?'

Across the pool, Focaria turns her back, rises from the water, and reaches for her dress as she steps out of the pool. She plucks a clean towel off a bench and steps into an alcove to dry herself and dress. When I'm sure she can't hear me, I say, 'I don't think she ever loved me.'

Euterpe puts her arm around me. 'That's not true,' she says.

I don't want to talk about it, so I say, 'What's going to happen?'

'What do you mean?'

'Are we always going to have to work so hard?'

'Little One,' Euterpe sighs, 'you know I can't answer that.'

I press against her and whisper directly into her ear. 'Do you still think about running?'

She scowls and puts her finger to her lips, then looks around. Thalia and Urania are napping together with their heads barely out of the water. Simplex has walked off into another room, where I can hear his keys clicking on his belt, and plump Gracilis is curled up, asleep, on a bench. Focaria is nowhere to be seen.

'Focaria doesn't have a collar anymore,' I whisper. 'All three of us have saved some money.'

We hunch together with our heads just above the water. 'It's dangerous to talk about it,' she says under her breath. 'The three of us still don't look like each other.'

'What if,' I whisper, 'we pretend that she's your slave? Or that you're her slave?'

'And who would you be?'

'Your slave,' I whisper. 'Or your son.'

'Little One,' she sighs, 'there's no place to run *to*.'

'We could buy passage on a ship,' I say. 'We could go to Africa, where they all look like us.'

'All the sailors know us,' she says. 'We'd never even get on board.'

'Then we could walk out that road that leads to the cemetery,' I say, 'and just keep going.'

'The country is empty for miles around. We'd die.'

'We could take food and water with us. Focaria would know what to do . . .'

Euterpe presses our foreheads together.

'Little One,' she says, 'I'm not sure she'd come with us.'

'I thought you said she loved us . . .'

'She has more to lose than we do.' Euterpe squeezes the back of my neck. 'Her life *is* better now. She's old enough to earn her freedom, and she might even have enough money set aside to pay for it. If she runs now—'

'Who's running?'

Focaria squats next to us on the side of the pool. Euterpe and I spring apart, splashing.

'No one,' says Euterpe.

'Because that would be stupid,' Focaria says. 'You might as well cut your own throat.'

'We were just talking,' Euterpe says.

'Talking is dangerous,' says Focaria. 'You should know that by now.'

The two women exchange a long look – Euterpe peering up out of the water, Focaria squatting above her, her hair down. For the first time, Euterpe looks frightened of her lover.

'What are you going to do?' Euterpe says.

Focaria looks along the rim of the pool at Thalia and Urania, who still seem to be napping.

'I'm not going to do anything.' She kneels and takes Euterpe's face in her hands. 'I would never . . . *never* say anything. But if you do it, don't tell me. I won't come with you. If you go, you go without me.'

'I would never go without you,' Euterpe whispers. Under the water, she grasps my wrist. 'Neither of us would.'

They look into each other's eyes. Focaria kisses her suddenly on the mouth, then she releases Euterpe and pushes herself to her feet with a grunt, towering above us. Across the pool, Gracilis has opened his eyes on the bench, and he's staring at us.

'What are you looking at?' Focaria says.

In the narrow lane on the way back to the tavern, Focaria comes up to me where I'm walking with Euterpe, takes me by the hand, and pulls me back. Euterpe hesitates, but walks on. Focaria drags me to a stop, grabs me tightly by the shoulders, and shakes me.

'If you ever try to take her from me,' she says, 'I'll kill you.'

I look toward Euterpe, walking away, but Focaria shakes me again.

'I mean it,' she says. 'She's everything to me. You're nothing.'

Sparrow watches from above as an angry woman shakes a wide-eyed boy in a dirty doorway.

359

'I know,' I say.

'Don't make me choose,' she says.

'I won't!'

Focaria shoves me back, nearly knocking me off my feet.

'Go on,' she says, 'catch up to her.'

Sparrow flutters after me as I run to Euterpe and take her hand.

'What did she say to you?' she says.

'Nothing,' I say.

'Ladies,' Melpomene announces that afternoon, 'we'll be shutting our doors to the punters early tonight. After sunset we're locking ourselves in for a private party.'

We are each perched on a stool around one of the tables in the tavern, and Melpomene has poured each of us a cup of wine. None of us speaks, but we're all thinking the same thing – a private party will be more work, one way or another. Thalia and Urania exchange a glance, but say nothing. Focaria sits slightly apart, at the next table, staring into her wine. Euterpe lets out a long sigh, but she, too, says nothing. Behind us, Diggy fidgets in the corner.

'Calidus is hosting a comissatio for his younger brother, Marius,' continues Melpomene. She stands behind the counter, as imposing as a general addressing his troops.

'What's a comissatio?' says Thalia.

'A drinking party,' says Euterpe, before Melpomene can answer. 'For rich boys.'

'Calidus's younger brother Marius is coming into his majority,' Melpomene says, 'so Calidus is throwing a party for him and his friends.'

'So they'll all be boys,' says Euterpe.

'Our guests tonight,' Melpomene says, as if Euterpe hadn't spoken, 'are not going to be like our usual punters. They'll be younger than most of the men we entertain, and for most of them, this will be their first visit to a wolf.'

'So they'll all be virgins?' says Urania.

'What's a virgin?' I whisper to Euterpe, but she touches me to be silent.

Melpomene smiles slightly. 'I expect most of them have had a slave in their households. Which means,' she continues, forestalling any commentary, 'that they'll be expecting more from us than they can get at home.'

'Meaning what?' says Euterpe.

'Meaning something more special than some sullen kitchen girl,' says Melpomene. 'We need to put our best foot forward tonight.'

'Foot?' mutters Urania.

'Our Dominus is going to be with us tonight.' Melpomene comes around from behind the counter and poses with her palms pressed together at her waist. 'He's bringing his beloved younger brother and boys from some of the best families in the city. This is our chance to show that Helicon isn't just for sailors and slaves. This is a chance to show we can serve a better class of customer.'

She pauses for a reaction, but no one says anything, so she says, 'Perhaps you understand now why we've put so much time and money into this place, why we have a new menu and new plaster and new draperies. I want to raise our prices, and that means offering something more to better punters. It also means,' she continues, 'better gratuities.'

'But not tonight,' says Euterpe.

This catches Melpomene off guard.

'Calidus owns the place,' Euterpe continues. 'He's not paying for this party, is he?'

After a moment, Melpomene says, 'No, he's not.'

'So none of these rich boys are expecting to spend any money tonight.'

'Not tonight, no.' Melpomene lifts her chin. 'We shouldn't expect anything extra.'

'So nobody's making any money tonight. Not even you.'

'Think of it as an investment.' Melpomene looks at each of us in turn. 'If we show the rich boys of Carthago Nova what we can do, we will all make more money in the long run.'

Still staring in her wine cup, Focaria says, 'You've got to spend money to make money.'

'That's right,' says Melpomene.

Euterpe gives Focaria a withering look, then turns to Melpomene. 'Only it's not money we're spending,' she says.

'Look.' Melpomene snatches a stool from another table and sits with us. 'If we do well tonight, there will be more private parties, where they *will* pay.' She smiles, just us girls together. 'Which will be less work and more money for all of us.'

The others look to Euterpe, who says nothing.

'I can threaten you with beatings and worse,' Melpomene says, 'but I don't want to. I don't want to be that kind of Domina.'

We all slide glances at each other – Melpomene is not our Domina – but we say nothing. She goes on as if she hasn't noticed.

'I need you to give these boys the night of their lives, not because you have to, not because I'm threatening you, but because it's in your own best interest.' She lays her hand on Urania's wrist. 'Isn't your cell nicer now?'

Euterpe watches as Urania says, 'Yes.'

Melpomene moves to Thalia. 'Didn't I get you a new mattress?' Thalia glances at Euterpe and nods.

Melpomene moves her gaze to Euterpe, but she knows not to reach across the table and touch her. 'I got lids for all the chamber pots, didn't I?'

'You did,' Euterpe says.

'These things cost money,' Melpomene says. 'And the only reason Calidus is willing to spend it is because we've been making more punters happy and making more money than we ever did under that brute Audo. Antinous,' she says, touching the back of my hand, 'are you making better tips?'

362

I can feel Euterpe's gaze on me, but I can't look at her. I shrug. Melpomene squeezes my hand.

'Inch by inch,' she says, 'step by step, we are making this the best tavern in the city.' She smiles at all of us. 'We should be proud.' She sits up straight and beckons Digitus from his corner. 'Diggy, pour everyone another cup.'

Digitus hobbles to the counter for the pitcher, then hobbles round the table, topping everyone up. Then he steps back, clutching the pitcher to his chest. Melpomene lifts her eyebrows at the assembled wolves, and we all pick up our cups.

'To Helicon,' she says.

Not long after dark, I hear the rich boys before I see them. Their shouts and laughter echo up the street and through my window, so I stand on my little table to see torchlight rippling under the eaves of the shops and houses in the street. The noise and torchlight swell beyond our wall, and then I hear pounding on the garden door and the voice of Calidus shouting for someone to open up. Diggy limps out and hauls back the bolt, then presses himself against the wall as the boys pour through, followed by a pair of slaves carrying torches. The boys are all wearing the nicest tunics I've ever seen, and in the middle of them, dressed in the nicest tunic of all, is Marius, the boy I saw in the atrium at Dominus's house. His hair is oiled and coiffed, he's wearing rings and a bracelet, and he's laughing and shouting louder than any of the others. They spread across the garden, poking into corners, trampling Focaria's plants, and calling out the garden's most sordid features at the top of their lungs.

'This latrine stinks!'

'The kitchen's worse!'

'What's up there?'

The boys all look up at the second floor, and I duck away from the window.

'Lads!' Calidus shouts, and I peek out the window again. He comes in last and shuts and bolts the door. 'This way!' He waves them into the tavern. Yapping like puppies, the boys flow in a jostling, shoving pool through the archway under my window. I jump down off my table, and I can feel the floorboards vibrating under my feet as they fill the room below.

'Who are these young reprobates?' roars Focaria, at her prickly best.

'Your worst nightmare,' laughs Calidus, and everyone cheers.

The boys below are as uproarious as punters on a busy night, only at a higher pitch. I lie down on my bed to wait for my first guest. I've already had a couple of punters earlier this afternoon, before we locked the shutters, but since then I have bent over my washbasin and scrubbed my face, underarms, groin, and backside. I have reapplied my make-up, oiled my skin, dabbed myself with scent, sweetened my breath with mint leaves. My curtain is open, and my new lamp, embossed with a pair of grappling lovers, is lit. From my mattress, I stare up at the new blue and yellow draperies that stretch corner to corner of the ceiling like a low-hanging cloud. They don't make the work any more bearable. They only make the cell seem smaller and closer, like a perfumed trap.

But no one comes. Down below, some of the boys are singing, rather uncertainly, as Calidus teaches them the words to one of filthier songs the punters like to sing. Some of their voices are piping and high, some are deep, some wobble up and down in pitch. All of them sound strange to me. Could I ever have been one of them? Did I ever have a chance to be a boy like that? Then, two or three at a time to reinforce their courage, they start to come upstairs, whispering and giggling in the hall as they peer into the cells where Melpomene, Urania, Thalia, and Euterpe wait for them – gowned and scented and made-up, kneeling or sitting on their new mattresses, overhung by draperies, in the steady glow of their new lamps. Melpomene has warned us that, unlike

364

our regular punters, these boys might need a little friendly encouragement to cross the threshold.

'I've been waiting for you,' I hear Melpomene say in her plummiest voice.

'I'm happy to see you,' says Thalia.

'Come in, if you're going to,' says Urania.

'Don't be afraid,' says Euterpe.

I'm kneeling on my mattress, too, when at last one boy peeks round the edge of my door. It's Marius himself, the young man of the hour. He glances over his shoulder at his mates, then turns back to me, staring at me wide-eyed. In the atrium he looked assured and arrogant, but here, in my doorway, he regards me as if I might be the chained dog on the doorstep of his father's house. Beware of the wolf. I lower my head and look up at him invitingly. I pat the mattress beside me. *Are you new?* I almost say. *Do you understand me?* But then he jerks away, out of sight. I hear urgent whispers and laughter in the hall, but he never returns, so I lie down with my hands behind my head and listen to the exertions of the boys in the other cells. One of the boys whoops when he comes, one of them cries like a baby, another squeaks like a small, trapped animal. Was one of them Marius? I have no way to know. Then I hear feet pounding down the stairs and a cheer that shakes my bed as they return to the others below.

Now a steady torrent of feet pound up and down the stairs. Boys crowd the hallway and eavesdrop on their mates, peeking through the curtains, the bolder ones shouting encouragement. Cries and laughter fill the upper floor of the tavern like a swiftly rising tide, drowning out the wolves, who find themselves working with an audience, like gymnasts or gladiators. I catch snatches from my sister wolves: Urania sighing heavily, Euterpe saying with uncharacteristic sharpness, 'One at a time.' Even Melpomene has abandoned her usual theatrics, in the interest of moving boys through her cell as quickly as possible.

Lying on my mattress, I want to share the burden of my sisters, but I also hope that none of the boys enters my cell. I feel guilty and relieved all at once. This is the easiest night I've ever had as a wolf. If it weren't for the racket, I might even be able to sleep. During a lull, I hear Thalia crying across the hall, then Urania's footsteps as she enters her friend's cell. I get up and peek into the hall. Euterpe leans in her doorway with her eyes closed and her gown hanging open, fanning herself with her hand. I touch her lightly, and she flinches. Then she sighs and lays her hand on my shoulder.

'How many?' she says.

'None,' I say. 'None of them want me.'

We hear a single pair of footsteps coming up the stairs, and she pushes me toward my door. 'Go in your room,' she says. 'Keep out of sight.'

But before I can disappear, Melpomene comes into the hallway from the stairs, clutching her gown shut. Under her smeared make-up, her face is drawn and tense.

'Antinous!' she says. 'How many boys have you had?'

'None,' I say.

'Why not?' she demands.

'Leave him alone, Mel,' says Euterpe. 'They don't want him.'

The curtain to Thalia's cell slides back, and Urania appears in the doorway.

'None?' She levels her gaze at me. 'You could make more of an effort!' When Euterpe starts to protest, she says, 'He could! We're doing all the work!'

Behind her, Thalia is curled up on her mattress with her gown pulled tight around her like a cocoon.

'They don't know you're here,' Melpomene says, 'that's the problem.'

'No, it's not,' Euterpe says. 'Some of them may want to, but not in front of the other boys.'

Urania glares at me. 'Then go downstairs and take some of them

366

into the garden.' She wheels on Melpomene. 'Some of them are coming up *twice*,' she says. 'And *none* of them are tipping.'

'They're not going to,' sighs Melpomene, weary of having to explain this again. 'It's Calidus's party, none of these boys expect to pay.'

Urania ignores her. 'You need to pull your weight,' she barks at me. 'Suck some fucking cocks!' She steps back into Thalia's cell and yanks the curtain shut.

Melpomene grabs me by the arm. 'Go downstairs and help out.' She pushes me toward the stairs. 'Focaria and Digitus can't keep up.'

Euterpe opens her mouth to say something, but thinks better of it.

'What do you want me to do?' I say.

'Go around with a pitcher of wine.' Melpomene wipes the sweat off her forehead. 'Smile. Make eye contact.'

She gives me another shove, and Euterpe steps back into her cell. I start down the stairs as another pair of boys are coming up. We edge past each other, the boys looking me up and down and then bursting into laughter when they reach the top. I come into the tavern, as bright as an apple in my red tunic and my unsmeared make-up. To my right, in the smoky private room, boys are lolling on the benches along the large table while Marius holds court from the far end, loudly bragging about what he did upstairs.

'I've been up twice already!' he shouts. 'I'm going to have them all!'

The others give a ragged cheer and shout out 'Me too!' or 'I've been up three times!' Marius's gaze comes to rest on me, and I turn away into the main room, where boys perch on the little stools around the tables, their voices slurred, their eyes watery, their heads wobbling as they burst out laughing at nothing in particular. Without a word, Focaria hands me a pitcher of wine and shoves me into the room. I circulate, topping up cups. Most of the boys pay me no attention, well used to ignoring slaves who wait on them at home. One or two look me up and down, or whisper something to the next boy. Focaria, meanwhile, is frantically running plates of sausage in from the kitchen, where Digitus is furiously frying them. Calidus is circulating, too. He's drunk, but not as drunk as the boys. He stays on his feet, gliding restlessly back and forth between the tavern and the garden, where a few of the boys have gone to throw up or pass out. The two slaves who accompanied the boys are also in the garden, their torches extinguished for now. They're resting with their backs to the water tank and their legs stretched out in front of them. They're guzzling wine and stuffing themselves with sausage and joking with each other under their breath at the youthful goatishness of their masters.

I have never seen this many boys in one place all at once. Not even the rough boys on the corner or along the quay congregate in numbers like this. Most of these boys are older than I am, but a few are as young as me. Not only do they wear nicer clothes than the boys on the street, but, at least under the influence of drink, they are louder and more confident, moving through the tavern and the garden as if there is no place they can't go, no place they aren't welcome, nothing they can't say or do. Which, of course, there isn't. The rich boys are better fed and more robust than the lean and bony boys who haunt the corner, but the real difference is in their eyes. The corner boys have a narrow, watchful, guarded gaze that sees everything and misses nothing. They can gauge in an instant what a person's weakness is. The rich boys, on the other hand, have wide-open gazes that see almost nothing except themselves. They don't need to gauge the weakness of others, because everyone is weaker than them. They don't have to take anything, because everything is theirs already. They see me and don't see me at the same time, as I glide among them with my pitcher of wine, not a boy like them, but a walking piece of furniture, a speaking tool, a slave.

I carry the empty pitcher to the counter for Focaria to fill again, and Calidus comes up behind me and lays an almost friendly hand on my shoulder. I instinctively give him the Antinous Fellator look from the menu on the wall, thinking he wants to go upstairs. But he looks down at me as if he's sizing me up, almost as if he wants to ask me a favour.

'Tell me your name again.' His speech isn't slurred, but he speaks louder than necessary, even over the low roar of the drunken boys.

'Antinous, Dominus.'

'Antinous!' He mimes surprise. 'Who gave you that name?'

'Begging your pardon, Dominus,' I say, 'but you did.'

He laughs and squeezes my shoulder. He lifts his eyes to the menu on the wall. Thanks to the skill of Astius and his slave, the colours of the new paintings are vivid in the yellow lamplight. On the bench below the pictures, five boys sit slumped with their heads on each other's shoulders, their mouths hanging open, empty cups in their laps or dangling from their fingers, ready to drop.

'How many of them have had you?' Calidus says.

'None of them, Dominus.'

'None! Really?'

Focaria watches us from behind the counter. She's refilled the pitcher, but she knows not to interrupt Dominus, so she picks it up herself and begins to circle the room.

'I think they'd all rather have a woman, Dominus.'

'Not all of them,' he says. 'Come with me.'

Hand on shoulder, he directs me just inside the doorway of the private room. The air is close with lamp smoke and the smell of sweaty boy and piss. Marius is holding forth at the end of the room. Several boys have their heads down on the table, and the rest are slumped on the benches, laughing immoderately at everything Marius says.

A boy stumbles down the stairs as we enter, jostling Calidus, and he stops the boy.

'How many times have you been up there, you beast?' he says.

The boy only laughs and pulls himself free, and he pushes two boys aside on the bench, making a space for himself.

'Three times!' Marius calls out to his older brother. 'I've been up three times!'

'You said two before!' someone shouts, and the room fills with catcalls.

'Come here,' Calidus calls out, beckoning his brother. Marius mimes surprise, as if to say, 'Who, me?' But Calidus beckons more emphatically, and Marius comes round the table, pushing boys out of his way, stepping over one who has passed out on the floor. Calidus claps him on the shoulder.

'You need some fresh air,' he says. Then, to me, 'Antinous, show him where the latrine is.'

'I know where the latrine is,' says Marius. He pushes me away and sways across the main room, toward the archway to the garden. Calidus shoves me after him.

'Go,' he says, not sounding drunk at all.

I come into the garden to find Marius staring up at the moon. It hangs high overhead, dimming the stars around it, silvering the leaves of the trampled plants in the garden. The two slaves have disappeared, who knows where, but one boy still sits against the wall near the door to the street, crying quietly to himself. He looks up as I come out. Marius ignores him, but when I meet the boy's bleary gaze, he leaps to his feet and flees past us into the tavern. Marius and I are alone now, though I can hear Digitus moving about in the kitchen and I can smell sausage frying.

'So, where is this latrine?' Marius is looking at me now.

I point across the garden.

'Show me,' he says.

'Dominus,' I say.

Marius watches me pass. Behind me, he says, 'Don't call me that.'

'Dominus?' I turn back to him.

He grabs my arm tightly, almost painfully. 'I *said*, don't call me that.' He marches me past the door of the latrine and into the corner behind it, by the woodpile. We're in shadow here, out of the moonlight, and out of sight of the tavern. He looks back across the silvered garden, then he pushes me up against the wall of the latrine and kisses me hard on the mouth. He's taller than me, and I'm not sure what to do at first – this almost never happens with a punter – but then I start to kiss him back. He tastes of wine and sausage, so it's not unpleasant, but I can feel him trembling. I put my arms around him, but he pushes me away and stares at me across the distance between us, breathing hard. I start to sink to my knees, thinking that's what he wants, but he grabs me by the arms and hauls me upright. Still breathing hard, he lets go of me and turns slowly around. He reaches back and pulls me up against him from behind. My head only comes up to between his shoulder blades, but even so, he pulls one of my hands across his chest and puts my other hand between his legs, where he's already hard. Then he leans forward and braces himself against the woodpile.

'Do it,' he whispers.

'Dominus?'

This has *never* happened before. I've had punters reach around and stroke me and even make me come, but I've never had one ask me to enter him. It just isn't done. It's not what I'm for. It would make him lower than me, and there can be no one lower than me.

'Don't call me that,' he hisses. 'Just do it.'

'I . . . I can't,' I say.

'Why not?' he says, irritated and desperate all at once.

'You're too tall,' I say.

Marius pushes away from the woodpile and crouches on all fours in the weeds, pushing up his backside.

'How about now?' he says over his shoulder.

I kneel behind him and reach around for his cock again. My mouth is dry.

'Yes, Dominus.'

'Call me Marius,' he says. '*Do it.*'

I try to pull my hand away from his cock, but he grips my wrist.

'Muh . . . Marius,' I say. 'I need my hand for a moment.'

He lets go of me, and I spit on my hand and stroke myself, trying to make myself hard. On the night she made me a wolf, and on many occasions since, Melpomene has drummed into me that a man can penetrate another man, but he can never allow himself to be penetrated. A man who fucks is still a man, but a man who is fucked is a woman, or worse. That's what *I'm* for, she's told me, over and over again. Punters come to fuck me, not to be fucked *by* me.

'Well?' says Marius.

I spit on my hand again to lubricate myself, and I enter the young Dominus. He gasps and lifts his hips to meet me. It's not like the time when Melpomene took me in her mouth, when my cock was wrapped in something warm and wet and alive. Rather, it's like pushing through a tight ring of muscle into a hot void.

'Harder,' says Marius. My thoughts race, but not in the usual way. Sparrow does not take flight, but if he were watching us from above, at my pale backside bobbing in the shadow of the latrine, he would be laughing. And he'd be right to laugh, because it *is* funny. The world has turned upside down, and the slave is fucking the master. The boy is fucking the man. Antinous is fucking the emperor. For the first time in my life, I'm doing to him what everyone else does to me. Does it hurt him like it still hurts me? I don't care. Does he like it? I don't care about that either. Does he feel afraid and humiliated and numb, the way I do? God, I hope so. I almost start to laugh out loud, but I catch myself, knowing how dangerous that would be. I press my lips together to keep the laughter from spilling out, thinking, *If they could see me now!* Would Melpomene be proud? Would Audo be angry? Would Nazarius think the slave is at last getting his proper revenge? I know what Renatus would think, and a little gasp of laughter escapes in spite of myself, which I disguise as a groan of pleasure.

Marius is breathing harder and bucking faster. I'm enjoying myself, but not in the way you think, reader, not in the way a punter does. I am aware of the dirt under my toes, I'm aware of the stink of the latrine, I'm aware of the rumble of voices in the tavern, I'm aware of the cool night-time air on the back of my legs. I'm looking at the stars overhead, I'm thinking of a million things at once, and not one of them is the boy underneath me. For all I care, I could be sitting outside the little temple on the hillside, shying stones at cats. I could be swimming in the harbour with the fisherman's boys. I could be flying over the countryside like a god, hand in hand with the Syrian girl, both of us naked as the day we were born, both of us laughing, both of us free.

Then Marius whimpers and shudders and comes in my hand. He bucks me off him and scrambles away from me into the weeds. He sits with his back to the woodpile, his chest heaving, and he stares at me in the dark with wide, fearful eyes. An instant later, he has me pinned to the wall of the latrine with his arm across my throat, choking me. He pushes his face close to mine, his breath humid with wine and sausage, his eyes full of rage.

'If you *ever*,' he hisses, 'tell anyone about this, *I will kill you.*'

I can't speak, I can barely breathe, and yet I'm thinking, *This is the second time today someone has threatened to kill me.* Now Sparrow is hovering overhead, watching.

'I will have you lashed, then I will have your bones broken, one at a time. Then I'll have you crucified. Do you understand?'

All I can do is gag and wheeze. I see stars erupting in blackness. Up above, Sparrow can hear me choking. Marius presses his lips to my ear.

'In Rome,' he whispers, 'they burn little rent boys like you alive.'

Then he kisses me again, hard, on the mouth, and I feel smothered and helpless. I'm certain that I'm about to die. Up above, Sparrow can see my arms and legs jerking.

Marius releases me suddenly, and I collapse into the weeds, panting for breath. The young Dominus pushes himself to his feet and yanks his tunic down.

'Stay out here till I'm inside.' He starts to walk away, then stops. 'Do you know how to count?'

I whimper something out of the weeds.

'Count to a hundred,' Marius says. 'Remember what I said.' Then he's gone, striding away in the moonlight.

I don't have to count to anything, because I can barely move. All I can see is stars beyond the roof of the latrine, dimmed by the moon, and all I can hear is my own ragged breath. My windpipe still feels raw and constricted, and the back of my head is throbbing where Marius banged it against the side of the latrine. I am limp in the grass, and either my skin is tingling or there are a thousand tiny creatures crawling all over me.

'Help me,' I whisper to no one.

My breath slows, and I return to myself, but now I'm aware that someone is near me. I lift my head, and there, squatting in the moonlight just beyond the latrine, is Calidus. Digitus is hovering behind him, wringing his hands.

'He rode you hard, did he?' Calidus says.

I lift myself up on my elbows. Behind him, Digitus is nodding furiously at me, indicating what I should say.

'Yes, Dominus,' I gasp.

'Good,' says Calidus. 'He's a man now. That's the way it should be.'

'Yes, Dominus.'

'My brother is going places.' He smiles at me in the starlight. 'He'll be a decurion someday. Maybe even a senator.'

He tosses something at me, and it clinks into the weeds next to my leg. 'That's for you.' Calidus stands, wobbling a bit when he's upright. 'Just think, Antinous,' he says. 'Someday you can tell people you were fucked by a senator.' Laughing to himself, he brushes past Digitus, who dances out of his way, muttering 'Dominus' over and over. When our master is gone, Diggy kneels beside me and helps me sit up. I hang on to him, afraid that if I lie back down, I'll never get up again.

'I see what happen,' Digitus says in his heavy accent. 'He hurt you?'

I draw a couple of deep breaths before I say, 'No.' *No more than usual.*

Digitus roots about in the weeds for the little purse, and before it even occurs to me to stop him, he plucks out a coin.

'I no say anything.' He holds the coin up in the moonlight in his three-fingered hand. 'Yes?'

I nod, and he pushes the purse into my hands. He puts his finger to his lips, then he stands and hauls me to my feet. I'm still dizzy, so he holds me under my arms until I can stand on my own. As he walks me across the garden, he slips the purse inside my tunic. He points up at the second floor, where we can see the lamplit windows of the wolves.

'Hide this.' He taps the purse inside my tunic. 'No say anything.'

I nod, and he turns me loose in the archway. As he limps back to the kitchen, Focaria comes rushing out and nearly knocks me over.

'Where the fuck have you been?' She rushes past me with an empty platter.

Inside, I duck behind the counter where I can't see the boys and they can't see me. They're quieter now, and when I pass the doorway to the private room, I see half a dozen of them sprawled across the table or under it, while the ones who remain sitting upright carry on a woozy conversation in mumbles and grunts. Marius isn't one of them.

There is still a line of boys up the stairs, and they barely make way for me as I edge past them. At the top, I turn into the hallway, where the curtains are drawn across the doorways of all four of my sister wolves' cells. Clutching the purse to my belly inside my tunic, I walk past each curtain, past the panting boys and the wolves gasping weary encouragement. When I reach my own cell, I pull my curtain shut and blow out my lamp. Up the hall, I hear one of the boys shout, then the thump of feet on the floorboard, then the voice of Marius, shouting in the hallway, 'That's four! I've done them all!' As the boys in the stairway give him a drunken cheer, I lift my mattress and slide the purse, without counting it, inside the slit where I hide my money. Then I crawl under my bed and curl my knees up to my chest. I can't see it in the dark, but I rest my fingers against the sparrow I scratched into the wall, and I listen to the receding tide of the party below until I fall asleep.

Next morning, neither Focaria nor Melpomene come with us to the baths. Melpomene stays behind to talk to Calidus, who returns blinking and hungover only hours after he left with his young guests. Focaria is helping Digitus with the shopping, since the private party emptied the kitchen. The other wolves are all especially sore and exhausted this morning, and each one keeps her own counsel on the way to the baths, pulling her hood over her head and staring at her feet as we move through the street.

No one notices the vivid purple bruise across the base of my throat until we're in the caldarium and I've stripped off my tunic and lowered myself into the warm water. Bruises aren't unusual, of course, and each of the others is carrying one or two herself this morning. But mine stands out, even among a group of wolves.

'Who did this to you?' Euterpe crouches in the water next to me. Even Thalia and Urania slide closer around the rim of the pool to have a look.

'Was it Calidus?' Urania says.

'The other one,' I say hoarsely. 'Marius.' The inside of my throat is still raw. When Euterpe touches me, I flinch.

'Oh, Little One,' she says. When she leans to kiss my forehead, she puts her hand on my other bruise, the one on the back of my head where Marius banged it against the wall of the latrine, and I push her away, splashing water over the lip of the pool.

'Don't call me that!' My voice is high-pitched and frantic, it reverberates around the vault of the caldarium. The others all sit very still in the trembling water. The bath slave Gracilis, wiping down the benches across the pool, lifts his head. I feel tears coming on, but I sink into the water up to my nose, glaring at the others to keep away. Even so, they gather round, at a distance.

'What did he do?' says Urania.

I shake my head.

The wolves exchange a look.

'What did he do?' says Euterpe.

I lift my mouth out of the water. 'He didn't do anything.'

'Nothing?' says Thalia.

'He made me do something to him.' I'm aware of my voice whispering around the vault. 'He said he'd kill me if I said.' I slide back under the water up to my nose again, watching the other wolves as they work it out.

'Did he ask you to . . . ?' Euterpe says, and I lift my head out of the water and shout, 'He said he'd kill me!'

'You *fucked* him?' says Thalia.

'Lucky you,' says Urania.

'Enough,' Euterpe says.

'Mel's going to work us like a pack of mules,' says Urania, 'and then she's going to sell us.' She points at me. 'But she's going to keep him.'

'Leave him alone,' Euterpe says.

'I can't handle another night like that.' Urania grabs Euterpe's arm. 'I'd *rather* be sold.'

377

'Don't say that!' says Thalia, clutching her friend's arm.

'I mean it.' Urania shakes Thalia off, sending waves across the pool. 'I can't do it.'

'It won't be like that every night,' says Thalia.

'It already is,' says Urania. 'Mel has us doing more punters than we ever did with Audo.'

'It's true,' says Euterpe. 'There will be more private parties.'

'How do you know?' says Thalia.

'What do you think Mel and Calidus are talking about right now?' Euterpe glances across the pool, where Simplex has joined Gracilis, the two of them listening to us while pretending to work. Euterpe lowers her voice, and the others, even me, slip closer to her in the water.

'Brutus tells me the church is trying to get rid of all the other indoor whores in town,' she says. 'Soon it's just going to be the wolves under the arches. And us.'

'They'll get rid of us, too,' says Urania. 'They'll sell us.'

'We belong to the bishop's brother,' Euterpe says, 'and as long as we make money for his new basilica, I think they'll keep us.' She lowers her voice again. 'But they'll want us to be more discreet, which is why there will be more private parties. They can lock the punters in, so there's less uproar on the street.'

'And more work for us,' says Thalia.

'And no tips,' says Urania.

I sit up suddenly, lifting my head free of the water. My heart is pounding and my mouth is dry. The caldarium seems over-heated and oppressive, and I can scarcely breathe. I can feel Marius's forearm crushing my windpipe, and Sparrow flutters frantically against the dome above, unable to find the way out. I want to jump out of the pool, leaving my red tunic behind, and flee naked into the street. I want to run as fast as I can, it doesn't matter where, until the tavern, the punters, the city, everything and everyone I know is far behind me. The others widen their eyes, as if a wild animal has suddenly erupted from the water.

'I hate it.' I am beyond tears. 'I want to die.'

Euterpe slides up to me in the water and puts her arm around me. The others move closer, too. Across the pool, Simplex and Gracilis are openly staring at us.

'Listen,' Euterpe says, 'I want to tell you all a story.'

'Your stories don't matter!' I shout. 'They never change anything!'

My words ricochet round the bath. I mean to wound her, to drive her away, but Euterpe settles closer to me in the water and beckons the others closer, too. She looks at the bath slaves, who exchange a look and settle down near us.

'This one's different,' she says. 'This one really happened.'

In the dripping echo of the caldarium, Euterpe tells us a story from the earliest days of the city of Rome. At the time I thought she'd made it up, but years later, in this library where I write, I will come across it again, in a volume of the historian Livy.

This happened many centuries ago, Euterpe begins, when Rome was still just one city among all the other cities, and it was forever fighting with its neighbours. Back then, she says, it didn't even have professional soldiers like Audo. All its wars were fought by farmers like Urania's father or by tradesmen like Nazarius, common men who left their families and their businesses to wage war on behalf of their fellow Romans. They'd fight for a few months, and even if they weren't killed or crippled, they'd come back to find their farms and shops struggling without them, and they'd have to borrow money from some rich senator to feed their families and keep their farms and shops afloat. When the loans came due, and the men couldn't pay, they'd lose their farms and businesses to the very men they had been fighting to protect, and they and their families were pitched out onto the street. Some of them even sold themselves into slavery to pay their debts.

We all listen, nodding silently. Nothing changes. The unfairness of life is burned like a cattle brand into the flesh of slaves, whores, and women.

The ordinary men, Euterpe continues, demanded relief from their debts and a voice in their own government. But the senators didn't want to give it to them, and they threatened the commoners with violence and expulsion from the city. Just as this confrontation between the senators and the commoners was reaching its pitch, scouts came hurrying into Rome to say that an army of Volscians was on its way to destroy the city.

What are Volscians? says Urania.

Men from another city, says Euterpe. Rome's bitterest enemy at the time. Now listen.

The fate of Rome is at stake, the senators told the commoners. The lives and honour of your wives and children are at risk if we continue this foolish argument. Quickly, form ranks, take up arms, and help us drive our enemy away.

She pauses for effect. Over her shoulder, I see Gracilis and Simplex crouching nearby, listening.

Not a single commoner stepped forward. Instead, Euterpe says, lifting her finger from the water for emphasis, they did something else: *all the commoners left the city*. They gathered their wives and children and trooped out to a hill outside the walls, called the Sacred Mountain. They left their shops empty and their farms unattended, and they made a camp for themselves on the hilltop and settled in as if they had no intention of ever coming back. Behind them, in Rome, they left all the rich men and their wives and children to see what their lives would be like without shopkeepers and farmers. Let the rich grow their own grain, said the commoners. Let them bake their own bread, clean their own laundry, butcher their own meat. Let them fight their own wars.

But the Volscians are coming! cried the senators. They'll take the city!

Let them, said the commoners. One master is just the same as another.

So the senators, Euterpe said, sent an emissary, a man the commoners trusted named Agrippa. He said that the people of a city are like a body, senators and commoners alike, and that even if the hands and mouth and teeth of the body get tired of doing all the work to feed the stomach, the hands and mouth and teeth in turn can't live either unless the stomach is fed.

Bullshit, says Urania. The rich aren't like the stomach. More like the asshole.

Everyone laughs, even Euterpe. It *is* bullshit, she says. But finally the commoners agreed to come back and fight the Volscians – but *only if* the senators agreed to create two new officers, called tribunes. These men would be elected from among the commoners, and *only* the commoners. No senator could *ever* be a tribune, and not only that, the tribunes would have the authority to veto anything the senators decided.

And they agreed to that? says Urania, sceptically. The senators?

They had to, says Euterpe, or lose the city.

We all sit quietly for a moment in the water. By the side of the pool, Gracilis and Simplex are rapt.

So the commoners came back, I say.

They did, says Euterpe, and they went to war and they defeated the Volscians. But more importantly, she continues, lowering her voice and drawing us all closer in the water, *they stuck together*, and because they stuck together, they won the right to have some say in how they were ruled.

We're all quiet for a moment. Little overlapping waves circle out from each of us and lap against the sides of the pool. The two bath slaves look as if they might get into the water with us.

'So what are you saying?' says Urania. 'You want us to leave the tavern and go camp on a hillside?'

'No,' says Euterpe.

'Because they'd just bring us back and beat us,' says Urania. 'Or sell us. Or worse.'

'I know,' says Euterpe.

'Were any of them slaves?' I say. 'The commoners?'

'No, Little One,' says Euterpe. 'None of them were slaves.'

'Have slaves ever done anything like that?' asks Thalia.

'Spartacus,' says Simplex. He's squatting by the side of the caldarium, the bundle of keys hung from his waist touching the marble. Gracilis squats beside him, keeping an eye on the doorways.

'Who's Spartacus?' asks Thalia.

'A slave,' says Simplex, keeping his voice low, 'who led an army of gladiators against the Romans.'

'Did he win?' says Urania.

'He kept 'em on the run for a couple years,' says Simplex. He's gripping the lip of the pool between his feet with both hands.

'But did he *win*?' says Urania.

'No,' says Euterpe. 'He didn't.'

'The Romans crucified them all,' says Simplex.

'Are any of us gladiators?' says Urania. She looks at the squatting man. 'Are you?'

He shrugs.

'So much for that idea,' says Urania.

'There are other ways,' says Euterpe. 'Things we can do if we stick together.'

'Go slow,' says Gracilis. He's gripping the edge of the pool now too, next to his mate. 'We do it all the time.'

'Go slow?' says Thalia. 'What does that mean?'

'Keep working,' says Gracilis, 'but go slower.' He smiles, revealing missing teeth. 'It really pisses them off.'

'I like that,' says Euterpe. 'We take more time with each punter.'

'What do you mean?' says Urania.

'Talk to them,' Euterpe says. 'Make conversation. Every punter likes to talk about himself. Keep him in your cell longer, make the others wait.'

'That's it?' says Urania.

'Take more time between punters,' says Euterpe. 'Keep your curtain drawn longer. Splash your water a bit, make them think you're washing. Or go down and use the latrine instead of the chamber pot. If Diggy brings you something to eat during the night, take longer over it.'

'Stay longer at the baths,' says Simplex.

We all turn to look at him. He shrugs again.

'Take an extra day with our monthlies,' says Urania.

'Yes!' says Euterpe. 'Good.'

'Let Quartus talk as long as he likes,' says Thalia, and we all laugh.

'Who pays a wolf to talk?' Gracilis says, and Simplex shushes him.

'What about Mel?' says Thalia. 'She'll see what we're doing. She won't like it.'

'She'll be busy with her own punters,' Urania says. 'She'll be stuck in her cell with the curtain closed.'

'And she'll be up and down the stairs all night,' says Euterpe, 'checking on Focaria and Diggy.'

'What if she starts checking up on us?' says Thalia.

'Let her,' says Euterpe. 'That slows her down, too.'

'That's part of it, right?' says Urania. 'Make her work harder, make her see what we're going through.'

'That's it,' says Euterpe.

'She could just sell us,' says Thalia. 'She said she would, if she had to.'

'She doesn't own us,' says Urania. 'It's not up to her.'

'She'd have to get Calidus to do it,' says Euterpe. 'She'd have to persuade him to buy a whole new tavern full of wolves, and I don't think he would. If things slow down, he'll blame her first.'

'So it would be easier for him to get rid of her,' says Urania.

'Yes,' says Euterpe.

'So she has to listen to us,' says Urania, putting her arm around Thalia.

'But,' I say, 'what if . . . ?'

They all look at me.

'Say it, Little One.' Euterpe squeezes me.

'What if they just sell one of us,' I say, 'as a warning to the others?'

No one says anything for a moment. From Sparrow's point of view, I see myself up on the stage in the theatre, naked and shackled, terrified about where I will end up next, all alone, away from everyone I know and love. From the stalls, the shopkeepers and their customers all laugh at me.

'They could do that any time anyway,' says Euterpe. 'We already face that risk every day.'

Urania and Thalia huddle together in the water, their arms around each other's waists. Behind them, I see both bath slaves nodding in agreement.

'So why not risk something for ourselves,' Euterpe says, 'for something *we* want?'

No one says anything for a moment. Simplex shifts slightly, and his keys clink against the lip of the pool.

'We're not *refusing* to do anything,' says Euterpe. 'We're just doing it *slower*.'

'What do we say,' Thalia says, 'when Mel asks what's going on?'

'Nothing.' Urania gives one of her rare smiles. 'Let her figure it out.'

'The important thing is,' says Euterpe, 'is that we *all* do it. It's important that we all stick together.'

'Like the commoners,' I say. 'On the hilltop.'

'Exactly.' Euterpe squeezes me. 'Like the men on the hilltop.'

'I don't know,' says Thalia.

Urania hugs her under the water. 'What do we have to lose?' she says.

'Everything?' says Thalia.

'It's worth risking everything,' says Urania. 'I can't go on like this.' She looks at Euterpe. 'I'll do it.'

'Me too,' I say.

We all look at Thalia, and after a moment, she nods. Then we all turn to look at the bath slaves squatting on the side of the pool. Gracilis puts his finger to his lips and winks. Simplex mimes locking his lips with a key, then throwing the key over his shoulder.

That night our regular punters come roaring back, angry about having been locked out the night before. It's a little frightening at first, because they're even louder than usual, but they vent most of their anger at Focaria, who happily vents it back at them.

'I heard you were running a school here last night,' shouts Nazarius.

'No more than usual,' Focaria shouts back.

'Are you going to rap me across my knuckles?' someone else shouts.

'Not unless you pay in advance,' says Focaria. Much laughter.

Melpomene is up and down the stairs more than usual, making it easier for the rest of us to start working slower. At first I'm not sure Euterpe's idea is going to work, at least for me – a punter, it turns out, isn't as interested in talking with a boy as he is with a woman. So instead of trying to engage each one in conversation, I simply keep my curtain shut longer between each one, making the next punter wait in the hall while I noisily splash about in my washbasin. Late in the evening, I sneak across the hall into the empty cell and crouch in the corner next to the door, where no one can see me if he looks in. I'm startled when someone walks in on me, but it's only Thalia, who has had the same idea, and we huddle together in the corner. Quartus comes looking for her, plaintively calling her name in the hallway. The two of us get the giggles, and we put our hands over our mouths

385

so he can't hear us. When he runs back downstairs to ask frantically where she's gone – 'Has . . . has Thalia been . . . *sold*?' – she gives me a quick kiss on the forehead, then sneaks back into her cell.

'Where were you?' says Diggy, who has come up to look for her.

'Right here,' she says. 'Where else would I be?'

When Quartus comes bounding back up the stairs, she not only asks him to read her one of his pilfered poems, she asks him to read it again.

'Really?' He can scarcely believe his luck.

Euterpe, as soon as each punter has finished, asks him, 'What's your hurry?' With a smile and a wink, she encourages him to stretch out next to her on the cot and talk for a while. For the first time in weeks, I hear the rumbling murmur of Brutus as he sits next to her cot with his legs stretched out before him. I hear her laugh.

Urania, meanwhile, starts telling each of her punters the tavern might start shutting down for private parties all the time, catering only to those who can pay to rent the whole place for the night, leaving the ordinary punter to seek satisfaction from the toothless and diseased old wolves under the arches.

'You didn't hear it from me,' she tells them, 'but from now on, they're going to let only rich boys have us.'

It doesn't take long, of course, for the men to repeat this to Focaria, who repeats it to Melpomene on one of her trips downstairs. Melpomene has to raise her voice, already ragged from the night before, to make herself heard over the drunken uproar.

'Who told you that?' she cries. Even from my hiding place upstairs, I can hear how weary she is.

'Is it true?' one of the men shouts.

'It was just the one night,' she says. 'For the birthday of our owner's younger brother . . .'

'Calidus is running for aedile,' someone shouts. 'He's just buying the votes of all those boys' fathers.'

'Well, he lost *my* vote,' shouts someone else.

'You've never voted in your life!'

'Lads! Lads!' Melpomene's voice is cracking. 'It was just one night . . .'

All the men shout her down, jeering at the expense of that pretty boy Calidus and his pretty boy brother and all those pretty rich boys with soft hands and easy lives. They proceed to slander our Domini – their looks, their advantages, their ambition – at length and in obscene detail.

'I hear young Marius has fucked every slave in his father's household, man and boy.'

'I hear Calidus has fucked every slave in the household *and* his younger brother.'

'I hear their father fucks them both!'

'And his brother the bishop *fucks them all*!'

With that, the tavern erupts. Sitting in the corner of the empty cell with my knees drawn up to my chest, I can feel the floor beneath me shake as all the men start laughing and roaring at once. I hear grunts and blows and the clatter of breaking crockery, and nearly lost in the riot, the plaintive cries of Melpomene and Focaria and Digitus as they do their best to clear the room and stop the punters from destroying the place. I push myself up and peek into the hallway. Thalia and Urania are also standing in their doorways. Then Euterpe pulls back her curtain and steps out, too, wrapping her gown tightly around her. None of us say anything. Then Euterpe smiles, steps back into her cell, and draws the curtain. Urania comes around into Thalia's cell, giving me a wink. I cross the hall into my own cell and put out my lamp.

In the morning, Melpomene oversleeps. She's face down on her mattress when I rise to go downstairs. I tiptoe through overturned tables, broken stools, and smashed wine cups. After using the latrine, I peek into the kitchen. Focaria and Digitus are still sleeping, too, Focaria curled into a ball in her old spot next to the oven, Diggy twitching like a dreaming dog in the corner where I used to sleep. I help myself to a couple of pears and take them into the garden, where I listen to roosters crowing up and down the street. Our own strutting rooster answers ear-splittingly back. One by one, the other wolves come down – Urania first, stretching and yawning like an underfed cat, then Thalia, rubbing her eyes. Euterpe arrives, puts her finger to her lips, and steps carefully into the kitchen, returning with enough bread and cheese for everybody. As the sky brightens overhead, we sit cross-legged in the dirt near the water tank and share a meal, keeping our voices low.

'Can we do that every night?' Thalia sounds worried.

'We won't have to,' says Urania.

'One way or the other,' says Euterpe, 'it will be settled soon.'

'I'm scared,' says Thalia.

'So am I,' says Urania, 'but what else can we do?'

'It was funny when Quartus came up and couldn't find you,' I say.

'Yes, it was funny,' says Euterpe. 'Where were you?' she says to Thalia.

'I was with Mouse.' Thalia smiles in spite of herself. 'We were hiding in the empty cell.'

'We were trying not to laugh,' I say.

'"Oh, Thalia!"' says Urania, mincingly. '"My pussy cat! My little dove! Where are you?"'

Our laughter is interrupted by Focaria's sharp voice.

'What are you doing?' she says.

We all look up. Focaria stands in the middle of the garden, her hair undone and wild around her face. She has red circles under her eyes and a bruise along her jaw. Euterpe starts to push herself to her feet, but Focaria holds up a rigid finger.

'Don't,' she says.

Euterpe sinks to her knees. The rest of us fall silent. Focaria glances up at Melpomene's window, then takes another step toward us.

'What are you doing?' She keeps her voice low. Behind her, Digitus, looking even more haggard than usual, peers round the edge of the kitchen doorway.

'What are you talking about?' says Urania.

'For fuck's sake.' Focaria grips the top of my head and twists my face up to hers. 'What's going on?' she hisses.

My eyes slide toward Euterpe, but Focaria rattles my head, making my bruises throb. 'I'm asking you.'

Euterpe stands and pulls Focaria's hand off me. 'That's enough.'

'Which one of you bitches,' says Focaria, 'told the punters they weren't welcome anymore?' She glares round at all of us. 'Was it you?' she says to Thalia, who looks at the ground. 'You?' she says to Urania, who lifts her face defiantly. But before she can speak, Euterpe touches her arm and says, 'One of them wanted to know why we were closed the night before, and I told him. That's all.'

'Why the fuck did you do that?'

'It's the truth,' Urania says.

Focaria glances back at Melpomene's window again. 'She's *furious*,' she says. 'So am I. We'll have to work all day to be ready for tonight.'

'I'm sorry.' Euterpe lifts her hand, but Focaria swats her away.

'If you give her a chance,' Focaria says, 'she's going to make our lives better. She has big plans for this place. She has big plans for all of us.'

'Do they include this?' Euterpe pulls me to my feet and jerks down the neckline of my tunic. The bruise across the base of my throat, where Marius choked me with his forearm, has turned a deep, sickly green.

'So what?' says Focaria. 'He takes his lumps like the rest of us.' Her eyes are the coldest blue they've ever been. 'I've given him worse bruises than that.'

'We can't work at this pace,' says Euterpe.

'We won't,' says Urania.

'It's killing us,' says Thalia, near tears.

Focaria looks round at us again, letting her gaze come to rest on Euterpe.

'This is about him, isn't it?' She looks me up and down as if weighing me by the pound, then smiles ferociously at Euterpe. 'It's always about him.'

'It's about all of us,' says Urania.

'Shut the fuck up,' says Focaria. She steps back. 'Things have finally started to get good for me, and you're all going to ruin it. You're going to ruin everything, for all of us. And for what.' She looks at me as if she wants me dead. 'For *him*.' She starts back across the garden, pausing just before she gets to the kitchen.

'Think about what you're doing,' she says. She shoves Digitus out of her way and disappears into the shadows.

When she rises, Melpomene says nothing, but only passes through the garden in her mantle, tossing the hood over her head as she steps into the street. Urania, Thalia, and I look to Euterpe, who watches her go and says, 'We go to the baths. As usual.'

In the echoing drip of the caldarium, we gather round her again in the water. Even Simplex and Gracilis come and crouch by the side of the pool. Euterpe, keeping her voice low, tells us we need to go slow for one more night.

'She needs to know we're serious,' she says.

'She wouldn't even look at us,' says Thalia.

'That's because she doesn't know what to do,' says Euterpe.

'She didn't expect this to happen,' says Urania.

I'm shivering in the water, even though it's warmer than usual. I'm crouching so low it laps at my bottom lip.

'What's she doing right now?' I say. 'Who is she talking to?'

I can imagine, and so can the others, but Euterpe says it out loud. 'For all we know, she and Calidus are buying four new wolves. For all we know, we'll be up for sale this afternoon.'

'Not likely,' volunteers Simplex, and we all turn to him.

'Not unless,' he continues, 'they buy some of the slags under the arches.'

'What are you saying?' asks Euterpe.

'The bishop really is getting rid of all the other whores in town,' Simplex says. 'You girls are the only proper wolves left in Carthago.'

'They'd have to . . .' Gracilis starts to say, and we all shift our gazes to him. 'They'd have to send away to another city for girls like you.' He nods at me. 'And you.'

'We have something they need,' says Euterpe, 'something they can't get easily anywhere else.' She lifts herself a little higher in the water. 'I say we try it one more night. Urania?'

'Yes,' says Urania, without hesitation.

'Little One?'

I nod without saying anything.

'Thalia?'

We all turn to her. She, too, is trembling in the water.

'There are worse things,' says Gracilis, 'than being sold.'

Thalia draws a breath. She nods.

'All right.' Euterpe settles into the water. 'Let's take our time going back.'

Thalia nestles close to her friend, putting her head on Urania's shoulder. Euterpe and I start to settle in together, too. Gracilis gets up and walks away, but Simplex crouches next to us at the lip of the pool and touches Euterpe on the shoulder.

'Why don't you come with me for a moment,' he says.

Euterpe sighs and says, 'Not today, Simplex.'

But Simplex lays his hand on her shoulder. His touch is more friendly than carnal.

'It's not that,' he says. 'I want to show you something.'

Euterpe shifts in the water and looks up at him.

391

'Put your mantle on if you want,' he says.

They gaze at each other, and something passes between them that I don't understand. Then Euterpe says, 'Stay here, Little One,' and pushes herself up out of the water. She throws her mantle round her shoulders and follows Simplex into the archway on the far side of the caldarium. I think about scooting over next to Urania and Thalia, but instead I stare into the shadowy archway and listen. All I hear is the jingle of Simplex's keys.

Before I can get worried, though, Euterpe comes back alone, sheds her mantle onto a bench, and steps into the water again. Thalia and Urania ignore her. They seem to be asleep.

'What did he want?' I whisper.

'I'll tell you later,' says Euterpe.

When we return to the garden, Melpomene is in urgent conference with Focaria in the kitchen doorway, but as soon as we come in, she peels away and marches into the tavern, without speaking, without even looking at us. Euterpe throws back the hood of her mantle and steps up to Focaria.

'What did you tell her?'

'Nothing,' says Focaria. She starts to turn away, but Euterpe grabs her arm.

'*Nothing*,' says Focaria.

'What about Diggy?' Euterpe says.

'He's too terrified to say anything.' Focaria pulls her arm free. 'You should be, too.'

When we come into the tavern, Melpomene is waiting for us, palms pressed together as if preparing to declaim an opening argument in court.

'Ladies,' she says. 'Sit.'

She has already dispensed four cups of wine around one of the tables. The wolves loosen their mantles and sit, and I hunch on one of the stools among them, my hands clasped between my knees.

392

'It's true,' Melpomene says. 'There will be more private parties. Calidus was impressed with what we did the other night. He sees the value in trying something new.'

Thalia and Urania exchange a look. I stare at my knuckles, which I am squeezing bloodless. Only Euterpe lifts her chin and meets Melpomene's gaze.

'I know why you're worried,' says Melpomene, 'and I am prepared to be reasonable.'

Spine erect, chin held high, she turns on the ball of her foot and marches round the end of the counter. She lifts a small wooden box from under it onto the countertop. She tilts it toward us so that we can see that it has a narrow slot in the top.

'It's the moneybox,' says Euterpe. 'So what?'

'It's a *second* moneybox,' says Melpomene, turning it round so that we can see there's no lock on it. 'It's for the four of you, to keep upstairs.'

'I don't understand,' says Urania.

'It's for the nights when we have private parties,' says Melpomene. 'I'm having Astius the painter make a sign to go with it, to encourage our guests to leave a little something extra before they head downstairs.'

'One moneybox,' says Euterpe. 'For the four of us.'

'At the end of the evening,' says Melpomene, 'you can divide the money any way you like. That's up to you.'

'What about you?' says Thalia. 'Do you get a share?'

'I won't take anything from it,' says Melpomene. 'Calidus pays me now to run this place. Everything that goes in here –' she rests her hand on the box – 'belongs only to the four of you.'

'What about—?' Urania starts to say. Euterpe gives her a sharp look, but Urania continues, 'What about the nights when we don't have private parties?'

'Then keep it in the empty cell, out of sight,' says Melpomene, 'and make your own tips, the way you always have. Or –' she taps the box – 'put it out if you want to. It's up to you.'

I look sidelong at Euterpe. She's sitting with her spine as erect as Melpomene's, her lips pressed together.

'I was one of you once,' says Melpomene. 'I still do the same work you do. I know how you feel.'

'It's fair,' says Thalia meekly, with a glance at Euterpe.

'I need you all to work as hard as you can,' says Melpomene, 'whether it's our regular punters or private parties. I could beat you into doing it, the way Audo used to. I could always find wolves who will do what I tell them to.'

Now Urania glances at Euterpe, who is as still as a statue.

'I don't have to do this,' says Melpomene, 'but like I say, I'm prepared to be reasonable.' She pushes the box to the edge of the counter and lifts her hands away from it, like a magician's flourish. 'Talk it over among yourselves.'

Melpomene walks away. We hear her mount the stairs, we hear her close her curtain. None of us says anything for a moment, but we all look at Euterpe. She stares at the moneybox, silently.

'It's something,' says Urania.

'Isn't this what we wanted?' says Thalia.

'The men on the hilltop,' I say, and everyone looks at me. 'Did they get everything they wanted?'

Euterpe closes her eyes, then opens them again. She stands.

'Do whatever you want,' she says.

We have another long night. The punters are still determined to make up for lost time from the night of the comissatio, and they take it out on us. I try to work slower, and after my first couple of punters, I sneak across the hall into the empty cell. Melpomene has carried the new moneybox upstairs and left it in here, so I sit in the blind corner again and pull the box onto my lap, tipping my head back against the new plaster. But tonight Thalia does not join me, and I listen to my sisters working as hard as they ever have all along the hall. Even Euterpe seems to be working at her usual rate, although she's quieter than usual. Only when Brutus turns up does she seem to take a little longer, and I hear them murmuring together briefly before he disappears down the stairs. Then I hear someone yank open the curtain of my cell and curse when he sees that it's empty. I stand and step into the hall behind him. He turns – he's a regular – and looks puzzled.

'I thought you was in here,' he says.

'I am,' I say, and I lead him into the cell.

Late that night, I crawl under my bed to sleep, and I hear Focaria come up into the hall after latching the shutters downstairs. I hear her pull aside Euterpe's curtain and stand in her doorway. I hear Euterpe say, very distinctly, 'Not tonight.' I lift my head from the floor. There's a long, breathless silence, then I hear Focaria's tread, away from Euterpe's cell and down the stairs. I wait to hear Euterpe close her curtain again, but she never does. I am just about to slide out from under my bed and go into her cell when I hear her rise from her bed, step into the hall, and lift my curtain.

'May I come in?' she whispers.

'Yes,' I say, and she crouches and peers at me under the bed. I say nothing and slide closer to the wall. She slides in next to me, wearing her gown, smelling of sweat and the men she's had that night. We lie there breathing and gazing at each other in the stifling dark. Her eyes catch no light, they are just holes in her face. Mine must be the same.

'Little One.' She lays her hand on my face.

'Yes,' I say.

She presses her forehead to mine. 'If I run, will you come with me?'

My heart starts to beat faster.

'Is Focaria coming?' I whisper.

'No,' she whispers back. 'I'm not going to tell her.'

I wrap my arms around her neck.

'When?'

'Tomorrow.'

'How?'

'Brutus,' she says. 'He'll meet us at the baths and take us out of the city in his cart before anyone knows we're gone.'

'Why would he do that?'

'I'm paying him.'

'When did you ask him?'

'I've asked him before,' she says. 'Several times, and he always said he would.' She draws a breath. 'Tonight I told him I was ready.'

I can barely speak, but I manage to say, 'What about Thalia and Urania?'

'We can't tell them.' She presses her forehead tightly against mine. 'Do you understand?'

'Yes.'

'You can't tell anyone.'

'I won't.' I'm starting to cry. 'Don't leave me.'

'I can't stay anymore, I have to go.' She kisses me. '*We* have to go. It's the only way we can be safe.'

In the dark under my bed, we are forehead to forehead, breathing each other's breath, feeling each other's heartbeat. My throat still hurts where Marius choked me. My heart is pounding so hard I'm afraid someone else will hear us.

'Will you come?' she whispers.

Where is Sparrow? He takes me away when I'm frightened or in pain, his image is scratched into the wall behind me, but right now he's nowhere to be found. Do I really have to decide this on my own?

'I'm afraid,' I say.

'So am I,' she says. 'But will you come?'

I feel the floor under me. I feel the bed above me. I hear the breathless, humid silence of my cell. I feel its walls around me like a shell, and I wonder if I can crack it open and wander out of it like some naked, glistening, defenceless creature and go abroad in the world, where no one knows me and everyone wants to hurt me. I don't think I can, but then I don't think I can live in this shell without Euterpe. If she goes, I'll just lie in this room until I die. If she goes, I have no reason to live.

'Yes,' I say. 'I'll come.'

We spend the night in Euterpe's bed, and in the morning, we lie awake long past cockcrow without speaking, listening as the other wolves stir and rise. Urania is first, coming out of Thalia's cell and pausing in the hall to yawn dramatically. She goes downstairs, and a moment later, we hear the trickle of Thalia using her chamber pot. I start to say something, but Euterpe puts her hand over my mouth until we hear the brisk rattle of Melpomene opening her curtain. A moment later, we hear her going down the stairs, and a moment after that, we hear her through Euterpe's window, saying something to Urania in the garden. Euterpe tries to hold me, but I rise from her bed, clear a space on her little table, and stand on it to look out the window. Urania is hovering near the kitchen door, rubbing her upper arms in the cool morning air and waiting for Focaria to feed her. Melpomene is in the middle of the garden, clasping her hands over her head and arching her back. In the street beyond the wall, I can see women gathering at the fountain, and I can hear the distant splashing of the water and the murmur of their conversation.

'What do you see?' says Euterpe.

I gesture for her to be quiet. Focaria has appeared in the kitchen doorway, and she's handing Urania a bowl with bread and cheese in it. Urania says something, and Focaria flips her hand, *that's all you're going to get*. Urania carries the bowl out of sight under the window, and a moment later we hear her coming up the stairs.

'Get down, Little One,' says Euterpe. 'Someone will see you.'

I wave my hand again, because now Focaria is calling to Melpomene, who shakes back her hair, rolls her shoulders, and walks to the kitchen doorway. They start to speak, but they're interrupted by Digitus, who comes out of the kitchen and squeezes past them. They stand silently and watch him as he fetches the buckets and yoke from the water tank, then unbolts the door and limps out into the street, leaving the door ajar behind him. I watch him join the queue at the fountain, then I look back down at the two women. Focaria has stepped closer to Melpomene, and she is talking urgently, gesturing with her hands. I can't hear what she's saying, but Melpomene is listening intently. As Focaria keeps talking, Melpomene looks up at the second storey, and I duck away from the window.

'What?' whispers Euterpe.

'Focaria's saying something to Mel,' I whisper. The table wobbles under my weight, and I steady myself with my fingers over the windowsill. 'I think they know.'

'That's not possible,' Euterpe says, and then she hisses, '*Don't . . .*' as I peek over the windowsill again. Focaria is still talking, and Melpomene is still listening, gazing at her feet, her arms crossed. She lifts her head, and I flinch again in the window, but she doesn't look up at me. Instead she touches Focaria's arm and starts talking over the cook until finally Focaria stops. Focaria stares hard at Melpomene, pursing her lips, breathing deeply through her nose. I know that look. It's the look she has before she hits me. Melpomene stands close to her, talking quickly, stroking her arm. Focaria looks away, nods. Melpomene turns away from her toward the tavern. Focaria opens her mouth to say something else, but Melpomene waves her off as she disappears through the archway below. As I hear her walking through the tavern, I feel Euterpe tugging on my tunic, trying to pull me down off the table. But as I watch from the window a moment longer, Focaria lifts her furious gaze to the second floor, first to the window of my cell, off to the right, then to Euterpe's window. This time I don't duck away, but keep looking, hoping she can't see me in the shadow under the eaves. But she stares hard at the window, and I can't help the feeling that we are staring at each other.

Melpomene comes to the top of the stairs and goes into her cell. Euterpe catches me under my arms and lifts me off the table with a grunt, nearly dropping me to the floor. We stand breathlessly, listening to Melpomene moving about next door. Across the hall, we hear the low murmur of Thalia and Urania talking as they eat. Then we hear the rustle of Melpomene's mantle, and we hear her step into the hall.

'I'm going out,' she says loudly. 'I won't be coming to the baths this morning. Euterpe, you're in charge.'

Euterpe and I clutch each other in the middle of her cell.

'Euterpe, are you awake?' Melpomene says. 'I said you're in charge.'

'Yes,' Euterpe calls out.

'Good.' Melpomene starts down the stairs, calling out, 'I'll be back at noon.'

'She knows,' I whisper.

'She doesn't,' Euterpe says.

'But what if she—'

Euterpe catches my face in her hands. 'If she knew, we'd already be on our way to the slave dealer.' She kisses me. 'Now go downstairs and fetch our breakfast.'

'I can't . . .'

'Yes, you can,' she says. 'You fake it with the punters every night. You can fake it with Focaria just this once.'

It's not the same, and she knows it. But I nod and lift her curtain.

Coming down the stairs, I draw deep breaths to calm myself. I've lied to Focaria many times, about all sorts of things. Why should this be any different? I pass through the tavern, which shows signs of last night – an overturned table, more broken cups on the floor – and as I come into the garden, Digitus is struggling through the door under the yoke, carrying two sloshing buckets of water.

399

He's not as good at it as I was, but it's too late now to teach him the trick of it.

Focaria is watching me from the kitchen, and I almost stop in my tracks. I draw another deep breath and ignore her, passing the kitchen to go into the latrine. In the reeking shadow, buzzing with flies, I stand on tiptoe and try to make myself pee. My bladder feels full, and at first it won't come, but at last I squeeze a few squirts into the hole. Then I go out into the fresher air of the garden, where Focaria is waiting in the kitchen doorway with a bowl of bread and cheese for Euterpe and me. I make myself meet her gaze as she hands it to me.

'I gave you a little extra this morning,' she says.

I stammer something.

'You've had a rough couple of nights,' she says, and even more uncharacteristically, she ruffles my hair. 'Tell her I'm sorry,' she says.

I look up at her, unable to speak.

'She'll know why,' she says, and she turns away into the kitchen.

Coming up the stairs, I pass Thalia and Urania coming down, on their way to the garden. Urania is still yawning, but Thalia nudges me girlishly with her hip in passing. I try to make a joke, but it catches in my throat. In spite of Euterpe forbidding me to, I want to tell them everything. But then they're behind me at the bottom of the stairs, laughing at something Urania said. At the top of the stairs, I carry the bread and cheese into Euterpe's cell and sag onto her bed with the bowl in my lap. Euterpe is bent over her little table, cinching a leather pouch full of coins.

'Focaria says she's sorry,' I say.

Euterpe looks at me.

'She says you'll know why.'

Euterpe considers this, hefting the pouch in her hand.

'Eat,' she says. 'It may be the last food we get for a while.'

The dry bread tastes like dust. I offer her the bowl, and without looking she says, 'You eat it all.'

'But you just said—'

'I'll be fine,' she says sharply. 'Eat it all.'

She turns abruptly and leaves the cell, crossing the hall to the empty cell across from mine, where I hear her pour a basin of water and scrub off her make-up. I slouch on her bed, trying my best to eat, but the dry bread and the crumbs of cheese stick like stones in my throat, no matter how much water I drink from Euterpe's cup to wash it down. By the time Euterpe comes back with her face scrubbed and shining, I've only finished half the bowl.

'I can't eat any more,' I say.

'It's all right.' She takes the bowl, lifts a piece of cheese, and takes a bite.

'Go into your cell,' she says, chewing, 'and put on your old tunic. Leave that one on the bed. Then go scrub your face.' She swallows and looks down at me. 'Now, Little One.'

I slide off the bed and slip round into my cell. I close the curtain, even though we're the only ones up here. I strip my red tunic over my head and lay it carefully on the bed. I stand naked in my cell for a moment, looking down at the empty tunic. Maybe the next Antinous will wear it. Maybe they won't even notice I'm gone.

I lift my old tunic off the hook near the door and struggle into it. It's a little too tight for me now. Then I go across the hall and wash myself in the basin of water, scrubbing at my make-up with the smelly old sponge that all the wolves use. The mirror is hanging from the hook on the wall with the reflective side out, and I watch as my dripping face emerges from behind the mask of Antinous Fellator. It's not the same boy I saw in the mirror that first time, lean and bright-eyed and sly. Now he's older, fuller in the face, and sadder.

'Are you done yet?' Euterpe calls out.

I say nothing and turn away from the mirror. Euterpe is standing in the middle of my cell, wearing her mantle already.

'Where do you keep your money?' she says.

I kneel beside my bed, lift my mattress, and pull out my bundle of coins. Euterpe takes it, tests the knot and tightens it, and sticks it inside her mantle. Then she pats the mattress and says, 'Sit.'

I put my hands under my thighs so she can't see them shaking. She pinches up her mantle and kneels within it, then plucks my shoes from under the table and starts to strap one of them onto my foot. She looks up at me.

'Are you scared?' she says.

I nod.

'Good,' she says. 'Me too. It will keep us alert, and we'll need to be alert for a long time. Do you understand?'

I nod. She tightens the knot on my strap and picks up the other shoe.

'When we get to the baths,' she says, strapping it on, 'we'll wait for Urania and Thalia to get into the water, but we won't get undressed. Instead we'll keep going through the next room, and Simplex will let us out a back exit into a side street. Brutus will be waiting there with his cart.'

'Simplex . . . ?'

'He showed me the back exit yesterday,' she says, tightening my shoe. 'He said he'd let me out anytime, if I paid him.'

She pushes herself to her feet and takes my shoulders.

'If we get caught . . .' she says, and when I inhale sharply, she grips me tighter.

'*Listen*. If we get caught,' she says, 'I took you against your will. It's all my fault. I made you come with me. Let me hear you say it.'

I take a deep breath. 'She . . .' I choke on it and she squeezes my shoulders. 'She made me come with her.' She nods at me, encouraging. 'I didn't want to come.'

Euterpe closes her eyes, folds me in her arms, and kisses me on the neck.

'I love you, Little One,' she murmurs.

I hold her as tightly as I can, for as long as I can, until she peels my arms from around her neck and tugs me to my feet.

'Let's go,' she says.

Carrying our bundles of coins in her mantle, Euterpe waits in the hall as I retrieve Thalia and Urania's mantles from their cells, then we descend the stairs into the tavern without talking. My heart is beating hard, and my mouth is dry. Euterpe walks with her chin lifted and her gaze resolutely straight ahead, but walking behind her, I take it all in – the massive counter, the stained and scarred tabletops, the wobbly stools. I look back one last time at the painting of the wolves – at the women and men of various hues grappling with each other, and especially at Antinous Fellator, the boy who doesn't really look like me, staring doe-eyed at a faceless punter. Either way, whether we escape or we're caught, I will never see this room again. This troubles me, though I know it shouldn't. This was a world of pain and fear and violence, but it is the only world I know. How do I know my new world won't be worse?

In the garden, Thalia and Urania are resting with their backs against the water tank and their legs stretched out in front of them. The morning shadow is receding toward them, and their feet are already in the sunlight. Thalia is napping with her head on Urania's shoulder, but Urania sees us right away. She sighs when she sees I'm carrying the mantles.

'So soon?' she says.

'I thought we could soak a little longer this morning,' says Euterpe. 'We've earned it.'

Urania jostles Thalia awake, and she also sighs when she sees the mantles. Urania pushes herself up, then reaches down to pull up Thalia. They each take a mantle from me and shrug it on.

'Are you angry at us?' Thalia says.

Euterpe says nothing. She's staring at the kitchen door, where we hear the clatter of a pot.

'Euterpe . . . ?' says Thalia.

'No.' Euterpe turns away from the kitchen. 'I'm not angry.'

'Shall I call her?' says Urania.

'Who?' says Euterpe.

'Focaria.' Urania lifts her chin toward the kitchen. 'Is she coming with us today?'

'No,' Euterpe says. 'Let's go.'

She turns both Urania and Thalia by the elbow toward the garden door. I look back at the kitchen, and Euterpe tugs me along. Urania slides back the bolt, and Euterpe ushers us into the street, pulling the door shut behind us without looking back.

'Let's put our hoods up today,' she says, and all three of the wolves lift their hoods. Euterpe guides me ahead of her, and we start up the street in single file, threading through the morning crowd. For once I wish I had a hood, too, because I don't want anyone to see me, I want my vision blinkered like a mule's. I make myself stare at the heels of Thalia's shoes, flashing beneath the hem of her mantle, and I try not to look around me. I try not to think of what and who I'm passing. But the street presses in on me anyway, and it's louder and more vivid than it has ever been before. I can hear every word of Priscianus enumerating the differing qualities of two types of oil for a customer. I can hear all the details as Afra whispers a salacious story to the women at the fountain. I can hear the scrape of the barber's razor under the chin of his customer. I can taste the hot metal from the tinsmith's shop at the back of my tongue. I can hear the splashing urine under the feet of Nazarius's treaders. I can smell the flour dust and the baking bread from Renatus's yard. I can feel the rumble of the millstone in the joints of my limbs. I breathe like an overheated dog and lower my gaze to the paving stones gliding slowly under the thin soles of my shoes, as if I were Sparrow, soaring over the grid of the city.

In the narrow, crosstown lane, Euterpe slips beside me and puts her arm around my shoulder.

404

'Steady, Little One,' she murmurs.

Ahead of us, Urania is stepping carefully round the dog shit in the lane, and Thalia lifts the hem of her mantle and tiptoes in her footsteps. From the shadow of the lane, we can see the bright, busy street ahead, where the doorkeeper of the baths leans in the doorway. As we come into the sunlit street, Thalia and Urania wait for us on the pavement. Euterpe stands behind them with her arm still round my shoulders, squinting in the sunlight, looking both ways.

'All right,' she says, and we hustle through a break in the traffic as a group, me in the middle, surrounded by the swinging skirts of the mantles. Thalia and Urania plunge into the doorway while Euterpe pauses to pay the doorkeeper, who gives her a wince of a smile and drops the coins into the moneybox. Then we enter the dank entrance, pass over the worn mosaic of the changing room, and into the humid, dripping caldarium. Only Gracilis is present, and he just nods and turns back to his sweeping. Thalia has already stripped off and is lowering herself into the water. Urania has shed her mantle in a heap on a bench, and she's taking a moment to tie up her hair.

'Where is he?' I whisper, and Euterpe squeezes my shoulder.

'Gracilis,' she says. 'Where's Simplex?'

Gracilis looks up. 'Simplex?'

'Yes.' Euterpe's voice is taut. 'Where is he?'

Gracilis points through the far archway. 'Through there.'

'This way, Little One,' says Euterpe, and she pushes me across the warm marble toward the arch.

'Where are you going?' says Thalia.

'He needs to use the latrine,' Euterpe calls out, her fingers digging painfully into my shoulder.

'Should've thought of that before, Mouse,' Urania calls out as she settles into the water.

We pass through the far doorway and into what used to be the steam room – low-ceilinged, lined with stone benches – but which is now a storeroom, full of boxes and brooms and stacks of towels. Simplex is lifting a box as we come in, shifting it to one side to get at another behind it. He pauses with the box in his arms, surprised to see us, looking us up and down – Euterpe in her mantle, me in my old tunic. Then he sets the box aside and stands up slowly.

'So soon?' he whispers.

'Yes,' says Euterpe, and Simplex glances toward the arch and puts his finger to his lips.

'Him, too?' he whispers.

Euterpe whispers, 'I'll pay whatever you want.'

He puts his finger to his lips again, then he comes to us silently and ushers us ahead of him through another low arch, into a dim, narrow, windowless passage, where he directs us to the right. The air is close and musty in here, and I'm suddenly even more afraid than I already was. My legs are trembling under me, and I stop suddenly and put my hand on the wall. Sparrow is fluttering all around me, his wings beating frantically against the walls and the ceiling. Euterpe wraps me in her arms, bending over me without speaking.

'What's the problem?' whispers Simplex behind us.

'We could go back,' I whisper. 'It's not too late.'

'Hush,' she says, and holds me tight.

'You don't have much time,' Simplex says. 'The others will notice.'

Euterpe slides around me and moves deeper into the dark, feeling the outside wall. She stops and puts her hand on a wooden door.

'It's here, Little One.' She beckons me deeper into the shadow. 'We're almost there.'

If my legs could work, I'd run back into the caldarium and fling myself into the pool, but I can't move. Simplex pushes past me, unhooking his keys from his belt.

'Let's go back,' I say again, louder this time. As Sparrow's wings thunder all around my head, I hear Simplex's keys jingling, then I hear one of them slide into the lock.

'What's it going to be, then?' he says.

I hear the click of coins as Euterpe hands them to Simplex. 'Unlock it,' she says, and instantly the lock grinds, the door scrapes, and a dazzling seam of light opens in the wall, blinding me, illuminating the dust floating in the hall, showing me the brilliant street beyond. Simplex is a shadow behind the door, but Euterpe steps into the shaft of light, her mantle gleaming.

'Is your man there?' Simplex says.

'Yes.' Euterpe holds her hand out to me. 'Little One,' she says. 'I won't go without you.'

Before I can even think about it, I've gone to her, and she ushers me out into the street, where I stand, trembling and blinking in the sunlight. Before Simplex closes the door, he holds his hand out with the coins Euterpe just gave him.

'Are you sure?' she says.

'Take them,' he says. 'You'll need them more than I do.'

With one hand Euterpe takes the coins, and with her other, she draws Simplex to her and kisses him on the mouth.

'*Now* she kisses me,' he says, and he shuts the door and grinds the lock.

In the street I'm blinking at the hairy, dripping nose of Potiscus, the mule. The beast is wearing a bridle and a cracked leather harness, and behind it is Brutus's cart. Today a piece of stained canvas has been stretched over the top. The carter is nowhere to be seen, though, and Euterpe starts to look frantically up and down the lane.

'Brutus?' Her voice is trembling.

'Here.' The cart shakes as Brutus slides off the back, where he'd been sitting. Euterpe sags with relief, and she gives him a nervous smile. He nods, and Euterpe hands him the coins she just took from Simplex. He hefts the coins in his palm and raises his eyebrows at her, and she lifts her leather purse out of her mantle and hands him a few more. Brutus tests each coin between his teeth, then sticks them in a pouch at his belt. Without speaking, he beckons us to the back of the cart, where he lifts me in and then hands Euterpe in after me. She lays her palm along his rough cheek, her eyes brimming, but he gently removes her hand and slides her deeper into the cart.

'Keep quiet,' he says. 'I'll tell you when you can get out.' Then he jerks a flap of canvas over the back of the cart, tying it down as Euterpe and I settle in cross-legged on the rough boards. The floor of the cart is covered with grit and dust, and there's a tangle of old rope in the corner. We hear the scrape of his feet as he walks up to the mule.

'Git up, Potiscus,' he says.

With the slow clop of hooves, the cart lurches forward under us. Euterpe scoots around to sit beside me, the two of us steadying each other as the cart rocks and rumbles up the quiet street.

'Where is he taking us?' I whisper.

'Hush,' says Euterpe, but then she says, 'To the eastern gate, where the road leads north to Lucentum.'

'What's Lucentum?' I say.

'Another port,' she says. 'A punter told me there are ships to Africa there.'

'Africa,' I say.

'Yes.' She presses my head to her shoulder. 'Now be quiet.'

The cart turns again, into a busier, noisier street. It's hot in the cart, and sunlight spears through holes in the canvas. Over the crunch and rumble of the wheels, I hear snatches of conversation, the steady rap of a hammer, someone singing, someone laughing. A barking dog follows us for a little while, making both Euterpe and I sit up straight and stare at the canvas across the back of the cart. Then Brutus shouts and throws a stone, and the dog disappears yelping into the distance. As Euterpe and I rock together, I can hear her breathing unsteadily through her nose. I want to tell her I love her. I want to say, I know you love me. But I don't say anything.

The cart turns into a shadowed lane, and the spears of sunlight disappear. Now the only sound is the rattle and squeak of the cart reverberating off the walls. Euterpe is holding me so tightly it hurts, and I wriggle a little to loosen her grip. She looks down at me wide-eyed, as if surprised to see me there, then she tips her head against the side of the cart.

'What have I done?' she whispers.

Now the cart enters a busy street again, turning right and lurching over the ruts in the middle of the pavement before settling into them. Sunlight pierces again through the holes in the canvas.

'Make way,' Brutus calls. 'Git up, you lazy beast.'

'How far is the gate?' I say.

'It can't be much longer,' says Euterpe.

In the warm twilight under the canvas, I can hear footsteps and conversation, a saw rasping through wood, the ring of hammers on metal. I can smell baking bread and hear the rumble of a millstone. I sit up straight.

'Whoa, easy now,' Brutus says, and the cart begins to slow. 'Whoa.'

The cart stops. I hear the splash of a fountain and the laughter of women. I smell urine. I hear men singing, call and response, *Here I come, walking slow, I ain't goin' nowhere . . .*

I twist around in the cart and grab Euterpe by the shoulders. Her eyes widen. I can hardly breathe. My throat is so dry I can hardly speak.

'*He brought us back,*' I say.

Now there are footsteps behind the cart and the rasp of rope being undone. The canvas flap is tossed back, and silhouettes reach for us out of the glare.

'Here they are,' Brutus says, and Euterpe and I, crying and clutching each other, scramble deeper into the cart. But hands grab us and yank us apart, pulling us across the splintery floorboards and into the sunlight. I scream wordlessly, swinging my fists and punching with my feet, but Brutus wraps his arms around me from behind and lifts me into the air, where my legs kick uselessly. Then he clamps his rough palm over my mouth to stop me screaming, and here I am once more, where I stupidly hoped I'd never be again, crushed against a man, helpless and barely able to breathe, while Sparrow takes flight and watches the street from above. Around the cart is a ring of passers-by, stopped and silenced by the unfolding scene. The women are watching from the trickling fountain, and Nazarius watches from the doorway of his shop. His men have stopped singing, and some of them are crowded behind the counter, watching. The schoolboys under the portico are standing on their benches behind their gawping schoolmaster, the corner boys stand on tiptoe to see between the people in the crowd in front of them. What Sparrow sees, what they all see, is a cart stopped at the entrance to the narrow passage that leads to the theatre, to the slave dealer. The tall doorkeeper from Dominus's house has pinned Euterpe's arms behind her back, while Calidus in his fancy tunic and Melpomene in her mantle look on. Euterpe screams something at Brutus, who will not meet her eye. Instead he looks at the ground and holds the boy, one arm clamped round his waist and squeezing the breath out of him, his other hand clamped tightly over his mouth. The boy has stopped struggling, and his legs hang limp above the pavement. His eyes are wide and unseeing.

Euterpe is panting, but she doesn't struggle against the man holding her from behind. Through her tears she widens her eyes at Melpomene.

'It's my fault,' she sobs. 'I made him come. It was all my idea. Don't hurt him . . .'

'Oh my dear,' says Melpomene. 'None of that matters now.'

'Shut her up,' Calidus says. The doorkeeper clutches Euterpe's arms in one hand and, with the other, he slips a gag over her head and into her mouth. She tries to scream through it. She stares

410

wide-eyed at the boy hanging in Brutus's arms. Tears pour down her cheeks, snot drips from her nose.

Melpomene, lips pursed, steps up and reaches into Euterpe's mantle. She lifts her eyes over Euterpe's head as she feels around, then smiles and pulls out the bundle of coins wrapped in a piece of cloth. She holds it up and says to Calidus, 'For Brutus?'

Calidus nods, and Melpomene sets the bundle on the back of the cart and nods at Brutus, who stares fixedly at the ground. Her eyes slip over the boy, who can barely see her. Then she turns back to Euterpe, and as she feels inside the mantle again, she says to Euterpe in a low voice, 'Brutus told Focaria what you were going to do.'

She pauses as she finds the other coin pouch, the leather one.

'And Focaria told me,' she says as she lifts the pouch by its drawstring out of the front of Euterpe's mantle, deft as a magician. 'I thought you ought to know that.'

Melpomene hefts the pouch in the air, to the appreciative murmurs of the crowd. Look how rich wolves are!

Euterpe's head sags over her chest. Her tears splash on the paving stones. Her shoulders heave. All her weight hangs in the grip of the doorkeeper behind her. If he were to let go of her, she'd fall to her knees.

'Your Honour?' Brutus at last lifts his face, looking at Calidus. He flicks his eyes at the bundle of coins on the back of his cart.

'Whatever.' Calidus flips his hand at the man. 'My gratitude.'

Brutus lifts his hand tentatively from the boy's mouth, and when the boy doesn't scream, Brutus lowers him to the ground. Hovering above, his heart fluttering, Sparrow watches the boy sag to his knees, his head wobbling on his neck. His back to Euterpe, Brutus picks up the clinking bundle, flips down the canvas flap, and walks back to the head of his mule.

'Git,' he says, tugging on its bridle. 'Git now.'

The mule leans into its harness, another slave who will never escape, and as the cart starts to crunch forward on its wheels, Melpomene hands Calidus the leather pouch of coins.

'Your Honour,' she says, dipping her head. 'That should be enough to buy another Euterpe.'

'Hm,' says Calidus, wrapping the drawstring around his hand and hefting it. He's not impressed, reader. The money was always his, after all. It was never really Euterpe's.

'Why not sell him, too?' Calidus tips his head at the boy kneeling slack-mouthed in the street. 'He's been nothing but trouble.'

'Oh, Your Honour,' Melpomene says brightly. 'Did Focaria tell you that?'

The young Dominus shrugs, and Melpomene says, 'Antinous is worth it. We'll never find another one like him. Her, on the other hand . . .' She gestures at Euterpe.

Both arms in the grip of the doorkeeper, Euterpe lifts her head and looks at the boy through her tears. She cries to him through the gag, but the boy isn't there. He can't see her or hear her. He is Sparrow, hanging in the air over their heads, looking on, feeling nothing.

'All right, then.' Calidus snaps his fingers, and the doorkeeper shakes Euterpe to make her stand up straight. The gag distends her mouth. Her eyes are wide and frantic. Then the doorkeeper swings her around, making her head snap, and marches her ahead of him into the narrow passage that leads to the theatre. Calidus follows, humming tunelessly and dangling the pouch of coins.

'The peace of God be with you all,' he sings out to the crowd as he goes.

Melpomene bends over the boy in the street and shakes him by the shoulder, and the crowd begins to dissolve around them. Sparrow watches from above as the women turn back to the fountain, whispering with each other. The schoolboys are driven off their benches by the schoolmaster's stick. Nazarius steps back into the shadows of his shop, where his men start singing again. Directly below Sparrow, Melpomene slaps the boy.

'Antinous!'

I look up to see Melpomene's eyes fixed on mine. My cheek is stinging, and I lift my fingers to touch it. She slaps me again, and I cry out. She grasps my wrist and drags me to my feet.

'Let's go,' she says briskly, and she pulls me along, toward the garden door up the street. I stumble after her, panting, my cheek burning. I'm exhausted, my limbs are weak. It's as if I've been running all morning. The sunlight weighs on my shoulders, trying to drive me to my knees. Every eye in the street penetrates me like the sharp end of a spear. As we pass the fountain, the women put their heads together and whisper as they watch us, and I stare back at them slack-mouthed as if I've never seen anything like them before in my life.

'I'm not angry at you,' Melpomene is saying. Her grip is tight but not painful. She leans forward against the weight of the stumbling boy, as if into a stiff wind.

'She was going to get you killed.' She shakes me to make me look up at her. 'I just saved your life. Someday you'll thank me.'

At the garden door, she swings me round her and pins my shoulders against the wall.

'When we go in,' she says, 'I need to talk to Focaria, without you. I need you to go straight up to your room and lie down. All right?'

I stare past her shoulder and say nothing.

'*Listen.*' She grips my jaw painfully and makes me look at her. 'Go upstairs and lie down. Do you hear me?'

I nod.

'All right.' Grasping my shoulder, she pushes me through the door. Inside, she lets go of me to pull the bolt across, and I take off, running across the garden toward the kitchen.

'Antinous!' Melpomene lunges and misses, tripping herself in the skirts of her mantle and falling flat on her chest.

'Focaria!' I shout. 'They're selling her!'

Behind me Melpomene is tearing the mantle off her shoulders and crawling out of it on her hands and knees, as if shedding her skin. I burst through the kitchen doorway and skid to a stop on the flagstones.

'What did you do?' I'm breathless and crying. 'They're selling her!'

Focaria is at the table, gutting fish. She stares at me wide-eyed, gripping the knife with her slimy fingers.

'What are *you* doing here?' she says.

'They're *selling* her!' I scream. '*What did you do?*'

Her eyes shift from me, and I turn to see Melpomene panting in the doorway. She lifts her palms to Focaria.

'Listen to me,' Melpomene says, and she starts slowly into the kitchen.

Focaria shifts her eyes back and forth between Melpomene and me. She opens her mouth wide and drops the knife on the table.

'No,' she gasps. 'No no no no no no no.' She thrusts her bloody fingers into her hair. Melpomene touches her, and Focaria recoils, retreating round the table into the corner by the oven, where I used to sleep.

'No!' she shouts. Her eyes are wide. She's tearing at her hair.

'*Listen,*' says Melpomene. As she edges toward Focaria, she carefully pushes the knife across the table through the fish guts, out of Focaria's reach.

'You were supposed to sell *him*!' Focaria thrusts her finger in my direction. I'm standing at the far end of the table, my chest heaving, tears pouring from my eyes. I'm choking on my own snot. I'm trembling all over.

'That was never going to happen.' Melpomene keeps her voice tight and low, and she backs Focaria into the corner without touching her. 'I need him. I'll get you another Euterpe.'

'No no no no no!' Focaria wails, rhythmically slapping her forehead.

'It's all for the best,' Melpomene croons, still not touching her. 'A month from now you won't remember her.' She glances at me over her shoulder. 'Neither will he.'

She turns back to Focaria, and I step up to the table, pick up the slimy knife, hold it high in both hands over my head, and drive it between Melpomene's shoulder blades.

Melpomene jerks erect. She lifts her head and sucks her breath in sharply. She whirls and strikes my face with the back of her fist, knocking me against the wall at the end of the kitchen. I curl into a ball on the floor like an animal, putting my hands over my head as Sparrow flutters frantically into every corner of the kitchen, heart hammering, wings flailing. He watches as Melpomene staggers against the table, her mouth working, breathing in short, harsh gasps. Leaning against the table, she arches her back and gropes for the knife behind her.

'Take it out!' she gasps. 'Take it out!'

Focaria comes out of the shadows behind her, her hair wild, her eyes wide. She lays a hand on Melpomene's shoulder and pulls the knife out with the other. Melpomene gasps and nearly sinks to her knees, but she steadies herself with both hands on the table.

'How deep is it?' she says, panting. 'Is it deep?'

'Not deep enough,' says Focaria, and with one hand she grips Melpomene's hair and pulls her head back, and with the other she draws the knife across her throat, opening a deep red seam that gushes blood and bubbles of air. Most of the blood spills down her chest and into her gown, but from a corner of the cut, a little fountain pumps into the air over her head, once, twice, three times, until it droops and dies. The kitchen fills with the iron smell of blood as Sparrow flails overhead and I lie trembling in a ball on the floor. Focaria lets go of Melpomene's hair and steps back. Melpomene drops as if all her strings have been cut, and I see Audo holding a man by his throat and cutting his face, I hear the *snick snick snick* of a blade gutting a man beyond the garden door, I see Clio bleeding

415

and screaming in her cell, I see Focaria and Urania kneeling over Audo and smothering him as he twitches and gouges the dirt with his heels. Melpomene lands hard on her knees, her head flops back, and she sags backwards onto the floor, her legs twisted under her. Her hand trails off the edge of the table and lands in her lap, where it twitches once, twice, three times, and then lies still.

Then Sparrow at last finds his way out the kitchen door, and he soars high above the garden and watches as, far below, a woman drags a kicking, screaming boy by his hair straight through the rows of plants and slams him against the side of the water tank. She yanks the lid off the tank and tosses it aside, then hauls the boy over the edge and plunges his head into the water, holding it under as he kicks and waves his hands, splashing water everywhere, turning the dirt beside the tank to mud. The boy's elbow catches the woman in the face, and she falls back, releasing him. He slides gasping down the side of the tank, his hair plastered to his head, his tunic soaked. The woman kneels near him, her hands pressed to her face, blood streaming from her nose. The boy, blinking and gasping, scuttles back away from her through the mud. He tries to stand, but he falls again and lies there on his elbows, watching her, his chest heaving.

'You broke my nose,' Focaria says.

I wipe the water from my face and try to stand again, but the best I can do is kneel. I want to say something, but all I can do is cough and gasp.

Focaria swipes the blood from under her nose.

'You've ruined everything,' she says.

'You . . .' I gasp. 'You gave her up.'

Focaria lunges for me, and I scramble back. But she catches me and straddles me in the dirt, pinning my arms to my sides. Blood drips from her nose onto my face.

'You little fuck, you've ruined everything,' she says. Her eyes are blazing.

416

I try to wriggle out from under her, but she's too heavy. She puts her hands around my throat.

'Euterpe will be angry at you,' I manage to say, but Focaria only tightens her grip.

'I should have killed you the day Audo brought you into my kitchen,' she hisses.

As her thumbs squeeze my windpipe, I gasp, 'I know where her money is!'

Her thumbs loosen.

'Whose money?' she says. 'Euterpe's?'

I manage to pull one arm free and grab her wrist.

'Mel's.' I swallow hard. 'You're going to need it.'

Focaria takes her hands away from my throat, but she continues to straddle me, panting and bleeding. She points her finger between my eyes.

'Are you lying to me?' she says.

My hair pressed into the dirt, I shake my head from side to side.

'You're going to help me,' she says. 'And maybe for her sake I'll let you live.'

In the kitchen, Melpomene lies in a wide, flat pool of blood. Tendrils of it seep along the seams between the flagstones. Clutching my wrist with one hand, Focaria lifts her old iron collar from the wall, where Melpomene left it hanging as a reminder, and tosses it on Melpomene's chest. Then she drags me out of the kitchen to the woodpile and thrusts a bundle of wood into my arms. She grabs an armload herself and pushes me ahead of her into the kitchen, where we dump the wood on and around Melpomene's body.

'Keep going,' she says, shoving me ahead of her, and we make several trips until we have carried all the wood into the kitchen, leaving only a damp patch of dirt in the weeds. We stack the wood in the corners and under the table, tracking bloody footprints all over the floor, leaving a narrow path to the smouldering oven. My hands are bleeding and splintered when we're done, and my tunic is filthy with dirt and mud. Focaria grabs my arm again and yanks it painfully up behind my back.

'Where's her mantle?' she says.

'In the garden,' I say, and she drags me out into the garden, where I show her the mantle, lying in a heap near the door. Still hanging onto my wrist, she crouches over me. Her upper lip is smeared with blood, and her nose is swollen and purple.

'Show me where Mel's money is,' she says, and she drags me stumbling and crying through the tavern and up the stairs. She pushes me ahead of her into Melpomene's cell, and I fall to my knees. She swats the back of my head.

'Quickly!' she says. 'They'll be back soon.'

I crawl into the corner, where Melpomene's drapery puddles on the floor. Under the drapery is a loose board, and I pry it up and lift out a pouch of coins, then another, then another, the lifetime savings of a wolf.

'Is that all of it?' Focaria is tearing a wide strip off Melpomene's sheet.

I nod, but Focaria thrusts me aside and reaches into the hole herself. She pulls out another pouch, and she hits me with it. I scuttle back from her, pressing my back against the drapery on the wall.

'I didn't know!' I cry, though I did.

She yanks the sheet off Melpomene's bed and, grimacing, tears a long strip off it. Then she places the four pouches onto the strip and jerks them up into a bundle with a tight knot.

'Take me with you,' I say. Tears are streaming down my cheeks and off my chin. My nose is dripping.

Focaria doesn't even look at me.

'We can find her,' I say, snuffling back my snot. 'We can find out where they sold her, and we can—'

Focaria crosses the cell and hauls me by the tunic onto the bed. She straddles me again, pressing me into Melpomene's mattress.

'Don't you dare say her name.' *This* is the coldest blue her eyes have ever been. 'She's gone.' She punches me in the face. 'She's dead, and you killed her.' She punches me again.

I'm sobbing now, 'I'm sorry, I'm sorry, I'm sorry . . .'

Focaria pulls her fist back again, but instead of hitting me, she yanks the pillow out from under my head and presses it over my face. I scream into the pillow, I kick my legs, I claw at her arms. It's my worst fear come true, it's the way I always thought I was going to die, crushed under someone else's flesh, unable to move, unable to breathe. But it's not Audo or a punter who is crushing me, it's my mother, or one of them, the woman who fed me and cleaned me and taught me, who hit me and cursed me and protected me, who hated the same man we all hated and loved the same woman I loved, who inhabited my earliest memory and is now bringing about my last moment. Sparrow watches as the woman straddles the boy on the bed the way a wolf straddles a punter, but the boy isn't trembling in ecstasy, he's shuddering the way Audo did, choking, breathless, his legs going limp, his hands falling away. Now even Sparrow's eyes go dim, and his ears hear nothing but the useless beating of his wings and the pounding of his own blood. Then silence descends like a shroud, and his eyes go black.

IV

I wake to the smell of smoke, the shouting of men, and the splintering of wood. I rub my eyes, already stinging from the haze hanging in Melpomene's cell. I don't understand what is happening, I'm not even sure where I am. Incandescent sparks swirl through the window above me and ignite the drapery hanging from the ceiling, turning it instantly to flame. I scramble off the mattress and out the door as the flaming drapery twists to the floor and ignites the mattress behind me. The curtain in the doorway ignites as well, heat roars out of the cell, and I curl into a ball on the hallway floor and cover my head. Above me a churning overcast of black smoke is descending, and below me, a jumble of men's shouts rises from the tavern. I crawl away from the heat to the end of the hall, and one of the voices, sharp and rasping, funnels up the stairway: '*Is anyone up there?*' I try to shout back, but my chest is full of scalding smoke and all I can do is choke and cough.

Then two hands are clutching at me, dragging me down the stairs by my tunic, banging my elbows and knees on every step. At the bottom, the man heaves me over his bony shoulder and charges through a crowd of shouting, frantic men.

'Are there any others?' someone shouts, and the man, in the voice of Renatus the baker, shouts back, 'I don't know.'

He pushes through the splintered shutters and into the street, and as I hang, retching and coughing, over his shoulder, he carries me round the corner, brushing the tintinnabulum as we pass, making it spin. He is coughing, too, and by the time he reaches the frantic crowd outside the garden door, he is staggering. More hands reach out and lift me off his shoulder, other hands grab Renatus, and together the two of us are lowered to the pavement, our backs against the wall of Priscianus's house. In front of us, a chain of men snakes along the street from the fountain and through the garden door. Each man is handing along to the next a brimming bucket or pot of water, using every vessel on the street.

Between their legs and through the wide-open garden door, I see, with my stinging eyes, the blackened walls of the kitchen and above them, a fountain of flame and black smoke roiling skyward where the roof used to be. Sparks sail high overhead, caught by the wind. Even at this distance, under the acrid smell of flaming wood and plaster, I can detect the aroma of burning meat. I've spent my life so far watching Focaria burn sausages and chicken and pork, and I can't help thinking of Melpomene cooking in the flames, her blood boiling off the floor, her flesh melting from her limbs, her bones blackening and cracking. More smoke pours through holes in the roof of the tavern, and more flames lick out of the windows of the cells. Orange embers float like fireflies over nearby roofs, and above all the other voices shouting, I hear Priscianus screaming hoarsely, over and over again, 'Save my shop! Save my shop!'

Then someone is crouching before me, blocking my view. It is a woman, and she puts a cup of water to my lips and makes me drink. I cough most of it out, and she waits a moment, pats my back, then tips the cup to my lips again. This time I keep it down, and she offers the cup to Renatus, who gulps down a mouthful.

'Was there anyone else, brother?' Balbina says, and Renatus coughs a moment before he answers.

'I don't know,' he gasps. 'The smoke . . . I couldn't see . . .'

'Where . . .' I say, and the baker and his sister turn to me.

'Where what?' says Balbina, resting her hand on my shoulder. 'Where's who?'

'Focaria,' I manage to say.

'If she was in there . . .' Renatus nods toward the burning kitchen. '. . . she's gone.'

'Drink,' says Balbina, putting the cup to my lips again. 'Don't talk.'

I force a little water down my ravaged throat. 'She tried . . .' I say. 'She tried to . . .'

'It's too late now.' Renatus's chest heaves. 'Where she is now, the flames are . . .' A pause. ' . . . are even hotter than that. And they . . .' Another pause. '. . . burn forever.'

'Not now, brother.' Balbina lays her hand on his shoulder.

'Melpomene . . .' I start to say, but then, beyond the line of men, the wall of the kitchen collapses in an eruption of flame. A roiling wave of sparks and black smoke drives the men in the garden back out through the door, where they pile up in a clot of limbs and shouting faces before they burst into the street. The smoke pours out the door and over the garden wall and through the crowd to where Balbina, Renatus, and I sit against the wall, blinding me and choking me until, at last, I pass out.

I wake again on the cold floor of a dim room. Motes of dust dance in a shaft of light slanting through a narrow window, and as I take shallow breaths through my raw throat, I stare at cobwebs in a corner of the ceiling and hear murmuring voices. I push myself up on my hands, and the voices stop. The room is narrow and lined with shelves stacked with folded linen. Against the door at the other end, beyond the dusty shaft of sunlight, I see Thalia and Urania sitting in their mantles, holding hands. Digitus huddles in a corner near them with his knees drawn up to his chest, staring dully at nothing.

I struggle to sit up, and I start coughing again. My hands sting with cuts. My face is sore where Focaria hit me. My tunic is torn and blackened with soot. The three at the far end of the room all

425

look at me, but none of them, not even Thalia, come to my aid. In that moment, even before they have spoken, I know I have lost them. I can tell from the way they look at me – Urania's dead gaze, Thalia's sad, wounded eyes – that they blame me for what is about to become of them. With her free hand, Thalia reaches into her mantle for something, doesn't find it, and pulls her hand out again, fidgeting instead with a fold of the material. Digitus doesn't even look in my direction. He's been through this before, and he's not wasting any time on me.

Finally I stop coughing, and I stare back at them, propped on my stinging hands.

'Urania . . .' I say hoarsely.

'Not Urania,' she says. 'Not anymore.' She levels her dead gaze at me. 'Now I'm just Izar, the pig farmer's daughter.'

'Thalia . . . ?' I say.

'Not anymore,' says Urania. 'She's Taesis. Just another useless girl from Egypt.'

'Taesis,' I say. 'I never knew . . .'

'You never asked,' says Urania.

'What did you do, Mouse?' Thalia's voice is wobbly, as if she's about to cry.

Urania folds Thalia's hand in the crook of her arm. 'Yes, Mouse,' she says, her voice level with contempt. 'What did you *do*?'

'Why didn't you tell us you were going to run?' Thalia is crying now. 'We would have come with you.'

I'm light-headed and bruised, and my chest and throat are still burning inside. I sit up and push my back against the wall behind me. I'm going to find no comfort at the far end of the room. Thalia's reaching inside her mantle again, and I realize she's feeling for her chi-rho medallion. But she never carried it to the baths, and now it's a lump of melted brass in the smouldering ruins of the tavern. She starts to sob, and Urania puts her arm around her.

'It was Euterpe's idea,' I say hoarsely.

'That's a lie,' says Urania.

'She wouldn't leave without us!' says Thalia.

It's true, I want to say, *she would*, but instead I say, 'What is this place?'

No one answers me at first, though Digitus slides his eyes in my direction.

'The house of Dominus,' Urania says finally. 'They're deciding what to do with us.'

'Where's Focaria?' I say.

'She's dead!' cries Thalia. 'She burned alive!'

Her fingers stray inside her mantle for the lost medallion again, and Urania roughly plucks her hand away.

'Stop it,' she says. 'It's gone.'

Thalia buries her face in Urania's mantle and sobs. Urania narrows her eyes at me.

'Where's Melpomene?' she says.

Reader, what could I say? If I told her the truth – *Melpomene is dead, and Focaria and I killed her* – Urania would be obligated to tell Calidus, or Granatus, or the aedile, or whoever asked her. In that case – as Focaria had put it not long before at the baths – I might as well cut my own throat. Telling her only part of the truth – *Melpomene is dead* – would be just as bad, because everyone would want to know how I knew. I could try to hide behind my fear and pain, hoping that no one would expect a terrified boy who had just been pulled from a fire to be able to explain what had happened. But Urania knew me too well. Looking down the length of the dim storeroom, I knew she knew that I was trying to think of an answer.

Digitus saves me. 'I see her!' he exclaims, and Urania and I turn to the dim corner where Diggy is sitting. Even Thalia lifts her face, wiping her tears with the back of her hand. Digitus is suddenly sitting upright and animated, as if a puppeteer has started working his strings.

'I am in bakery,' he says, waving his hands. 'Man come in and
he say, tavern is burning! Renatus, he yell for slaves to follow him,
and I follow too. We run down street, and I see her come other
way, from tavern . . .'

'Melpomene?' Urania scowls at him sceptically.

'Yes!' says Digitus. 'I see her!'

'You saw her face?' says Urania.

'Yes!' insists Digitus. 'Well, maybe no. She had hood up . . .'
He mimes a hood with both hands. 'But it was her . . . her . . .'
He gestures at his shoulders, searching for the word.

'Her mantle?' says Urania.

'Yes!' Digitus shakes his finger. 'It was *her* mantle! I call to her,
I say, Domina! Tavern is burning! But she just . . .' He flaps his
hands. 'She keep walking, away from tavern, very fast. Then crowd
catch me up and . . .' He shrugs and lets his hands flop to the
floor, and he slumps against the wall again, as if the puppeteer has
let him drop.

Urania levels her gaze at me.

'What happened, Antinous?' she says, and now I know for
certain I've lost her. She has never called me Antinous before.
The reprieve Digitus gave me is over, and now I have to think of
something to say.

But before I have to answer, we hear a key rattling in the lock
of the door. Thalia recoils and Urania puts an arm around her, and
they scuttle into the corner with Digitus as the door scrapes open.
Silhouetted against the brighter light outside is Dominus's doorkeeper. He looks down at the two wolves and the kitchen slave
watching him from the corner. Then he lifts his gaze down the
length of the room and points at me.

'You,' he says.

*   *   *

His hand heavy on my shoulder, the doorkeeper pushes me ahead of him through Dominus's gaudy, immaculate house.

'Don't touch anything,' he says.

I hear a woman's voice, and through an open doorway I see an older woman sitting in a gloomy room with a young girl standing between her knees. The woman is showing the girl how to spin wool with a distaff and spindle, guiding the girl's hands with her own while the girl concentrates with her tongue between her lips. At the sound of our footsteps, the woman looks through the doorway, and our eyes meet. Is she Granatus's wife? Is the girl his daughter? As the girl fumbles with the spindle, the woman says something to someone I can't see, and the door shuts, as if on its own.

The doorkeeper directs me through the atrium, where a shaft of late afternoon light slants across the bronze statue of the boy pouring water into the pool, gilding his head and the pot on his shoulder. In the corner, the Christian altar is unlit, but Christ is watching me, looking sceptical, his two fingers raised as if in warning. I'm still unsteady on my legs, but my head is clearer, and while my throat is still sore, I can breathe a little more deeply. I know that what is about to happen is going to determine if I live or die, and I also know that I am about to face it entirely alone. Euterpe cannot protect me any longer, if she ever could, and – if I'm being honest, reader – it's her fault I'm here. The other woman who might have protected me, because I was useful to her, is gone too, by my own hand. If Melpomene were here, she might tell me how to work the situation to my own advantage, or at least how to avoid being crucified or burned alive. But if her spirit is looking on, from whatever afterlife she has gone to – the tenebrous underworld of the old gods or the flaming lake of the Christians – she has no reason to wish me well, and who can blame her? As for Focaria – who knows where she is right now? Maybe they've caught her already. Maybe she's already dead. Or maybe she's wearing a dead woman's mantle and walking as fast as she can through the scrubland outside the city. Maybe she's watching the city sink beneath the waves from the deck of a ship under sail, having used a dead woman's money to buy her passage as far away from Carthago Nova as she can afford.

Coming round the pool in the middle of the atrium, we step up into Dominus's office, and my eyes meet those of Marius, who is sitting with his feet up on the desk, eating an apple and reading a book. His slave, the sullen boy I met once before, is slouching in another chair behind him, and he sits up as the doorkeeper and I come in. Marius lets his eyes drift down the length of my body from head to toe, then he looks back at the scroll in his lap.

'Didn't I tell you they burn boys like you?' he says, and as I pass behind Marius, the slave boy laughs out loud, bouncing up and down in his seat.

He's still laughing as the doorkeeper and I pass into the garden. I squint and hold my hand up against the slanting light, and the doorkeeper directs me along a winding, pebbled path between spiky, flowering bushes and trees pendulous with figs, apples, and pears, their fragrance overwhelmed by the smell of smoke from my tunic. The doorkeeper pushes me across a narrow little bridge over a clear pool full of lilies and flashing, golden fish, and I hear voices ahead. Four men halt their conversation and turn to watch us approach. Two of them, Granatus in a tunic and the thin, grey aedile in his overlarge toga, are sitting on one bench, while Calidus is pacing on the neatly trimmed grass behind them. On another bench, a slight distance away, the bishop sits perfectly erect with his hands loosely clasped in the lap of his black robe. My footsteps, and the footsteps of the doorkeeper, crunch on the path as we approach.

My heart flutters in my chest like Sparrow's wings, but he does not take flight. Instead, I am thinking, *This is the moment, and these are the men who will decide my fate.* Except for Marius, who stays in the office behind me, none of these men have had me, not that that would make any difference. Whether they fucked me or not, I have no reason to expect any sympathy from them. I am here to explain a disaster to them, one which I helped to cause, though I can't tell them the truth about that. Worse yet, I don't know what they already know, which means that at any moment, I could be caught out in a lie. Even worse than that, they expect me to lie. In the aftermath of a crime, a slave is only considered to be telling the truth when he is being tortured. Focaria enjoyed telling me that once.

So, I think, *I have that to look forward to.* Ahead of me, Granatus and the aedile lift their chins as I approach, while behind their bench, Calidus stops pacing and looks at me the way Audo used to, as if he wants to pound me into the ground with his fists. The bishop does not move, but watches me with his hands very still in his lap. All around me other people rise out of the foliage, both men and women, naked or near naked, lifting their faces to the sky, and there are even more figures looming in the shadow of the colonnade, contorted as if in ecstasy or in pain. It takes me a moment to realize that they are statues like the bronze boy in the fountain, only brightly painted. Behind Calidus, at the very back of the house where the shadow is deepest, is the largest painting I have ever seen, crowded with dark, colourful figures. It's nothing like the paintings in the tavern, but in the dim light, I can't make out what the figures are doing. Euterpe could have told me the story behind it.

It's a hero, Little One, she would have said, Ulysses and his men outwitting a monster twice their size, or the young Alexander leading his wild Macedonians against a Persian army of vastly superior numbers.

That won't do him any fucking good, says Focaria. Look at him, torn and burned and filthy. You and your fucking stories.

431

Then, although I can't imagine why she would help me now, I hear the voice of Melpomene in my ears like the single, clear tone of a bell.

Look around you, Antinous, she says. We paid for all of this.

The doorkeeper jerks on my shoulder to stop me. No one speaks for a moment. Sparrow flutters again and goes still. I stand before these men on unsteady legs, with splintered hands, a bruised face, and a scalded windpipe, in a torn and dirty tunic, a runaway, a catamite, and a murderer. I have never been more myself than I am right now.

'What's your name, pusus?' says the aedile.

'Antinous, Dominus,' I say.

'I'm not your Dominus,' he says. 'You address me as "Your Honour".'

'My apologies, Your Honour.' I lower my head. 'I am Antinous.'

'Look at me.'

I lift my head. The aedile watches me steadily with his grey eyes.

'How did the fire start?' he says.

I turn my head and cough a bit, but it's a performance. Melpomene, if I hadn't killed her, would have been proud.

'Speak up,' says the aedile.

'I don't know, Your Honour.' I clear my throat. 'I was asleep in my cell, and when I woke up, everything was on fire.' This is the truth, sort of.

'Oh, fuck me.' The other three men turn to see red-faced Calidus charging round the bench where his father sits. 'What the fuck happened?' he's shouting. Behind me, the doorkeeper lays his hand on my shoulder. It's not to comfort me, but to hold me steady so Calidus can pummel me. The aedile looks annoyed. The bishop says nothing. Granatus jumps up and puts himself in front of his son, gripping his upper arms and holding him back.

'Shut up!' Granatus says. 'Sit down!'

But Calidus is so angry he's willing to scuffle with his own father, who barely holds him back, digging his feet into the rattling pebbles of the path. Calidus reaches over the older man's shoulder.

'What are we waiting for?' he shouts. 'Let's torture the little fuck!'

With a grunt, Granatus heaves with all his strength, and Calidus staggers back on his heels. When he starts forward again, his father slaps him hard, snapping Calidus's head to one side and nearly driving him to his knees. Calidus gasps, doubled over. The aedile perches on the edge of his bench, as if he's ready to flee or join in. The bishop, meanwhile, keeps his eyes on me, and though his expression has barely changed, he almost looks as if he's surprised at how quietly I am standing. As it happens, so am I. Usually, when the air is heavy with the threat of violence, Sparrow takes flight. But now I don't even feel the flutter of his wings in my chest. Instead, my heart beats slow and steady. Right now, at this moment, it's just me.

The older Dominus hooks his son's elbow and walks him back into the shadow of the colonnade, where he stands him up in front of the dim painting and lectures him in a low voice, shaking his finger in the younger man's face. Meanwhile, the aedile turns to me.

'Come closer,' he says.

I hesitate and look at the ground. Another performance.

'I won't hurt you,' the aedile says, and the doorkeeper shoves me forward. I step to within arm's reach of the aedile. He sits up straighter and fusses with his toga.

'You're filthy,' he says. 'Your tunic is in a shocking state.'

'The fire, Your Honour.'

'Let me see your hands.'

I hold them up, palms down, and he says, 'Turn them over.'

I turn them over, and he takes my hands in his, tugging me toward him.

'How did you get these cuts?'

'In the fire, Your Honour. Trying to get out.'

'And these bruises on your face. Who hit you?'

'No one, Your Honour. I fell down the stairs.'

These are my first overt lies. I'm hoping they don't know that Renatus pulled me from the burning tavern. Still surveying my hands, the aedile says, 'They found a burned body in the kitchen. Do you know who it was?'

Here is a fork in the road. If I say I know who it was, I have to say how I know, which leads to another fork. If I say it's Melpomene, I have to invent a story for her death. If I say it's Focaria, then I have to invent a story for that as well. I also have to consider the possibility that they have caught Focaria already, and they know whose body they found in the smoking debris of the kitchen. The easiest thing to do, the slave's default, is to say that I don't know, and stick to my story that I was asleep in my cell when everything happened. But instead, I astonish myself.

'Focaria,' I say.

'What was her name?' The aedile lets go of my hands.

'Just Focaria,' I say. 'She was the cook. She didn't have a name.'

'How do you know it's her?' The bishop is speaking now. Calidus and the older Dominus have stopped hissing at each other in the shadows of the colonnade, and they are listening.

I turn to the bishop. 'Thalia told me, Your Honour.' I'm pleased at my own cleverness and hoping it doesn't show. 'She told me Focaria got burned up in the fire.'

'Who's Thalia?' says the bishop.

'One of the other wolves.'

'When did she tell you this?'

'Just now, Your Honour.' I glance back toward the house, to indicate the storeroom where they are keeping us. 'Before they brought me out here.'

'You address the bishop as "Your Grace",' says the aedile, but the bishop makes a gesture – *it doesn't matter* – while keeping his gaze directed at me.

'So you were in your cell,' says the aedile. 'What happened before that?'

'They caught us, Your Honour.' I turn back to him. 'Euterpe . . .' At the mention of her name a tremor enters my voice, and I cough to cover it up. 'Euterpe tried to run and she made me go with her.'

The aedile frowns. 'After that,' he says. 'When Melpomene took you back to the tavern.'

'I went up to my cell, Your Honour.'

The aedile sighs and looks at the bishop. 'The boy's an idiot,' he says.

'He's lying!' Calidus shouts from under the colonnade.

'Shut up,' says his father.

'He's frightened,' says the bishop. 'I would be too, if I were him.' He beckons. 'Come here, pusus.'

From behind, the doorkeeper twists me toward the bishop. I take a few unsteady steps. Yet another performance.

'What happened,' says the bishop, 'right after Melpomene brought you back to the tavern, but before you went up to your cell?'

Of all the men in this overstuffed garden, the bishop is the one who worries me the most. With his mouth obscured by his beard, I can't really make out his expression, but he seems to watch me the way Astius the painter did – keenly, but without the carnal intent of a punter. I am a puzzle to be solved and then disposed of. I have to lie to this man, but I know he's the one person in the garden who is most likely to catch me at it. More than anything else at this moment, I want to look away from him, but looking away from him would be the worst possible thing to do.

'Your Grace,' I say. 'As soon as we came in the door, Melpomene sent me upstairs.'

'All right,' says the bishop. 'Then what did she do?'

'She went into the kitchen.'

'She let you go upstairs on your own?' says the aedile.

I answer him without looking away from the bishop. 'Yes, Your Honour.'

'Why didn't you run?' he says. 'You were already trying to escape.'

I risk turning away from the bishop to look at the aedile. Granatus and Calidus are standing behind him now, and the older Dominus has his hand on his son's shoulder. Calidus is grinding his teeth but saying nothing.

'I beg your pardon, Your Honour,' I say, 'but I wasn't. Eu-Euterpe took me with her. I didn't know she was trying to escape.'

I have to work to keep my voice from catching. This is what Euterpe told me to say, but it feels as if I am betraying her, condemning her to who knows what. For all I know, I am killing her, the same way I killed Melpomene.

'So you went upstairs,' says the bishop. 'Did you hear anything?'

I turn back to him.

'I heard Focaria and Melpomene yelling at each other.'

'What were they saying?'

'I'm sorry, Your Grace, but I couldn't tell.'

Calidus snorts.

'Then what happened?' says the bishop.

'The yelling got louder, Your Grace, and then it stopped.'

'And then?' says the bishop.

This is where it could all go wrong, but what did I have to lose, reader? Whether they believed me or not, I was either going to be killed or sold. I might as well try to save my life.

'I stood on the table under my window,' I say, 'and I saw Melpomene come out of the kitchen and leave the garden through the door into the street.'

'Liar!' shouts Calidus, but his father holds him back. 'He said he was sleeping! He said . . .'

Without looking at his nephew, the bishop holds his finger up for silence. Calidus seethes, but says nothing more.

'You're sure it was her?' says the bishop. 'You saw her face?'

Now I am one of the devious slaves in a play by Plautus, wondering which lie is most plausible, and least likely to get me hurt. I remember what Digitus said just now, in the linen storeroom, and I decide to hedge my bets. For all I know, he's already told them he saw Melpomene with her hood over her face in the street.

'No, Your Grace,' I say. 'She had her hood up. But it was Melpomene's mantle.'

'And then?' says the bishop.

'And then, Your Grace,' I say, 'I lay down on my bed and went to sleep.'

'In the middle of the day?' cries Calidus. 'After what just happened to him?'

We all turn to look at Calidus, even the bishop. Granatus clutches at him, but Calidus bats his hand away and comes around the bench where the aedile is sitting. He looms over me, and he talks above my head to the others.

'Melpomene had just helped me catch Euterpe and this little cocksucker,' he says. 'Why would she kill the cook and burn the place down? It doesn't make any sense!'

'Begging your pardon, Dominus,' I say. 'But she didn't.'

He grabs me by the hair and twists my face up to his. 'There's a burnt body in the ashes of the kitchen,' he says, 'but you already know that.'

I stand on my toes to keep him from pulling my hair out by the roots.

'Let him go,' says the aedile, but Calidus only twists my hair.

'I always knew this boy was trouble.' He clutches me by the throat and lifts me off my feet.

Sparrow takes flight, watching the scene from above. Granatus and the aedile hover around Calidus and the struggling boy, without touching either of them. The doorkeeper backs away. The bishop raises his hand without standing.

'Nephew!' he says sharply.

Calidus tightens his grip on the boy's throat. Sparrow watches the boy clutch at Calidus's wrist and kick his feet. The bishop stands.

'Put him down!' he says. 'Now!'

Calidus drops the boy, and I fall in a heap on the pebbles of the path, gasping.

'Step away,' says the bishop. Calidus glares at his uncle, but turns away. His father tries to grab him, but Calidus waves him off. The aedile sits down again.

'Just so you know, I've already heard from Priscianus,' Calidus announces to everyone. 'He's suing us for the loss of his shop.'

'For the love of God, son,' says Granatus, 'will you shut up?'

'Can you speak?' The bishop is standing over me, blocking the low sun.

I rub my throat and nod. The pebbles of the path are pressing into my hip. As I struggle to rise, the bishop backs reflexively away from me. He sits down on the bench again. The doorkeeper hooks my arm and pulls me to my feet.

'How do you know Melpomene didn't kill the cook?' the bishop says.

I stand on wobbly legs, my eyes lowered to the path. I feel their gazes on me. Through my bruised throat I say, 'I heard her, Your Grace.' I pause to swallow, and then I say, 'After Melpomene left, I heard Focaria crying in the kitchen.'

'Why was she crying?' says the bishop.

I meet his gaze. 'She loved Euterpe,' I say, 'and Euterpe loved her.'

The bishop closes his eyes as if in pain.

'I think she was sad,' I say, 'that they were never going to see each other again.'

The bishop holds his hand up to keep me from saying anything more. He does not want to hear about this.

'So Focaria set herself on fire?' Calidus cries. 'We're supposed to believe that?'

'I don't know, Dominus,' I say, watching the bishop, who is still sitting with his eyes closed. 'I only know I heard her crying as I went to sleep.'

'This is bullshit!' Calidus shouts, but he doesn't come around the bench again. 'She's out there somewhere, laughing at us! Why are we listening to this . . . to this . . .'

The bishop, his eyes still closed, holds up his hand, and Calidus falls silent. All of us are watching the bishop, whose lips seem to be moving under his beard as if he's praying.

'Where is Euterpe now?' says Granatus.

'I sold her,' says Calidus. 'This morning, to a merchant. They're probably at sea already.'

'Without consulting me?' says his father, and the aedile says, 'Citizens, this is getting out of control . . .'

The aedile, Granatus, and Calidus all start to talk at once. The doorkeeper stands a few paces away from me, as still as one of the statues in the bushes.

I keep my eyes on the bishop. His eyes still closed, he smooths his moustache and beard with his palm, once, twice, as if to still his lips. Then he opens his eyes, and I feel my heart start to flutter under his gaze. Have I gone too far? Have I lied too much or too little? I've tried to complicate my lies to make them sound real and contradictory, the way the truth usually is, because I'm certain that if I tie them all neatly together, they will sound more like lies. At the same time, I'm trying to make it sound as if I don't understand what's going on, that I'm just a confused and frightened boy. Melpomene has taught me well. The bishop stares long and hard at me, and I stare back, not daring to look away.

'Enough,' the bishop says.

The other men keep arguing and talking over each other.

The bishop raises his voice. 'Enough!'

The other men fall silent.

'None of this matters.' The bishop stands. 'It doesn't matter whose body is in the kitchen, or which of the wolves got away. It doesn't matter who set the fire or why. The tavern was always unwholesome – if necessary – but now I hear that it was a cesspit of even more sinful and disgusting passions than I had imagined. It's a good thing that it's gone.'

Calidus and his father protest simultaneously – 'Uncle!' 'Brother!' – but the bishop shouts them both down.

'Enough!' He points his beard in my direction. 'This wretched boy has done me a service. It is a blot on my conscience that I have allowed this place to operate under my nose, knowing what went on there.' He looks at the other men. 'Now it's over. Get rid of him, and get rid of the other wolves. Your days of peddling filth and defilement are over.'

Calidus and his father look at each other, but say nothing. The aedile rises from his bench.

'Your Grace,' he says, 'the curia will need to decide . . .'

'The curia is as guilty as I am in this matter,' says the bishop. 'But I take responsibility. At the insistence of the Church, you have shut down every other tavern in the city, while allowing my brother's to stay open, with my implicit consent. But the requirements of our faith are paramount in this matter, since it involves the immortal souls of everyone involved. Not the least of which is mine.'

He takes a step toward me. For a moment I think he might even touch me, but then I realize that he would rather cut his hand off than do that.

'The martyr Cyprian,' he says, 'wrote that a bishop must be blameless in order to serve as a steward of God. And yet I am a foul sinner, almost as much as this boy is. But I may yet be washed clean.' He draws a breath. 'Sell the other wolves. Sell him. Send him out of the city. That's the end of it.'

He turns, crunching pebbles under his shoe, and starts to walk toward the house. The doorkeeper lowers his head and steps out of his way.

'Uncle,' Calidus calls out, 'why not just kill him?' He sounds disappointed.

The bishop hesitates and speaks over his shoulder, without quite looking back. 'If you do that,' he says, 'I will prosecute you for murder.'

He resumes walking, then stops again.

'As long as he still lives,' the bishop says, 'this boy, too, might be washed clean.'

Then he rounds the trickling fountain and steps into the shadows of the house.

Did he believe me, reader? I will never know, and neither will you. All that matters is that I did the best I could, in an impossible situation, and that in the end, whether it was a result of my lies or not, the bishop spared my life, and he spared the lives of Thalia, Urania, and Digitus. Which was the best we could hope for under the circumstances.

Perhaps you're also wondering, why did I protect Focaria? Why did I let her walk away, a murderess, carrying her victim's money? Why not tell the bishop that Focaria slit Melpomene's throat in a rage, which is only the truth, even if it's not all of it? I could just as easily have lied about that as I did about whose body was in the kitchen. I had no reason to wish her well. Yes, Focaria was my teacher, and a mother to me, of a sort, but she never loved me like Euterpe did, and in the end, she tried to kill me. And if they caught her, of course, she would have told them that I killed Melpomene, which was partly true. But I don't think that occurred to me in the moment. And now I don't remember. It was all so long ago.

Sometimes, when I'm feeling uncharacteristically good about myself, and about the things I've done in my life – a whore, a pimp, a murderer – I tell myself I protected Focaria as an act of love for Euterpe. It's what she would have done had she been standing in the garden surrounded by men. She would have sacrificed herself to let someone she loved get away. She would have done the same for me, or for Thalia or Urania, and maybe even

441

for Melpomene. 'That's what love is,' she told me, and all these years later, I still can't make up my mind if Euterpe was a saint or a fool. Perhaps they're the same thing.

As for myself, I have been a fool more often than not, but I have never been a saint.

It was always going to end like this, with me standing naked on the slaver's stage, wearing a sign I can't read around my neck and iron shackles around my ankles, watched by the small group of buyers in the well of the theatre, and by the larger crowd of idlers who have nothing else to do, and by the merchants in the ranks of stalls who used to sell me fruit and hares and spices, and by Musa the moneylender and his slave Deodatus, and by Opitria – who, if I'd ever paid her to predict my future, would no doubt have told me that this was coming. I'm flanked on stage on one side by Digitus, who looks embarrassed with his tunic off, and on the other by Thalia and Urania, who hold hands with each other until the dealer breaks their grip with his quirt.

Quartus the scribe, crying with happiness, buys Thalia. He dances up on stage to hand over his pouch of coins – supplemented, no doubt, by a ruinous loan from Musa – and he embraces her even before her shackles are unlocked. Thalia is crying, too, as Quartus leads her away. She looks over her shoulder at Urania, who stares after her and says nothing. After a short bidding war, Urania is purchased by a visiting merchant from far-off Alexandria. I call her name as she's led away – her real name, Izar – but she does not look back at me.

For what it's worth, I fetch the highest price that morning, because I am something of a rarity. I am no longer Antinous or Antiochus or even Mouse, but I am young, healthy, and highly trained in an unusual profession. Early in the bidding, Balbina makes an effort to buy me. Her brother hovers over her shoulder and hectors her, and she brushes him off. But she quickly has to give up, because whatever my immortal soul might be worth to her, she can't match the price that men are willing to pay for my specialized skills. As her brother leads her away, she looks up at me in tears and calls out something that I can't hear over the jeering and laughter of the crowd.

In the end, my fate comes down to two slave traders from out of town, one from the Gaulish city of Arelate and the other from the city of Tarraco, which is up the coast of Hispania from Carthago Nova. Both men come up on stage to take a closer look at me, parting my hair to check for lice and scars, assessing my teeth, tapping my chest. They squat to squeeze my legs, to part my backside to check for piles, to finger my penis and testicles. Staring over their heads into the theatre, I see men whose cocks I've sucked, I see boys who have called me names in the street, I see women who have covered their children's eyes when I passed. But I am not ashamed, reader, to be inspected in public like this, because how is it any different from what punters have been doing to me, every night for a year? Is it really any different to be naked in front of a hundred people than it is to be naked in front of one?

The man from Arelate and the man from Tarraco stand in a little triangle with the slave dealer at the focus, and the two men bid silently against each other with short, sharp gestures of their hands. Finally the man from Arelate gives up, and he steps out of the triangle and tosses his hands in the air. The man from Tarraco slaps hands with the dealer to seal the bid, and the slaver snaps his fingers for his assistant to come over with the key and unlock my shackles and take away the sign around my neck. I bend to pick up my filthy tunic and put it on, and when I stand erect again, my new Dominus is looking me up and down with his hands on his hips. He is short and bald and round-bodied, but his legs are shapely, and he looks solid. His tunic is expensive but simple and unadorned, unlike the tunics Calidus wears, and he has a satchel slung over his shoulder. When I have put my tunic on, he reaches into the satchel, produces a length of rope, and steps up to me.

'What do they call you?' He starts to bind my hands with the rope, tightly, but not painfully.

'Antinous,' I say. 'Dominus.'

'That's a grand name for a wolf.'

'My Dominus chose it for me,' I say. 'I mean, my previous Dominus.'

'My name is Tatius.' He drops the loop of a tether around my neck, pulling it snug but not too tight. 'Are you a Jew, Antinous?'

'I don't know, Dominus. I might be a Syrian.'

'Even better,' Tatius says, and he picks up the end of the tether. He looks me up and down again and nods.

'I have a buyer in Tarraco, a very important man, who likes dark little Eastern boys like you.'

'Yes, Dominus.'

'If he likes the look of you as much as I think he will,' Tatius says, 'you won't be Antinous anymore, you'll be Ganymede. He calls all his boys Ganymede.' He looks at me sidelong. 'I don't suppose you know any Greek? Do you know who Ganymede was?'

'No, Dominus.'

The slaver's assistant comes back with the receipt for my sale, and Tatius takes the papyrus, glances at it and nods, and the assistant goes away.

'Ganymede was a pretty boy like you.' He rolls the papyrus up. 'He was chosen by the immortal Zeus to be his lover.' He slips the papyrus into his satchel, then he looks at me. 'If you're lucky, this man will choose you to be his Ganymede, and I will make a great deal more money than I just paid for you.' He gently tugs the tether. 'Let's go.'

As we descend the steps from the stage, I look back up at Digitus standing all alone, still shackled, his tunic in a heap at his feet, hands clasped over his crotch. He sees me looking at him, and he calls out, 'You no worry about me, you little bastard boy!' The crowd laughs at him, and he laughs desperately back at them.

'Digitus like cat!' he shouts at them, and at me. 'He always land on his feet!'

At the end of Tatius's tether, I walk one last time down the street where I have spent most of my life. The crier is out today, strutting like a rooster in the crossroads, declaiming in his staccato singsong, 'One HUNdred denarii for INformation about MelPOMene, a FREEDwoman and a WOLF . . .' I glimpse Nazarius, joking with two women from behind his counter, and I hear the men singing deeper in his shop. Tatius leads me past the trickling fountain, where there are only a few women still gathering the day's water. I don't recognize any of them, and none of them pay any attention to me as we pass. Across the street from the fountain, Priscianus's shop is half burned out – the roof is gone, the insides are blackened, his jars of oil scattered and smashed and burnt. But a couple of the walls are still standing, and the shop looks like a melon that has been smashed open and left to rot in the sun.

The blackened, burnt-out shell of the tavern is still smoking, a thin grey haze that wafts this way and that with the breeze, overwhelming every other smell in the street. The garden wall is sooty and scorched and still standing, but the door has been wrenched off its hinges. Inside, a group of slaves wearing cloth masks over their noses and mouths are pulling blackened bricks and jagged lengths of wood out of the two mounds that used to be the kitchen and the tavern itself, tossing the bricks in one pile and the wood in another. One slave wanders back and forth from the water tank, pouring hissing bucketfuls of water on hot spots in the mounds, using the same bucket I carried back and forth for years.

'What do you know about that?' Tatius says over his shoulder.

'Nothing, Dominus,' I say.

Tatius laughs. 'You're discreet,' he says. 'That's good.'

Then we are passing through the murmuring beggars who live in the shadow of the city gate, and a moment later, we are crossing the quay and have left the city behind us.

I spend my last night in Carthago Nova in a cage on the afterdeck of a ship tied up to the quay.

'I have big plans for this one,' Tatius tells the captain, 'so don't put him below with the others.'

The cage is not as uncomfortable as it sounds. I don't have room to stand, but the ship's watchman has given me a mat to lie on and something to eat, some salt fish and wine. That night we seem to be the only people on deck, and I wonder where the rest of the crew have gone, now that the tavern is in ruins and the bishop has closed all the other taverns in the city. The ship rocks gently under me, an unusual but not unpleasant sensation, and it occurs to me that I am going to leave the city the same way I came into it.

The curious thing about being in this cage is that despite the fact that I can scarcely move, I can see in all directions and hear everything. It is a mild night, and there is enough headroom for me to sit up. In one direction I see the black bulk of a mountain blotting out the stars, while in another direction the stars come all the way down to the horizon, in the space between the two black mountains at the harbour mouth. Looking back across the quay, I see lamps hanging in the gaping mouths of warehouses, and in the distance, I hear voices singing. Beyond the city wall, I see the darkened roofs of houses, and on the hill above the theatre, I see the old temple of Asclepius imprinted against the stars, not far from where Melpomene initiated me into the life of a wolf.

As the night wears on, the singing in the distance dwindles away and dies. The watchman falls asleep on the deck, and I can hear his steady breathing. Now and then, from below, I hear a rustle or a sigh or a moan. The only other sounds are the creaking of the ship, the slap of water against the quay, and the rattling of palms in the breeze off the sea. I curl into a ball inside the cage and stare at the stars bobbing beyond the stern of the ship, up and down, up and down, and I look for the shape of wings against the sky. Will Sparrow come with me tomorrow, or will he stay here, in the city? As my own breathing steadies and my eyelids begin to fall, I realize I'm not bothered. Sparrow will come again when I need him, I'm sure of it. I am Sparrow, and Sparrow is me. It's the only thing I am sure of anymore. Perhaps he will even watch over me as I sleep.

In the depths of the night, I am awakened by the rattle of the lock, and I lift my head to see Euterpe opening the door of the cage. Her eyes are as bright as the stars overhead and she is smiling, and before I can speak, she has put her hand over my mouth to keep me from exclaiming aloud. She draws me out of the cage and we embrace, and I am wrapped once again in her warmth and her familiar smell. Then she leads me across the deck of the ship, and she smiles again and puts her finger to her lips as we step over the sleeping watchman and jump silently from the ship to the quay.

Then we pass under the rattling palms and through the gate into the city, and we come to the ruins of the tavern, where the shattered walls are already grown over with plants from the garden, gone wild. The ruins no longer smell of smoke, but of thyme and rosemary and oregano, and over the trickling of the nearby fountain, I hear two women's voices, and out of the dark come Thalia and Urania, still wearing their mantles, their eyes shining like Euterpe's, bright as the stars. My sisters and I embrace one last time, and Urania says she's taking Thalia back to her village in the countryside, where her father will take them in, and where he will beg Urania's forgiveness for selling her in the first place. Before they go, Urania bends down to kiss me and whisper in my ear, 'I forgive you, Mouse.' Then Euterpe takes my hand and leads me away, and I look back over my shoulder to see Thalia and Urania running hand in hand down the middle of the street, laughing, their mantles glowing in the starlight.

Then Euterpe and I round the corner and pass quickly along the street behind the warehouses of the harbour until we come to the aqueduct, where the wolves who work under the arches rise out of the shadows and salute us, wishing us well on our journey and asking us to remember them always. Then we run laughing across the bridge and along the road between the steep mountain on one side and the silent lagoon on the other. Two fishermen and their boat are silhouetted against the stars reflected in the water, and they salute us, too. We pass between the little houses of the dead, and only when we come to the low wall of the cemetery do I start to feel afraid, thinking of Audo wrapped in his shroud and sleeping restlessly in his shallow grave by the waterside. But Euterpe holds my hand and tells me not to worry, and when a shadowy figure rises from among the tombs and glides toward us, she only laughs.

'What took you so long,' says Focaria, tossing back the hood of Melpomene's mantle and throwing her arms around Euterpe. The two women kiss, and then Focaria puts her hand on my shoulder and says, 'Do you forgive me, Pusus?' and I say, 'Of course I do.' Then my two mothers each take one of my hands, and we run together up the road until the mountain and the lagoon and the tavern and the city are lost in the night behind us, and they swing me between them, laughing, their hands firm and warm in mine, with the promise that we will never stop running and that they will never let me go.

Author's Note

This is a work of fiction, not history. That said, the work of many scholars, each of whom knows vastly more than I ever will about classical and late antiquity, was essential to the writing of *Sparrow*. Here are some of the books that helped me create the world of Carthago Nova: *The Fires of Vesuvius: Pompeii Lost and Found*, by Mary Beard; *A Social and Cultural History of Late Antiquity*, by Douglas Boin; *Trade and Taboo: Disreputable Professions in the Roman Mediterranean*, by Sarah Bond; *Slaves and Masters in the Roman Empire: A Study in Social Control*, by K. R. Bradley; *The World of Late Antiquity* and *The Body and Society*, by Peter Brown; *Running the Roman Home*, by Alexandra Croom; *Ideas of Slavery from Aristotle to Augustine*, by Peter Garnsey; *Slavery in Early Christianity*, by Jennifer Glancy; *From Shame to Sin: The Christian Transformation of Sexual Morality in Late Antiquity* and *Slavery in the Late Roman World, AD 275–425*, by Kyle Harper; *The Roman Street: Urban Life and Society in Pompeii, Herculaneum, and Rome*, by Jeremy Hartnett; *Slavery in the Roman World*, by Sandra Joshel; *The Material Life of Roman Slaves*, by Sandra R. Joshel and Lauren Hackworth Petersen; *Race and Ethnicity in the Classical World*, edited by Rebecca F. Kennedy, C. Sydnor Roy and Max Goldman; *Invisible Romans*, by Robert Knapp; *Late Roman Spain and Its Cities*, by Michael Kulikowski; *The Brothel of Pompeii: Sex, Class, and Gender at the Margins of Roman Society*, by Sarah Levin-Richardson; *The Economy of Prostitution in the Roman World:*

A Study of Social History and the Brothel, by Thomas A. J. McGinn; *Goddesses, Whores, Wives, and Slaves*, by Sarah B. Pomeroy; *Sexuality in Greek and Roman Culture*, by Marilyn B. Skinner; and *Roman Homosexuality*, by Craig A. Williams.

The book also benefited from the following works: *Sex Work Matters: Exploring Money, Power and Intimacy in the Sex Industry*, edited by Melissa Hope Ditmore, Antonia Levy and Alys Willman; *The Classic Slave Narratives*, edited by Henry Louis Gates, Jr.; *Paid For: My Journey Through Prostitution*, by Rachel Moran; *Slavery and Social Death: A Comparative Study*, by Orlando Patterson; *The Boy Who Was Raised as a Dog and Other Stories from a Child Psychiatrist's Notebook*, by Bruce D. Perry and Maria Szalavitz; and *Domination and the Arts of Resistance: Hidden Transcripts*, by James C. Scott. Any of my misuses of this scholarship, deliberate or otherwise, are my responsibility alone.

I am extremely lucky to have landed with Ravi Mirchandani at Picador, and I'm grateful for the hard work and support of everyone at Pan Macmillan, especially Marta Catalano, Elena Battista and Jon Mitchell. Gillian Stern's enthusiasm and expert editorial advice were vital to the final draft. The copyeditor, Fraser Crichton, and the proofreader, Mary Chamberlain, saved me from many of my own mistakes. I loved Stuart Wilson's cover design the moment I saw it.

I'm also grateful to several good friends who read early versions of the book: Kate Christensen, Jim Crace, Matt Cutts and John Marks. Neil Olson, my friend and agent of more than thirty years, has never said no to my ideas, no matter how odd, and he has never given up on me. I owe him more than I can say.

Finally, *Sparrow* would not exist without the wise counsel of my wife, Mimi Mayer. She tells me when I have done something well, she tells me in no uncertain terms when I haven't and she's talked me down from the ledge, let's say, more than once. That is why this book is dedicated to her, with all my love.